**Critical Praise for *After the Storm*
by Lenora Worth:**

"Suitable for CBA readers, this title
is also a good pick for romance collections
and those who enjoyed Kristen Heitzmann's *Halos*
or Hannah Alexander's *Hideaway*."
—*Library Journal*

"Worth takes readers on a thrilling ride...."
—*Romantic Times*

"...an inspirational romance and mystery thriller
rolled into one.... For a sweet, heartwarming story
that is full of suspense, I recommend *After the Storm*."
—*Romance Reviews Today*

**Critical Praise for Other Titles
by Lenora Worth**

"Talented new writer Lenora Worth
combines heart-stealing characters and a tragic secret
to make this page turner worth every reader's while."
—*Romantic Times* on *The Wedding Quilt*

"Ms. Worth puts a most unique spin
on the secret baby theme to make this
wonderful love story positively shine."
—*Romantic Times* on *Logan's Child*

"Lenora Worth creates another gem—a great, easy,
entertaining read for everyone, inspirational or not."
—*Romantic Times* on *His Brother's Wife*

LENORA WORTH

AFTER THE THE STORM

Steeple
Hill®

Published by Steeple Hill Books™

STEEPLE HILL BOOKS

Steeple Hill®

ISBN 0-373-81096-2

AFTER THE STORM

Copyright © 2004 by Lenora H. Nazworth

www.SteepleHill.com

Printed in U.S.A.

In Memory of Sandra Canfield
and Suzannah Davis.
I miss you both so much.

❧ *Chapter One* ❧

He was lost.

Jared Murdock didn't need a map to tell him that he'd been lost for a very long time. But sitting here on this steep, rain-drenched North Georgia mountain road brought it all tumbling toward him, like a mud slide unleashed.

"It wasn't supposed to rain this hard," he grumbled as he once again put his right foot on the gas pedal of the sleek black Escalade. Jared pressed firmly, but the big tires on the SUV kept right on spinning deeper and deeper into the mud hole in which he'd managed to get himself stuck.

"So much for four-wheel drive," he said out loud, hitting his fist against the leather-encased steering wheel.

He knew he was close to the cabin his travel agent had rented for him on one of the foothills of Dover Mountain, but with the darkness and the storm, Jared couldn't tell if he'd made the right turn or not. Apparently *not*.

It had been such a long time since he'd been here. At least twenty years. That had been the summer before

Jared had headed off to the University of Georgia. He'd come here to hike and fish with his grandfather before football and studies took up all of his time.

And then there had been so little time to get together after that. Wishing now he'd taken the time, Jared stared out into the angry night.

Maybe he'd been lost ever since, Jared mused now as he watched the storm's violent slashes of rain and wind descend over the ominous-looking woods and hills. The crash of thunder and lightning rumbled over the earth, shaking the windows of his vehicle.

Jared saw a flicker of dancing fire rushing out of the heavens, and then a tree deep in the forest split in half. "That one hit too close for comfort."

There was only one thing left to do. He'd have to walk the short distance up the steep mountain road to the cabin. That would have to be better than sitting here in the rain and dark inside his vehicle, an easy target for a tree to land on. He'd find the cabin, get a roaring fire going, get some sleep, then come back for the Escalade in the morning.

Things always looked better in the morning. Wasn't that what his grandmother used to say? "The light comes after the darkness, Jared," she would tell him. Grandmother Murdock had passed away while Jared was in college.

And his grandfather had passed away a couple of months ago. The grief of that washed at him like the rain hitting his windshield, fast and furious.

Jared turned off the motor and got out to go around the SUV, water and mud sluicing against the treads of his hiking boots. The downpour would have him soaked to the bone in minutes, but he didn't have much choice.

Lifting the hood of his leather jacket, he opened the back door and got out his duffel bag. At least he'd dressed warmly and he had warm clothes to spare in the aged leather bag—if he could keep it dry. And there should be some food waiting in the cabin, according to the travel agent. At least coffee and soup, if nothing else.

Trying to remember what the woman had told him earlier, Jared searched the road and woods as he trudged up the ever-winding incline. It had been so long since he'd been here and the mountain refused to give him any clues.

Nor had the perky travel agent, who'd wondered over the phone why Jared wanted to stay at such a down-and-out tourist spot as Dover Mountain. "It used to be the place to go for a quiet retreat, but now it's fallen on hard times. It's awfully isolated there, Mr. Murdock. Certainly off the beaten path."

"Just find me a cabin," he'd growled into the phone.

She'd called back a few minutes later, her enthusiasm back in full force. "There are several to choose from. Some of them are privately owned now, but some of them are rentals. Yours is the second one on the left, back off the road."

Or had she said the second one on the right?

Jared was too bone weary to remember what she'd said, or which cabin he'd always shared with his grandfather. But he hoped he'd guessed the right one when he'd tried to describe it to the confused agent. It didn't really matter now, anyway. He'd been too frustrated earlier to care whether or not the woman found him the same cabin. He only knew that he wanted to come back to this spot, this mountain, maybe in honor and celebration of his grandfather, maybe out of a sense of duty and guilt.

Tired. He was so tired. And he'd only wanted to get away. Lately the events in his life had just about worn him to a frazzle. And besides, he did his best thinking when he was alone, with no distractions. The adventurer in him liked the solitude of climbing rock faces and hiking through dense woods. But tonight his soul was crying out for something more, for something he'd lost the day his grandfather had died.

Actually, he'd lost part of himself long before Grandfather Claude had died. Meredith had seen to that.

During the next month, Jared intended to think his way out of having to end a fifteen-year partnership with his friend Mack Purcell. Well, at least now he didn't have to come up with a plan to save Murdock and Purcell Media Consultants; his ex-partner owned the company outright. Now Mack would have to decide what to do about expanding the company in a strained economy. Jared was out of the picture. Completely. Once he'd signed the final papers earlier today, selling out his shares to his partner, there had been no turning back. Jared should have felt relief, but instead he'd just felt drained and sick. Old and washed-out. Empty and betrayed.

We took too many risks, Jared thought now as the wind and rain whistled around his dark hair. And Mack had taken the one risk that had ended their friendship forever. Only, that risk had nothing to do with business. It had been strictly personal.

Nothing like a best friend stealing a fiancée right out from under a man's nose to bring that man to a crashing midlife crisis.

"I'm too young for this," Jared reasoned as he battled the cold wind and the even colder water hitting his face. Too young for a crisis, but too stupid to see what had been so clear and right in front of his eyes.

Well, he could see now. Or at least by the time he'd trailed all the hills and bluffs of Dover Mountain, he'd have it all figured out.

The cold air caused Jared's eyes to tear up and his nose to turn red. It was a wet spring night, unusually cold for April. Not a good night to be out on a lonely mountain road. Instead of helping him get his mind off things, being here only brought home the problems he'd left behind in his fancy Atlanta penthouse and the memories he'd tried so hard to leave behind in his mind. Maybe he should just turn around and go back to the city. But he didn't want to turn around. Jared's failures were chasing him up this mountain as surely as the driving storm was chasing at the trees.

He turned to the right and saw a single light shining from a cabin up the lane.

Always leave a light burning.

His grandparents had taught Jared that. Always leave the door open for hope, they'd said. Jared had come back here in hopes of finding some of the faith and strength his grandparents had tried to instill in him. And maybe finally to face his own shortcomings. He wondered if he'd be able to conquer those shortcomings.

Or even to make it up this drenched mountain to that beckoning light.

She was in trouble.

Alisha Emerson held one hand to her protruding stomach as yet another pain shot through her with the ferocity of a lit fuse. With her other hand, Alisha held the wall as she struggled toward the bedroom. Could this be it? Was her baby coming? But it wasn't time yet. The doctor and the midwife had both told her another two weeks.

In spite of the chilly Saturday night, sweat trickled down Alisha's face. She could feel the cold sweat of fear and anticipation moving down her back. She wished that she'd had a phone installed six months ago when she'd moved here, but Alisha knew it was too late to do any second-guessing now. She had refused a phone because she wanted to save money, and she didn't want to talk to anyone. She didn't want anyone to find her. Or call her. She'd been trying to protect herself and her unborn child. But now, she wished she'd thought ahead, just in case.

She'd thought she had everything planned out. Mrs. Wilkes had offered to let her oldest daughter, Geneva, come to stay with Alisha just before the baby came and even afterward. But Geneva wasn't due back in Dover Mountain for another week. She lived in Fort Stewart with her new husband, but had planned on coming home to stay during the spring while he went away on temporary duty in Iraq. The girl had readily agreed to the job, since she could use the money Alisha had offered, and since it would help to ease her own loneliness, too.

Lonely.

Alisha had never felt so lonely in her life. With a groan, she made it to the bedroom where a single kerosene lamp burned on a small grapevine table. At least she had that one source of light, since the storm had knocked out the electricity. The next round of labor pains knocked *her* down on the bed. Alisha grabbed the baby-blue chenille bedspread that had belonged to her mother, her fingers digging against the worn, plush fabric. Even the pain brought her a small measure of comfort on this dark night, since she knew that meant she'd soon have her baby in her arms.

But she wanted that baby to be born safe and warm, without any problems. She needed help. She'd never make it up the mountain to the Wilkeses' trailer with this terrible storm brewing outside. She probably couldn't even make it to the next cabin up the hill. And if she did, she might not find anyone there anyway. Loretta Wilkes had told her a renter was coming to stay for a month or so. But Alisha wasn't sure when the renter was due to arrive.

And besides, she didn't like strangers.

"Lord, I need Your help now," she whispered in a fevered prayer. *"I need You, Lord. You brought me here, You protected my baby in the womb. Please protect this birth. Please, Lord, bless this birth. Send me somebody, Lord."*

Alisha's prayer became a constant plea as she struggled through the first stages of labor. Her water hadn't broken yet, so if she could hold on until morning, she might have a chance. She could at least go out on the road and wait for someone to come down the mountain then. The few commuters to Dalton and the other surrounding towns usually drove down the mountain around five each morning, but then with this storm...

Alisha let out a gasp as another realization hit her almost as hard as her labor pains. "Tomorrow's Sunday." No one would be coming down the mountain. They'd all be headed to church.

Tomorrow was Easter Sunday.

Telling herself not to worry, she realized this could just be false labor. She'd read about that. It was probably a false alarm, a welcoming warning of the real thing. No need to get all worried until things got worse.

Things got worse in the next hour. The pain in her stomach felt like a vise grip pressing on her center, her fear increased with each beat of her heart, and her back was hurting all over. She twisted to her side to relieve the pressure on her back, but the pain seemed to keep on coming.

Outside, the storm hit with the same intensity as the pains in her stomach. She could hear the wind moaning, could hear falling limbs crashing against the shingled roof of the tiny cabin. Thunder and lightning banged and hissed through the night, making her own pain seem more frantic and fast-paced.

Grimacing, she shifted so she could see the windup clock by the bed. Well after midnight, but still a long time until morning. Trying to stay calm, Alisha began timing her contractions. They were coming about every ten minutes and lasting about thirty seconds. From everything she'd read in her pregnancy books, this was all right for now. If she could just stand the pain. She didn't think beyond what she would do if they started coming faster and lasting longer. She didn't think beyond the timings.

"But I have to think," she said to the silent, creaking cabin. "I have to be prepared. Didn't I learn that lesson a long time ago?"

Deciding to take matters into her own hands, Alisha managed to get up and gather some clean blankets and sheets and place them on the rocking chair by the bed. She held onto the wall by the window for a while, watching the driving rain just past the tiny porch. The woods and trees looked so angry and full of turmoil as water and wind covered them in a heavy whitewash. Alisha longed to go out into the rain, to be washed clean again. To be pure and fresh again. To find some beauty. Every now and again, the wind would pick up and the rain would blow past the window in a great huffing breath of swirls and water.

As she stood there, Alisha realized that she was utterly and completely alone. After a while, another contraction hit her. She held on to the wall, her gaze on the trees being tossed about out in the forest, her prayers trapped inside her throat as she worked against the increasing pain and fear. Then she went back to the bed and tried to rest.

A few minutes later, Alisha lay back as another contraction passed, her eyes focused on the driftwood-and-seashell cross hanging on the planked wall across from the bed. Her now-deceased mother had given her the beautiful cross when Alisha had gotten married over ten years earlier.

"Never forget who gives us strength, honey," her diminutive mother had told her in a tear-strained voice.

Keep your eyes on the cross, Alisha told herself now. Don't think about the bad stuff. Don't think about him. He's gone now. He can't hurt you anymore. He can't hurt your baby. Keep your eyes on the cross. God will not leave you comfortless.

But she had to wonder, would God help her tonight? Or would He bring about His own certain justice to make her pay for her sins?

"For my child, Lord," she said into the night. *"I'm asking for the sake of my child. He is little and innocent. Please, Lord, don't punish my child."*

She must have drifted into a moment of sleep. She woke quickly, but lay still, breathing deeply, the pain subsided for now. When she got a bit of energy, she'd have to go to the kitchen and boil some water. And she'd need more towels and some sterilized scissors. She wasn't sure how she was going to deliver this baby all by herself, but if her contractions got worse, she'd have to do the best she could. She felt thankful that she was in good physical shape from exercising and from walking up and down this mountain every day, come rain or shine. Besides, thousands of women had done the same, hadn't they?

Frantically, she sat up and searched the small room for one of her baby books. Finding one on the aged dresser, she struggled to step across the space and grab it. She'd just have to follow the step-by-step instructions shown in the book and hope that everything went okay.

Keeping that thought in mind, she stood against the dresser, taking in her haggard appearance in the cracked mirror, then quickly threaded her long auburn hair into a haphazard braid and tied it with a ribbon she found in a drawer. Then she sat back against the bed, her fingers hurriedly turning pages to the spot that listed what to do if you have to give birth alone.

Another pain racked her body, causing Alisha to feel the need to find release. Dropping the book beside the bed, she gritted her teeth and groaned. She wanted to push, but was afraid she shouldn't do that yet, so she lay back down on the bed and held to the wrinkled spread, trying to remember the breathing exercises she'd memorized from reading her pregnancy books over and over. She needed to pant so she wouldn't bear down.

Even as she huffed and counted and tried to focus, Alisha felt a lone tear moving down her left cheek. It fell with a big, cold splotch onto the yellow-flowered flannel of her nightgown, just over her heart. It didn't take long for other tears to follow. She could feel the wetness on her cheeks and neck, at first warm but soon turning icy cold against her hot skin.

"Mama, I'm so afraid," she said, her eyes trying to focus on the cross through her tears. "Mama, I need you. I need someone to help me—"

Her plea ended in a scream as her water broke and a huge wave of nausea and panic hit her with all the force of the next contraction. Dazed, she glanced down to check for the color of the water. It was pink-tinged amniotic fluid, which meant her baby was getting ready to be born. But...how long would she be in labor? No one could answer that. No one was here *to* answer that.

She listened for answers, but only heard the hissing of the fire in the nearby den and the now-soft dance of the rain falling outside. That and her own labored breathing.

Alisha gripped the spread, then lifted a hand up to the old iron frame over her head. She was about to give birth, alone in a cabin on a mountainside, in the worst rainstorm they'd seen in these parts this spring.

Alisha prayed into the muted light. *"Dear God, what have I done? Why did I come back here?"*

"Now, why did I come this way?" Jared wondered out loud as the wet wind hit him in the face and laughed around his freezing ears. It was bitter cold and icy. The rain wasn't falling as heavily now, but the temperature was dropping by the minute. From the looks of the de-bris-strewn road, the wind that had just moved through had to have left some damage.

"Power outages," Jared thought.

If he was back in Atlanta working, he'd probably be stuck at his downtown office for the duration of this torrential storm that was covering the whole northwestern part of Georgia. When trees started snapping and the roads became flooded, things didn't go too smoothly in Atlanta. There were sure to be problems all along the many roads to and from the city. He felt sure a tornado had struck somewhere close. The forceful storm that had passed through here had been full of high winds.

Jared's clients would need damage control, with both site evaluations and press releases assuring their customers that in spite of the dollar amount of damage from the fierce storm, it would be business as usual. But then, it had always been business as usual.

That *had been* his job after all, making sure that big companies always came out ahead. It was his job to make million-dollar corporations look good, look even better than they really were. It was his job to put a positive spin on any given situation, good or bad, just to keep above the competition. But he didn't have a job and a company to go back to after this extended vacation, he reminded himself. He'd walked away, too angry and too bitter to keep fighting with his growing restlessness and his partner's obvious betrayal.

"You figure it out," he'd told Mack just before he walked out the door. "You got what you wanted. You got the company we built together. I'm done with it."

And Mack got—no, make that took—something else, Jared thought, his bitterness as moving and liquid as this storm.

"Yeah, but you've made a killing," Mack reminded him. "On both the company and this deal—selling out to me. Not to mention the hefty inheritance your grand-father left you."

Jared heard the resentment in the other man's voice. He wanted to remind Mack of what *he'd* received from this deal—the woman who'd planned on marrying Jared until things got too rough for her.

"Yes, I can finally travel around the world," Jared retorted, "and you still get to clean up other people's messes."

While I run to the hills like the coward I've become.

Well, Mack was right about one thing. Jared had sold out, all right. He'd handed his ex-partner the keys to the kingdom, along with the woman who would be queen. Had Meredith really expected Jared to stay and fight?

No, Meredith should be happy now. Happy that she'd secured her future and that she'd be a society doll at last.

She *should* be happy, but after their parting words yesterday, Jared wondered if the woman he'd had a five-year relationship with would ever be truly happy.

"Mack gives me the things you never could," she'd told Jared the night months ago she revealed she was in love with his partner instead of him. "He gives me security and love. We have a good future. He's ready to make a commitment to me."

Hadn't Jared offered her all of that? Maybe not in words, but in deeds, at least? Obviously, he hadn't made it plain to Meredith that he had her best intentions at heart, that he *was* committed to her.

"I can't do this, Jared," she told him, her blue eyes tearing up. "You can't expect me to put our lives on hold, our wedding on hold, while you play nursemaid to your sick grandfather." Then she'd pouted. "Mr. Murdock has plenty of money to hire nurses around-the-clock. Why do you feel you have to be there with him most of the time?"

"Because the man raised me," Jared said, his voice hissing with pain and disbelief. "He's given me his life, Meredith. Now it's time for me to return the favor."

But Meredith didn't understand the connection, the concept of that kind of devotion. She thought Jared was being oversolicitous, overprotective of his aging grandfather. She also saw Jared's wanting to wait as an excuse not to get married.

In his soul, Jared knew Meredith had been right. Mack could make her happy. Would make her happy. While Jared had mostly made her miserable.

"I've waited so many years, Jared. I'm tired of waiting."

Stalking up the muddy dirt lane, Jared reached the little cedar-walled cabin. It looked quaint and idyllic, sitting there in the night, its slanted, shingled roof covered with pine needles, its little porch settled under the eaves with a soft smile of welcome. Two high-backed rocking chairs graced the small porch, one sitting on each side of the wide screened doorway. A stack of firewood lay underneath one of the wide, paned windows on one side, while on the other side, an old rickety swing rocked gently in the freezing wind.

Jared stepped up onto the porch, following the glare of the single light that had brought him here, then touched a knuckle to the wooden door behind the screen. Even if this wasn't his cabin, maybe someone in there could direct him to it. Or at least invite him in out of the cold.

She was so cold. Alisha shivered on the small bed, her body weary as she stretched a hand toward the stack of blankets she'd dropped on the chair in the corner. Just as she reached out longingly to the soft warmth of a handmade quilt, an intense pain coursed up her spine, causing her to suck in her breath and cry out. She couldn't reach the quilt. She needed it, needed the warmth she knew it could bring.

Alisha got up, bent over double, shivering and sweating at the same time now, but determined to get to her favorite quilt. The contractions were only three minutes apart. She could feel her lower body pushing and changing, could feel her baby dropping. Her mind was playing tricks on her now. She thought she heard a tapping at her door.

At first fear gripped her, every bit as intense and dangerous as the pain knifing through her stomach and legs. But then the fear was quickly replaced by hope. Someone had come to help her!

"Who is it?" she said, but the words were a weak whisper.

Did it matter who was at her door? Or was she just imagining that tapping noise? Was this her punishment then, to go mad while giving childbirth? To never know the sweet baby she'd dreamed about? To die alone here on this mountain, away from the city she'd once loved, away from her family and friends, without ever holding her little child in her arms?

"I won't let that happen," she said as she once again tried to reach for the flowered quilt. "I won't—"

The pain became too much for her weary, frightened body. Alisha grasped air, just missing the stack of blankets and quilts in the padded rocker by the bed. Grasped and gasped, just as the knock at her door became louder. Then she felt her body falling, falling toward the hard, cold wood of the planked floor, felt the waves of pain ripping her apart as she tried to touch the fringed fibers of her mother's quilt. The effort was too much. Her fingers brushed against the comfort she needed as her body turned treacherous and tried to break in two. Alisha accepted and gave in to the pain as she screamed out, a soft sorrow covering her as she fell into darkness.

Jared heard a scream coming from inside the cabin. Shocked into action, he hammered hard on the door. "Hello, is everything all right in there? Hello?"

He leaned in, listening. Then he heard another sound that brought a racing warning to his heart. A moan.

Someone was hurt.

Without thinking, he dropped his soaked duffel bag onto the porch and rammed his body full force against the sturdy door. He heard the splintering of wood as he fell through the door, his shoulder bruised and throbbing, then rolled over on the floor, his body briefly touching on a braided circular rug centered before the dying embers of the fireplace. He felt a gush of welcoming warmth before he jumped up and shouted out again.

"Hello? Where are you?"

"In...here."

The reply was feminine and weak. Wondering if someone had broken in and left a victim, Jared rushed around the big, long room, noting in his confusion that the place was tidy and clean, with no signs of a struggle.

But that scream of pain still gripped at his system, so he forgot the formal tour as he raced toward the room down the hallway, just past a small bathroom.

The room with the single lamplight.

Jared stopped in the doorway, his eyes adjusting to the muted light as he took in the bedroom. A small iron-framed bed, with the sheets and covers tossed back. A pile of blankets and quilts on a chair. A long, battered dresser lined with trinkets and books. A cross on the pine-paneled wall.

"You're safe now," he said into the still room. "You can come out."

"Down...here."

Jared moved around the bed toward the chair in the corner, his gaze taking in the dark shadows.

And then he saw her.

A woman with long red hair, lying in a heap on the floor, her hand reaching up toward the rocking chair.

Bending down, Jared pulled her head around. "Are you all right?"

She tried to open her eyes, tried to speak, but in the next instant she gritted her teeth in pain and clutched a hand toward her stomach.

Her rounded, very pregnant stomach.

"What—"

"Help me, please," she whispered through pale lips, her eyes wide with fear and pain. "Help me, mister. I'm...having a baby."

❧ Chapter Two ❧

Jared immediately lifted the woman up, then gently sat her down on the bed. Even heavy with pregnancy, she didn't seem to weigh very much. She looked petite and fragile. Her hair had come partially loose from her braid and it fell in gentle reddish-gold waves and ringlets around her heart-shaped, freckled-nosed face and down her shoulders.

"Are you sure you're in labor?" he asked as he grabbed the covers and pulled them up over her body. Before she could answer, he saw the wet, stained sheets, his gaze moving from the bed to her face again.

"I'm very much in labor," she said, fear making the words a mere whisper. "And so glad you came along." Then she gave him a weak smile. "You're soaked to the bone. Go by the...fire."

"Don't worry about me," Jared replied as he ran a hand through his drenched hair to get it off his face.

"Cold out there," she whispered, a visible shiver going through her body. "A cold Easter."

"What can I do?" Jared asked, looking around for a

phone while he dripped puddles of water on the plank floor. "Have you called anyone?"

"No phone," she said as she gripped the covers, her eyes going wide.

She had green eyes, Jared saw. And right now they were filled with fear and concern.

"You don't have a telephone?" He hadn't meant the words to sound so harsh, but who in this day and age didn't have a telephone, even on a remote mountain?

"I never needed one before," she replied with a bit of defensive fire. "The baby's coming early. We have to go to plan B."

Jared let out a sigh then took off his wet jacket, dropping it on a thick rug at the foot of the bed. "What was plan A?"

"Dr. Sloane and a midwife—Miss Mozelle—to assist."

"And where is Dr. Sloane? Where is the midwife?"

Grimacing, she grabbed the bed railing, her next words coming out in a gasp of pain. "Up the mountain. Can't make it."

"I have a cell phone," he said, grabbing at the inside of the jacket he'd just dropped on the floor.

"No good. The reception here is terrible, even on a good clear day."

Jared had to try anyway. Frantically he tried dialing 911 on the fancy silver gadget—several times. He got only a weak signal message, then the phone blinked out of commission completely. With this storm, even if there was a tower close by, it probably wouldn't be very receptive anyway. Tucking the useless phone back into the hidden pocket, he said, "Okay, then what's plan B?"

"You and I get to do it. And I'm making up the rest as I...go."

She collapsed into another contraction while Jared watched helplessly, grimacing at the intensity of her pain. What now? He didn't think he was ready for plan B.

Jared decided he'd ask questions later. And he had a lot of questions. Right now, this woman was going into labor and she needed his help.

"Okay, what do I do?"

"Ever lived on a farm?"

"No. I grew up in Atlanta."

"Atlanta?" Her eyes grew wide again, and seemed even more green. Warily, she stared at him with a wild, anxious expression. "Where...what part of Atlanta?"

"North of the city. Buckhead."

That seemed to satisfy her, even though she still looked almost afraid of him. Her eyes darted across the room, then back to his face, questioning and unsure.

"Look, you're going to be fine," Jared said, thinking she was probably worried about a stranger helping to deliver her baby. "I've never done this before with any animals or humans, but surely between the two of us, we can manage to bring your baby into the world."

"I hope so," she said, forcing a weak smile. "He must be ready to get going." She grimaced, her gaze searching his face. "Do you have children?"

"No. I'm...not married."

She stared up at him, as if measuring his credentials. "Why not?"

Jared shrugged, thinking that was a very good question. He could see Meredith's tear-streaked face, could still hear her weak excuses. "Just never worked out that way. I've come close a couple of times, but—"

"You don't have to explain," she replied, her eyes widening with pain. "At least not right now."

"Okay, then. How are you *right now?*"

"Not so hot. Waiting for the next wave."

"You mean, a contraction?"

She nodded. "Book, down on the floor."

Jared followed the direction of her finger. Moving around the bed, he glanced down and saw a big, dog-eared paperback book lying open-faced by the bed. He reached to pick it up, amazed by the title. "A how-to book, huh?"

"Yes. Find the page about giving birth at home."

Jared stared sharp-eyed at the woman, then started searching the pages of the book. He was usually pretty good with directions, but...this? Delivering a baby? Suddenly, he realized the magnitude of the situation. What if he did something wrong, something to harm her or the baby?

"Are you sure we can't get you to a hospital?" he asked. "My car's stalled out in a big mud hole, but if you have one—"

"I don't have a car."

No phone. No car. This woman definitely lived the old-fashioned way.

"Do you think you could hold on until I try to get my SUV out of the bog?"

"No," she said in a loud moan of pain. "No. This baby is coming now. Right now. Even if you got your car going, we'd never make it down the mountain to a hospital—the roads are probably washed out. I don't think I could even make it the half mile to the doc's clinic in the village. Now, are you going to argue with me or are you going to help me?"

Jared didn't know how to answer that. He knew he'd have to assist her, but there must be a better way.

"Look, mister," the woman said after the contraction had stopped, "all night long I've been praying for God to send me somebody. And now that *you're* here, I don't have time for you to decide if you're up to the task. I need you to boil some water and get a pair of scissors out of the drawer by the sink in the kitchen. Then I need you to prop my bottom up with those sheets in that chair. Then I need you to—"

She stopped, mortification covering her face in a soft blush. "You'll have to look in that closet by the rocking chair. There's a piece of netting in there I was saving to put over the baby's bassinet, to protect against bugs. You can place that over my...my...private parts."

Jared had to smile at that endearing euphemism. "You want me to help you give birth through netting?"

"For modesty's sake," she said, her tone reasonable and defiant all at the same time. "I don't know you, after all."

"I'm Jared," he said, enamored by her need to use discretion. Under the circumstances, he didn't see how it could matter, but his grandmother had taught him to be a gentleman and so he'd abide by this woman's wishes. "Jared Murdock," he added. "I'll try to keep my eyes closed until the big moment."

"I'd appreciate that." She leaned back, her face filled with weariness and strain. "I'm...Alisha Emerson." Then she waited, as if expecting him to say or do something.

Jared thought he saw that trace of fear back in her eyes. Hoping to ease her worries, he said, "Nice to meet you, Alisha, although I must admit I never dreamed—"

She relaxed, a great sigh of relief seeming to wash over her body as she lay back and closed her eyes. "It's about to start again. I have to do my breathing and concentrate. Soon I'm going to have to push. You'd better get those things we need."

Before Jared could turn and do her bidding she let out a wail and sat up, huffing and holding her stomach. Jared rushed to the side of the bed. "Are you—"

She waved him away without a word, her pretty face contorted in agony. Jared watched her for a minute, noticing that she was focused on the cross hanging on the opposite wall from the bed. She'd said she'd prayed for God to send her someone to help her.

"Did it have to be me?" Jared asked the heavens as he went about finding a kettle to boil water. After fumbling with lighting the ancient stove, he continued to ponder that question. Alisha Emerson was obviously a woman who believed God actually sent people to help other people in need. Jared couldn't wrap his practical, logical brain around that concept, but then nothing about this night was logical or practical. He'd booked this trip on impulse and anger, emotions he tried to avoid, hoping to find something familiar and comforting in these old woods, but he had taken a wrong turn and found the wrong cabin.

Or maybe the right one, he thought as he set the kettle to boil then hurried back to the bedroom and Alisha.

He didn't seem to know her.

Alisha fell back as the contraction passed, thankful that the handsome stranger from Atlanta hadn't recognized her name. She'd been so afraid, but this fear had nothing to do with having a stranger in her cabin. It had everything to do with wanting to keep the world at bay, though. Especially the world she'd left behind.

But she had lived on the other side of town, south of Atlanta, in Riverdale. People from Buckhead rarely kept up with the happenings south of Hartsfield International Airport.

But what if he did remember her? What if he'd read something in the papers? Connected on the name? There had been a couple of short, terse articles in the *Atlanta Journal-Constitution* just a few months ago. After that, things had died down. And she'd left the city for good.

It didn't matter now. She had to take her chances. She needed this man's help and he seemed willing to do what he could. At least, she wouldn't have to go through this alone. Her baby had a better chance now. Believing God would show her the way, Alisha said a prayer of thanks, then hoped she wouldn't regret letting Jared Murdock help her deliver this baby.

He came barreling back into the bedroom, dropping the scissors on a rag he'd brought from the kitchen. Carefully, he placed both on the table by the bed before he went to the closet. "The water is hot. I put it on low to let it keep boiling. Now where did you say that netting is?"

She pointed toward the small add-on closet. "Up on the top shelf."

Alisha took the minutes between contractions to study her birthing partner. Tall, rugged, muscular. He had been wearing a nice black leather jacket, but it was gone now. His light-blue sweater, damp in spots from the rain, looked to be cashmere. His hair, still wet and glistening, was almost as dark as the jacket he'd had on. And so were his eyes. They reminded her of jagged coal waiting to become diamond chips. He was a big man with a nice smile. And he looked expensive.

Buckhead meant he came from money. Probably old money. That gave her some sense of peace. Jared Murdock probably didn't travel in the same circles as the people she'd left behind. The people who couldn't know where she was now.

"Got it," he said, tugging out the gauzy white fabric. "Want me to drape it over...you?"

"Please," Alisha said, clutching her stomach again. "You need to get yourself dry, too."

"Don't worry about me. I'll dry out by the fire later. Let's just take care of you right now."

Alisha nodded her thanks, then grabbed the blanket as another wave of pain centered in her stomach.

Jared hurriedly helped her lift her hips so he could push a couple of cushiony blankets underneath her, then with his eyes on her face, he gently placed the sheer net material over her exposed legs. "I guess I can deliver this baby by touch," he teased.

"I don't care how you do it," Alisha replied, her back locked in a spasm as she gritted out the words. "Just so it gets done."

"Okay, I'm think I'm as ready as I'll ever be."

Alisha nodded, then took a long breath. "Good, 'cause here comes another one. We'd better get *me* ready—we've got extra sheets, the gauze over my legs and waist. What else? Did you sterilize the scissors?"

"Yes, and wrapped them in a clean ironed rag." He shrugged. "I read that in the book. It said to iron a rag to help sterilize it. Found the iron on a corner shelf, right by the clean dish towels. Since we had no power, I heated the iron on the gas stove."

"You're doing good for a beginner."

"So are you." Then he glanced down at her. "I mean, this is your first child, right?"

She nodded, huffed, concentrated on trying not to push as painful memories tore through her with the same consistency of the pain in her center. "Yes, my first."

"What about...where's your husband?"

She stilled. "He's...dead."

His reaction was pure polite shock. "Oh, I'm sorry. That must be tough."

She swallowed, closed her eyes to the truth. "It happened a while back, right after I found out I was pregnant." *Eight months ago, to be exact.*

"Any other relatives nearby?"

"No." She wanted to tell him she had no one but herself and the baby she had to protect, and that she didn't need anyone either, by the way, but she didn't say that. Instead she closed her eyes and willed her heart to stop racing.

"You don't have to talk about it now," he said, obviously sensing her agitation and probably mistaking it for grief. Well, she *was* grieving. For so many reasons.

"Thank you," she managed through a groan. Then to distract herself from the sharp cut of clawing memories, she said, "Music. Could you put a cassette in the player? It's over by the window."

She watched as Jared turned and spotted the pile of old cassettes she kept in a wicker basket by a bigger basket of books. "I guess you don't buy CDs, huh?" he asked over his shoulder. "Just lots of books and old cassettes."

"No, can't afford CDs." She struggled to talk. "Bought those secondhand in the village. Player's secondhand, too."

He gave her another questioning stare, as if he couldn't quite figure her out, then said, "What would you like to hear?"

"Harps."

"Harps?"

"There's a mountain music one in there somewhere. Harps and fiddles, guitars and mandolins. Soothing—"

Pain caused that word to come out in a scream.

"Okay," Jared said, spinning into action. "Breathe through it while I put on those harps."

Groaning, Alisha reached out a hand toward him. "I don't think I can breathe through this. I...can feel the head—"

"Oh, oh, okay." Jared turned as soft music filled the room. "Hang on, now. Everything is going to be just fine."

Even in her fit of pain and trying not to push, Alisha had to smile. The man looked positively terrified.

But then, so was she.

It had all been over in a matter of minutes.

Jared stood at the kitchen window, looking out into the sloping woods behind the tiny cabin. The Easter dawn glistened through the trees and shrubs, the sun's first tentative rays giving the drenched forest an ethereal, mist-filled glow. The storm had passed, but it had left a soggy, whitewashed stillness that was only interrupted by the sound now and then of ancient tree limbs hitting against the cabin walls in a gust of defiant wind.

There was a pretty garden in the backyard, complete with an aged wooden bird feeder shaped like a tiny house, and a squirrel feeder made so a corncob could be placed where the squirrels were sure to find it. A couple of cardinals dug through the soggy feed, strewing it on the ground below. A wooden picnic table and two sturdy chairs sat near an ancient oak tree. Delicate crushed blossoms from flowering plants lay about on the table and chairs and ground. Everything was covered with a fine sheen of water. It was as if the whole world was frozen in a lake of flower blossoms and trees.

The coffee he'd set to brewing earlier smelled fresh and enticing, causing Jared to turn from the window. It would probably be strong, but he really needed a cup. He wasn't surprised to find his hands shaking as he tried to pour from the aged percolator. He'd just witnessed something he couldn't explain.

And on Easter morning at that.

He'd witnessed the birth of a child. A tiny little baby. A boy.

"One more push," he remembered telling Alisha after the baby's head began to crown and it was safe for her to finally give in to the urge. "You're doing great. And don't worry, I've got the baby. I've got the head in my hands."

Jared grinned, still amazed at how tiny that little head had been. So tiny and so soft, with reddish-brown tufts of wet hair.

And then after all the huffing and puffing and pushing, out came the whole baby. Jared stood there, his eyes wide as he stared up at Alisha, a grin splitting his face. "It's a boy."

She cried, of course. With joy. With relief. Then she instructed him on how to open the baby's nasal passages. At first, Jared panicked. Weren't newborns supposed to cry?

"Keep rubbing on him," she gently ordered, the trace of concern in her voice making the words shrill. Then because he could tell she was about to panic, Jared handed the naked baby to her. Alisha cooed and cried and even blew on the baby's little nose.

And that's when he'd heard the first soft wail.

It was the sound of a tiny miracle.

"He's okay, I think," Alisha shouted, tears rolling down her face.

Quickly, Jared cut the cord and wrapped the baby in fresh clean blankets to hand up to his mother. After delivering the placenta, he helped Alisha get herself and the bedding cleaned up—she insisted he turn away while she struggled with a clean gown and underclothing. Then he let her hold the little boy for a while before she suggested he give the baby a quick bath, too.

That had been over two hours ago.

Since then, he'd had time to get to know this tiny cabin full of books and knickknacks. The books ranged from the classics to a stack of romance novels. There were also some textbooks scattered here and there, mostly to do with physiology and social work. The knickknacks ranged from antique dishes to dime-store finds.

Her home, just like the woman, was a paradox to Jared. How could she live here with no phone and no transportation, and yet seem so well-educated and worldly?

Jared drained his coffee and went for more, too weary to figure out Alisha Emerson, but too keyed up to sleep or eat.

Deciding he'd better check on mother and child, he took his cup of coffee into the bedroom. Standing just inside the wide door, he smiled at the sight of Alisha sleeping peacefully. Then Jared walked to the white wicker bassinet over by the bed and peeked inside.

The baby slept wrapped in swaddled blankets. The baby he had delivered, and bathed and held.

Jared held out one of his hands and looked at the size of it, marveling that he'd held that little head inside it just hours before. Bringing a child into the world truly was a miraculous thing. Being a part of that, being a witness to that, had left Jared shaken and changed. He couldn't put his finger on the change inside him. He just knew it was there.

Not one to put too much store in religion, Jared thought about Mother's Day. It was only a few weeks away. That, and this Easter morning, made him think of his deceased parents. They'd died in a plane crash when Jared was a small boy. He'd lived with his grandparents after that, in the big, rambling mansion in Buckhead. Mother's Day had always been hard for him. He couldn't remember his mother, nor his father, for that matter.

He thought about Christmas, too. Maybe because Grandmother Fancy Murdock had always insisted on telling him those particular Bible stories when he was growing up. He'd heard the story from the book of Luke about the birth of Jesus, of course. But not until this night had Jared ever considered how that story could affect his own life. This morning, he stood reliving the whole Easter story, and remembered how Christ had suffered and died on a cross, then had risen on the third day.

Was that what humans had to do? Did they suffer, then rise triumphant over their adversities? Over their sins?

Jared closed his eyes, wonder coursing through his system. Then he opened his eyes to the bright sunshine washing over the hills and trees. The first green buds of spring were sprinkled throughout the woods like confetti. What a glorious morning to witness the birth of a child! It was the calm after the storm. Everything was glowing and glistening in the fresh, dewy morning light.

"Thank you," he said to whoever might be listening up there.

He'd never had time to turn to a higher source for inspiration or guidance. Coming from an uppercrust, well-respected family, Jared had always hurried through life. His grandparents believed, but Jared hadn't followed through with that tradition on a regular basis. He'd been too busy keeping up with all his social and business obligations. And he'd always had the best, from prep school to an expensive college education. Jared had been handed everything life had to offer. He'd accepted all of it with an inbred arrogance that made him think he deserved it.

Maybe there was something to be said for being overly educated and overly rich. And overly cynical. Maybe he didn't deserve anything, after all.

"No tests or trial by fire for me, Lord," he whispered as he glanced down at the sleeping baby. At least not until now.

Was this his test, then? Was all the turmoil that had brought him here just the beginning of some sort of faith journey for Jared? He had to wonder. And he had to have answers, concrete answers. Yet as he stared down at this little baby and remembered Alisha's screams of agony, followed by her tears of joy, Jared finally understood that some things didn't require an answer. Some things just…were. Some things had to be accepted without question. Life. Death. Betrayal. Forgiveness. Renewal.

But…he always had questions.

"You did a fine job."

Hearing Alisha's soft Southern-tinged words, Jared turned from the baby to her, his breath hitching inside his chest. "So did you."

She smiled as she snuggled underneath the now-clean bedding. "He's so beautiful, isn't he?"

Jared nodded, thinking, And so is his mother, then sank down in the chair he'd pulled to the bed during all the earlier commotion. "He certainly is. And he seems in good shape, all things considered."

"Yes. As soon as we can, though, we have to get the doctor here."

"Of course. Or I'll take both of you to the nearest hospital myself. That is, if you're feeling up to the trip."

"Need to rest some more, I think," she said with a sleepy yawn. "So tired. Just need to see Dr. Sloane."

"No wonder you're tired. You worked very hard."

"Couldn't have done it without you. You...will always hold a special place in my heart. And in his." She waved a hand toward the baby. "What's your middle name?"

Surprised, he said, "Callum. Jared Callum Murdock. There's a lot of Irish and Scottish blood on my father's side of the family."

"Callum," she said. "Then that's what we'll call him. Callum Andrew Emerson. Andrew was my father's name."

Jared watched as she drifted back to sleep, her words echoing in his mind like the music of the mandolins and fiddles she had listened to during her labor. She was going to name her son after him. That brought him comfort and made him feel proud.

He hadn't felt proud, really proud, for a very long time now. And in spite of the awesome events that had transpired since he'd first arrived at this cabin, Jared knew that sooner or later he was going to have to go back to Atlanta and accept everything he'd left behind, so he could start fresh.

Soon. But not just yet. He wanted to sit here a while longer and watch Alisha sleep. He wanted to keep an eye on the little tyke nestled inside the old bassinet. Just for a few more precious minutes, Jared wanted to experience the peace of this beautiful spring morning.

He could ignore the fallen tree limbs in the nearby woods and his vehicle stuck out on the narrow, rutted road. He could ignore the piercing chill of this last snap of cold before spring was officially here. He could ignore the pounding pressure of guilt and worry inside his own head. But he couldn't ignore the soft breathing of this beautiful and brave woman, nor could he ignore the sweet heartbeat of the infant sleeping right next to her.

But mostly, he couldn't ignore the questions. He wanted to know all about Alisha Emerson. And he especially wanted to know what had brought her here to Dover Mountain.

❧ Chapter Three ❧

He heard the screams in his sleep.

Jared opened his eyes, disorientation making him wonder where he was for just a minute. Then he remembered what had happened here last night. He'd helped Alisha Emerson give birth to a little boy.

Alisha was having a nightmare. She moaned and cried out again. "No, no. My baby—no!"

Jumping up out of the chair in the den where he'd been drifting in and out of sleep, Jared ran into the bedroom. He grabbed her arm and gently shook her. "Alisha! Alisha, wake up!"

Her eyes flew open while her arms went up in defense. "No—" She stopped, looking around the room with wild eyes before her gaze came back to him. Then her hand flew to her mouth. "Where's Callum?"

"He's right here, in his bed," Jared said, his hand still on her arm. His gaze held hers and he saw the alarm in her eyes. A fine sheen of cold sweat covered her face. She was shaking; he could feel it through the heavy flannel of her flowered nightgown. Wanting to reassure her, he said, "Your baby is fine, just fine."

Alisha fell back against the pillows then closed her eyes again. "I was having a bad dream. They were...trying to take Callum from me."

"Who?" Jared asked, concerned as he saw the flush of anxiety moving across her face. "Who was trying to take him?"

She shook her head. "Just some people, in the dream. It wasn't real. Thank goodness it wasn't real."

Jared touched a hand to her forehead. "You feel warm. You might have a fever."

"No, I'm just—it was the dream." She shrugged, fluffed her long hair, then fell back against the pillow. "I guess all new mothers feel this way, right?"

"Considering your long night of labor, here alone until I came, it's understandable you'd have nightmares."

He watched as she held her eyes shut, as if she were trying to block out what she'd just seen inside her head. "Are you sure you're okay?"

"I'm fine." Finally, she opened her eyes. They were a clear, vivid green now, devoid of any fear or apprehension. "I'm hungry."

"Of course, you'd be hungry," he said, relaxing a little. "I'll make you some soup."

"Not too spicy," she said in a raw whisper. "I'm nursing him."

"Right." He nodded, grinned. "I read in the baby book all about colic and late-night crying bouts. And that's just the baby."

She managed a weak smile. "Very funny."

"That's better," Jared told her, hoping to keep her cheered up. He'd also read about postpartum blues in the book. Maybe that was why Alisha had had such a vivid nightmare. New mothers were as protective as she-cats, he imagined. And no wonder, after all the hormonal changes and the nurturing feelings pregnancy brought out. Who knew women went through so much to have children? He'd gained a healthy respect for motherhood just from reading the how-to book. And felt a pang of regret that he'd never found the right woman to spend his life with, to make a family with. He'd come close with Meredith, but somehow Jared couldn't picture sophisticated, worldly Meredith Reynolds as a mother.

Hearing a little whimper from the bassinet, Jared forgot his own regrets and grinned again. "I think Callum might be hungry, too."

"Oh, hand him to me." Alisha struggled to a sitting position. "He probably needs changing. There's some disposable newborn diapers in the closet. A gift from one of the villagers. I plan on using cloth diapers, but those will do for now."

"Those *will* come in handy." Jared reached into the bassinet and carefully lifted the tiny baby out. "Hello there, little fellow. Want to see your mommy?"

Callum smacked his little lips and proceeded to wail even louder.

"I take that as a yes," Jared said as he brought the baby over to Alisha. "Here you go." After he'd made sure she had a good grip and was safely settled in, he found the diapers and some wet wipes in the closet and brought both to the bed. "I'll go find you something to eat, so you can have some privacy. Call if you need anything."

"I will," Alisha said, her gaze on her baby. "And Jared?"

He turned at the door, the sight of mother and child taking his breath away. "Hmm?"

"Thank you."

He nodded, his throat locked up with some emotion he couldn't identify. It felt both unfamiliar and painful all at the same time. "I'll go get that soup started."

Alisha couldn't stop staring at her baby. He was so pretty, so perfect, so beautiful. A fierce, all-consuming need to love and protect him coursed through her tired body, giving her a new determination and a new surge of energy. That's why she'd requested some food, even though she wasn't sure if she could actually eat. She had to be strong for her baby. And that meant taking care of herself. Her nightmare had brought that back full force.

"Mommy is going to take good care of you, too," she said as she moved a hand over his little arm down to his fingers. The tiny fingers sprang to life at her touch, automatically reaching out to grasp the warmth of her hand. "I love you," she told the baby. "I know you can't understand that concept right now, but I love you so very much. Everything I did, everything I had to do, was for you." She watched his face, seeing shades of his father's image in the shape of his tiny jaw, in the slant of his eyes. That image brought her both pain and longing. "Things will be different for us, Callum. I promise."

Things had to be different for them now. They were safe and protected here on Dover Mountain. Secure and isolated, just the way she wanted it. She wouldn't let dark dreams or unnecessary fears worry her now.

But what about Jared Murdock? a voice in her head shouted. He knows you now. He knows you and Callum.

I have to trust him, Alisha thought, clinging to that one hope. But she needed to be careful, very careful. She was so thankful that Jared had shown up and helped her with this birth. Thankful but wary. Wary, but when she thought about what could have happened if he hadn't been here last night, Alisha couldn't help but be grateful.

God had sent Jared for a reason. Alisha didn't want to question that, but worry and fear pushed at her resolve to be grateful and accept the gift of Jared's help.

"He won't be here long," she whispered in Callum's ear. "He'll be long gone soon and he'll forget all about us, won't he, little boy?"

Then we can get on with our life together, at last.

Jared would never forget the sight of Alisha holding her baby. As he watched the chicken noodle soup he'd found in an overhead cabinet coming to a boil, he accepted and recognized the foreign feelings that had clogged his throat and left him unable to speak.

Those feelings were regret and loneliness. He regretted that he didn't have a family to love. He longed for something, someone to make this sorrow in his soul go away. A sorrow he'd only just realized existed underneath his quiet, determined work ethics. A sorrow that had only magnified after his beloved grandfather's death and Meredith's betrayal.

All this time, he'd thought he was doing the right thing, working hard day and night. He'd had relationships with women, but they'd been shallow and one-sided, mostly for companionship and show. The last one had ended badly, very badly. He'd almost married Meredith, though. He could have settled down with her, even if he wasn't so sure he really loved her. But Meredith hadn't loved him enough and she'd told him that,

along with a few other revelations. Jared was still reeling from those revelations and from his partner's betrayal. Maybe that was why he was feeling so...
confused.

Up until this moment, Jared had never *needed* anything long-term and lasting. He'd always had his work,
and he'd had his quiet time with his grandfather. In his
mind, he'd pictured a marriage with the woman he
thought he was compatible with, but there was no
hurry, no urgency. Now even that hope was gone.

Why now, Lord?

Why did he have to wish for things he'd never
needed before when his whole world was falling apart
around him?

Maybe because his whole world *was* falling apart?
Maybe because he had nothing left to lose, even though
he could quite possibly lose so much?

"If I don't have my work, I have nothing," he said out
loud. *Nothing.* It was a somber, sobering realization.
Nothing but a big pile of old money and even older
properties, and a big house that he rarely stayed in since
he had a penthouse in the city, things left to him by his
wealthy grandfather.

Things. A legacy that he should be proud of. A legacy that had helped him start his own business right out
of college. And now, even when that business that he
was no longer a part of was being threatened by his
partner's reckless decisions, Jared knew he'd bounce
back. He'd walked away from the partnership a very
rich man, in spite of Mack's bold, risky ventures. But selling out hadn't been about the money. It had been about
his pride, plain and simple. Jared had old money to fall
back on. But that was all he had now.

He'd told himself getting out while he was ahead was a good thing. He'd be free from the yoke of constant worry, the yoke of having to be responsible for so many people and things. And after the final fight with Mack, after the full betrayal had been disclosed, Jared had wanted nothing more than just to escape.

But now, now he could see so much more clearly. He wanted that sweet picture he'd seen in the bedroom. Mother and child. He didn't just want to deliver a baby. He wanted to be a father.

The soup hissed and sizzled as it boiled over on the stove. Jared grabbed a potholder and moved the pot away from the flame of the gas burner. The piping-hot soup brought him back to reality. He had to figure out how to get past the last few months of uncertainty and anger, and he had to decide what he was going to do now that he no longer had a company to run. That's what Jared needed to concentrate on now.

Not some silly notion of a family.

He looked at the windup clock over the stove. Almost ten. Maybe the roads were beginning to dry out a bit. He could go get the doctor at least. It would be good to get out in the crisp, clean mountain air and clear his head.

And his heart.

"The soup was great," Alisha said later as she shifted on the bed. "I think I should get up and walk around a bit now."

"I'll help you," Jared replied as he hurried across the room. "Do you need to go—"

"Not yet." She blushed, but managed a smile. "Isn't it funny, about you and me?"

"Oh, how so?"

Not knowing how to approach the matter, she said, "Well, we've been as intimate in some ways as two people can be, and yet, you're still a stranger to me. Help me up, and then you can tell me all about yourself."

He nodded. "Okay, but only if you do the same for me."

Alisha realized her mistake the minute she saw the eager gaze in his dark eyes. She *couldn't* tell him about herself. That would be asking for trouble. But even without knowing everything there was to know about Jared Murdock, she knew this one thing. *He* would want to know. Everything. And she couldn't tell him anything.

She'd just have to steer the conversation and questions back to him.

Jared pulled back the covers and gave her an arm. "Should I carry you?"

"No, the book—"

"I know, I know. The book says to walk around. But if you're not able to do that, I can carry you."

She laughed as she slowly eased her feet to the floor. "What would be the point in trying to walk if you wind up carrying me?"

He gave her a playful look. "I guess that doesn't make any sense."

They managed to get her to a standing position. "Whoa. I'm just a bit dizzy." She held to Jared, acutely aware of the warmth radiating from his touch. "After I walk, I'll let you drive up the mountain to get the doctor. If you can't drive it, at least you can walk it in the daylight. It's about half a mile." She took a steadying breath. "Most folks will be in church, with it being Easter Sunday. But Dr. Sloane...he doesn't go to church. You'll probably find him either in the clinic or at the Hilltop Diner."

"I'll get to him, either way," Jared promised as he eased her along the room. "Want to go into the den and see the yard out the big window?"

She nodded as they slowly made their way up the narrow hallway. When they reached the long, wide den, she took in the room, and felt comforted by what she saw. Jared had straightened things up. The small kitchen lining one wall was sparkling clean, all the mismatched Fiesta-ware dishes placed against the drain and up in the open dish cabinet beside the sink. The crocheted blue-and-brown-patterned afghan she'd knitted years ago was neatly draped over the old patchwork sofa. Her beloved books were stacked in precise rows across the battered old coffee table. A fire was roaring in the fireplace on the far wall, and he'd fixed the door latch. She could still remember hearing the splintering of the wood when he'd crashed through it last night. Thankfully.

Wanting to tell Jared how grateful she was, Alisha debated and decided she'd get too emotional right now if she tried to put her feelings into words. She'd never been good with words, but she'd thank him properly later. So she said, "Oh, that fire feels nice. I see you found the firewood."

He guided her further into the room. "Yes. Don't you have any other source of heat?"

"Furnace in the kitchen closet. But I turned off the pilot light since the weather was beginning to warm. Of course, I wasn't expecting these cooler temperatures the storm brought in."

"I'll see if I can relight it so you and the baby will be warm. This should be the last cold snap before spring."

"I hope so," Alisha said. "I love spring on this mountain." She lifted her head to the welcoming fire. "I had the cabin remodeled when I moved in, but there are still some things that need updating."

"We can certainly agree on that. Why don't you have a phone?"

Oh, boy. Here he goes with the questions, she thought. What should she tell him? Alisha didn't like lying, so she decided to tell the truth, but only what he needed to know. "It's just hard getting service up here. We're so remote. Getting a phone line almost requires an act of congress."

That much was true, at least. Of course, she knew the village had most of the modern conveniences, including computers and Internet access, but only a few people living here went all out for that. Alisha wasn't one of them.

"Well, then we'll just have to petition Congress," Jared said. "With a baby, you will definitely need a phone."

"You're right. I'll take care of it as soon as I'm back on my feet and back at work."

He kept a hand on her arm as they stopped in front of the big bay window that looked out over the front yard. "You work?"

"Yes," she said, debating how much to tell him while her gaze took in the battered and broken limbs the storm had left all around her yard. "In the village, at the only store in town. Dover Mountain Mini-Mart and Grocery. It's like a general store—everybody calls it that—or a really small Wal-Mart. We carry a little bit of everything."

"What do you do there?"

"Whatever Mr. Curtis needs me to do," she said with a laugh, glad she could tell him that much at least. "I help customers, stock inventory, sell my own homemade jellies and jams and crafts. And bread. I make good bread. There's some in the cupboard by the refrigerator."

"Really now? I'll keep that in mind for lunch."

She liked the teasing light in his eyes. But she didn't like the curiosity.

"Tell me about you," she said by way of changing the subject.

He shrugged, stared out at the dripping trees. "I own—correction—I used to own my own company. Murdock and Purcell Media Consultants. I just sold my half to my partner. He has a new partner already, though."

Alisha saw the dark light of his eyes. So he didn't like to talk about himself, either. "What did you do? I mean, who did you consult?"

He smiled then, his rugged features looking younger. "We did the consulting. We had clients who deal in television and radio, the Internet, any form of communication and media. We'd make suggestions to them on everything from advertising to investments."

"Sounds important."

He looked down at the African violet she kept on the windowsill. "It *was* important, to the people who depended on me, and to me."

"And did you have a lot of people depending on you?"

"Yes."

"Then why'd you give it up?"

She saw the darkness leap from his eyes, saw the way the smile drained right off his face and turned into a frown. "I got tired," he replied, the words low and gravelly. "And disillusioned, I guess."

"I can certainly understand both those feelings."

He kept his head down, then turned so fast she almost had to step backward. "So...back to *your* job. Sounds as if you practically run the general store."

"I try," she admitted. She wanted to know more about him, but decided she wouldn't press him for information. He might get suspicious and turn the tables on her. So she told him only superficial things. "I do like to stay busy, and the store is so ancient. No computers, no digital anything. Just the steady cling of the hand-cranked cash register. It's very peaceful and soothing, spending my days there. And Mr. and Mrs. Curtis have already told me I can bring the baby to work with me for as long as I need. They live off the back of the store, so I can put Callum in a crib right near the door to their apartment."

"That would be convenient," he said, nodding. "Do they like children?"

"Oh, yes." She smiled softly. "They raised three of their own and now have lots of grandchildren coming to visit. One more won't matter a bit to them. And Mrs. Curtis can help me with him. She loves babies."

"They sound like a wonderful couple."

"They are. But I love all of the people here. They're all like that, helpful and caring." And protective. But she didn't mention that particular quality to him. "I feel like I have a whole new family."

"What made you come here?"

She didn't want to answer that, because she couldn't answer that. But she could tell him one of the main reasons she'd decided to live on the mountain. "This cabin has been in my mother's family for generations."

He gave her a surprised look, but didn't press her. "And now it's yours?"

"It's all I have left," she said, suddenly tired herself, her body drained, but her mind even more so. "I think I need to get back to bed."

He turned her around, then urged her back toward the bedroom. "It must be hard, going through this without your husband."

"Harder than I ever imagined," she said. And that was the truth. "But I'm going to make it," she added, her conviction ringing hollow in her ears. She *hoped* she was going to make it.

"Will you be okay here alone while I go for the doctor?"

"Yes. I'm just going to sleep." She let him help her down onto the feather mattress. "Could you pull the baby's bed close, so I can see him?"

"Sure." Jared did her bidding, bringing the rickety bassinet to the side of the bed, by the nightstand. "Can you get to him from there if you need to?"

She nodded. "I'll be able to sit up and reach in for him."

"Well, just be careful. Now which way is the doctor?"

Jared found his truck right where he'd left it. The cold air made him breathe puffs of fog, but the sight of his bogged-down SUV made him say hot words. "No wonder I couldn't get it out last night," he hollered to the wind.

The big truck's two front tires had slipped into a muddy rut just off the badly paved lane that served as a road. The darkness and the bushy thickets along the road had covered the mud hole last night, which in turn had caused him to shift farther into the gaping hole and get all four wheels stuck. From the looks of it, it would take a winch and a tow truck to get the vehicle out.

And the radio weatherman had said this storm's aftermath would be very bad. Power outages might last for another day and night at least. All over half of the state, the roads were closed, trees were down, schools would be closed on Monday for a three-day weekend due to water and wind damage and lack of electricity. Everything was closed, which meant Jared was stuck on this mountain.

Well, he'd wanted to get away. And he'd told the travel agent to find him the most remote, most isolated spot she could find in the fringes of the Blue Ridge Mountains, the one spot he remembered from his youth. He was at least three hours from Atlanta, almost to the Tennessee border.

When Jared decided to get away from it all, he certainly did it right. But being back here soothed his frazzled mind. He'd had happy times on this mountain with his grandfather. Times he'd long since forgotten due to work and everyday distractions.

He turned and started walking up the slippery slope of a road that wound toward the little village on top of the mountain. He didn't want to leave Alisha alone for too long, so Jared tried to hurry. Even though he hadn't been mountain climbing in years, he was in pretty good shape physically from working out at a downtown Atlanta health club three times a week. But that didn't seem to matter in this early-morning cold. In spite of the wool sock-hat Alisha had given him and the collar of his heavy leather coat pulled up around his face, Jared felt as if he were frozen solid. His cheeks burned and his lungs hurt. But he kept on walking, right past the road that probably led to his own cabin, right past the rickety, run-down trailer that Alisha had told him belonged to the Wilkeses.

She'd also told him that the Wilkes family took care of the five different cabins the village rented out to tourists. He'd need to see Mr. and Mrs. Wilkes, she'd said, if he had trouble getting into his own cabin. If that ever happened, he reasoned now, thinking he couldn't leave Alisha helpless and with a baby to take care of. Surely the doctor could suggest someone to sit with her, someone better equipped to deal with all of it.

Someone who wasn't highly attracted to her and mystified by her, Jared thought as he huffed another short breath.

Thinking back over their earlier conversation, Jared remembered how evasive she'd been in answering his questions. She obviously valued her privacy. And she obviously loved living here in the quiet of the mountain, safely away from the outside world.

But why? his logical brain had to ask. Why was she here? Alisha was an intelligent, beautiful woman. A woman who had chosen to live alone in a remote cabin, without transportation or a phone.

Was she so destitute that she couldn't afford those things? Or was it something else?

Thinking maybe he'd get some answers from the doctor, Jared finally reached the summit and the center of the small town. He'd like to help Alisha. He'd like to get to know Alisha.

And he'd really like to know what she was hiding.

❧ Chapter Four ❧

Jared pounded on the wide, creaking, glass-and-wood doors of the Dover Mountain Mini-Mart and Grocery, then pushed, surprised to find the store open this early on a Sunday morning. The indoor heat hit him with a dry, hot rush as he left the cold behind. The door was unlocked, but the place was dark and deserted. "Hello," he called, glancing down the crowded aisles. "Anybody here?"

"In the back," came a voice that sounded as aged and cracked as some of the old pickle barrels sitting around the place looked. "What can I do for you, fellow?"

Jared followed the sound of the voice to a rocking chair beside a puffing wood-burning buckstove. This whole store creaked and swayed and puffed, he decided, wondering how it had stood up through last night's storm.

"Mr. Curtis?" he asked as he took off the sock-hat and ran a hand through his hair, his gaze on the old man who sat smoking a pipe while he steadily rocked back and forth.

"That'd be me," the old man said, his grin revealing a gap-toothed smile. "Warren J. That's what they call me. And who are you, stranger?"

Jared liked the directness of the other man's question. "I'm Jared Murdock. I came in last night. Rented the second cabin on the left—"

"Number 202," Mr. Curtis said, nodding. "Heard we had some city fellow coming to stay for a while. Don't get many people from the city, mostly hunters or fishermen during the different seasons. Get a few rafters who like to ride the river in the summertime—too cold for that today, though. Goin' to do some fishing and hiking, camping maybe?"

"I haven't decided," Jared replied, trying to get past the niceties. "Mr. Curtis, I got stuck in the storm and I went to the wrong cabin last night and...well, I helped Alisha Emerson deliver her baby."

"What now?" Mr. Curtis shot up out of the rocking chair so fast, Jared had to catch the man to keep him from falling into the roaring heat from the furnace. "Let me get Letty." He whirled in a mist of pipe smoke and overalls, his brogans carrying him to the back of the store with a clamoring clarity. "Letty, Letty Martha, come on out here, you hear?"

Jared heard a shrill voice responding. "Coming. Coming. Do we actually have a customer this morning? Well, I did tell you we'd need to open up just in case people needed things." She stopped talking for a full second. "I was just about to go for a walk to survey the damage—before I change for church. We might not have electricity, but this *is* Easter Sunday. We'll hold the service out underneath the trees if we have to."

Jared waited, listening to the voice calling out from the back. Did the woman ever take a breath?

Warren J. stomped a brogan against the plank floor, causing the whole store to shake. "Not just a customer, honey. A man who says Alisha had her baby last night."

That brought a rustling movement from the back. Letty Martha appeared in the doorway, wearing a bright pink nylon windsuit over a thick white turtleneck sweater. Even thicker white-and-purple bunny-rabbit-decorated socks folded like a ruffle against her battered athletic shoes. Pushing at the tufts of gray hair surrounding her jovial face, she gave her husband a direct head-to-toe look. "Did you say Alisha had her baby?"

"That's what I said," Warren J. replied, clearly agitated as he turned back to Jared. "And this here man, what did you say your name was now, son?"

"Jared Murdock," Jared said, mustering a reassuring smile toward Letty Martha.

"This Jared says he helped deliver the baby," Warren J. said, his watery eyes suspicious and full of utter disbelief.

"I don't believe it," Letty said, echoing the look in her husband's eyes, her hand flying to her mouth. "Surely you're joking us, mister. A baby born on Easter morning?"

"I'm not joking," Jared said, hands on his hips. "Alisha wanted me to stop by and tell you first, but I need to find Dr. Sloane." At the panicked look in the couple's eyes, he held up a hand. "Mother and child are both doing fine as far as I can tell, but we still want the doctor to check them."

Letty Martha and Warren J. both swung into action, almost colliding with each other in their nervousness and haste.

"I'll call Doc right now," Warren J. said as he held out two hands to steady his plump wife.

"And the midwife, too," Letty Martha said, wagging a veined finger in the air. "Alisha wanted Miss Mozelle there, too, remember."

"Well, I can only call them one at a time," Warren J. replied in a curt voice. "I can hardly see without a light."

Letty found a candle, lit it and held it to the phone so her husband could see. "Now then, do it, do it," Letty Martha said, waving her hands in the air after her husband stubbornly took the candle from her. Turning back to Jared, she let out a laugh. "You'd think we'd never before had a baby born around here."

Jared had to smile at that while he remembered his own nervousness from the night before. "I guess anytime a baby is born, things become a bit exciting."

"You can say that again," Letty replied, her hand reaching out to pull him down into one of the matching rocking chairs. "Sit down here and tell me everything. How is the darling? How's the mama? That Alisha, she is such a sweet little thing, isn't she? And been through so much—"

Letty Martha froze as if someone had put her in a trance, her vivid sky-blue eyes centered on her husband. Jared turned just in time to see the warning in her husband's eyes, as well as the finger he had pressed to his lips, silently telling Letty Martha to be quiet.

Jared looked from the man with the phone to the woman in the rocking chair opposite him. "What's wrong?" he asked, wondering if he was going to get a straight answer after all.

"Nothing, nothing," Letty Martha said, waving her hands again. "I ramble on and on about everything.

Warren J. was just reminding me to mind my manners. Now, would you like a good strong cup of coffee and a slice of apple bread?"

Jared could only nod and watch as, before he could decline, she disappeared in a puff of pink, an aura of almond-scented lotion following in her wake.

"Phone's still not working," Warren J. said as he ambled back over to the furnace. "You'll have to walk to the doctor's clinic. It's just around the corner, but he might not be there, what with this storm and all. Just about everything in town—and that ain't much, mind you—is shut down 'cause the power's out."

"What about his residence?" Jared asked, trying to be patient.

"It's back behind the clinic," Warren J. replied, rocking back and forth on his heels. "A white two-story house."

"I'll find him," Jared said as Letty Martha came back in with his coffee and a large chunk of moist-looking brown bread, centered on a pink-and-purple-checked napkin. Apparently, pink and purple were Letty's favorite colors.

"Eat, eat," Letty Martha suggested, a serene smile on her face. "Did you walk all the way up that mountain?" At Jared's nod, she added, "Take a quick rest, then. That's a hard trek, even on a good day."

Jared took a quick bite of the wonderful apple bread, then drank deeply of the fresh coffee. Chewing quickly, he thought he should just hurry to get the doctor. He'd only stopped in here to let them know about Alisha— at her insistence—and to make sure he was headed in the right direction toward the clinic.

But now he really wanted to know why Warren J. Curtis had made his wife hush before she could tell Jared exactly what Alisha had been through. Jared knew she'd been through a lot, losing her husband, moving here, then giving birth to a child alone, but there seemed to be more behind the story. He'd seen the look in Warren J.'s eyes. It had been a definite warning. Jared got the distinct impression that this lovely couple was in on some sort of secret.

Some sort of secret about Alisha Emerson.

While Jared talked to the Curtises, another man stood looking out at the silent town.

He knew a secret.

He stood at the window of the run-down house, staring out at the cold, wet landscape. Without electricity, there was no chance of getting anything done today. The roads were empty and dead silent, the ridges and woods eerie-looking and treacherous with fallen debris and limbs. Besides, he wasn't in the mood to work anyway. And he sure wasn't going to church to celebrate Easter with all the fine folks of Dover Mountain.

He hated storms and he didn't like God very much either.

"Could go on back to bed," he told himself as he shivered in his undershirt and flannel pajama bottoms. If that aggravating phone company got the lines back up, he could go back to his latest obsession, surfing the Internet, hanging out in chat rooms, finding out secrets people didn't necessarily want to be found out.

Like Alisha Emerson, for example. Alisha Emerson, the pretty, pregnant woman who'd mysteriously appeared on Dover Mountain in the fall and set up house in an old cabin that she claimed had belonged to her mother's people.

Well, he'd done some digging around. Thanks to a few blabbermouths around here, and his ability to track people's background information, he knew a few things about Alisha Emerson. And he intended to find out more. He had a plan. And that plan included wanting more than he was getting, wasting his time and his talent on this trash pile of a mountain. And if what he'd heard—what someone had let slip—was true, Alisha Emerson could help with those plans. He'd already tried to get closer to her. He'd been friendly and sympathetic to her plight, but the woman was stubborn and quiet. She liked to keep to herself, didn't hold with sharing much personal stuff. That was okay. He'd learned enough when she'd first come here. And he could be patient as far as the rest. He could bide his time.

But first, he had to get all his ducks in a row. He had to be armed with enough information to make it worth his while. Enough information to make Alisha Emerson sweat just a little bit. Once he had her convinced, she'd give in to him. She'd be his then. He'd get back everything he'd lost, and together they could leave this dreadful place.

Speaking of sweating, he was freezing now. That's how it went, hot and cold. Hot and cold. Shaking one minute and calm and still, burning, the next. He was just about to turn around and head back to his bedroom when he saw a movement coming up the road, headed toward the store just around the corner. He squinted against the cold, cracked window.

"Now, who's that?" he wondered as he watched the tall man wearing a black leather overcoat go trudging up the muddy, potholed road to the south. There was a stranger on the mountain.

Tourists. Dover Mountain only got a few, but he hated them. They were just so nosy and demanding. A real pain to deal with. But this one looked like he had money, at least.

He snorted and scratched at his belly. "Some city fellow got lost in the storm. How tragic." He laughed, thought about offering the man some help, but then decided he just felt too miserable for the effort. "You got yourself this far, I reckon. You can keep on moving."

Besides, soon he'd have plenty of money himself. Wouldn't have to depend on strangers for handouts, wouldn't have to depend on this town, or these people to keep him above water. Soon, he'd be on his way off this sad little mountain and on to better things. No more worries. No more nagging memories. Freedom at last.

And all thanks to the beautiful Alisha Emerson.

Jared found Dr. Sloane. He had to pound on the door of the white house several times, but when the doctor finally came to the door, Jared was shocked at what he saw, and more than a little relieved that this man hadn't had anything to do with Alisha's delivery.

Dr. Sloane's face was the color of saffron, yellowed and aged like dried newspaper. His hazel eyes sank back against his jaundiced skin like two pebbles trapped in stagnant water. His thick silver-streaked hair stood up in oily clumps around his forehead. He looked to be around fifty or so, but he was apparently suffering from what Jared could only guess was a tremendous hangover. Was this the best medical help the people of Dover Mountain could get?

"What you want?" the doctor asked, his bloodshot eyes moving over Jared's face with contempt. "The clinic's closed on Sundays, and I can't open up, anyway. I don't have electricity, so I can only deal with true emergencies." He moved to shut the door.

"I have an emergency," Jared said, his hand coming up to block the door. Hoping he'd be wrong, he asked, "You are Dr. Sloane, right?"

"Yep, but—"

Jared held the door. "Alisha Emerson had her baby last night. I helped deliver the boy. We just need you to come and check on them both, that is, if you think you're able."

Dr. Sloane's head came up, his skin becoming a strange florid shade as he glared up at Jared. "I'm perfectly capable of seeing to Alisha's needs, thank you." Then he pointed a finger in Jared's face. "And just who exactly are you? We don't cotton to strangers here, you know."

"I'm beginning to see that, yes," Jared said. "I'm Jared Murdock. I live in Atlanta—"

"Where in Atlanta?"

It was almost the same question Alisha had asked him last night. "Buckhead. In a house that's been in my family for close to seventy years." Jared didn't go into detail about his uptown penthouse. It was none of this man's business, anyway.

The doctor teetered on his bare feet, his liver-spotted hands pulling tightly at the sash of his threadbare plaid flannel bathrobe. "Old money, huh? Y'all think you can come up here and take over this mountain—tourists and troublemakers—"

"I'm not a troublemaker, and I'm really not a tourist," Jared replied, anger making the words harsh. "But if you don't get in gear and come with me to see about Alisha, I'm going to make trouble, a lot of trouble."

"I don't take to threats," the doctor said, leaning in so close Jared could smell the leftover alcohol on his breath. And see the fury in his eyes.

As they stood staring each other down, Jared heard church bells ringing, then the soft, sweet sound of voices lifted in a song. The Easter service had begun, and the sound of the celebration echoed out over the mountain, reminding Jared of Alisha's gospel music. Reminding him that he'd left her alone.

"Do you care about Alisha and her baby?" Jared asked the doctor, doubt and worry making him think Alisha was better off without this old coot. No wonder Alisha had insisted on having a midwife present, too.

That brought the doctor's head back up and Jared thought he saw tears in the man's weary eyes. But the clarity came back, as if the doctor had come to his senses and realized his job. "I care. We all do. Never doubt that for a minute."

The softening tone in the man's voice gave Jared a little bit of reassurance. "Then will you hurry up and come back down the mountain with me. I had to walk—my SUV is stuck in a mud hole, and the roads are muddy and slick. Do you think you can make it to her cabin with me?"

"Let me change," the doctor said, spinning around. Then he turned back to stare at Jared. "You can come on in, make a pot of coffee. I got a percolator and a gas stove to brew it nice and hot."

There was a plea inside the suggestion.

"Good idea," Jared said as he entered the narrow hallway of the old home. "For both our sakes."

Alisha heard the knocking at her door, and thinking it was Jared, called out to him. "Come in."

"It's me, Miss Alisha."

"Rayanne?" Alisha sat up in the bed. "I'm back in the bedroom, honey."

She waited, her gaze moving protectively over little Callum as she heard the girl coming up the hallway toward the bedroom. As Rayanne Wilkes entered the bedroom, Alisha thought of the tough road the girl had ahead of her. Rayanne was also pregnant, unwed, and due in about three or four weeks.

Taking in the sight of the girl all bundled up in a worn green wool coat and an old, moth-eaten yellow knitted scarf, Alisha asked, "What are you doing out in this cold, wet weather, sweetie?"

"Word's out you had a baby last night," Rayanne said, her smile shy as always, her green eyes dancing. She lifted the heavy scarf away from her face, static causing strands of her limp blond hair to fly out. "Mama sent me right away. I put some cookies and sandwiches on the kitchen table."

The Wilkes family had very little money and no hope of climbing out of debt anytime soon. They lived in an old mobile home back off the road, up on a beautiful ridge just past Alisha's cabin. With four of their five children still living at home, and with their only income coming from part-time jobs and cleaning and maintaining the village's five remote rental cabins, the Wilkeses were barely squeaking by. And yet, Loretta Wilkes had somehow found food for Alisha.

Touched by the kindness, Alisha said, "That's awfully nice of your mama," Alisha said. "She didn't have to do that."

"She wanted to," Rayanne said, moving around the room toward the bassinet. "Mr. Curtis came himself to tell us. Wanted one of us to come and sit with you while that man who helped you went for the doctor."

"Jared Murdock," Alisha replied, memories settling around her as she stared up at Rayanne. "I guess he found Dr. Sloane all right?"

"Don't know," Rayanne said. "Half the town's at the church, attending Easter services out in the prayer garden. Of course, we both know Dr. Sloane won't be there." Then she spotted the baby and leaned in toward the crib as she let out a squeal. "Oh, ain't he the prettiest little thing?"

Alisha felt tears pricking her eyes, and wasn't surprised to see the same in Rayanne's eyes. "You'll soon have your own."

Rayanne nodded, the mist turning to real tears. "I guess so."

"What about Jimmy?" Alisha asked, her tone gentle and without judgment.

"He ain't offered to marry me, if that's what you're wondering," Rayanne said as she sank down in the chair by the bed, her eyes still on little Callum.

Jimmy Barrett was Rayanne's boyfriend and the father of her child. And in Alisha's mind, he was the worst kind of trouble. He drove a souped-up Camaro and ran the roads up and down the mountain, back and forth, day and night. What little money he made went for beer and more fancy equipment for his computer games and elaborate stereo system. "Has he offered to help with the expenses, at least?"

"No." Rayanne shook her head, then sniffed. "He ain't offered nothing, and my daddy's pretty steamed about that."

"Rightly so," Alisha replied, remembering when the

teenaged girl had first come to her seeking help. "Rayanne, I'm glad you're keeping your baby, but honey, you know if it gets to be too much, there are plenty of couples who could give your baby a good home—"

"No," Rayanne said, coming up off the bed in spite of her rounded belly. "I told you already, I can't do that, Miss Alisha. I can't give up my baby to strangers. Mama said we'd make do. I'll find work somewhere, and Mama will help me."

"I know your mother will do her best," Alisha said, nodding, her hand reaching out to the girl. "And you know I'll help you out, too."

"Yes, ma'am," Rayanne said, settling back on the bed, her hand clutching Alisha's. "I appreciate everything you've already done. And I ain't told no one about the money you loaned me."

"Good," Alisha replied, relief washing over her. Then at Rayanne's evasive look, she asked, "Not even Jimmy?"

Rayanne glanced away. "He found some of it in my purse. But I told him Mama gave it to me. He made me give some over to him, for cigarettes and gas. Said I owed him since he had to take me down the mountain to that free clinic you suggested in Dalton."

Anger coursed through Alisha's veins like a raging river, but she couldn't let Rayanne see that anger. It had been a long, hard battle, counseling this girl at church every week, and Alisha knew the real battle was still to come. She couldn't bad-mouth Jimmy Barrett, whether she liked the man or not, at least not to Rayanne. The girl was in love with Jimmy. But Jimmy was older than Rayanne, and a sweet-talker with street smarts at that. Rayanne had been taken in by his charm and cunning. And now the girl was paying for her impulsive actions and her need to be loved and accepted. Big-time.

But we all have to pay, sooner or later, Alisha reasoned. We all pay for our sins.

Don't let my baby suffer because of me, Lord, she said silently. *And don't let Rayanne pay because she made one mistake*. "Jimmy needs to own up to his responsibilities," she told the girl, her voice calm in spite of the flutter of rage still moving through her system.

"I think he'll come around after the baby is born," Rayanne said in a hopeful tone. "I mean, how could anyone resist something so little and sweet?" As she spoke she gazed down at Alisha's son. "What did you name him?"

"Callum," Alisha answered, the anger simmering down as she looked at her son. "Callum Andrew Emerson."

"Callum," Rayanne said, a dreamy look in her eyes. "Where'd you come up with a name like that?"

Alisha lowered her head and smiled softly. "The man who helped deliver him—his middle name is Callum."

"Ah, that's so sweet, Miss Alisha. Is this man...is he handsome?"

Seeing the girl's sly grin, Alisha laughed. "He is a very nice-looking man, yes. And a true gentleman."

A man who grew up in Atlanta, the very place I'm trying to forget, she reminded herself.

Rayanne watched Alisha, then touched a hand to Callum's little arm. "Do you wish his daddy was here?"

A shiver moving like a fingertip down her spine, Alisha wasn't sure how to answer that question. "I know his daddy would be so proud," she said, tears once again brimming in her eyes.

"We're a pair, ain't we, Miss Alisha?" Rayanne said, one hand holding to Callum as she reached the other to Alisha. "All alone, with no daddies for our babies."

"We are a pair," Alisha said, the tender longing in the girl's eyes making her own heart ache. "But we're going to be fine, Rayanne. Remember, I promised to help you."

Rayanne nodded. "And you told me, no matter how bad things get, God is watching over me."

"That's right," Alisha replied, remembering a time when she thought God had abandoned her. "You made a mistake, but your child shouldn't have to pay for that mistake. And if you turn to God and try to do right by this baby, things will work out for the best."

"I hope you're right," Rayanne said, her hand touching her stomach. "I pray you are."

Alisha echoed that prayer in her own soul. She wanted to do right by her child, and she surely wanted God to guide her along the way. It had taken her a while to see that God was here with her, and now that she'd turned back to Him for the help and guidance she needed, she could only hope God had not turned away from her pleas, from her need to raise this child with love and faith as his cornerstones.

And she could only hope that God had forgiven her for her awful, awful sins and the secret that could destroy her son if anyone ever found out the truth.

✎ Chapter Five ✎

It was past noon before Jared made it back to the cabin with Dr. Sloane and Miss Mozelle in tow. Together, he and the doctor had gone to find the midwife, in spite of Dr. Sloane's protests that he didn't need "that strange woman" meddling in his work.

"Alisha wants her there," Jared had told the ornery man. And after meeting the distinguished Dr. Joseph Sloane, Jared wanted a second opinion himself.

To his credit, however, Dr. Sloane had cleaned up and sobered up with record speed. And the man didn't seem to have a problem walking the half-mile distance to Alisha's cabin.

"Been walking this mountain since I learned how to walk," Dr. Sloane had informed him as they skirted their way past deep rutted puddles and fallen limbs. "Walking is good for your health," the doctor had reminded him.

Jared hadn't lost the irony of that reminder. He wanted to retort with, "Well, alcohol is not good for your health or for anyone living on this mountain who needs your help." But something had stopped him. Something in Dr. Sloane's demeanor set Jared to wondering why the man did drink. Jared decided he couldn't be cruel to someone who was willing to go out after a storm, with a hangover, to help another human being. Maybe Doc Sloane had some redeeming qualities after all.

And then there was Miss Mozelle. If she had a last name, no one had bothered to give it to Jared. Even though she had to be older than the doctor by twenty years, she didn't look as old and wizened as Dr. Sloane. But then, Jared didn't think anyone could top the doctor's sallow, sunken face.

The midwife had skin the color of a rich mocha coffee, and eyes as brown and rich as tree bark. She wore several knitted shawls and scarves, a bright red one on her braided head, a green-and-yellow one around her shoulders and another longer thick black one for warmth. Underneath them, she had on a long denim gathered skirt and sturdy hiking boots. And she carried a large tapestry bag, her walk proud and queenlike. She also stood at least a half a foot over the shrunken Dr. Sloane.

"I was born and raised in that house," she told Jared as she pointed to her large square gray-washed house with the long wide front porch. "My great-grandfather was a full-blooded Cherokee. He married a freed slave woman and they had seven children. My father was a hardworking, proud man who farmed the land down in that small valley beyond our house, and my sweet mother was a schoolteacher to the black and Native American children on the mountain."

Miss Mozelle was obviously very proud of her mixed Native and African-American heritage. Interesting African masks were hanging on the porch walls, mixed in with Cherokee artifacts that seemed to depict a story of some sort. The colorful masks, broken arrowheads and shiny beads, all strung and hung with leather, glinted and swayed as the weak sun tried to break through the cold, dark skies.

Not knowing what to say to the intimidating woman, Jared nodded toward the mountains off in the distance, past a plummeting drop-off that fell to a deep gully and flowing stream below. "You have a splendid view."

"Gets even better this time of year. Like being smack in the middle of a flower garden on top of the world," she said, her laughter as thick as dripping syrup. "Right up here close to the good Lord. I like it that way."

Dr. Sloane snorted his disapproval then, and he was still arguing and snorting now, as they stepped up onto Alisha's cabin porch. "You can stay right here until I call for you, woman," he told Miss Mozelle with a lift of one bushy brow.

Miss Mozelle stopped to catch her breath, her keen eyes centered on the doctor. "I aim to go in there and tend to Alisha."

"Not if I don't need you, you aren't."

"I don't care about you or what you need, silly man. Alisha done told me she wanted me by her side when that baby comes. And that baby done come, and I'm going in there to see to both the mother and the child. Now go on in, or step aside."

Dr. Sloane stood up ramrod straight, that faint glint of rage back in his eyes. "Why, you—"

"Uh, excuse me," Jared said, getting between these two very stubborn forces. "Could we concentrate on Alisha and the baby? I've been out all morning, trying to round both of you up, and I'm worried about her being in there all by herself. Can we go inside, please?"

Both of them turned at the same time and ran into each other.

"After you," Dr. Sloane said, his words stretched with sarcasm and annoyance as he gave an elaborate bow to Miss Mozelle.

"Why, thank you," Miss Mozelle replied, sweeping past him like a regal queen dismissing a lowly subject. Then she opened the door and hollered, "I'm here, baby. Miss Mozelle gonna take care of you, precious."

The doctor snorted and scowled, but he hurried to catch up. "That woman thinks she knows everything there is to know in the world, especially about mothers and babies. And considering that she never married and had any, it's a puzzle as to why these women around here trust her at all."

Jared shook his head, wondering what kind of time-warp he'd walked into, and wishing he'd had the travel agent book him a safe, cozy cabin in Vail or Aspen, or a nice warm spot on an exotic island, instead of here in the North Georgia mountains. These people didn't live by the rules and standards of the outside world. Here on this remote mountain, they seemed to live in a world of their own. And they seemed determined to keep the real world out of their affairs.

Very tight-knit and closemouthed, these villagers.

When he entered the tiny cabin, he saw just how tight-knit. And just how suspicious. The room was full of people, mostly women and a few men looking uncomfortable and closed, while the women fussed and gushed and fluffed and shifted. But all of that stopped when Jared walked in. The room went silent as all faces turned to him. Jared nodded a greeting then looked around.

There was food everywhere. Bread, cakes, pies, soup, a pot roast, a big batch of chocolate chip cookies— Jared couldn't believe the amount. Alisha would never be able to eat all of this.

"Hello," he heard a timid voice say from just inside the hallway toward the bedroom. "You must be Jared."

Jared turned from the stares and nods of the people gathered in Alisha's cabin, to find a young, blond-haired girl staring up at him. A very pregnant, young, blond-haired girl. Thinking he sure wasn't ready to assist in yet another delivery, Jared could only nod. "Yes, that's me."

"Well, what took you so long?" the girl asked, one skinny hand on the hip of her baggy jeans.

Jared took off his cap, then unbuttoned his jacket, suddenly hot and stuffy. "I...I had to find the doctor and Miss Mozelle and, well, it's still wet and messy out there." Not used to having to make excuses or give explanations, Jared grew silent and went into a staring war with the defiant young girl.

"We're glad you're here now, mister," another feminine voice said from the kitchen.

Jared looked up to find an older replica of the pregnant girl staring at him. The woman's hair had probably been blond once, but it was now a wash between gray and gold, and pulled up in a haphazard bun around the top of her head. Her clothes looked old and washed-out, too. A faded polyester dress printed with huge cabbage roses covered her sunken frame. In spite of her plain, wrinkled face, her smile was fresh and sincere.

"I'm Loretta Wilkes, and that's my daughter, Rayanne," she said, waving a hand toward the hovering girl. "Rayanne, quit staring and go see if Alisha needs anything."

Rayanne shrugged and turned to head toward the bedroom.

The woman's eyes swept over Jared's face again. "We just came straight here from the church services."

"I heard the singing as we were walking back," Jared replied, remembering the sweet, clear sound of "Shall We Gather by the River."

"In spite of the storm and the cold, we had a good turnout for Easter-Sunday." She laughed then, pushing at loose strands of hair, one hand going out to a man who approached with a plate of pie. "Reverend Stripling, this is Jared Murdock, the man who helped Alisha last night."

The jovial young-looking reverend pumped Jared's outstretched hand, balancing his pie with the other hand. "Nice to meet you. We sure appreciate what you did for Alisha."

"Well, it's nice to meet you, too," Jared said. "Both of you." Then he extended a hand to Mrs. Wilkes. "I guess I need to get the key to my cabin from you."

"Yes, got it right here," Mrs. Wilkes said, digging into a big blue vinyl tote bag that stated I Love Quilting on its side. Producing the key, which was attached to a white furry rabbit's-foot keychain, she said, "We don't get many visitors this time of year when it's still chilly out. Most folks like to come in late spring or during the summer—family-type outings."

Jared saw the curiosity in the woman's hazel eyes. "I don't have family," he said, his tone hesitant.

"That's a shame," Loretta replied. "Me, I got family to spare. I'm kin to most of the people on this mountain." She laughed again, the sound like a soft melody.

"And it looks as if a lot of them are here with you today," Jared said as a small boy of about seven whizzed by him, a blue plastic Richard Petty Nascar race car in his hand.

Loretta grabbed the boy without batting an eye. "Robert, slow down there." After giving the boy a stern warning, she turned back to Jared. "Yes, sir. Sorry I had to bring along the two younger ones. Can't leave them with their older brother. They fight too much." She motioned around the room. "That's my husband, Tate. He's holding our boy, Joshua. And I think you know Mrs. Curtis from the store."

Mrs. Curtis smiled brightly, but didn't bother to carry on any conversation. When Jared smiled back, the older woman quickly averted her eyes.

"And Langford and Dorothy Lindsay—they run the Hilltop Diner, across from the store."

Trying to be polite, Jared waved and spoke to the big-chested black man and his petite, smiling wife as they lifted their hands and nodded toward him, their direct stares intimidating and obvious. Jared felt as if he were being put to some sort of test. They didn't like having an outsider among them.

But in this case, they couldn't turn him away. Jared had helped Alisha. And since the whole mountain seemed to love and admire Alisha Emerson, these people had to be grateful and courteous to him.

For now, anyway.

The rest of the day went by for Alisha in a blur of shapes and sounds. Visitors came and went, careful not to linger too long or get too close to the tiny newborn baby.

Dr. Sloane examined her, then declared she was doing okay, all things considered. And he pronounced little

Callum as being near perfect—no problems there either that he could tell. He seemed to want to linger, his eyes centered on the baby, his expression solemn and quiet, even though his hands shook. Alisha could clearly see that he had a hangover. Again.

Then Miss Mozelle gave Alisha another examination, using her own unique brand of medicine—part folklore and old wives' tale, part prayer and healing, and always, always, with the firm belief that God was in complete control.

Jared walked in just as Miss Mozelle lifted Callum out of his tiny cradle and held him to her heart. Amazed, Alisha watched as the woman gently rocked the baby back and forth, cooing to him in some ancient dialect that had a soothing rhythm to it. Jared shot Alisha a puzzled, questioning look, but remained silent and respectful. Miss Mozelle had that kind of effect on people.

"She's saying a Cherokee prayer for him," Alisha explained in a soft whisper. "To ward off evil."

Miss Mozelle kissed the baby, then put him safely back into his little bed, seemingly satisfied that she'd done her job.

"Take this here," she told Alisha later, handing her a packet made of cheesecloth tacked together with string. "It's wild cherry bark. Brew you some tea—it's good for the blood. You need to rebuild your blood now, honey. Lady's slipper leaves will do the same, but I ain't got any of them right now." Then she'd wagged a long finger. "And remember, if the colic takes little Callum, just wrap a warm towel around his tummy. That'll soothe it right away."

"Thank you, Miss Mozelle," Alisha said, grateful for the kind woman's knowledge and wisdom. Alisha felt

safe with Miss Mozelle. But sometimes she also felt raw
and exposed to the woman's keen intuitions. From the
moment they'd met, Miss Mozelle had watched her
closely, as if she already knew why Alisha had come
home to Dover Mountain. Alisha had confided in the
wise older woman, to a certain degree, at least. There
were some things she couldn't share with anyone, not
even Miss Mozelle.

"You got some healing to do, don't you, precious?
That's all right by me. Me and the good Lord, we're
watching out for you. You can rest easy now." Miss
Mozelle told Alisha that later in the afternoon, after
she'd sent all the well-wishers on their way, telling them
mother and child needed to rest.

All the well-wishers but one, of course.

Jared Murdock was still here. Maybe Miss Mozelle
had finally met her match.

As if Alisha's thinking about the man had summoned
him, he appeared in the bedroom door with a soft smile
on his rugged face. "Did you get any rest?"

Alisha stretched, then grinned. "Yes, I did, actually.
Callum had his lunch feeding and then we both had a
nice nap. But I think I need to get up and move around
some more now though. Miss Mozelle——"

He held up a hand. "I know, I know. She said you had
to keep the blood circulating through your system.
Said—let's see if I can remember—the only way to get
over being weak is to get on with being strong."

Alisha had heard that same advice many times since
coming here. And she supposed that was exactly what
she'd done all along. She'd been weak once, but now
she had to be strong. For her son's sake.

"Miss Mozelle is an amazing woman," Alisha said as she slowly eased up off the bed. Taking the thick floral wrapper that Jared handed to her, she allowed him to help her pull it over her flannel gown.

"Everyone seems scared of her," Jared replied, his touch on her arm comforting and warm.

"As well they should be. Miss Mozelle believes in the old ways of the mountain people."

"I kind of gathered that."

"She's had a hard life here on the mountain, but she's educated. Her father, Jasper Cooleridge, wanted all of his children to have an education, but especially his first-born. She attended Spelman College in Atlanta."

Jared looked surprised. "Wow, that's one of the best African-American colleges in the South."

Alisha laughed, fluffed her braid. "Yes, and she'd be the first to tell you that." Clasping her hands, she continued. Telling him about Miss Mozelle was much safer than talking about herself. "Her father died the year before she started school, but her mother urged Miss Mozelle to go on to college. She was studying to become a doctor—something unheard of for a black woman in that day and time—then her mother passed away during Mozelle's junior year at college. Mozelle didn't hesitate. She came home to Dover Mountain to take care of her three younger siblings.

"Once they were old enough to look after themselves, she finished up at Spelman, then went to nursing school. She became certified as a nurse/midwife at Emory University, while she worked part-time as a waitress in a diner near the college. She could have worked in Atlanta, but she came home to the mountain."

"Is she married?"

"No, she never married. Doesn't have children, either. Her life was always devoted to her family. These last twenty years have been devoted to helping Dr. Sloane deliver babies safely. Actually, she helps him with most of his patients."

Alisha wondered if that's how her life would be here on the mountain. Would she spend the next thirty-five or forty years alone the way Miss Mozelle had?

"You look so sad," Jared said, bringing her mind back to the woman who'd helped her heal.

Alisha managed a smile for him, and reminded herself that she was safe and she had a beautiful baby boy. She wasn't alone. She had nothing to complain about. So she went back to talking about her friend. "I just admire her so much. She sacrificed a lot. She's worked hard all her life, fighting for the things she believes in. She marched in Selma, Alabama, with Dr. Martin Luther King."

Jared crossed his hands over his sweater. "Impressive. No wonder she doesn't take any bunk from anyone."

"No. She's strong and sure, and she's done a fine job with her two younger brothers and her sister. Their parents left them a trust fund for college. But Miss Mozelle never used that money. She worked her way through nursing school and midwife certification. She gave her money to the other three for their education. Now they're all married with children and good steady jobs, scattered around the country. And they send her monthly checks—which she puts away in case they need the money back someday."

"Why'd she become a midwife?"

"She doesn't talk about that very much, but I think she wanted to do something to help the poor women on this mountain. I think she relies on her instincts, her knowledge, and the old ways a lot. All the women on the mountain trust her to do the right thing—if Miss Mozelle can't help you, she'll get you to the nearest doctor or clinic so you'll be all right."

"Well, I'm glad she's here," Jared said as he sank back against the window frame. "I have my doubts about Dr. Sloane."

"He's a kind soul really, once you get past the crusty exterior."

"And the alcohol on his breath."

Alisha decided not to tell Jared all there was to know about Dr. Sloane. The man was so tormented, nothing could reach him now. Best to be discreet and not gossip about the doctor's private miseries. "He's very efficient when he's sober," she said. "But then, even though they constantly argue and fuss at each other, Dr. Sloane and Miss Mozelle have helped out everyone on Dover Mountain at one time or another."

"And they haven't come to blows yet, I guess. That's good," Jared replied, his brain awhirl with more questions. "Only, you got stuck with me instead."

"We did okay," she said, her gaze moving over to the baby sleeping within her reach. "Miss Mozelle says Callum is twice blessed."

"Oh, really, how so?"

She lowered her head, embarrassed even to say it. "She says he has me for a mother, and now he has you for a protector."

Alisha could tell this made Jared uncomfortable, too. He stood up straight, stared at the baby, glanced back at Alisha, then settled back on the wall again, obviously at a loss for words.

"You don't have to listen to that kind of talk," she said, a tiny bit of disappointment moving through her system as she eased toward the hall. "I love Miss Mozelle, but she can be a bit overwhelming if you don't know her. Just remember, she has a heart of gold, but not even she can predict the future. She'd tell you herself only God knows that. She's the one who got me back involved in the church."

At his look of interest, Alisha wished she hadn't mentioned that. Jared Murdock didn't need to know the details of *her* life.

"So you attend regularly then?"

"Yes," she said, deciding this was a safe topic. "I attend and I volunteer two afternoons a week as a mentor for the youth group. Those teenagers need some positive guidance."

He helped her make her way across the den toward the fireplace. "What do you do to help them?"

"I mostly listen," Alisha said, her body protesting the short walk, her legs wobbly and weak. "You know, teenagers are the same anywhere. The big city, a small mountain town. It doesn't matter where they live or how much money or social standing they have, they all have the same problems."

"Such as Rayanne's being pregnant?"

She nodded, one hand on the pain in her back as she eased down into a chair by the fire. "Yes. Poor girl. Sixteen and having a baby. And the father refuses to marry her. I could just shake that Jimmy Barrett. He sure led her right down the garden path."

"I take it you don't approve of the boy."

She glanced over at Jared, not sure what to expect since she didn't know where he stood in the faith and good works department, but all she saw in his dark eyes was polite curiosity. "No, I don't approve of him. He's twenty-three years old and a charmer. He makes pretty good money doing yard work and working on cars, but he's lazy and only wants to have a good time, spends his spare time on the computer, e-mailing his friends, and he spends most of his money on music, beer and video games. He hasn't offered either marriage or money to Rayanne."

"So you counsel her?"

"I try. She doesn't want to give the baby up for adoption, but her parents are having a hard time as it is. Her father, Tate, worked at the local outlet store and manufacturing company at the base of the mountain, but then it shut down and put a lot of people out of work, including him. Now they just clean and maintain the few cabins we have left to rent to tourists and take on odd jobs here and there to make extra money."

She could almost see his mind churning with more questions. "What type of manufacturing?"

"Carpets and drapery. It was a spin-off plant from the Dalton carpet factories, and an outlet store for carpet and drapery samples on the side, but the owner didn't have very good business sense. He was the last descendant of the original settlers on the mountain, the last of the Dovers. He lived in a fancy house in Dalton, and only came here to check on things when it was absolutely necessary, but he just couldn't get it together and he ran up a lot of debts trying to keep the factory running. Then things got pretty bad with the economy and they had to shut it down.

"He went bankrupt and now Dover Mountain doesn't have any sort of employment opportunities.

People have been forced to move closer to Dalton and Rome, some as far away as Atlanta, and some with no place to go, living off welfare. It's really bad."

"And yet, you came back here."

Alisha stared down at the fire. She had her reasons for coming back here, but she wasn't ready to explain them to him. Hoping to change the subject, she asked, "Why did you come here, Jared?"

His face went blank, his eyes downcast and evasive. He sat silent, his hands clasped for a full minute before he said, "I honestly don't know."

"Or you just don't want to talk about it," she replied.

"Maybe not." He got up to stir the fire, his broad back effectively shutting her out.

Alisha watched him, acutely aware of how his masculine presence filled the tiny cabin. He was a stranger who'd shown up in a raging rainstorm. A stranger who now held a strong bond with her newborn son. And her.

A stranger who didn't want to explain why he'd come here. He didn't want to be a protector.

So we're both hiding out, Alisha decided, wondering what exactly Jared Murdock was running from. And hoping she didn't have to tell him why *she* was hiding here on this beautiful mountain.

Miss Mozelle had said Callum was twice blessed, but what if it was the other way around? What if between Alisha and Jared and their secrets, her child was destined to become twice cursed?

⮞ Chapter Six ⮜

Jared stood at the window of his cabin, watching the sun set over the damp trees outside. In spite of the weak sun that had come and gone all day, the temperature was still in the mid-forties. This last freeze of the season was coming on with a vengeance as the bone-chilling dusk took over. The woods and hills, shimmering wet against the last rays of the setting sun, looked as if they'd been scattered with shards of brilliant golden crystal. Every now and then, he could hear the distinct sound of a forest animal crashing into the underbrush. Mother Nature had rearranged things in the woods, causing havoc.

But there was good news—the power was back on and everything in the cabin seemed to be in good working order.

And he had a pretty landscape before him. He had a good view of a sloping ridge on the backside of the property to the west, and a breathtaking display of the distant vistas of the Blue Ridge Mountains to the east. A gentle, meandering stream ran down into a small valley right beside the secluded property. He could take long walks or he could hike up the many trails carved out on the foothills all around Dover Mountain.

Or he could just stand here and stare out at this strange and mysterious world.

"Why did I come here?" he asked himself now, a fresh cup of coffee in his hand. He'd finally gotten into his cabin a few hours ago, and even though he was exhausted physically, his mental state was on high alert. Probably from drinking way too much of the dark brew in his cup.

"So what do I do now?"

The woods gave him no answers. Even the wind had died down now that darkness was coming.

Better yet, he wondered, what was he doing standing here alone when he should be back at that other cabin, taking care of Alisha and Callum?

"She has help now," Jared said, just to stop the silence.

Miss Mozelle had declared she was the *doula*. Apparently being a midwife entailed arranging for a house mother to watch over the mother and child during the time after the birth, and Miss Mozelle now had things organized down to a science until the oldest Wilkes daughter, Geneva—the person Miss Mozelle had appointed to this important position—could get here next week. Tonight, Miss Mozelle, the head *doula*-midwife-boss, was spending the night—just to make sure everybody was functioning correctly, she'd explained in her no-nonsense way—and then Loretta Wilkes would take over tomorrow night. In fact, Alisha would have guests for the rest of the week, and then Geneva, who sounded capable since Miss Mozelle had drilled her and trained her for this very purpose, according to Alisha, would settle in for two weeks. Alisha's friends were there to help her. She didn't need Jared any longer.

But he needed...he needed to be there.

Jared couldn't understand why it felt so urgent, so important for him to go back and see Alisha and Callum, but he felt it with every fiber of his being.

He has you as a protector now.

Jared remembered Alisha's words to him earlier.

Maybe he did feel a need to protect Callum. After all, it wasn't every day a man helped deliver a baby. Jared was still in awe of the whole situation. What would have happened if he hadn't come along at that precise time?

He didn't want to think about that now. Turning back from the growing darkness, he checked the fire, then wondered about getting some dinner. The flame was roaring at a nice, crisp pace in the small fireplace. All in all, this cabin was a cozy retreat. The walls were an aged, varnished pine. The main room was similar to Alisha's, but smaller. It had a phone, but no television. Just a transistor radio that apparently could only reach one country-and-western station that spent a lot of its airtime giving weather updates. There was a tiny bath in the hall and a nice bedroom with an iron-framed bed covered with what looked like a handmade quilt patterned in rich browns and reds. The mattress was old and sagging, but the room was clean and sparse, just the way Jared liked things.

This cabin, however, didn't have the lived-in, cozy look of Alisha's. Hers was definitely a home, with its many stacks of books and magazines and its flowers and dainty feminine treasures. This cabin was just a retreat, a place to sleep and eat, not to come home to. A place for someone looking to get away from everything and everyone.

"Congratulations," Jared said, raising his coffee cup to the fire. "You've certainly succeeded there."

He was about to open a can of beef stew he'd found in a welcome basket on the counter, when he heard a knock at the door. Surprised, Jared dropped the handheld can opener he'd dug from a drawer and went to the door. He opened it to find a teenage boy standing there, grinning.

"Hello," Jared said, waiting.

"Hey," the kid replied, shifting on battered sneakers covering feet too big for his scrawny body. "I'm David, Rayanne's brother. Miss Mozelle wanted me to come get you."

Alarm coursed through Jared's system. "Is everything all right with Alisha and the baby?"

"Oh, they're fine," the boy said, his hazel eyes glistening as he waved a scrawny hand in the air. "She...well, Miss Alisha...wants you to come on back to the cabin for dinner. Said she's got enough to feed an army and you'd be hungry, what with being up all night and traipsing around this mountain all day."

Jared relaxed, his hand on the door, a surge of warmth coursing through his system. Alisha wanted him to come back. "I see. That's nice of her. Thanks for coming to tell me."

"I'll walk you back over there, if you need me to," David offered with a shrug and a flip of his long shaggy brown bangs.

Jared turned to look around. "Let me make sure this fire is secure behind the screen here and I'll shut things down and get my coat."

"Okay." The boy grinned again, stomping against the bitter cold.

"You can come in while you wait," Jared offered.

David rushed into the room, his eyes roving about. "You from Atlanta, huh?"

"Yes." Jared nodded, amused, stoked the fire, then replaced the protective screen.

"I never been there, but Rayanne has. She went with our older sister, Geneva."

"It's a big, busy, crowded place."

"Yeah, Jimmy—that's Rayanne's boyfriend—he says he's gonna live there one day in a fancy apartment. Says he's gonna get a good job and go out on the town every night."

"Quite ambitious," Jared replied, remembering Alisha's distaste over Rayanne's choice of suitors. "What about you?" he asked the boy.

"Me?" David looked surprised anyone would care. "I dunno. We ain't got much money right now. I want a computer system, like Jimmy's got. I'd like to learn how to make computers or something like that, I reckon."

"Computers are important in this day and time," Jared said as he pulled his coat off an antique hall tree by the door. "Considering Alisha doesn't even have a phone, I'm surprised you'd have access up here, though."

"Oh, we got all the modern conveniences," David replied defensively. "Some people have computers and such, and some don't. It's just, well, Miss Alisha, she don't care about stuff like that. Said she had all that once, and now she just wants some peace and quiet."

Jared stored that bit of information, and again wondered why Alisha lived the way she did.

David kept talking, unaware that he was feeding tidbits to a man starving for answers. "We just got some new lines running," the boy replied as they headed for the door. "Fiber optics?"

He asked it as a question, as if he wasn't quite sure he had the right word.

"Yes. The world runs on fiber optics and broadbands now," Jared said as he turned off the lights, leaving on one lamp by the sofa. He didn't bother locking the door, since he felt quite sure the cabin was safe. Besides, he didn't have anything very valuable with him.

David shrugged again. "Don't know much about that, but I sure would like to learn more. We got one computer in my science class at school, but I've heard about how some schools have a computer for each kid. I'd like to get a job working around computers, someday." His voice trailed off, his *someday* sounding a long way down the road.

Jared wondered just how big the boy's dreams were, and if he'd ever achieve them. To encourage the boy, he said, "Then I suggest you study hard, get a good education, maybe at a technical college like Georgia Tech, for example, and work hard to make that dream come true."

David stopped in the yard, his eyes going wide. "You think I could do that, really? Even though my daddy says we're as broke as an old picket fence?"

"I don't see why not," Jared replied, very much aware that he'd never had to struggle for anything. He'd taken for granted going to the University of Georgia, taken everything in life for granted, for that matter. It had all been given to him without question. He'd never had anything taken from him. Except his company and his pride, he reminded himself grimly.

But you handed that over, he also reminded himself. You just gave up, sold out, and walked away without so much as a fight. Not wanting to dwell on these feelings of inadequacy, he turned back to David. "You know, David, Georgia has a very good scholarship program now. You can have your education paid for by the state, if you work hard and study."

"I probably won't get the grades," David said, his head down. "Jimmy says I'm stupid. He tries to show me how to do things on his computer, but then I mess up and, well I guess he's right. I ain't too swift at math and science and things like that."

Jared was beginning to see why Alisha didn't like Jimmy Barrett. In spite of the broken English, David seemed bright to Jared. "Ah, now, I think you're smart enough. You just need some help in applying what's in your brain to everyday life. I wouldn't listen to Jimmy if I were you. After all, from what I hear, he's not living up to his own responsibilities."

David looked confused, then nodded. "Yeah, my daddy don't even like to talk about that. But hey, that's life here on the mountain, you know."

Jared didn't know, but he was beginning to understand. He'd been dropped in the middle of the kind of life he'd never been exposed to at all. He'd given up on so many things lately, his business, his relationship with Meredith, his friendship with Mack. He'd given up and walked away to wallow in self-pity and self-condemnation. To brood about his lot in life. His empty lot.

But now he was here. And he was beginning to think there was a reason for that. As if her voice was moving on the night air, Jared remembered something his churchgoing grandmother had said to him long ago, when he was being a snarly teenager who refused to attend worship with her. "One day, son, you'll be tested. I might not live to see it, but it will come. I want you to pass the test, Jared."

When he'd gotten old enough to make his own decisions, Jared had quit going to church with his grandmother, much to her dismay. But his grandparents had never forced him to do anything. They'd spoiled him, because they'd felt he needed love after losing his parents. He'd just moved through the good life, following the traditions that had been passed down in the Murdock family since before the Civil War. Not one to dwell too much on a higher source of strength or power, Jared still had to wonder if God was now trying to bring him down a peg or two. Or test him.

"It's working," he said, causing David to shift his gaze toward Jared, a questioning look on his face.

"Did you say something, Mr. Murdock?"

"No, David. Just mumbling to myself."

"My mama does that all the time."

Jared had to smile at that. And while he was smiling, he decided he'd find a way to help David with his studies. At least while he was here for the next few weeks. It would give him something concrete and constructive to do, instead of standing around thinking he had to be the conquering hero for Alisha and her baby.

Jared was nobody's protector. But he could at least help this mixed-up kid out while he was here.

"You sure were mighty keen on asking that stranger back here for supper," Miss Mozelle told Alisha.

Alisha sat by the fire in one of the worn high-back gold corduroy chairs she'd found at a garage sale, little Callum safely tucked in her arms. "I just want to repay him. He did deliver my baby." She looked down at the sleeping child, still amazed that he was so beautiful and healthy.

"And did a right fine job, if I do say so myself." Miss Mozelle never looked up from putting bright aqua and orange plates around the oak kitchen table. "He's an interesting one, that Mr. Murdock."

Alisha didn't need to look at the woman to know she was fishing for information. Not personal information about Jared Murdock. Miss Mozelle had a way of finding out things such as that on her own. But information regarding what Alisha planned on doing about the stranger who'd now become a part of her life.

"Yes, he is," she said, careful to keep her voice blank and calm. "He's from Atlanta."

That brought Miss Mozelle's turban-covered head up. "What part?"

"North," Alisha said, glancing over at her. "Buckhead. Old money, apparently."

Miss Mozelle stood back, one hand on her slender hip. "That ain't near Riverdale, thankfully."

"Yes, that's what I thought, too." Alisha shifted Callum's tiny weight. "There's no way—"

"He don't know a thing about you, child. He's curious, but that's only because he's interested. I can feel that in my heart."

"Are you sure?" Alisha said, her pulse picking up tempo as she thought of all the possibilities, good and bad. "I mean, Atlanta and the surroundings towns— that's a big area of space."

"Did he act like he knew you?"

"No, but I think he has some secrets of his own. He doesn't like to talk about himself, but then, neither do I."

"Then keep it that way, suga'. You hold tight to your secrets and let him do the same. Makes things equal. If anything else needs to be said, ask God to guide the way."

Alisha smiled, relaxed. "Well, Jared is only going to be here a few weeks. Probably just through the end of the month."

Miss Mozelle came over to sit down on the footstool in front of the fire, her elegant hands draped over her gathered skirt. "That's plenty of time to let something slip. Better be careful."

"I will," Alisha said. Then she reached for one of Miss Mozelle's comforting hands. "Thank you."

Miss Mozelle took Alisha's hand and turned it over in hers. "For what, honey?"

"For never asking questions. For letting me keep my secrets. For keeping what you know to yourself."

"That's between you and God," Miss Mozelle said, squeezing Alisha's hand tight. "I'm just here to watch and pray, and if you want to share anything else, I'll listen and pray some more."

"And you are so very good at both listening and praying," Alisha replied. Then she smiled again. "Does my hair look decent?"

Miss Mozelle's wide pink lips parted in a grin. "Ah, fancying up for a gentleman, now ain't we?"

"No," Alisha replied, feeling the heat of a blush on her face. "I just...well, last night I wasn't at my best."

"I reckon not."

"I'd like to look nice for supper."

"You look beautiful, precious," Miss Mozelle said, letting go of Alisha's hand to stand. "Pot roast is nice and hot. That man better get himself on over here."

They heard a knock at the door then.

"Right on time. I like that in a man," Miss Mozelle said, her chuckle shaking her elaborate, mosaic-patterned turban as she headed for the door.

Alisha said another prayer of thanks, for Jared being right on time last night, too. And then she settled back in her chair and looked forward to seeing Jared again.

It had been so long since she'd enjoyed the company of a gentleman.

Jared entered the cabin, then turned back to David. "Thanks for keeping me company on the walk. Will you be okay getting home?"

"Oh, yessir. I know all the trails on this old mountain." The kid backed up, then spun around. "Oh, I almost forgot. My daddy and Mr. Burgess will get your truck out of that bog first thing tomorrow."

"I appreciate that," Jared said, reaching out to shake the boy's hand. Grinning, David pumped Jared's hand.

"Thanks, David," Alisha called from the chair, waving to the boy. "And thanks for coming to check on us."

David grinned and waved. "Somebody'll be over tomorrow, too, just in case y'all need anything."

Jared turned to take off his coat, his eyes scanning the now-familiar cabin. "Seems as if I just left here."

Doubt clouded Alisha's peaceful mood. "You didn't have to come back. I mean if you're tired—"

"I am that," he admitted as he came to sit down on the old floral sofa, his dark gaze moving over Callum. "But I was also restless, alone in my cabin. I was worried about you and the baby."

Miss Mozelle, who appeared not only to be *doula,* but also fierce chaperon, sank down on the footstool, her eyes glowing. "She's gonna be just fine. And look at that fine boy. He eats, sleeps, sighs. A perfect little angel. That's 'cause his mama took good care of herself, eating right, walking and exercising. Had a pretty good delivery, all things considered." She gave Jared a long, assessing look, as if to say, "Even with you helping."

Alisha gave Jared an amused smile, and was relieved to see him relax, his expression soft, his dark eyes centered on her before he looked down at Callum again. The way he looked at her made her heart beat too fast, but the tenderness in his eyes when he gazed at her son made her grateful. She had to swallow and remember to breathe. "He sure goes through a lot of diapers," she said to keep things on an even keel.

"We'll get 'em washed up," Miss Mozelle replied, completely calm, her gaze sweeping over Jared. "Ever changed a baby?"

"No, I can't say that I have. But then I never delivered a baby either until last night."

"First time for everything." She pushed off the stool. "Supper is ready. Baby, you think you can sit at the table?"

Alisha looked at the hard oak chairs, then grimaced. "I think I'll take my plate here by the fire."

"Me, too," Jared said, getting up to help Miss Mozelle serve the food. Then he turned back. "Want me to put Callum in the bassinet?"

"Yes," Alisha said, waiting as Jared leaned down to take Callum from her. His nearness caught Alisha off guard. Their eyes met as he gathered baby blankets, tucking them around Callum's arms and legs. Alisha sank back, her breath hitching. Jared smelled clean and fresh, like the mountain air on a warm day. He made her feel warm all over, too.

"Hold his head," Miss Mozelle gently ordered. "Okay, then." The older woman gave him another scrutinizing look as she watched him carefully lay the baby in the bassinet. "I'll let you two eat by the fire and I'll sit over here in the kitchen."

"You can eat with us," Jared said as he dipped pot roast dripping with rich brown gravy, then added potatoes and carrots for Alisha.

Alisha remembered that he was a gentleman. Miss Mozelle beamed her approval at his suggestion. "That's kind of you, but I like my plate in front of me, not on my lap. Y'all get on over there and enjoy this food now, before it gets cold. I'll be fine right here, minding my own business."

Alisha knew exactly what the crafty woman would be doing. She'd be watching. Observing. Analyzing. Figuring. Miss Mozelle would let her instincts and her intuition take over, and if she decided she didn't approve of Jared Murdock, she wouldn't hesitate to let Alisha know. But she wouldn't judge too harshly, either.

Alisha took the plate Jared offered her. "Thanks."

"Take her some of that tea I brewed," Miss Mozelle ordered from her perch.

Jared did as he was told, his eyes twinkling as he poured the steaming dark brew from a large ceramic teapot into a bright yellow cup.

"And she needs a napkin."

Jared got an aqua-colored linen napkin off the counter, then grabbed another one for himself. Then he sat down on the footstool by the fire, his expression eager as he lifted a forkful of tender roast to his mouth.

"Hold it, mister," Miss Mozelle said, clapping her hands so loud, Jared dropped his fork of food and stared over at her in surprise. "We gotta say grace."

"Of course." Jared waited, his smile now frozen on the verge of impatience.

Alisha closed her eyes and bowed her head, amusement coloring her mind. Jared was in for a wait. Miss Mozelle liked to pray long and loud. Sure enough, by the time the woman was finished asking God to bless this house, this family, this new baby, this man who'd been sent to minister to both, this town, the whole mountain, and the whole country and world, and lastly, herself, Alisha could hear a soft sigh emitting from Jared's close-mouthed silence.

Just as Miss Mozelle finished with a long amen, Alisha opened one eye to peek over at Jared. He had his head lowered, but both eyes were open now as he stared across at Alisha and frowned. She smiled and put a finger to her lips. It wouldn't do for Miss Mozelle to catch them making light of her very serious and much-needed blessing.

Jared grinned, then winked, his dazzling smile making Alisha grin, too.

"Now, let's eat before I have to warm all this up again," Miss Mozelle declared in her rich, flowing voice, her eyes sharply surveying them both for any signs of dissent.

"Thank you. That was lovely," Alisha said, grateful for the comfort of her dear friend.

"Yes, and very thorough," Jared said, careful to avoid looking at Miss Mozelle.

"I believe in covering all my bases with the Lord," the woman said, her hand on her steaming cup of tea.

"Probably a good idea," Jared agreed, finally able to chew his meat. "Umm, this is very good."

"Loretta cooked it," Miss Mozelle said before Alisha could respond. "She's a fine cook."

"They seem like a nice family," Jared said.

"Where's your family?"

At Miss Mozelle's pointed question, he looked down at his plate. "My parents are both dead. Killed in a plane crash when I was ten years old. My grandparents raised me, but they've both passed on. My grandmother died when I was in college, and I just buried my grandfather a couple of months ago. There's really no one left."

Alisha's heart went out to him. Another thing they had in common, then. They were both alone in the world, and hiding out from their sorrow. "I'm sorry," she said to Jared, her tone low. "Both of my parents are dead, too. First my father, then my mother a few years later."

"It's tough," he replied, sympathy and understanding darkening his eyes to a midnight black. He swiped his napkin across his mouth. "Mine were so involved with each other, they traveled everywhere together, and... they died together."

"Oh, I sure hate to hear that, bless 'em," Miss Mozelle said, echoing Alisha's thoughts. The room was silent for a while, then she asked, "Now, what do you do for a living?"

"I *did* own my own company. Media consultant. And I still watch over the holdings my grandfather left."

Miss Mozelle nodded as she took in the information. "Hmph, don't know a thing about any media. All this television and Internet junk, you can keep that. Makes these young folks around here lazy and shiftless. Give me a good book and some good music any day."

He nodded, smiled politely, tried to chew before she asked him something else. "I guess I'd had enough of all that myself. I sold my share of the company just before I came here."

"What you aim to do with the rest of your life?" Miss Mozelle asked, one hand going to her hip.

"I don't really know," he responded, his eyes downcast.

"I always wanted to be a social worker," Alisha blurted out, then wished she could take the words back.

Jared gave her a scrutinizing look. "Why haven't you done that, then?"

"I...I never finished college," she explained. "I had started, but I had to drop out."

Thankfully, Miss Mozelle interrupted. "Jared, let me fill that cup of tea for you. I declare, my manners done gone out the window tonight. Now, tell me some more about your grandparents. They must have been mighty fine folks, to take you in and raise you like that. Bless 'em."

Alisha ate her food as Jared described his life back in Atlanta. Her appetite was better tonight, now that she'd had some rest. While she ate, she watched Jared's face and listened to him answering the questions she'd longed to ask. His expression was caught between exasperation and amusement as he tried to make conversation with Alisha, only to have Miss Mozelle answer him or question him before Alisha could even open her mouth. The poor man had no way of knowing that her friend was just trying to protect Alisha's privacy.

Finally, he gave up and sat silent, shoveling food in his mouth, probably to keep from laughing or shouting out loud. He was a quiet, polite stranger from the city, but Alisha knew she shared a strong bond with him now. Which could prove to be dangerous for her. She didn't want to bond with anyone except her baby.

"Who wants pound cake and peaches?" Miss Mozelle said as she pushed up from the table, her own expression bordering on a sly smile.

"That sounds good." Jared got up to take his and Alisha's plates over to the deep, old-fashioned sink..

"Want some coffee with it?"

"No," Jared replied. "I've had enough coffee for one day. I'd love a glass of milk, though."

"Milk and pound cake," Miss Mozelle said, her cackling laughter filling the tiny cabin and causing little Callum to jump in his sleep. Then she turned to Alisha, an approving smile on her dark, smooth face. "He's all right, this one, suga'."

"Oh?" Jared said, turning to both of them, his hands on his hips. "What makes me all right in your mind, Miss Mozelle? Besides me delivering babies and everything?"

"Any man who likes milk with his pound cake is all right in my book," the woman explained. "That was my sweet daddy's favorite combination in the world. Milk and pound cake. So if you like the same thing my daddy did, that means you're not only smart, but a good man, too, Mr. Jared Murdock."

Jared turned to Alisha and let out a long mock sigh of relief, his hands falling to his side. She laughed, then motioned him close. "You just passed a big test."

He nodded. "I know. But something tells me it's the first of many to come."

❧ Chapter Seven ❧

Earlier today, he had watched out the window as they all paraded by. All the nosy do-gooders going to see the new baby. They made him sick, all of them. This place was like a prison, a prison full of dull, lifeless people who didn't care about the outside world or what it had to offer.

Well, he cared. He wanted off this mountain, away from the despair and boredom, and now he had the perfect opportunity to get what he wanted. If that stranger didn't get in the way, of course.

He'd watched people coming and going, and he knew for a fact that the stranger had been back to visit Alisha Emerson. Tonight. He'd talked to that stupid kid, David, just in passing, in a polite, inquiring way, of course. David had been only too happy to tell him everything. But he had to see for himself. So he'd walked along the back trails to her cabin, seen them in there, all cozy and cuddled, sharing dinner together. And to make matters worse, that old she-hen Mozelle was staying with Alisha. No chance of paying Alisha a visit with that old battle-ax standing guard. Besides, if he showed up late at night for a visit, that might make people suspicious.

No, he had to be careful. He'd wait until the time was just right. He'd go see her, to make it look good. He'd use the right excuses—just checking on her and the baby, of course. He'd keep getting closer to her, gain her trust and confidence even more. And then he'd spring it on her. She'd be willing now. She'd do anything to protect that brat of hers.

Babies. He hated them, too. Whining bundles of mess, if you asked him. Never had any use for having a baby. Things might have been different for him. Long ago, he could have loved a child. But that had changed. Now, he would only use the child as leverage to get what he wanted. He refused to feel anything for the baby. All of his feelings were tied to Alisha and what she could do for him.

He moved from the window, intent on getting warm. He'd been out roaming around in the dark, in the cold, and he'd seen some things out there. Found some interesting things, too. These people on this mountain, so ignorant, so innocent, didn't know about how he prowled around at night, watching and waiting.

But they would know soon enough. Soon, everyone on Dover Mountain would recognize and know him. They'd give him the respect he was due. No more back-breaking work, no more having to bend to the rules of this forsaken place.

He couldn't wait to get out of here.

He was anxious to start his plan. Too anxious. He had to wait until everything fell into place. He had to do a little more grunt work, and then, he would be living on easy street. Away from Dover Mountain and the hicks who lived here. He'd waited so long and now it would be so very easy. It only took one secret and one woman willing to pay for that secret. She'd have to pay, and before it was all over, she'd be begging him to help her.

And that woman was Alisha Emerson. If that stranger from Atlanta didn't get in the way.

Jared felt something was wrong the minute he entered the cabin. Looking around, he felt the hair on the back of his neck stand up. What was it?

He checked the fire. It had burned down to a few red-hot embers. The room was warm near the fire, but it was beginning to chill in the dark corners. He went to turn on the lamp by the door so he could see to put more wood on the fire. Then it hit him. The lamp was off.

Jared had left the lamp on. He always left a lamp on. It was something his grandmother had taught him.

"Leave a lamp burning, Jared. That way, you can always find your way home again." It had been a gesture of love on his grandmother's part, but with Jared, it had become a habit born out of love and respect for his grandparents.

He thought back, remembered talking to David, remembered how he'd deliberately left that one particular lamp on. Curious, Jared went to the lamp and clicked the switch back on. Nothing happened. Jared glanced around, the feeling of unease still prevalent in his mind. Then he touched the light bulb. It wasn't hot, not even warm. Must have been off for a while. He twisted the bulb, then nodded. It was loose in the socket. That explained why it had gone out. Jared tightened the light back into the socket, then clicked the switch on and off, testing it. The light seemed to be intact now.

One problem solved, at least. Tomorrow he'd get his truck out of that mud hole and maybe then he could actually settle down to a much-needed vacation. Only, Jared had a feeling that the next few weeks on Dover Mountain would be anything but a vacation.

He thought back over the people he'd met so far, in awe of this tight-knit community. Living in the elite society of some of Atlanta's oldest and proudest families, he'd never stopped to think about how the rest of the world lived. He never before would have cared about a place like this village on top of a mountain, and his childhood memories could only reflect fishing and hunting with his grandfather. They'd always kept to themselves on those trips. But now that Jared had had a glimpse into the lives of the people who inhabited this mountain, and the strong sense of faith they possessed, he had to wonder about his own life, about his own decisions, and about his own lack of faith.

Jared felt some powerful forces at work here. Forces that had surely led him to this place. Why else would he have picked this particular spot for a vacation, for a getaway, after forgetting it for over twenty years. He'd traveled the world over in all that time, and he could have gone anywhere in the world this time.

Thinking back, Jared remembered the afternoon he'd called the travel agent. "Find me a spot in the mountains," he'd said. "Somewhere secluded and away from people. Somewhere I can go and think things through." Then an image had popped into his mind. An image of a quiet stream and his grandfather's amused chuckle. "Look up Dover Mountain," he'd suggested. "See what you can find there."

"I have the place," the chirpy woman had told him later, only too happy to accommodate one of her best clients. "Dover Mountain is quaint and rural, far from the maddening crowd. They have a few cabins, and they *are* trying to attract tourists to help pump much-needed money into the town, but Mr. Murdock, this isn't exactly a country club."

Explaining that he'd visited the mountain as a child, Jared had told her to book him a cabin. Then he'd packed a few clothes, and he'd headed up I-75. He'd done this without thinking things through, without a long-range plan, which wasn't like him at all. Jared Murdock always had a plan. But this time, he only knew he wanted to get away from all the problems and revelations he'd had to deal with over the last few months.

And now, here he sat, alone by the fire. With new concerns, new revelations clutching at his soul in the same way the bare branches clutched at his window just outside. Just enough to be irritating. Just enough to be intriguing.

He'd come here to be alone, and suddenly he was surrounded by strange, interesting, colorful characters. Good people. Simple people who'd worked hard all their lives. People who only asked for a decent way of life for their families.

People like Alisha Emerson and little Callum.

Jared knew he'd come here as an outsider, a stranger. He wasn't supposed to get involved with the townspeople. But because he'd helped Alisha, he *was* involved.

And he hadn't decided if that was good or bad.

Yet he couldn't wait to get out and walk around or maybe take a long run up one of the trails. He wanted to see the town after the fast-moving storm had washed away some of the fairy-tale facades. He wanted to find out why Dr. Sloane drank, why Miss Mozelle had never married. Why the Wilkes family seemed to be in a constant struggle. Why Rayanne's bad boyfriend wouldn't marry her and give her baby a name and a father.

But mostly, Jared wanted to find out more about Alisha. Because he'd noticed two things about her tonight. One, she didn't have any family pictures scattered around her cabin. Jared found that very odd. She had the other feminine, dainty things most women required in a home. She had stacks and stacks of books, and festive dinnerware, and hats and throws, comforters and pillows. But no pictures.

And two, when he'd leaned down close to her to take the baby, she'd almost cringed away, as if in fear. Until she'd looked up into Jared's eyes. Then her fear had changed into something else entirely.

Hope.

She hoped she was just imagining things.

Alisha sat up in bed, the old nightmare causing a dread she hadn't felt in many months to cloud her mind with a cold, dark fear. She'd first noticed the plant after Jared had left and Miss Mozelle had gathered blankets and pillows to make a bed on the couch.

"What's that?" Alisha asked her friend, her finger pointing toward the green plant in the straw basket by the front door.

"Oh, that," Miss Mozelle replied with a sniff. "It's an azalea plant, honey. I sure don't know where anybody found one that had survived that powerful storm, but you can plant it outside when the weather finally warms."

"Who brought it?"

"Why, I reckon Jared did. He set it inside the door after he went out to get more firewood. Said it would freeze for sure out there on the porch."

Jared hadn't mentioned the plant to Alisha. He must have brought it in when she'd gone to the bedroom for a diaper for the baby. Did he get her the plant as a gift? But that didn't make any sense. The local nursery was still selling firewood and outdoor pipe covers right now, not azalea bushes. Those weren't due to arrive until a couple of weeks from now, when all the springtime plants started coming in.

Alisha lay back, her nightmares crouching around her like unwanted shadows. An azalea plant. She hated azaleas. Hated the flowers she'd once loved. Hated the sight of their bright pink and purple blooms trailing the roads and yards during the spring. Now someone had left her one.

Was that someone Jared? Or had he just found the plant on her porch? She'd be sure to ask him that next time she saw him. If she saw him again.

The little bit of trust that had come during the long hours of labor was gone now. Jared had helped her, but she wasn't quite sure why he was here on the mountain in the first place. After all, he had come knocking at her door in the middle of the night. Fate? Coincidence? Or a carefully planned visit?

Alisha didn't want to distrust Jared Murdock, but she felt it to her bones, like an aching warning.

And she didn't want to hate azaleas. They were as much a part of the South as corn bread and grits. Lying here in the dark, she remembered how she'd planted the hearty bushes in her large, sloping yard back in Riverdale. Her azaleas had been the talk of the town. They had grown up to six feet tall, blooming like cotton candy for an achingly short time each spring. She'd tended them with such loving care, hoping to have them in her garden for a lifetime and beyond.

But now, just like those velvety soft blooms, her hopes and dreams were gone, to be replaced by a cold, sick fear. If the sight of one potted bush could bring all of it rushing back, how was she going to cope with raising a baby? Or protecting that baby?

Alisha got up to check on Callum. He slept with the face of a cherub. "Maybe I'm just being overly cautious," she whispered into the night. "Maybe it was an innocent gesture." And maybe Jared did just find the azalea bush on the porch.

She thought back. Had she let something slip in passing to someone, maybe about how she used to work in her garden, toiling away to make her azaleas grow and bloom?

That had to be it. Maybe she'd told Letty Martha or Loretta Wilkes something about azaleas and they were just being kind by giving her a new plant in honor of her baby's birth. But then, there had been no card.

Alisha lay back down, cold to the bone, and pulled the covers close. She'd just gotten settled when little Callum begin to rustle and wail. He must be ready for his midnight feeding. Alisha got up to get him, then turned to find Miss Mozelle standing there in a billowing flannel gown, her arms outstretched.

"Need some help, honey?"

"You can sit with me while I change him and feed him, if you want."

"You sound worried, child. What's wrong? Bad dream?"

"The same old dream."

"Bless your heart. Probably just the stress of delivery."

"No, it's more than that. I am worried, Miss Mozelle, but I can't put my finger on why exactly. Will you say a little prayer for my baby?"

"Of course, honey. You know I will."

Alisha thought back about what Miss Mozelle had said earlier, about Jared Murdock now being Callum's protector. She didn't know Jared that well, but she hoped and prayed Miss Mozelle was right. Because her baby needed a protector right now.

As Alisha settled in the rocking chair to nurse her baby, her thoughts once again turned to the potted plant sitting in the other room. As soon as she could, she'd get rid of the azalea. She didn't want to plant it in her yard. She didn't want to see it bloom. She just wanted to forget about it and all the nightmares the plant had conjured up. But in the back of her mind, the one thought was shouting at Alisha with a loud clarity that she couldn't escape.

Someone might know that she had once loved azaleas.

Could that same person possibly know something else about Alisha? Something from her past? And was that person Jared Murdock?

She hoped she was just imagining things, but the lush plant sitting by her door was very real. And so were her fears.

Jared held his foot to the gas pedal and pressed while Tate Wilkes and the man he'd introduced as Hank Burgess waved for him to give it the gas. Hank's big Dodge had a winch on the front, so it should be just a matter of minutes before the Escalade was out of the mud and back on the narrow, potholed road. Except that even after Jared gave it the gas and steered it back and forth, the SUV was still stuck solid in the middle of a deep, jagged rut.

Jared took his foot off the gas and turned toward Hank as the burly man came to the open window. "You got yourself stuck pretty good there, fellow."

"Yes, I did," Jared said, thinking this whole conversation was a bit redundant.

Hank shook his head. "City fellows. That's a mighty fancy vehicle, and expensive, too, but it don't do much just sitting there."

"I appreciate the help," Jared replied, the manners his grandmother had instilled in him kicking in, in spite of the way the other man was sneering at him. "What do we do now?"

"Well, let's try the winch again while I back my Dodge up. Give it a little more power."

"Okay." Jared nodded, his immediate impression of Hank Burgess less than favorable. But the man had come out on a cold morning to help him out of a jam. Jared could live with the insults and the sneers if Hank could live with him being a "city fellow."

Jared waited for Tate's signal, then pressed down on the gas pedal again, watching in the rearview mirror as Hank slowly started backing up the big white Dodge. This time, between the powerful winch and cable and the Dodge's big motor roaring to life, Jared was able to rock the SUV over the deep pockets of the mud hole and stop it on solid road.

Putting the Escalade in park, Jared got out of the SUV and extended a hand to Tate Wilkes. "Thanks. I was beginning to think I'd have to leave it there until spring finally came."

Tate grinned and took off his thick wool Atlanta Braves baseball cap. "That's a bad spot there. We need to fill it in, but nobody around here has the time or the money, I reckon. We don't have much in the way of funds for road improvement."

Jared liked Tate Wilkes. He had a ready smile and a friendly face. In spite of hard times, Tate seemed to be grounded and civil.

He couldn't say the same for Hank Burgess. Hank turned off the Dodge and hopped out, his expression caught somewhere between amused and downright unfriendly.

"Can I pay you?" Jared asked, hoping to reimburse the men for their trouble.

Hank seemed to be figuring an amount in his head.

"We don't expect any pay, Jared," Tate said before Hank could speak.

"Just try to keep that thing steady next time, stranger," Hank retorted, his big hands in the pockets of his sturdy gold barn jacket, his expression grim.

Tate spoke up. "Hank, he got stuck in the middle of that storm the other night. That coulda happened to the best of us."

"Yeah, I heard all about how it happened," Hank replied, his brown eyes centered on Jared. "Funny how you wound up at Alisha's place."

"And thank goodness he did," Tate said, giving Jared an apologetic look. "I don't even want to think about that poor woman there alone, having a baby."

"She had plenty of willing help, if she'd just asked for it," Hank said pointedly, his chest puffing up. "Everyone on this mountain cares about Alisha, but she's too stubborn to see it at times."

Jared suddenly understood why Hank didn't seem to like him. Hank had a thing for Alisha, obviously. "I'm just glad everything turned out okay," he said, his gaze land-ing on Hank, daring him to say anything more. Jared knew how intimidating that Murdock gaze could be. He'd used it on better men than Hank Burgess.

The other man stared back for a minute, then glanced away. "I gotta get to the garage."

Tate nodded. "Yep. I got to make the rounds to the cabins, make sure no pipes are busted, or any trees fell on anything. I sure don't need any property damage right now, with spring just around the corner."

"Need some help?" Jared asked Tate, hoping to move about this morning and explore the village. He didn't want to spend the morning inside his cabin.

Hank scoffed. "Didn't you come here to rest and relax?"

Jared shook his head. "I came here to get away from the city. But I like to stay busy. And I'd like to repay everyone for their hospitality."

"That's mighty nice of you," Hank said. Then he pivoted and headed for his truck. "Tate, you coming with me?"

Tate looked from Hank back to Jared. "Nah. I guess I'll take Jared here up on his offer. I could use an extra set of hands."

Hank gave Tate a mutinous glare, then cranked the Dodge and peeled out, headed back up the narrow mountain road.

"That one's a hot wire," Tate said by way of an excuse. "Always got a grudge against somebody or something. Thinks the rest of the world owes him, big-time."

"I got that impression," Jared said as they climbed into the Escalade. "Where to first, Tate?"

"Let's start with a good cup of coffee at the Hilltop Diner." He grinned, then pointed toward the road. "It's right across from the Mini-Mart—what we call the general store. After that, I'll give you the whole nickel tour of our fine city."

Jared nodded, turned the SUV around and headed up the road toward the village. As they passed Alisha's cabin, he noticed the big white Dodge parked in her yard.

Tate glanced over at Jared. "Hank. Well, his wife left him a couple years ago. Got a divorce. Ever since Alisha showed up here last fall, he's been trying to—"

"Date her?" Jared finished, a sick kind of dread clouding out the bright sunshine that spilled into the dark interior of the Escalade.

"Yeah, something like that. Hank ain't got the manners of a hog, but he owns the village garage, so he makes a decent enough living, I reckon. He might be a good catch."

Somehow, Jared doubted that. And he had to know. "How does Alisha feel about Hank?"

Tate grinned, the crow's-feet under his graying eyebrows crinkling. "Alisha don't want no part of Hank Burgess. She'll send him on his way quick enough."

That gave Jared a sense of relief. He couldn't picture Alisha with crude, rude Hank Burgess. She deserved better, much better, than some redneck auto mechanic.

Someone like you? a voice in his head asked. Maybe you'd make a better choice for Alisha?

Jared didn't think he was nearly good enough for Alisha Emerson, either. But then, he hadn't come here looking for that sort of thing.

Alisha hadn't been looking for company this morning, but company seemed to be looking for her. First, Dr. Sloane had come by to make sure she and Callum were both fit and sound. After Miss Mozelle and he had argued their way through examining Alisha and the baby, the doctor had walked back up the mountain. No sooner had he left than another visitor had shown up. Hank Burgess was sitting in her kitchen drinking coffee and eating breakfast.

Alisha gave Miss Mozelle a silent warning to behave, watching as the woman poured Hank a cup of coffee and cut him another slice of homemade cinnamon roll. Knowing how Miss Mozelle didn't approve of Hank's slovenly ways, Alisha prayed that the woman wouldn't come to blows with the mechanic.

"It was nice of you to come by, Hank," Alisha said, trying to be polite. "You're out awfully early this morning."

"Hmmph, ain't that the truth," Miss Mozelle said as she sat down on the couch, her look of utter disapproval apparent. "Everybody's out early today."

Hank cut his eyes toward Miss Mozelle, then grinned at Alisha. "I was helping that fellow Murdock get his fancy Cadillac SUV out of a big ol' mud hole." He puffed up, then said, "Sorry I didn't get by the other day. I was just so tired. We put in a long week at the garage." He gave her a meaningful look. "I'm gonna clear me a pretty profit this month."

"I understand," Alisha replied, ignoring his bragging. "And really, I'm fine. No need for everyone to keep checking up on me."

Hank leaned forward, his fork full of cinnamon roll hanging in midair. "We just wanna help you."

"I know," Alisha said, shifting little Callum in her arms. "And I do appreciate it so much. Everyone has been so good to me."

"Including that city dude, from what I hear," Hank said, his voice going low, his expression changing from friendly to surly in the blink of an eye.

"He's a right nice fellow," Miss Mozelle called out, her gaze on the fire. "A real gentleman, too." She said this with a little too much emphasis to suit Alisha.

And apparently Hank, too. "Well, I ain't no fancy gentleman, but I don't trust that fellow. He looks too slick. And what's he doing here anyway?"

"I 'speck that's his business," Miss Mozelle replied tartly. "He's a paying customer, so we can't send him back down the mountain."

Hank raised his fork in the air. "Yeah, but why would anyone want to come up here in this kind of weather? I mean, the man drives an Escalade, not that that mattered one hoot in this storm. He could have stayed in the city and watched this storm passing right out the window of his—what's he live in—mansion, town house, penthouse?" He asked this with a sly glance at Alisha.

So Hank was fishing for information about Jared. Alisha knew this tactic, had seen it before with Hank. He seemed to think she would eventually wind up with him, so any man who might be a threat was immediately suspect to his narrow-minded way of thinking. Especially a handsome, wealthy man from Atlanta. Hank distrusted anyone who came up the mountain from the city.

Miss Mozelle rose slowly, then brought her coffee cup to the sink. "It don't matter where the man lives, or why he came here for a vacation. What matters is that Jared Murdock helped Alisha deliver a healthy baby boy. And for that, we are so thankful to the Lord above."

Hank got up, glared at Miss Mozelle, then placed his cup by the sink with a clatter. "You and your preaching. Woman, I wasn't even talking to you. I came here to visit with Alisha."

Miss Mozelle's lips pursed in a tight, controlled way that Alisha recognized. This could get ugly. She tried to send her friend a silent warning, but it was too late.

"I know exactly what you came here for," Miss Mozelle said as she pointed a finger at Hank. "And I'm here to make sure this woman and this baby both get the proper rest they need. So you can just hightail it right back out that door, Hank Burgess."

Hank looked angry, too angry. He gave Miss Mozelle a look that would have frightened any other woman. "This is Alisha's house. I won't leave until she asks me to leave."

Miss Mozelle threw up a hand. "Well, I reckon you are sure right there." Then she purposely looked down at Alisha. "What you say, honey? Do you feel up to him staying and visiting some more?"

Alisha didn't want to hurt Hank's feelings, but she'd had to feed the baby after visiting with Dr. Sloane, and she'd barely finished when Hank had knocked on the door. But then, Hank had a way of just showing up out of the blue at the oddest of times. Caught between Miss Mozelle's overbearing protective nature and Hank's overwhelming methods of courtship, Alisha felt drained and tired.

Finally, she smiled and said, "I do thank you for stopping by, Hank, but it's about time to give Callum a little bath with a warm rag. Miss Mozelle and I need to do that by ourselves. Maybe you can come back another time when things aren't so...hectic."

Hank got the message, but he didn't like it. His brown eyes went one shade darker. "I'll just do that," he said to Alisha, his eyes on Miss Mozelle. "I'll make sure it's at a time when nobody else will be around to interrupt us, too."

After he left, Miss Mozelle whirled around, her hands on her hips. "I do believe that was a threat." Then she shot Alisha a cautious glance. "You shouldn't be alone with that man. I don't trust him one bit."

Alisha let out a sigh. "I wish Hank could understand that I'm not ready for anything near dating or a romantic relationship."

"Some people are born with thick skulls," Miss Mozelle said with a huff of breath. "That one, he ain't got the sense God gave him. Always in a mood. Spends all his time working on cars or playing them no-good computer games—you know, them kind where they chop up people and shoot them. I know. I hear things, you know."

Alisha nodded, an involuntary shudder rippling down her spine. Hank was harmless, and yet, sometimes he gave her an uneasy feeling. What would happen when she came right out and told him she wasn't interested in him?

Alisha didn't want to think about that, about Hank maybe being a violent man. She couldn't think about that now. The storm was gone and the temperature was getting back to normal. The sun was streaming in through the windows. It was a good morning to count her blessings and spend time with her son.

But when she looked out the front window on her way to the bathroom, she saw Hank's big truck still parked there in her front yard. Hank sat in the truck, staring up at her cabin for a minute before he cranked up and spun out of the yard, headed toward town.

∽ *Chapter Eight* ∽

The Hilltop Diner fit the term *hole-in-the-wall* perfectly. With its cracked brick walls and yellowed photos of past owners and patrons, it looked old and run-down, but the coffee was good and the pancakes melted in Jared's mouth. The eggs and bacon were both cooked to perfection, too. And no wonder.

The burly cook behind the counter, an African-American man named Langford Lindsay, looked intimidating, but he was singing "Just a Closer Walk with Thee" in such a sweet baritone that it must have caused the food to cook on its own from pure joy. It had all been served by Langford's wife, Dorothy, her smile beaming bright in spite of the fallen tree lying in the parking lot.

"Don't fret about that old pine," she'd told Tate when he commented on the damage. "Langford here's gonna chop that right up for firewood, even though pine ain't the best for burning, you know what I mean?"

"Let me know if you need any help," Tate had replied, his tone friendly and sincere. "We've got a mess of fallen trees all over this mountain, but we'll have plenty of wood come next winter."

Jared had noticed that about the people here. They seemed more than willing to help each other out. No questions asked. He wasn't accustomed to being around that type of honesty and caring. Most of the people he dealt with back in Atlanta always had ulterior motives for one reason or another. He took another bite of his pancakes, savoring the thought of not having any motives except those that would help him relax and have some downtime.

"Very good," Jared said now, nodding over at Tate Wilkes. "Do you eat here a lot?"

"Nah," the other man said, holding his coffee cup up for a refill. "Used to. But these days I don't have extra cash to blow on eating out. Mostly have a biscuit or cereal at home to save a few bucks. But I wanted to treat our one early spring visitor to breakfast, to thank you for helping Alisha."

"No, now." Jared held up a hand. "Let me pay. You helped get my truck out of that bog."

Tate stared over at him for a minute, then smiled. "Are we gonna sit here and argue about this?"

"No," Jared replied good-naturedly. "There is no argument. I'm paying and that's final."

Tate lowered his gaze. "I appreciate it." Then he pointed a finger. "I'm buying next time, though. I ain't so broke that I can't thank a friend with a meal."

"Fair enough," Jared said, glad to know the other man considered him a friend. And he wouldn't want to insult Tate by refusing his generosity a second time.

Tate grinned, then pointed a finger at Jared. "I bet you say that to people all the time—what was it—'and that's final'?"

"I used to," Jared admitted. "But I just retired from owning my own business for fifteen years. I'm a free man for the next month, at least."

"Wow, must be nice to retire at your age. You can't be a day past forty."

"Thirty-six." Jared sat back, warm and full, his fingers moving over the big white mug of steaming coffee Dorothy kept refilling. "I hadn't planned on retiring this early, but well, things happen."

Tate snagged another piece of crisp, brown bacon. "Tell me about it. We've got three hundred people living on this little mountain and about half of those used to work at the outlet mill. Some in the factory and some on the sales floor. When Mr. Kenneth Dover decided he'd had enough of this town, he shut that place down and cut his losses. Left most of us high and dry."

Jared placed his hands together on the worn linoleum table. "I saw the abandoned outlet building on the way in the other night. I hate to hear that. So there's no hope of getting something else going in the old building, some sort of industry?"

"No hope that I can tell," Tate replied. "Lucky for me, I had been doing part-time maintenance on the five cabins the town owns and operates. When the manager decided to move back down the mountain for a better-paying job at a resort, the mayor offered me the job full-time. And just in time, too. I'd been laid off about two weeks earlier." He shifted, took a long swig of coffee. "Thank goodness for Letty Martha's quick thinking." At Jared's puzzled look, he added, "She's the mayor now. Has been for about four years."

Jared let out a chuckle. "That sweet little old woman runs this town?"

Tate grinned. "Yes, sir. And does a right fine job of keeping all of us in line, let me tell you. City Hall is right next to the Mini-Mart. She just goes back and forth doing business in both. Post office is right there inside the store, too—just a little corner slot."

Jared laughed. "I suppose she's in charge of the mail, too, right?"

"Nah, Warren J. is postmaster around here. He's just nosy enough to do a good job, too. But Letty Martha, she runs this town."

"So she gave you the job as manager of the cabins?"

"Yep, she's sweet but shrewd, too, let me tell you. Dover Mountain Rustic Hideaways—that's the official name on the Web site. Can you believe we've even got a Web site? That Letty, she's a modern-day mayor. Ordered this big ol' computer system about a year ago. Made the money by holding an arts and crafts festival during the peak tourist season."

Curious, Jared asked, "Oh, and when is that?"

"'Bout a month or so from now," Tate replied. "Let this last little cold snap pass, and you'll start seeing more buds on them trees out there in the hills. And let me tell you something, it's a mighty pretty sight. Dogwoods, azaleas, sweet gum, oaks, all sorts of hardwood. Mountain laurel. And of course, the blue spruce. They don't call this the Blue Ridge Mountains for nothing."

Thinking this little village was sitting on a gold mine of tourist opportunities, Jared asked, "Does the town actually turn a profit on renting cabins?"

"Barely," Tate said, chuckling again. "But hey, it's a living."

"So you do that full-time now, managing the cabins?"

"That and odd jobs here and there. Hank owns a garage and I help him out some on the side. He's pretty much got a monopoly going there. These roads are hard on vehicles, so people are always needing new brakes and new tires. He makes out pretty good, but he tends to gouge the customer, if you know what I mean. I don't cotton to that, but a man's got to make his own way, somehow."

Jared sank back against the green vinyl booth. He could see Hank Burgess upping the price of a set of tires, or charging extra labor on a brake change. "Sounds as if Hank takes advantage of his customers."

"He does." Tate leaned close. "But...Hank has a burr up his bonnet anyway. He's been different since his wife left him. She ran away with some hunter who'd come up here from Marietta. Fellow was a doctor. Had money to burn. She used to work right here—that's how she met the man. Hank never got over her leaving him like that, so now he's determined to make a pile of money himself. Just to prove to her she should have stuck it out, I reckon."

"Twisted logic, don't you think?" Jared asked, his dislike of Hank Burgess even stronger, in spite of the man's hardships.

"Kinda. But then, she did a number on him." Tate shrugged. "'Course, that don't mean he's got to do a number on everybody who needs a mechanic. I've tried talking to him, tried to get him back into church, but Hank ain't having any of that. He's been burned too bad."

Jared could understand being burned by a woman. He'd certainly felt the sting of Meredith's rejection. But he hadn't been in love with Meredith. He could see that now that he'd walked away. His pride had been scorched, but his heart had almost given a sigh of relief. But then, there had been so many factors playing into their breakup. Factors Jared didn't want to think about right now.

He glanced over at Tate, wondering how the man kept such a positive attitude. "You go to church? Alisha mentioned she goes and volunteers a lot, too."

"Yep. We only got the one. First Church of Dover Mountain. First and only. Just about everybody attends. Reverend Stripling is a good man. After the storm, he insisted we have a quick Easter morning service out under the trees, since the power was out in the church. He's tried to bring new things into the church, like Alisha's counseling the teens around here. We need more of that type of thing." His eyes grew dark then. "Wish she'd been able to get through to Rayanne, but she's been a big help during all of this."

"She seems close to Rayanne," Jared said, seeing the pain and worry in Tate's eyes.

They sat silent for a few minutes, then Tate moved to get up. "Well, no use dwelling over spilled milk. We're gonna get through this rough spot, with the Lord's help."

"And a few friends," Jared replied as he grabbed the check just before Tate tried to steal it.

"Just thought I'd try," Tate said, sheepish.

"My treat," Jared told the other man. "It was worth it just to hear you talk about this place. I'm going to be here awhile, so I'd like to get to know everyone." And maybe he'd be able to help.

"You'll probably hear more than you want to hear," Tate replied. "Folks around here are tight-lipped, but we like to keep tabs on each other. When we do open up, we share everything."

Jared had to agree. He'd gotten some strange looks when he'd walked in the diner with Tate. He could tell the locals weren't sure about him. When he went up to the register to pay, Dorothy Lindsay greeted him with a warm smile. "How was it?"

"Great," Jared replied, taking in her crisp blue uniform and her tightly permed short curls. "Those pancakes melted in my mouth."

"A secret family recipe," Dorothy said, beaming with pride, her silver daisy earrings dangling against her cheeks. "Langford won't share that one."

Jared handed her a twenty and said, "Well, tell Langford there, between the pancakes and his singing, I think I've died and gone to heaven."

Dorothy threw back her head. "Hey, big daddy, you hear that?"

"What's that, sweet pea?" Langford said as he came barreling up the aisle, his massive arms bulging underneath his crisp T-shirt.

"This here city fellow likes your cooking and your singing."

Langford extended a beefy hand. "Well, then, come on back here for food and if you want to hear more of my singing, meet me in church Sunday."

Thrown by the man's bold sincerity, Jared shook his hand and laughed. "I just might. I know I'll be back here. Can't wait to try the chicken-fried steak."

"Good, good." Langford turned as a waitress called from the kitchen. "See you in church."

Jared watched the big man move slowly toward the back of the restaurant like a bull about to be let out of the pen. Dorothy handed him his change. "How's Miss Alisha and that boy?"

"Good, last time I checked," Jared replied. "Guess you heard—"

"I heard all right," Dorothy said, slapping a hand on the counter. "Mercy, mister. You sure picked a good night to get lost in a rainstorm. Bless you, though. We all love Alisha. She deserves some happy times, that's for sure."

Jared wanted to ask the woman more regarding that subject, but decided he'd had enough of warning looks and suddenly closemouthed villagers each time he asked questions about Alisha. So he just nodded. "Alisha seems like a lovely person."

"Yeah, she is that." Dorothy sent him a scrutinizing look. "You gonna be around awhile?"

"I plan on staying a few weeks," Jared said.

"We're having a cleanup day tomorrow. You seen all them downed trees, right? We could use an extra set of hands to get this place back in shape for spring."

"I'll be glad to help," Jared said, meaning it. "I'm not used to being idle. I plan to do some fishing, maybe a little hiking and rock climbing, but other than that—"

"We'll keep you busy," Dorothy said, nodding her approval. "Normally, we leave the tourists to their own devices, but since you done delivered our newest citizen, and it being Alisha and all, well, I think you gonna fit right in around here."

"I don't know about that," Jared said. "But I'm willing to help you get this place cleaned up."

"Just in time for spring," Dorothy said. "Good Friday and Easter came early this year, then that storm came through. We had a few buds and blossoms for the holiday. But now, all that rain will make this mountain spring to life. It's time for new beginnings all around."

"Maybe it is," Jared said. "Thanks again." Then he turned to walk toward where Tate was visiting with another diner.

Jared felt Dorothy's almond-shaped eyes following him all the way out the door.

"Uh-huh. You hurry on back now," he heard her call out.

"You were in such a rush for your dinner," Alisha told little Callum as she held the sweet-smelling baby up to her shoulder for a good, long burp. "Did you get enough this time?"

She was tired. No doubt about that. And she was definitely still sore. But Alisha felt so happy today she could just shout it to the mountains. "I love you," she whispered to Callum. Then she kissed his fuzzy head.

His hair was dark, probably would be brown like his daddy's. Thinking of Callum's father gave her a start, but she quickly put that out of her mind. Alisha held her hand to the baby's head, then brought him down so she could coo at him. "Look at that sunshine, little one. It's warmer today. I think spring is finally coming to this old hilltop."

Callum gave her a wide-eyed look, let out a big yawn, then drifted into a soft sleep, his little eyelids drooping as she gently rocked him in her arms.

"Nodding off on me again?" Alisha asked on a whisper. "No wonder. With that full belly, I'd need a nap myself." She tiptoed toward the bassinet, wishing she had room for an all-out nursery. But the cabin was too small for that. She'd found the bassinet at a secondhand store in a town a few miles down the mountain. Most of Callum's things had either been given to her or bought secondhand, but Alisha didn't mind that. Callum had everything he needed right now: a warm bed, clothes and diapers, food and nourishment, and a mother who loved him with a fierce intensity that took her breath away.

"Soon, Mama will have to decide what to do," Alisha said as she pulled a blue cotton blanket around him. "When you get older, we'll be better able to add on to the cabin, and you'll have a nice room of your own."

Until then she had to guard what little she had. She had to guard the money she'd tucked away for Callum. "One day at a time," Alisha said as she kissed her finger then placed that kiss on Callum's soft cheek. "We've made it this far. It's going to be okay."

She thought about the azalea bush out on her porch. She'd asked Miss Mozelle to take it back out since it was warm today. Alisha got knots in her stomach each time she thought about the plant. Who had brought it?

"Stop imagining the worst," she whispered to her reflection in the bedroom mirror. "It was just someone being kind."

Deciding to put that particular worry out of her mind, Alisha walked back up the hallway and into the kitchen. "Miss Mozelle, you don't have to wash those dishes."

"Yes, I do," the woman replied. "I like to talk to the Lord while I'm washing dishes. You ever do that?"

Alisha laughed. "Yes, while I'm washing dishes, while I'm washing clothes in that old washing machine on the back porch, while I'm hanging clothes on the line. While I'm taking a shower."

Miss Mozelle smiled, then lowered her turbaned head. "I guess you've perk near bent the Lord's ear right off, then."

"I have done my share of praying lately," Alisha admitted as she sat down on the sofa to fold freshly washed diapers. She was alternating between cloth diapers and the disposable ones some kind neighbor had given her, but she noticed there always seemed to be diapers around here—both dirty and clean. That just made her smile even more.

"You look content," Miss Mozelle said as she finished her work and dried her hands on a rooster-decorated kitchen towel. "Any more bad dreams?"

"No, I slept pretty good last night," Alisha said. "Your herbal tea is a wonder."

"Chamomile and rose hips. Good for the soul," Miss Mozelle replied. "I have to watch after your health, darlin'."

"Well, you're doing a good job," Alisha said. "But you don't have to stay here day and night. I know you need to be helping Dr. Sloane at the clinic."

"That man can do without me a day or two."

"Jared said Dr. Sloane had a hangover the other morning, after the storm."

"I don't doubt that," Miss Mozelle replied as she glanced down at her hands. "That man don't like storms, not one bit."

"It must be horrible, having to live with that terrible grief and guilt each time a storm passes through."

Miss Mozelle didn't look up. "It's been twenty-five years, but I guess some things a man just never forgets."

"He did all he could, from what you've told me."

"Yes, he did. I wish *I* could have done more."

Alisha's heart went out to both Miss Mozelle and Dr. Sloane. "Is that why you went back to school to become a midwife?"

Miss Mozelle's head shot up, then she slowly nodded. "I had to do something, honey. That man was so full of grief and self-hatred after he lost his wife and baby. I just wanted to be able to help other women here on this mountain. I wanted to help him."

Tears pricked at Alisha's eyes. "It's a tragedy. Losing a child at birth is hard." She swallowed, thinking of Callum. "But to lose your wife, too. I can't imagine that."

"And him being a doctor." Miss Mozelle stared into the fire. "That's what got to me. Seeing him crying out to her, holding the baby out for her to look at. And them both dead and gone already. I did everything he asked to assist, but it was a hard labor and I just stumbled in on them, tried to help best I could. And there was just no way of getting any other help up here with that terrible storm washing out the roads. Child, I never want to see that happen again. Never."

She got up, sniffed loudly, then turned with a serene smile on her face. "But we got us a fine baby, this time, in spite of this recent bad storm, Miss Alisha Emerson. Callum looks happy and healthy, so we can breathe a sigh of relief on that account, at least."

"Yes, we can," Alisha said, the sadness permeating the room being replaced with a whiff of joy. "And I can thank Jared Murdock for that."

"You sure can, again and in person," Miss Mozelle said, her hands on her hips as she stared out the window. "'Cause he's coming up the lane toward the front door right now."

"Thanks for lunch," Jared said later as he watched Alisha rocking little Callum. "I didn't stop by intent on eating, you know."

"I know." She smiled, kissed her son's fringe of fine hair. "But I'm glad you did come by. It gave Miss Mozelle a chance to go for a walk. That woman loves to walk."

"She's in good shape for her age," Jared replied, keenly aware that he was alone with Alisha and the baby. Now that things had settled down, Alisha seemed distant and aloof. Did he make her uncomfortable, he wondered.

"She urged me to walk while I was pregnant," Alisha said, her tone light and conversational in spite of the wariness in her eyes. "I think that's one reason I had such an easy birth."

"You consider *that* easy?"

She laughed and the sound made Jared think of wind chimes and tinkling bells. She had a joyous laugh that brightened her whole face. And made her so pretty. Her freckled skin glowed with a warm porcelain hue and her green eyes danced with mirth.

"That was easy, all things considered. I've seen worse," she added, her smile seeming to wither, the light leaving her expressive eyes.

"I don't mean to make fun or doubt you," he said, "but honestly, Alisha, I never knew what women go through just to give birth."

"But look at the reward," she said, lifting up out of the rocker to take Callum to his bed.

Jared watched from his spot in the high-backed wing chair as she gently placed her sleeping son down on the soft, sweet-smelling bassinet sheet. He waited until she had Callum tucked in, noting her long, braided hair and the pretty button-up pink sweater she wore over baggy blue jeans. "You look remarkable. No one would know you gave birth just days ago."

"I feel good," she told him, running a hand over the sprigs of deep red hair escaping from her braid. A soft blush colored her cheeks. "Miss Mozelle made me eat right and get plenty of exercise. She said I'd be back in shape in no time if I did that."

"I guess she was right." Jared could tell that even with the soft rounded belly left from giving birth, Alisha was a petite, small-framed woman. "Would you like to go for a walk, then? When Miss Mozelle returns?"

She looked surprised, then glanced outside as if she were unsure about going out. "It *is* a beautiful day. And I haven't actually left this cabin, except to go out onto the porch to wash clothes, since I had Callum."

"We could stroll around the yard at least."

"That would be nice."

Did he see a trace of doubt and fear in her eyes, in her expression? Was she still leery of a stranger being so intimately involved in her life now?

"I wonder..." Jared said as he watched her putting folded baby clothes in a wicker basket, her long braid falling over her shoulders each time she bent down.

"About what?"

Again, he thought he saw a spark of some unspoken fear cross her face. "I wonder what would have happened if we'd...if I'd just gone on to my cabin that night?"

Alisha turned to face him, all fear gone now. "You mean, you and I might not have ever known each other?"

"Something like that. Suppose you were still pregnant. You'd probably just be here at home, biding your time."

"And you'd be in your cabin, thinking about doing some fishing and hiking, like you said you might do."

"Yes. You wouldn't be at work, so I'd have less chance of seeing you, and I wouldn't have gotten to know everybody around here in such a hurry. Do you think our paths would have crossed at all?"

"Only if God saw fit for that to happen, I reckon."

"Is that why, then?"

She wouldn't look at him. She lowered her eyes to stare at the baby. "Why what?"

"Is that why I wound up at the wrong cabin? Do you believe God led me to you?"

She walked over to the couch, sank down to stare across at him. "I believe God answered my prayers that night. I have to believe that, Jared. It's the way I think. It's ingrained in my very being. I depend on God to guide me through everything in life."

"How do you do that?" he asked, genuinely wanting to understand. "I've never been able to rely on a higher being."

"But you love the outdoors, right?"

He nodded. "I've always loved hiking, camping, fishing. I can get away from everything and think things through out in the woods and water. I guess that started after my parents were killed. My grandfather was an avid outdoorsman."

"Then you have turned to a higher source." She waved a hand toward the window. "God made all of that."

"I suppose you're right," Jared admitted. "All that time I've been working through things, traveling around the world, mountain climbing, fishing, hiking, God was listening?"

She smiled. "I believe that, yes."

"So you rely on God for everything?"

Alisha put her hands together over her lap, then gave

him a direct, green-eyed look. "There was a time when I didn't rely on God at all. A time when I turned away from God and gave up asking for His help."

Jared was shocked to hear that. Alisha seemed so devout, so sure in her faith. "I can't believe that."

She nodded. "Oh, yes, believe it. I figured God had abandoned me, so I would just give Him the same regard."

"What happened?" he asked. "What would make you turn away from your faith?"

"And then turn back," she reminded him.

"Will you tell me?"

"No. I can't tell you." She picked at a pull on her sweater, her eyes evasive again. "But I will tell you this. I will never again doubt God, Jared. Never. I might doubt myself, blame myself for things I've done or caused, but I will never forget that God brought me back to Dover Mountain, and because of that...and your help...I have my son with me. At last."

Jared sat there watching her face. He saw the play of emotions moving over her like sunlight dappling a darkened forest. She smiled, grew quiet and almost forlorn, then smiled again, as if determined to send the darkness fluttering away.

Jared wondered what darkness she was fighting against. What was buried deep inside her, that certain something that brought a crystal-clear pain to her eyes?

That certain something that made her unable to trust him.

❧ Chapter Nine ❧

He should have known he couldn't trust her.

He'd watched Alisha today, from his spot up on the hill behind her house. Watched her walking around the property with that city fellow. Watched her as she laughed and talked and smiled.

She never did that with *him*. She acted as if she were too good for the likes of him. Didn't want him around, except of course when she needed advice or help. He knew how she felt because she'd dropped enough hints around town when she'd first arrived. A new single woman in town always brought out men looking for a good wife. But *she* claimed she didn't want to get involved. He'd heard it enough from stupid Rayanne and that crazy Wilkes clan, heard it all the time from Letty Martha and Warren J., and nosy Miss Mozelle, too. Better leave Alisha Emerson alone, they'd say. She's been through so much. And Rayanne, of course, was so much like Alisha must have been once.

Poor Rayanne, with her whining demands and her growing belly. She was turning out to be just like the rest. Always wanting more than a man could give.

He quickly pushed Rayanne and her problems out of his mind since that little bundle was pretty much tied up anyway. What was he going to do about Alisha? Better yet, what was he going to do about that meddling, smiling stranger? The man was getting mighty cozy, mighty fast. And he had money to spare, from the looks of things. That might be too tempting for poor all-alone Alisha now that she had a baby of her own to worry over.

He thought about it for a minute while he waited for his computer to boot up. Then he grinned.

Things happened to people up here in these hills. Accidents. Mistakes. Tragedies.

Maybe something needed to happen to Jared Murdock.

Something tragic.

That would take care of that little problem.

And he knew he was good at taking care of problems. One at a time.

First, he'd get Murdock out of the way.

Then he'd concentrate of taking care of Alisha Emerson.

"Jimmy, what are you doing here?"

Alisha turned from the washing machine to stare down at the man standing in her backyard. She'd been so involved in loading the machine, she hadn't even heard him come up.

"Came to pay my respects," Jimmy said, his movie-star grin a bit toward the lecherous side. While he grinned, his baby-blue eyes did a head-to-toe sweep of Alisha. "My, my, you look great. I'd never know you just had a baby."

She shivered, but held his eyes when they finally made it back to her face. This was why she didn't like

Jimmy. He was a womanizer, and he didn't care that Alisha was older than him and a friend to Rayanne. He flirted, he hinted, he got too close for comfort. When she'd first come to Dover Mountain, he'd made several passes at her and had even asked her out on a date. It didn't seem to matter that she was five years older than him, and expecting a baby. She'd refused, but that didn't seem to stop Jimmy from showing up now and then to test her resistance. And now, here he was sneaking up on her.

"What can I do for you?" she asked, trying to sound casual as she glanced around toward the kitchen. It wouldn't do for Miss Mozelle to come out here and find Jimmy Barrett hanging around.

He gave her another suggestive look, then shifted one battered cowboy boot on the bottom step, his thumbs hooked in the belt loops of his Levi's. "Nothing. Nothing a'tall. Rayanne's just been going on and on about that boy you had. Said I needed to come by and see the little fellow. Guess she thought I'd get the daddy bug or something." He shrugged, then added, "So I was passing by and here I am."

Alisha let out a sigh, then lifted her head. "Are you going to marry Rayanne, Jimmy?"

"That's between me and Rayanne, don't you think?"

"You're right," Alisha said, nodding in agreement. "But, Jimmy, she looked so sad and confused when she saw little Callum. She was thinking of her own child. Your baby needs a good home. Rayanne needs proper care. And you know her parents don't have a lot of extra money. You've got to help her."

"Yeah, yeah," Jimmy said, raising a hand in the air. "But I didn't come by here to discuss Rayanne and her family. Let me tell you, I get enough of that every time I go by there to pick her up. And I especially don't need you filling her head full of ideas of love and marriage."

"What's wrong with love and marriage?" Alisha asked, squaring her shoulders. "You were more than willing to conceive this child, now you should be responsible for it."

She saw the flash of fire in his eyes, followed by a hint of remorse. "You know what, Miss Alisha? I came just to please Rayanne, since she was pouting and whining about this. But I don't have to stay here and listen to you butting in to my business or giving me one of those canned counseling sessions."

"I'm sorry," Alisha said, hoping to convince him to do just that. He needed to listen to someone, and he surely needed counseling. "Can we start over? I do appreciate you coming to visit. Do you want to see the baby?"

The anger slipped off his face like water falling down a mountain, clean and slick. He gave her another grin. "I guess that's a safe enough topic. Rayanne wanted to come, but I didn't have time to go get her. I'll just take a little peek and be on my way." Then he handed her up a paper sack. "Oh, my mama sent over some baby stuff. Powder and lotion, stuff like that."

"That's nice," Alisha said. "Come on in and see Callum then, before you go."

She felt uncomfortable inviting the man in. Jimmy was too old for Rayanne, but too young for Alisha. She didn't want to give him the wrong message. But then, she suspected that Jimmy believed every woman he encountered fell in love with him. He had an ego the size of Tennessee.

She guided him into the kitchen and was met head-on with a sharp-eyed look of utter disapproval from Miss Mozelle. "What's he doing here?"

"Jimmy came by to see Callum," Alisha said, hoping to keep her tone light while she gave Miss Mozelle a warning look to behave. "And his mama sent over some things."

"Oh, I see," Miss Mozelle replied, placing her long arms across her midriff as she eyed Jimmy. "That's a good thing, I'm thinking. Won't be long before his *own* baby will be born."

Jimmy glared at Miss Mozelle, but didn't speak. The woman commanded respect, if nothing else. Most of the men on Dover Mountain gave her that respect and a wide berth, since she didn't have any qualms about calling them to task regarding their shoddy ways.

"He's sleeping," Alisha said, pointing to the bassinet by the sofa. "He seems to do that a lot."

Jimmy shrugged, then leaned toward the baby as if he were afraid Callum would bite him. "He sure is a little thing."

"But a mighty big responsibility," Miss Mozelle interjected with a huff.

Jimmy once again gave her a glance, then pivoted toward Alisha. "You seem to be doing okay on your own—being single and all."

Alisha thought she saw a questioning look pass through his glassy blue eyes. Maybe he wanted to be pushed in the right direction after all. Or maybe not. "Raising a child is not easy, Jimmy," she said, hoping to convince him to live up to his own coming fatherhood. "But the joys far outweigh the hardships. Callum is worth it all—everything."

That brought his head up. "You don't mention your husband very much. Must be depressing, knowing he'll never see his son. And you without any other family."

It was the way he said it, more than the mock sympathetic look he gave her, that set Alisha's nerve endings on edge. And set Miss Mozelle into a tizzy.

"Time to move on," Miss Mozelle said, grabbing Jimmy by the arm to escort him toward the front door. "You ain't got no business coming here to pester Miss Alisha. And don't tell me you came out of the goodness of your heart."

"Hey," Jimmy said, yanking his arm away. "I'm not through visiting. You know, old lady, you can't guard her all the time. Let the woman speak for herself."

Alisha looked from Jimmy's now-red face to Miss Mozelle's determined one. "It's okay, Miss Mozelle. I'll walk Jimmy to the door."

Alisha pushed Jimmy forward, then turned to put a finger to her mouth to stop Miss Mozelle from speaking. "I'll be right back."

When she had Jimmy out on the porch, she said, "I'm sorry. She's just being protective." But Alisha was very glad for her friend's intervention this time.

Jimmy gave Alisha a hard, calculating look. "Yes, and why is that? Rayanne tells me things, you know. Tells me how that midwife bosses everybody on this mountain around. It's people like her that keep this place from getting any better."

"No, it's people like Miss Mozelle who work hard and care about others that make this mountain a good place to live," Alisha said, her anger and dislike for this man coming back twofold. "She's been good to me, Jimmy. And if you do right by Rayanne, Miss Mozelle will be the first in line to help you, too."

"I don't need her help," Jimmy retorted as he pushed a hand through his long blond bangs. "Soon enough, I'm leaving Dover Mountain for good."

Alisha didn't like his smug expression. "Does Rayanne know about this?"

"She will when the time comes, I reckon." His smile was secretive and sure. "I've got some plans. Big plans."

"I hope you'll consider including Rayanne in those plans. You can't leave her all alone with a baby."

"I can if I want," Jimmy countered as he hopped down the steps. "Besides, I don't even know if that's *my* baby."

That shocked Alisha. "Oh, come on. You and Rayanne have been an item for a long time."

"Yeah, maybe. But we fight and break up, you know. And she goes off with other men sometimes."

"Not since she's been pregnant, surely?"

"I can't say anything for sure, Miss Alisha. Except that I'm leaving here real soon." He tipped a hand to his head, then gave her that killer smile again. "Real soon." With a quick wink, he trotted on down the steps and took off toward the red Camaro parked out on the road.

Alisha watched him take off in a swirl of spewing mud and squealing tires. Then she turned to find Miss Mozelle standing on the porch, frowning. "Three single men and a middle-aged doctor—well, he's single, too but he don't count—done come visiting you today, sugar. I'm telling you, they all been sniffing around like hunting hounds after a jackrabbit. It beats anything I ever seen. And you a new mama at that."

Alisha let out a chuckle. "Well, it's a good thing I'm not interested in any of them. With you acting as my chaperon and protector, I can safely say we've probably scared all of them off for good."

Miss Mozelle let out a grunt. "Well, good riddance, I say. Except for that Mr. Murdock. I think I like him. I'm still waiting to make a final judgment, mind you. But I do believe he's suitable."

"Why, thank you so very much for that rousing endorsement of my love life," Alisha replied, lowering her head to laugh.

That's when she saw it.

Another azalea bush.

"Where did that come from?" she asked Miss Mozelle, a hand trembling on the woman's arm.

Miss Mozelle squinted, her eyes on the plant. "I don't know. That ain't the same one?"

Alisha shook her head, then pointed. "No. It's over there by the firewood. This...this is a different plant." She remembered Jared offering to plant the first bush, earlier when they'd gone for a walk. She'd held him off, stating she didn't have a good spot for it.

And now this.

Miss Mozelle leaned down. "There's a card."

Alisha felt sick to her stomach, her heart racing so fast, she could feel the pulse quivering along her neck, the pounding blood inside her head causing her to feel faint. "What...what does the card say?"

Hoping against hope that this was just another innocent gift from a villager, she waited while Miss Mozelle read in silence.

The other woman finally looked up at her, her dark eyes wide. "It says, 'To replace what you've lost.' No name. Now ain't that strange?"

Alisha gasped, then reached for one of the rocking chairs as her world started spinning. Miss Mozelle caught her before she hit the porch floor.

"Let's get you inside, honey," the kind woman said, her grip strong as Alisha wavered against her. "It's gonna be all right. You just plumb tired out. That's all."

Alisha didn't hear Miss Mozelle's soft cooing. She couldn't feel the woman's gentle touch as Miss Mozelle guided her to the sofa and quickly wrapped her shivering body with a floral quilt. All she could hear was what had been written on that card, all she could see or feel was a haze of fear and pain.

To replace what you've lost.

That phrase kept going through her mind like a scream.

She'd heard that exact phrase once before, not so very long ago.

But the man who'd told her that in a cold, uncaring voice was now dead.

Her husband had told her that the day he'd brought home an azalea bush to replace...to replace the ones she'd lost when he'd mowed down her entire garden in a fit of rage.

Jared heard the car careening up the mountain road before he saw it. He was walking back from a long climb up one of the rock faces to the west. The sun was just about to set over the beautiful vista, but Jared's gaze lifted away from the peacefulness of that scene. He had to get out of the way of that fast-moving car, his climbing gear swaying and rattling as he jumped back. He could hear the powerful motor straining toward him as gears shifted into overdrive.

He waited at the driveway to his cabin, intent on finding out who was driving so fast on such a dangerous, twisting road. The red late-model Camaro came flying around the curve on two wheels, dirt and mud kicking out as the car bounced toward Jared. Jared stood there watching for the driver and was met by a set of cold blue eyes and an angry, defiant face.

"Get off the road," the driver called out through the open window as he passed Jared, a look of disgust evident on the handsome features. Jared thought he heard an expletive as the car and driver disappeared over the hill.

"Thanks for the warning," Jared said, turning to stare after the racing car. "Nice to meet you, too."

Whoever that was needed to slow down. And whoever that was sure had a bad case of road rage.

Shaking his head, Jared readjusted his shoulder sling, then walked on up to his cabin. He was tired, but it was a good tired. The weather had cleared up and the afternoon had been mild—the temperature in the mid-sixties. He'd worked with Tate Wilkes and a few of the other men all morning, picking up limbs and sawing up trees. After having lunch with Alisha and walking her around the yard, Jared had picked up the broken limbs and crushed flower blossoms on her property, then headed up the mountain to get some more exercise. He hadn't climbed far. Just high enough to get a good view of the surrounding hills and vistas. Just high enough to clear his head and give himself some time alone.

Alisha had suggested one of her favorite trails, so Jared had struck out, hoping to find some solitude. He'd found gentle waterfalls, beautiful just-budding dogwoods, spots of mountain laurel and lady's slippers, and challenging rock beds.

But he hadn't found solitude or a clear mind.

He couldn't stop thinking about Alisha Emerson.

At first, they'd had a nice walk around her yard. Jared liked being with Alisha. She was a very smart, very modern woman, in spite of her desire to live simply here on this mountain. They'd talked about books—one of her passions—and what she hoped to do after Callum got older. She wanted to go back to college, maybe continue counseling youths. They'd talked about the weather. Spring was definitely in the air. They'd talked about her garden. She couldn't wait to get back out in it. She wanted to plant roses, lots of roses. And bulbs. She liked lilies, especially daylilies. They'd been going along just great until Jared mentioned planting the azalea that sat in a pot on her porch.

"I'd be glad to do it," he told her, pointing to the budding plant. "You need to get that in the ground. It might bloom soon. Right now, it looks a little puny."

A change had come over Alisha then. She'd grown quiet and pensive, evasive again. "I...I haven't decided where to plant it yet. Azaleas...don't do well here. I can't seem to make them grow."

Then she'd told him she was tired. She wanted to go inside and check on Callum and Miss Mozelle. Jared had obliged her, then beat a hasty retreat.

Maybe he was wearing out his welcome at Alisha's cabin. He'd visited her every day since the birth. He couldn't keep that up, or she would become suspicious.

Suspicious of what? he asked himself. Of his motives? She was already that, he was sure. Jared didn't want to give Alisha the wrong impression, but he felt an obligation to make sure she and the baby were all right. That was it. Just an obligation. He wasn't ready for anything beyond that.

But he sure wouldn't mind seeing her every day.

Stop it, he silently told himself as he walked up onto the porch of the cabin to unhook his climbing harness. His equipment clinked and jingled, the noise echoing the chaos inside his head. He'd come here right off a bad relationship. He wouldn't take advantage of a kind woman like Alisha Emerson just to appease his own bruised pride. Alisha deserved better than that. She deserved better than him.

Telling himself he just wanted a warm shower and a good meal, Jared headed inside the cabin—and was met with a disturbing surprise.

The place had been ransacked. The lamps were overturned, the tables crushed and broken. He went into the kitchen to find catsup and mustard smeared all over the refrigerator and the countertops. The red smears were startling at first. They looked like blood, until he saw the empty catsup bottle tossed on the floor by the trash.

Hurrying to the bedroom, he found the bedding dumped on the floor and the mattress slashed. Oddly enough, his duffel bag was still intact inside the closet, even though some cash was missing from where he'd left it on the dresser this morning.

He'd locked the door this morning, since he hadn't been sure when he'd be back at the cabin.

"What a day," Jared said out loud. It had started with getting his Escalade out of a bog, and meeting the not-so-friendly Hank Burgess, then a meal with Tate and a few stares from the townsfolk. He'd worked hard helping the men remove debris, but Jared didn't remember any hostility from that quarter. Then lunch with Alisha and a walk with her. Since mid-afternoon, Jared had been alone on the trails and rocks leading up to the summit of the western side of the mountain.

And while he'd been doing that, someone had obviously been busy trying to destroy this cabin.

But why?

Kids seeking a thrill?

Or someone with a more purposeful intent?

Jared looked around at the destruction.

Maybe somebody was trying to scare him or send him a message. Maybe someone wanted him off Dover Mountain.

He thought about Alisha and his strong need to stay close to her and the baby. "Well, guess what?" he said into the growing dusk. "I'm not running away." Not this time.

Something wasn't right here. Something definitely wasn't right.

Jared intended to find out what that something was. And soon.

❧ *Chapter Ten* ❧

"Mister, you got yourself a mess here."

Deputy Dwight Parker took one look at Jared's cabin, then stepped out on the porch to spit a stream of brown tobacco juice into the bushes. He took off his pristine tan wool Stetson, then came back inside and closed the door. "This ain't the city, you understand. 'Bout all I can do is file the report and see what's what."

"What does that mean, exactly?" Jared asked, his impatience with the man's nonchalant attitude wearing very thin.

"That means I can file a report and see if we need to assign this to an investigator. Take about three days for that to make the rounds, then they can dust for prints, but I can't guarantee we'll find out who did this. We got people in and out of these places all the time."

Jared got the message. The deputy's department didn't have the resources to do much but declare this a break-in. "But what about the damage?" he asked. "I didn't lose anything but a couple of hundred dollars. I'll get over that. But look at this place."

The deputy nodded, the action causing his ruddy bulldog neck to bulge out over the collar of his khaki-colored uniform collar. "Yep. It'll take some major repair work. Sure didn't need this on top of that storm messing up everything around here."

"I'll replace the damaged furnishings," Jared said.

The other man cupped a meaty hand to his ear, a look of disbelief on his chubby face. "Come again?"

"You heard me," Jared said, tired and angry. "I'll buy new furnishings for the cabin, pay to have this cleaned up. I don't want the Wilkes family or the town to have to fork out funds for this."

The deputy nodded, his sharp little brown eyes growing wide. "Well, now, that's awful considerate of you, seeing as how you were the one who got robbed."

"But I'm okay," Jared replied. He didn't like the accusing tone in the officer's voice. "I just want to help out."

"I've been hearing that a lot about you," Deputy Parker replied. "You seem to want to contribute a whole lot for someone who just got here a few days ago. You're practically a hero—delivering babies, chopping up fallen trees. What's your angle here, mister?"

Jared couldn't believe what he was hearing. "I don't have an angle. I just wanted to get away for a vacation and—"

Parker chuckled out loud. "You got more than you bargained for, huh? Betcha thought you'd never be noticed in a place like this. Could just come and go whenever you wanted." He leaned forward. "Well, we notice things on Dover Mountain. We notice when someone new comes into town."

"Okay." Jared stretched the word out for emphasis. "I'm glad you notice things. Maybe you could notice that this cabin had been burglarized, and maybe you could think about finding out who did this and why?"

"A good enough question," the deputy countered, his face beet-red. "Are you saying I can't do my job?"

Jared laughed. "Deputy Parker, I'm not implying anything. I just thought you might make an effort."

"I'll get someone from CID to dust for fingerprints, I told you. But—"

"I know, I know. It will be hard to catch whoever did this."

The deputy held his hat in the air. "I'm wondering why? Why would anyone do this. We hardly ever get this kind of thing here. People here rarely lock their doors at night. Now you show up, and suddenly, I'm looking at a crime scene."

"Yes, it is a crime scene," Jared agreed. "But I didn't do anything to provoke this. I can't imagine why someone would want to tear up this cabin."

"Think they could have been looking for something?"

Again that accusing tone. "They took some money," Jared reminded him. "I don't have much else to take. Just a few clothes and books, a camera in here and some fishing equipment, hiking boots and climbing equipment out on the back porch."

"Did they take any of that?"

"No, that's the weird part."

"Bingo," the deputy said. "That's why I think *you* must have been a target. Somebody wanted to scare you, maybe."

Jared pointed toward the dresser where he'd left his money. "And take my cash."

"Probably just because it was there." The deputy put his hat on, obviously satisfied that he'd figured this out.

"This is mostly vandalism. Some punk kids out for a joy ride, I bet."

Jared thought about the red Camaro. "I did see a car near here when I got home this afternoon."

Parker turned at the door. "What kind of car?"

"A red Camaro. Going way too fast up the road."

Parker shook his head. "Oh, that'd be Jimmy Barrett. I've given that man more tickets than I care to remember."

Jimmy Barrett. Jared remembered Alisha talking about Rayanne's boyfriend. So that had been the charming Jimmy Barrett he'd seen today on the road. "Do you think he could have done this?"

The deputy chuckled, then shook his head. "Nah, this ain't Jimmy's thing. He's more into fast cars and even faster women. Works at Hank's garage, plays on the Internet a lot, that kind of thing. He's past the age of silly pranks." He turned to spit again, then turned back. "Unless, of course, you've given Jimmy some sort of motive for aggravating you."

Jared hit a hand on the kitchen table. "Why do I get the impression that you think *I'm* the criminal here?"

"Simple enough," the deputy replied. "I don't know you well enough to let you off the hook. You could be a drug runner or on the lam, for all I know. Nothing personal, just purely an observation."

"Well, your observation is wrong," Jared told him, coming face-to-face with the bulldog of a man. "I'm just a law-abiding citizen who needed a vacation."

"I've been wrong before," the deputy replied, his voice calm and steady. "You'll just have to prove that to me."

"Is that how things work in this town? A man is guilty until proven innocent?"

"Like I said, this ain't the big city," the deputy said. "But I highly doubt you'd do this damage yourself. On that we can agree. Now, the other—somebody having a strong reason to get you riled or drive you away—that could be our starting point here." He placed a hand on his hip. "You made anybody mad since you got here?"

Jared thought about what the deputy was saying. "I have to agree with you that my first reaction when I saw this was that someone was trying to scare me."

"Did they succeed?"

Jared wasn't one to scare easily. He'd always taken care of himself in just about any situation. No, he didn't run out of fear, but he sure walked away due to pride. "I'm not scared. Just aggravated and tired. And no, I don't think I've made anybody mad." He thought about Hank Burgess, but decided that scenario was just too bizarre. The man might have feelings toward Alisha, but would he be jealous enough toward Jared to do something like this? No, more like a fistfight or showdown on the main street, probably.

Deputy Parker, for all his slow, country hokiness, seemed to have good instincts. He eyed Jared with a curious stare. "What are you thinking, Murdock?"

Jared decided to level with the man. "I have gotten the impression that people around here don't trust me. I know this is a tight-knit community and I had planned on coming here and being low-key. I used to come here when I was a child, with my grandfather. But no one would even remember that. No one knows me here. Or at least, they didn't at first."

The deputy nodded. "But helping Alisha has put you in the limelight, so to speak. Out front."

"Yes. I've visited Alisha several times and maybe... maybe somebody doesn't like that."

"That makes sense," the deputy said, nodding. "Some of the single men on this mountain, well, they behave like mountain men for sure. Get real possessive when it comes to their women."

"But Alisha isn't close to any one in particular, that I can tell."

"Are you asking or telling?" the deputy asked, grinning. Then he nodded again. "Alisha is a right pretty little thing. Half the available men in town have tried to date her. Mister, you might be in more trouble than you think."

"I'm beginning to see your point," Jared said. "But this is a silly way of venting a jealous rage, don't you think?"

The deputy shrugged. "You never know. Depends on who's doing the venting. Things are different up on this mountain."

"I've noticed," Jared said as they started walking down the steps. "I guess I'll clean up what I can and find out about replacing the rest."

"Sounds like the best we can do." The deputy gave him that hard-edged stare again, then said, "Tell you what. Let me call the criminal investigations department to dust and look for any evidence the burglar might have left behind. Then I'll help you straighten the worst of it."

"Thank you," Jared said. He'd obviously passed one hurdle by being honest with the deputy. The man didn't seem as distrustful now.

A little while later, the deputy and the officer from CID went about their work with slow, steady precision while Jared stood in the kitchen, drinking a cup of coffee. Jared looked around for clues, something the intruder might have left behind. It was hard to tell, since he wasn't yet familiar enough with the place to notice anything out of the ordinary, other than the broken furniture and missing money, of course. His mind focused on clearing away the mess, he reached down by the front door and picked up a crushed flower blossom. It looked like an azalea blossom.

That made him think of Alisha and her aversion to planting her own azalea bush. He'd have to find out what that was all about. Maybe she was allergic to certain plants or something.

Deputy Parker walked up, staring at the blossom. "Looks like someone stepped on that."

Jared nodded. "It's got a tread mark on it."

"Want me to have it analyzed?" the deputy said, his tone full of mirth.

"I don't think so," Jared replied. "That might take way too much time and manpower, right?"

"Right." The deputy grinned. "We'll be on the watch for any more vandalism, I can promise you that."

Jared knew it was the best he could get, considering the deputy didn't seem in the least worried about what had happened.

"I'll let you know what the boys at the crime lab find," the deputy told him, causing Jared to drop the crushed blossom into the trash bag he'd been filling up. "We're stretched pretty thin up in these hills. Our unit covers the whole northwest side of the county. It might be a while."

"I appreciate it, anyway," Jared replied, thinking that at least the deputy seemed to be more willing now to investigate. Jared thanked the young CID officer, then watched the man drive away, headed back to Dalton.

When they got to the deputy's shiny green truck, Deputy Parker turned back to face Jared. "Just keep this one thing in mind, son. We all love Miss Alisha. She comes from good people. All her mama's relatives lived on this mountain at one time or another, but she's the only one left now. She's come back here for reasons of her own, and she just wants some peace and quiet. We aim to keep it that way."

"Is that a threat or a warning?" Jared asked.

"Take it either way," the deputy replied. Then he tipped his hat and got in his truck and left.

The next morning Jared got up early to haul trash and broken furniture down to the road, his mind taking in the contrast between the disorder he'd found in his cabin last night and the calming beauty of the spring morning. Three days after the storm, the mountain was reclaiming its landscape. The tree limbs and flower blossoms that had been tossed and scattered during the savage storm were now sinking into the hills and valleys, becoming part of the heavy vegetation and undergrowth in a way that spoke of nature's healing grace and reclamation.

Jared imagined how years of falling leaves and twigs, years of flowers blooming and then softly turning to decay, had sealed this mountain in a cloak of protection that echoed with each touch of the wind, that cried out with each chirp of a cardinal. It was a protection that carved a gentle path each time water flowed over the meandering stream by his cabin, a regeneration that produced seeds and started new plants each spring. Even after the storm, nature found new strength in the slow, steady everyday renewal of the forests and mountains.

It should have brought Jared comfort, but he only felt a raw, open need to put down roots himself, to let the wind and water wash over him and seal him with a renewing touch.

Jared did feel like an intruder here. But he had to get this cleared up, both the break-in and the source. He had to find out what had provoked this. And, like Alisha, he only wanted to be left alone.

He'd called Tate Wilkes first thing this morning to tell him about the break-in. Tate would bring his truck by to take some of the stuff to the nearby dump; then the weekly garbage truck would take care of the rest. After the deputy had done his part on the crime scene investigation, Jared had worked late into the night, cleaning up and washing away catsup and mustard stains off the kitchen table and counters. He didn't hold out much hope for finding out who had broken into his cabin, but he sure intended to be more watchful and alert from now on.

Jared had always had a keen mind. He had a good memory for details, too. And now that he'd had time to think back over everything that had happened, he knew his instincts were right. The people on this mountain were protecting Alisha Emerson, no doubt about that. They were cloaking her in a protective security, just as this mountain was cloaked in old oaks and spruce trees and the first jonquils of the season. On the surface, it looked pretty and completely natural. But underneath, there was a buried darkness that held at secrets with tenacious roots.

That darkness was now eating at Jared. He wanted to find out what lay beneath the bucolic surface of

Dover Mountain and its citizens. Whether they liked him or not. He had a feeling the dark secrets held the key to Alisha Emerson. And he especially wanted to find out more about her. Whether the villagers wanted him to or not.

But then, it didn't take a rocket scientist to figure that one out. Jared had had outright warnings from several villagers, even Deputy Parker.

That got Jared to wondering what had happened to Alisha's husband. Since she'd just had a baby, her husband hadn't been dead that long. She'd said a few months?

Again, Jared got a feeling of uneasiness. Something just wasn't adding up here. Alisha had no family pictures in her house and she never mentioned her husband. Plus, not one of the people who had warned Jared away from Alisha had mentioned her husband either. He could understand if she were still grieving and needed her privacy, but why wouldn't one of her friends state *that,* at least, as being her reason for not wanting to get involved? No, they'd all said pretty much the same thing. Alisha wanted some peace and quiet, *after everything she'd been through.* And they were going to make sure she got that.

Which meant Jared needed to stay away from her and respect that, too.

So now, in the awakening of a beautiful morning, he stood out at the side of the road, staring down the lane toward her cabin. He could just make out the roof and chimney through the trees and hills. He could see her bedroom window. He pictured Alisha in there, her long red hair cascading down her back like a waterfall; pictured her holding her baby close, a mother nurturing the child she loved.

"Wait a minute," Jared said to himself as he breathed in the fresh morning air. "Maybe I just need to ask Alisha herself about all of this. Maybe she'll be honest with me and tell me what's going on." And maybe she'd tell him that he was always welcome at her house, that he could come and visit her and the baby any time while he was here, regardless of the villagers' protective nature.

While he was here.

I'll be leaving soon, Jared reasoned. He'd go back to the city, delve into his holdings, decide if he wanted to start something new or just retire and live off his assets.

His assets. There was an understatement. He had money to spare, a nice stately home, cars, an address book that included everyone in the social register, and yet what did he have, really?

Jared remembered delivering little Callum. He remembered holding the tiny baby in his big hands, awe in every fiber of his being at this little creature who'd made such a grand entrance into the world, born on Easter morning in the middle of a storm.

Jared looked up, saw the sun's first rays tipping over a ridge to the east past Alisha's cabin, felt the warmth of it penetrating his skin. He closed his eyes, thinking that such moments were rare in a man's life. All the turmoil he'd been through over the last months, involving both his business and his personal life, seemed to lift away as the sun washed over his face. He turned his face to that sun, savoring the warmth, the grace of it, as it touched him and made him feel whole again.

The moment passed, the sun rose, and Jared opened his eyes to find himself standing on a mountain road, surrounded by a pile of garbage. He didn't miss the irony of the moment. He'd forgotten the garbage. He'd felt only the beauty, the simplicity of life in that brief moment of warmth.

That made him ache for something he'd never had before.

He looked back toward Alisha's cabin.

And he knew what that something was.

Alisha woke with a start to find sunshine streaming in her window. She got up quickly, the fear from her nightmare so real, she had to touch Callum to make sure he was alive and well.

"He's fine," she told herself as she grabbed her wrapper. She was chilled with a cold sweat in spite of the mild temperature this morning.

The dream had been so vivid. Colors everywhere. Azaleas blossoming so thick and fluffy and so hot-pink that she felt their cloying blooms whispering like feathers across her skin, rasping against her as she tried to escape through a never-ending garden maze. And in the dream, while she tried to claw her way out of the thick foliage, she could hear her baby crying off in the distance.

She'd tried to speak, to call out to him. "I'm coming, Callum. Mommy's here." But as was the case with dreams, the words were just a scream inside her mind, trapped there as she tried to say them out loud.

Then she'd heard the laughter. That cruel, whipping laughter that she remembered so well. Trevor. Her husband was looking for her, taunting her with his promises of cruelty. She had to get out of the garden. She had to find Callum.

Before *he* did.

"It's not real," she told herself as she lifted her child to her heart and held him clutched close in her arms. His warmth, so small yet so powerful, fought the chill away. He slept in perfect peace, his little mind unencumbered by the harsh realities of the world. He smiled in his sleep, a gentle parting rush of baby's breath that lifted out on a sigh to pierce Alisha's heart. "You're safe now," she told him as she kissed his downy head and laid him back in his little bed. "You're safe here with your mother."

Alisha went to the window to stare out. The world outside looked the same. The trees were budding a bright fresh green, a tender green that spoke of deep roots and billowing leaves. The sun was fresh and clear, dry and warming. Birds chirped and fussed in the trees. She saw a squirrel racing toward the promise of some long-lost acorn from the fall. The shadows were only those of a sun-dappled mountainside. Nothing dark and sinister here. Nothing to fear. She was okay. It was just another bad dream.

Needing to feel the fresh air on her fevered skin, Alisha tiptoed up the hallway and silently opened the front door, careful not to wake Miss Mozelle. Once outside, she went into the yard, her gaze scanning the trees and flowers out toward the road. From her driveway, she could just make out the porch of Jared's cabin sitting up on a slight bluff. Even from here, she could see the bright yellow of the jonquils popping up at random along the roads and in the yards. She wondered if Jared had slept well, wondered for the hundredth time why he was here on this mountain.

And reminded herself that she couldn't trust him. She had to be careful, so careful. She had to think of Callum and his safety. That meant putting Jared's intriguing face and deep laughter out of her mind. Just because the man was a gentleman and a kind person didn't mean

Alisha could trust him. She couldn't open up to him or share the details of her life with him. Her silence had become her symbol, her penance, her punishment. And she couldn't break that silence with Jared Murdock. Especially with Jared Murdock.

Jared had stumbled into her life and helped her through her labor and delivery. A stranger had come through a storm to her door at a time she'd needed him the most.

She still needed him, even after the storm.

That realization caused Alisha to gasp and bring her hand to her chest. She'd never thought she'd need a man's comfort again. But then she'd never really known any tenderness or comfort in her marriage.

But I can't need him. She had to keep telling herself that. She had to put these feelings of gratitude into a proper place, into the secret place of her soul, where she kept her wishes and dreams, a place where she could only look in and watch, as though she were outside looking into a beautiful room through a window.

But oh, how she wished she could go inside, to that room with that loving family, to live in that home of happiness and warmth and grace.

She lifted her face to the sun and felt the warmth of it through the cool morning breeze, then she closed her eyes and took in the scent of the ancient mountain, the scent of decay mixed with new growth, of rain mixed with dirt and roots and blossoms, and she prayed to the God who had made that sun and this earth. She prayed for her child. She prayed for her own salvation.

When Alisha opened her eyes, she saw the woods and the trees and the blossoms of spring. For just that brief moment, she felt as if everything was going to be all right in her world.

Then she turned back toward the house and saw the two azalea bushes sitting on her front porch.

To replace what you've lost.

Nothing could ever replace what Alisha had lost. She went cold inside as she turned away from the sun, and her dreams.

ᴑ Chapter Eleven ᴑ

A few days later, Geneva Ashton turned from the stove to stare at Alisha. "Are you happy here?" she asked, her hands wrapped across her midsection.

Alisha was momentarily surprised by the directness of the question. Geneva had graduated from high school and gone on to junior college before meeting and marrying an enlisted man. Alisha knew she was happy in her marriage and in being away from the mountain.

"I'm...content," Alisha replied, hoping her smile was reassuring to Geneva. "Especially now that I have Callum. Why do you ask?"

Geneva shrugged, pushed at her brown shagged hair. "Oh, I was just wondering. Me, I'm so glad to be away from this place. I love living near Savannah. I love knowing that I can travel with my husband, see the world. I guess I just don't understand how you could leave Atlanta and come back here."

Alisha's heart begin to pound with a rushed intensity. "How did you know I used to live in Atlanta?"

Geneva frowned. "Well, I guess everybody knows that, but Rayanne told me."

Alisha tried to brush it off. "Of course. I think I did mention it to her once or twice." When she was trying to convince the girl to get help for her baby. Wishing now she'd been more careful, Alisha decided she couldn't worry about this for the rest of her life. Although she probably would. "I lived on the outskirts of Atlanta, but it was still a small community much like this one." Not wanting to delve too much into her reasons, she added, "And I came back here because this is where my mother's people lived when she was a little girl. One of my aunts lived here in the cabin before I came back. She's in a nursing home in Marietta now though."

Geneva nodded at that. "I remember your aunt. You know, my mama thinks y'all are related somewhere down the way. Distant cousins or something."

"Your mother is probably right," Alisha said. "And I'd be proud to be related to Loretta."

Geneva touched a hand to her ribbed sweater sleeve, then picked at a pulled yarn. "Can I tell you something?"

"Of course." Alisha was used to others opening up to her. She was a good listener. Maybe that was why Reverend Stripling had pegged her for a youth counselor when she'd first come back here. That and her secret dream of being either a social worker or counselor.

Geneva turned to stir the chicken and dumplings she was making for dinner. With her back still to Alisha, she said, "I used to be ashamed of my folks."

Alisha could see the humiliation in the slump of Geneva's shoulders. She wasn't sure how to respond, since she'd felt the same way at one time. But that had changed. Now she longed for the comfort of her mother's arms, for the charm of her daddy's grinning, dimpled face. "We sometimes don't realize what a joy our relatives are until it's too late," she told Geneva, her tone wistful.

Geneva came to sit down on the footstool by the fireplace. "You're right there. When I first got away—" she stopped, shrugged again "—when I first left here, I was so glad to be out in the real world. But I had a lot to learn about people. We're really sheltered here, you know."

Alisha nodded. That was one of the reasons she'd come back here. To be sheltered.

Geneva continued. "Then I met Ryan and I was so afraid to bring him here to meet everyone." She lowered her blue eyes. "He comes from this strong upper-middle-class family—the typical four-bedroom ranch house in the gated subdivision. He was just so normal. I didn't want him to see how my family lives. How I'd grown up. You know, the battered old pickup parked in front of the double-wide."

Alisha reached out a hand to her friend. Although Geneva was a few years younger than her, they had a lot in common. "Well, obviously, you couldn't keep him away. Ryan seems to love your folks from what I've seen. What did you do?"

"I tried to stall him." Geneva lifted her head, then smiled. "But Ryan is so smart. He saw right through that and he told me that he would love my family, because he loved me. It was that simple for him. So I brought him home and sure enough, he just fit right in. I was so ashamed—but not of my folks. I was ashamed of myself this time." Tears sprang to her eyes. "And now I think of him off in some strange land, serving our country. And I'm so grateful that he's seen my mother's smile and had some of her pot roast and red velvet cake. That he's become friends with my brothers. And well, him and my daddy—they are just so close. What if I'd denied my family? I keep thinking that I would have been lying to Ryan, hiding a part of myself from him. Why was I so ashamed?"

Alisha sighed, then took Geneva's hand, her friend's comments hitting too close for comfort. "You realized you were wrong, Geneva. That's a good thing. And because of that, Ryan now knows everything about you and he loves you so much. You have a wonderful, loving family. I'm glad you've learned to appreciate that." She lowered her head. "We should all be able to appreciate family."

"I do," Geneva said, her head bobbing. "But I don't think I can ever live here again. I had to get away, Alisha. I felt so stifled, so hemmed in. And now, I'm worried about Rayanne. If that no-good Jimmy does marry her, what kind of life will she have, stuck here, with him running up and down the roads and carrying on with other women right in front of her? He only works when he feels like working and he bosses her around like he owns her. I'm just so worried."

Alisha understood why Geneva had asked her the question now. "You want your sister to have a better life, right? But you feel bad about pushing her. You don't want your parents to think you're ashamed of them?"

Geneva nodded. "Yes, I do want her to have a better life, but I can't force the issue. But then I look at you. You *chose* to live here, alone and with a baby. And you seem so sure and so secure. I want that for Rayanne, but I also want to beg her to come and live with Ryan and me at Fort Stewart. Only, I don't want to mess up things with Ryan by bringing all this into my house, even though he'd allow it for my sake. I'm thinking of taking her back with me, just until she has the baby. By that time, Ryan should be back home and maybe she'll want to stay near us and make something of her life. What should I do?"

Alisha leaned back in her chair. Callum was asleep in his little bed. The quiet cabin creaked and settled. Outside, it was a beautiful spring afternoon. And yet, she could feel the clawing of old fears reaching across her skin like dry, dead winter branches.

How could she tell her friend that *she'd* had no other choice? She'd had to come back to Dover Mountain. She also wanted to tell Geneva that she wasn't as sure and secure as she let on. But she put up a good front. She had to protect herself and Callum. This was the one place she could hide out from the world. Trevor hadn't even known about this place, precisely for the very reason Geneva had named.

Alisha had been ashamed of her heritage.

But that shame, as sinful as it had seemed, had turned out to be her one blessing, her one way of escape. Trevor was dead, and his family couldn't find her because they had no idea where she was. They'd only known her parents from a distance, hadn't wanted the association to go any further. And she'd never told Trevor that her mother had come from mountain people. He'd made enough fun of her as it was, taunting her because her father was a blue-collar worker who drove a delivery truck and her mother worked in a discount store.

Alisha had learned to stay quiet and let Trevor do the talking. He was so smart and sure, so arrogant, that she hadn't had to give out too many details of her history.

She'd learned how to stay in the background, almost invisible, while her handsome, shining example of a husband had boasted and preened for the world. They'd been the perfect family. Or the perfect facade of a loving, happy couple.

"Alisha?"

She looked up to find Geneva sitting there with a hopeful expression on her face. "Can you help me?"

Alisha patted Geneva's hand again. "I've talked to Rayanne about getting help. About moving away—maybe to a girls' home in Atlanta, or maybe giving up the baby—"

"She won't do that," Geneva said, shaking her head so fast her shining, layered hair flew around her face. "She's only seventeen and she's so afraid. I just wish I could have been here to keep that animal away from her."

Alarmed, Alisha lifted her head. "He didn't—"

"No, it was a mutual thing, but he still persuaded her and she gave in. He's a real charmer, that one."

Alisha remembered how Trevor had charmed her. And she longed to protect Rayanne. Jimmy Barrett had all the hallmarks of being an abusive husband. He was controlling and self-centered, hugely jealous and unreasonable about money and everything else. "I know, honey. But it's too late to worry about that. Rayanne is close to having that baby and we've got to help her, whether it's just by supporting her decisions or financially, somehow, we've got to help her. But I don't think that means you should bring her to your house in Savannah. You're still a newlywed yourself. That could cause problems between you and Ryan."

Geneva nodded, then got up to pace the room. "I know that. He doesn't like Jimmy and Jimmy hates

Ryan. When Rayanne just mentioned to Jimmy that she might come and stay with me, he went ballistic." Then she turned to stare down at Alisha. "Be careful, Alisha. Be careful in what you say to my sister. She tells Jimmy everything. If he thinks you're putting notions into her head, well..." Her voice trailed off as she shuddered. "I wish she could get away from him."

An answering shiver moved down Alisha's spine as she thought about all the intimate talks she'd had with Rayanne. Those talks were held in confidence as far as Alisha was concerned. She'd promised Rayanne that. But what about the girl? Rayanne might do or say the wrong thing, based on Alisha's advice. She'd almost let it slip to Jimmy that Alisha had loaned her money. What else had she told him?

I have to be more careful, Alisha thought. If Rayanne had told Jimmy about Alisha living near Atlanta, then it wouldn't be long before lots of other people knew, too. Some already knew, of course. Miss Mozelle and Dr. Sloane knew the worst of her terrible past, but they had to keep it quiet for professional reasons. Tate and Loretta knew the basics, but they also knew not to talk about Alisha's past to anyone. That left Mr. and Mrs. Curtis. Alisha had shared some things with them, working with them every day. But she felt she could trust them. They wouldn't talk, either.

But what about Jared? Alisha thought. Worry caused her to glance toward where her son slept so peacefully. Jared was from Atlanta, but she'd never told him she'd once lived there. What if someone else told him?

She looked up at Geneva, needing answers. "Have you met Jared Murdock yet?" And has anyone told him anything about me?

Geneva's smile mellowed into a dreamy grin. "Oh, yes. Sure have. Heard all about how he helped you. Also heard he's been visiting you on a regular basis."

"He hasn't been by in a while," Alisha said, not sure if she should be disappointed or relieved. She felt a little of both. But maybe Geneva would have information. Gossip did come in handy sometimes. "I guess he's finally getting in some fishing since the weather has turned off so pretty."

Geneva threw up her hands. "Oh, you don't know?"

Perplexed, Alisha shook her head. "Know what?"

"Mr. Murdock's had something besides fishing on his mind last couple of days. Somebody broke into his cabin the other night. Did a real number on the furniture and stole some money. Him and Daddy had to move some stuff from a warehouse to put in the cabin. Mr. Curtis let them have it—some end tables and a couch, I think. Deputy Parker came by to investigate, but you know how that goes. They'll probably never find out who did it. Everybody's been talking about it, though."

Alisha felt ill. Physically ill. She immediately leaned closer to Callum's bed, making a silent pledge to get a phone installed. And maybe some sort of alarm system, too. "But we've never had any problems with that type of thing. Do they know who might have done it, or why?"

Geneva shook her head. "Parker thinks someone's out to intimidate Mr. Murdock."

Alisha sank back against her chair, a hand to her heart. "Why would anyone want to do that?"

Geneva turned off the stove. "I don't know, but word is that Deputy Parker thinks Jared made too good of an impression, delivering a baby in a rainstorm, getting stuck in a mud hole. He's the first high-profile tourist we've had in these parts in a very long time, that's for sure. And it's obvious he's got the big bucks. Have you seen that SUV? Top of the line! Plus, he seems to be a really nice man. He's even offered to help David with his homework." She lifted her hands in the air then dropped them by her side, her tone exaggerated and frustrated. "But apparently, somebody on Dover Mountain doesn't appreciate nice, normal, *well-meaning* people coming to town."

Somebody had been in his cabin again.

Jared noticed it right away. Nothing had been destroyed this time, no food smears on the walls or furniture. But something was definitely different.

There was one lone azalea blossom lying on his kitchen table, a spot of glaring hot pink cascading out against the dark wood.

Why would someone leave a flower on his table?

Jared thought back over his day. He'd gotten up early to do some trout fishing out in the stream. No luck there, but then he'd hiked up one of the trails, stopping to cast his line every now and then in one of the many creek beds. Giving up, he'd come home around mid-afternoon, starving for a sandwich. Then he'd walked to the Wilkes house to visit with David and offer his help to the boy as a tutor. They'd chatted and discussed David's homework for over an hour, sitting out on an aged picnic table underneath the shade of an oak tree.

When Loretta Wilkes had come out to offer them some fresh lemonade, she'd mentioned Alisha. "Can you believe it's been a week since she had the baby?"

Jared could believe it. He'd tried to stay away, hoping to give Alisha some privacy, and yet he wanted to visit her and Callum. But the day after the break-in, he'd been busy helping Tate move furniture Warren J. had offered at no cost to replace the pieces that had been destroyed in the cabin. Of course, Jared had also had to field questions concerning the break-in. The Lindsays had been curious when he'd stopped to eat lunch in the Hilltop Diner, and so had Letty Martha, since she was the mayor. This latest hadn't exactly added to their trust of him. Maybe they thought, just as Deputy Parker seemed to, that Jared had somehow brought trouble with him to Dover Mountain.

"I've been busy," he'd told Loretta. "Letty Martha is worried about the break-in."

"Have you seen her?" Loretta had asked him, a hopeful expression coloring her vivid eyes.

It had taken Jared only a minute to figure out she wasn't referring to the colorful mayor of Dover Mountain.

"Who? Alisha? Not in a couple of days," Jared had admitted. "I didn't want to impose."

But this afternoon, he'd come home with one purpose. He was going to take a long shower and go visit Alisha. He knew Geneva was there with her now, so they should be able to relax and get to know each other without benefit of the ever-watchful eye of dear Miss Mozelle. At least, that had been his plan a few minutes ago when he'd unlocked the door and entered the cabin.

Until he'd seen the flower blossom on the table.

As far as Jared knew, no one had told Alisha about the break-in. Maybe Alisha needed to be warned about this though, since her cabin wasn't far from his.

Who in the world was doing this and why? They'd changed the locks. Jared had helped Tate do it. He knew the locks were different now. Had someone found the extra set of keys Tate had had made at the general store?

Was this yet another message of some sort?

Who wanted him gone so badly?

And what did that have to do with azaleas?

Then a sickening thought hit Jared straight in the middle of his gut.

Someone had left azalea plants for Alisha.

Could that same someone have left this single blossom for Jared?

It was time to talk to Alisha. It was time to try and find out what was going on here. He'd have to be careful. He'd feel her out first, asking her specific questions before he told her about the azalea he'd found on his table. He didn't want to scare her until he was sure there might be a connection.

Because if there was a connection, they could both be in danger—Alisha and the baby.

And that was a thought Jared just couldn't accept.

Alisha waited as Geneva opened the door, her dread turning to fear now that she'd heard about the break-in at Jared's cabin.

"It's Mr. Murdock," Geneva whispered over her shoulder, the door held open a couple of inches. "Are you up to a visit?"

Alisha wanted to send him away, and yet, she needed to see his face, needed to know in her heart that he wasn't involved in some sort of conspiracy against her, or that he hadn't been harmed in any way.

"Let him in," she told Geneva. Then she quickly ran a hand through her damp hair. She'd had her first good long shower over an hour ago, so at least she was clean and fresh.

Jared walked into the room, filling the cabin with a masculine presence that made Geneva's eyes go wide behind his back. "Hello," he said to Alisha, his gaze sweeping her with an appreciative look. "You look rested."

"I'm doing great," Alisha replied, a feeling of joy rushing through her like one of those streams moving down the mountain. "Callum was a bit restless earlier, but he's down for a nap now. Haven't seen you in a while. How's the vacation coming?"

Jared laughed, glanced over at Geneva. "It's been interesting."

Geneva extended a hand. "I'm Geneva Ashton. Tate and Loretta's oldest."

Jared nodded, shook her hand. "You have a lovely family."

"I sure do," Geneva said, a faint blush rising up her cheeks. "Thanks for helping David with his schoolwork. That boy needs to build up his confidence."

"He's smart," Jared said, knocking his index finger against his temple. "We just need to convince him of that."

Alisha glanced from Geneva to Jared. "You're helping David?"

"Just with his math," Jared said, looking sheepish. "He thinks he's dumb, but it's all a matter of knowing the right equations."

"That's awfully nice of you," Alisha replied, impressed all over again by Jared's generous nature.

Jared nodded, glanced back over at Geneva. Then he turned to Alisha. "Want to go for a walk?"

"Sure she does," Geneva answered, then lifted a brow toward Alisha. "Go ahead. I'll listen out for Callum."

Alisha knew she should say no, but it was such a pretty day. And she needed some fresh air and exercise. Or at least that was the excuse she used. "Okay, but just around the yard."

"Okay." He smiled at her again and she felt the heat of that smile piercing her heart. Jared Murdock was a handsome, successful man. A different sort of man. A gentleman. These things she could see plain enough. But there was no going beyond that. He'd be gone soon, and she had to take care of Callum.

"Coming?" he asked, causing her to snap to attention.

"Yes. Let me get a sweater."

Hurriedly, she went to the bedroom and brushed her damp hair, then grabbed a white sweater to go over her button-up green corduroy shirtwaist. She should be warm enough since the dress hung to her ankles, just over her lace-up black booties and socks. Not exactly dressed to attract a handsome man, Alisha thought, then chastised herself for even caring.

But she did care. She could admit that as she came back up the hallway to find Jared bending over her son, a warm smile on his rugged face. He'd helped her bring that child into the world, had helped her through what had started out as the loneliest night of her life. How could she not care about him? Especially now when he was cooing to her child like a loving, proud father.

Alisha swallowed, took a breath, prayed for strength.

Jared glanced up as she entered. "Ready?"

"Yes." Turning to Geneva, she frowned at the girl's wide-eyed interest. "Holler out if he wakes up."

"I will," Geneva said. "And y'all go on for a long walk. We have two bottles of pumped milk in the refrigerator. I can feed the little fellow."

"We'll be nearby," Alisha told her as Jared held open the front door.

Alisha moved quickly down the steps, refusing to look at the azalea bushes still in the pots on each side of the porch.

"Which way?" Jared asked as they stepped into the yard.

Did she just image that he'd made a point of looking at those just-blooming bushes? "We could go in back, to the garden," Alisha offered. It was more private there, and there were no azaleas anywhere around. "And up the way, just over the ridge, there's a pretty spot. I'd still be able to hear Geneva from there."

He nodded, took her hand. His touch warmed her and made little sparkles of awareness shoot up and down her spine. "Maybe we could just walk up there and back first, then sit in the garden. If you're up to that."

"It's not a bad hike," she said, glancing up the sloping ridge toward the trees. "That'd be nice. When I'm feeling better, I'll take you up to the ruins. There used to be a church up there, but it burned down. Or at least part of it did." She stopped, feeling a hesitation in him as he looked toward the summit. "Ready?"

"Yes." Then he guided her around toward the back of the house. "Alisha, I need to ask you something."

Her heart hammered like a woodpecker against her chest. Was this it? Was he going to ask her outright about her past? Did he already know who she was, what she'd done? Or had somebody been talking?

TESTED BY FIRE

in D.C. but we'll be flying back into Chicago to-morrow.''

''Did you say 'we'll'?'' Finn grabbed onto the word hopefully.

''I can't talk now, but I needed to tell you so you wouldn't worry. They're both safe and sound, praise the Lord,'' Diane said, her voice cracking slightly.

''And John? He's all right, too?''

There was a moment's hesitation. ''He's fine.'' Finn heard someone say something to her in the background.

''Finn, if you're thinking about meeting the plane, I think you should reconsider. They're both pretty exhausted.''

Something in her voice didn't sound quite right. ut Finn was still overw~~~~ed by ~ ohn and N ~l we~

Like what you see?
Then send for TWO FREE larger-print books!

YOURS FREE!

You'll get a great mystery gift with your two free larger-print books!

Steeple Hill Reader Service™ — Here's How It Works:

Accepting your 2 free larger-print Love Inspired® books and gift places you under no obligation to buy anything. You may keep the books and gift and return the shipping statement marked "cancel." If you do not cancel, about a month later we will send you 4 additional larger-print books and bill you just $4.49 each in the U.S., or $4.99 each in Canada, plus 25¢ shipping & handling per book and applicable taxes if any.* That's the complete price, and — compared to cover prices of $5.24 each in the U.S. and $6.24 each in Canada — it's quite a bargain! You may cancel at any time, but if you choose to continue, every month we'll send you 4 more books, which you may either purchase at the discount price...or return to us and cancel your subscription.

*Terms and prices subject to change without notice. Sales tax applicable in N.Y. Canadian residents will be charged applicable provincial taxes and GST.

"Go ahead," she said, the words barely audible amid the noise of chirping birds and buzzing bees. The woods were busy today. Maybe somebody else might have been busy, too, and she'd lose a man who could have been a good friend because of it.

"I guess you've heard about the break-in at my cabin?"

"Geneva told me. Any news on who did it?" And does it have anything to do with me? she wanted to add.

"No, no word, and I'm not holding my breath on that."

He stopped to stare over at her as they reached the shade of the tree-lined foothills. "It's so strange, but I don't think that's the first time someone's been inside my cabin. I remember leaving a light on the first night I was there and when I got home from having dinner with you, the light was off. I might be imagining things, but I think someone deliberately turned it off."

Alisha clutched her hands to her stomach, suddenly chilled as they strolled up the winding trail. "Are you sure?"

"No, not really, but why would anyone have any reason to harass me?"

"Is that what you wanted to ask me?"

"I thought you might know. You've lived here for a while. And I've heard—"

She stopped, her hand on his arm. "What have you heard?"

He looked surprised, curious. "I've heard that several of the bachelors around here feel very strongly about you and me being friends. They don't like it. I'm thinking most of the townspeople don't really like it, either."

She felt relief coursing through her body, strong and refreshing. "Oh, is that all?" She laughed, a rush of the same relief escaping in a big breath. "Jared, no one has any claims on me. Besides, I'm not even interested in dating right now, for obvious reasons."

They had reached a crest now, where a small opening allowed them a view of the surrounding hills and valleys. The spot looked worn-down, as if someone had recently been here. But it was clear and flat and from here, they could see down on the backyard and the cabin, which brought Alisha a small measure of comfort.

"What happened to your husband?"

The question shook her, causing her to gasp.

"Alisha, are you all right? Maybe we shouldn't have walked up this far."

"It's not that," she said, waving him away as she stumbled to a jutting rock to lean against it. She wanted to be honest with Jared, but she couldn't risk it. "It's just hard to talk about his death."

"How did he die?"

She looked up, wondering how she'd learned to live with her secrets. But she also wondered if she could ever learn to live with the truth. What if she just came out and told Jared the whole awful, sordid story? That way, they could end this bond now and forever. He'd never want to be near her again once he found out. Maybe that would be the best way for both of them. Just tell him and watch him walk away in disgust.

She was about to do just that when she heard Geneva's voice, calling up to them. "Alisha? Alisha, where are you?"

Alisha jumped up to call back. She could see Geneva out in the backyard. "Up here," she shouted, waving.

Geneva spotted her, then motioned for her to come back.

"I have to go," she told Jared as she rushed by him on the path.

"Of course." He was right behind her, helping her over the rough spots.

Alisha only wished she could allow him to help her over the rough spots of her past. But that was her burden to bear. All alone and forever.

As she hurried back down the path, the woods and trees she loved suddenly became ominous and shadowy.

Why did she always feel as if someone was watching her?

✑ Chapter Twelve ✑

He'd watched them. Alisha and that stranger. Jared Murdock. An interesting man, that one. Rich and powerful. Good-looking, too. The kind of man a woman would just naturally turn to. Would Alisha run off with Jared Murdock? She might, if Murdock kept sniffing around, taking her on long walks, having nice, intimate meals with her.

He'd thought Murdock would be gone by now. But everyone in town was talking about the man as if he were some sort of saint. Said he'd come up here to get away from the city, to fish and do some hiking and mountain climbing, but now he was doing more than that. He was being so helpful, so *nice*. Said Jared Murdock had made quite an impression on the villagers.

Even though some of the villagers had made it plain they didn't trust outsiders.

He'd given the man ample enough hints, hadn't he? First, the break-in, then the azalea on the table. What more did the man need to know he wasn't welcome here?

"He doesn't scare easily," a friend had told him.

"We'll just see about that." He'd met that kind before. Had seen 'em come and go on this old mountain. They thought they could just traipse around like they owned the place, throw their money around, then leave. Everyone always left anyway. He knew that from personal experience, didn't he?

He had to make Jared leave, one way or another. Had to get the man out of the picture. If not, all his plans for Alisha would be for nothing. Nothing.

And nothing was what he had right now. He wanted more. He wanted it all to be the way he dreamed about it being. He wanted to take Alisha and get off this mountain. Take Alisha and that big bank account she was trying so hard to hide.

He took another sip from the bottle he carried, then turned to sneak back up the path. He'd watched and waited, and bided his time last night. Everything was all set to get rid of Murdock once and for all—one more scare, this one more intent, more damaging.

Murdock shouldn't have shown up at Alisha's house again. He'd seen Geneva motioning to Alisha. He'd watched as Alisha and Murdock had hurried back down the footpath to her cabin. That meant Murdock would be occupied for a while at least.

But soon, that aggravating man would be gone.

Tonight, he'd make his next move.

"He has a fever," Alisha said, her mind racing with all sorts of possibilities as she paced the floor with Callum in her arms. "I don't understand. He was fussy last night, but then he seemed fine this morning. We need to get him to Dr. Sloane."

Jared held a hand on her arm, his eyes on the crying baby. "Why don't we take him into Dalton, to a pediatrician? I don't trust Dr. Sloane."

Jared's suggestion and Geneva's worried expression only mirrored what Alisha was feeling in her heart. Dr. Sloane was a good doctor when he was sober. He'd been by just about every day to check on Callum. But when he wasn't sober Alisha couldn't take her baby to her friend. Callum needed someone more qualified, someone who wasn't lost in pain and need.

"He's got a point, Alisha," Geneva said. She glanced up at Jared. "I was supposed to drive them into Dalton anyway at the end of the week, for Callum's two-week checkup."

"I'd already found a good pediatrician there," Alisha told Jared. "And Miss Mozelle thought it would be a good idea to set Callum up for regular visits anyway, just in case." She whirled, searching for the spiral notebook where she kept addresses and phone numbers. "I can't even call them to see if I can bring him in. I usually make phone calls from the store. I need to get that phone installed."

Feeling as if the cabin walls were closing in on her, she looked down at Callum's flushed face. "Here I thought I was protecting you, when I've actually been putting you in danger by not having things safe. We need a phone and we need a reliable doctor."

Jared stepped forward, his hand halting her pacing. "We'll take care of both of those, Alisha. C'mon. Get yourself ready to go to Dalton. I'm going to get my truck. I'll drive you to the pediatrician's, then I'll find out about getting you a phone installed." He leaned close, his expression calm in spite of the determined light in his dark eyes. "And on the drive to Dalton, maybe you can explain to me why you don't have a car or a phone."

Alisha watched as he walked out the front door, her mind racing with indecision. Should she tell Jared the truth? Or did she tell him only what he needed to know? *Dear Lord, I've carried this terrible shame so long, I don't know what the truth is anymore.*

Mistaking her agitation for worry, Geneva took Callum from her. "It's going to be all right. I bet he's just got an ear infection or a touch of a cold. You go get what you need while I make sure he's dry and dressed."

"Thank you," Alisha said, tears misting her eyes as she hurried up the hallway to the bedroom, all of her old insecurities coming back to laugh in her face.

Jared wanted answers. She could understand that. To anyone from the outside world, the way she lived here like a hermit probably seemed strange and hard to understand. But how could she explain that she'd once been a part of that outside world, she'd had the luxuries of modern life, and they hadn't helped her or saved her? She'd had too much noise, too many telephones and televisions, too much loudness. She'd craved silence.

How could she explain that she'd come here with nothing but a duffel bag and a broken heart? That she hadn't wanted any material possessions, hadn't needed those things anymore. She'd only wanted rest and quiet, safety and security.

Dover Mountain had given her that. She could walk to work and she felt safe in her little isolated cabin. The neighbors checked on her, watched out for her.

But now, things were changing. Callum was here and he needed things——a phone for emergencies, transportation for doctor's appointments and other things.

"One day at a time," she whispered, telling herself she would do what she had to do for her son. She'd been doing that since the day she'd found out she was carrying him.

Hearing Callum cry out, she rushed back into the tiny den and took him in her arms to wait for Jared.

She had to trust Jared now. But could she trust him enough to tell him the whole story?

He wanted her to trust him.

Jared pushed the powerful Escalade to the max, hoping to make it the fifty miles to Dalton in record time. Callum was sleeping safely in his little car seat—a hand-me-down from the Wilkes family. Alisha had given him a tiny drop of infant pain reliever she'd had on hand in one of the gift bags from a neighbor, so his fever seemed to be going down.

Jared looked at her in the rearview mirror. She had insisted on sitting in the back seat so she could be near Callum. "How you doing?" Jared asked, his eyes holding hers in the reflection.

"I'm okay. Better now that we're almost there." She leaned up close, so he could hear her. "Thank you for the cell phone." She'd called ahead once they were out on the road and near a signal, to let the doctor know they were coming.

"No problem. We have to get you a phone installed, though. You realize that, don't you?"

"Yes." She lowered her eyes, glanced at her son. "I know you don't understand me, Jared. But when I first came back to Dover Mountain, I wanted to be away from all of that." She lifted a hand in the air in explanation. "I didn't want to hear the phone ring. I didn't need a car then."

"I *can* understand that," he said, meaning it. "You seem to want a simple life and there's nothing wrong with that. But you have a baby now, and this is just one example of what having a child entails."

She lifted her chin, her expression both defiant and defensive. "You're right there." After checking on Callum with a hand to his little head, she slipped between the captain seats and settled in beside Jared. "He seems to be resting okay. Maybe he'll sleep until we get there."

Jared watched as she buckled her seat belt, then stared ahead. "You can't tell me, can you?"

She flashed him with a frantic look. "Tell you what?"

"What's really going on, Alisha? You can't tell me, and nobody else *will* tell me. Somebody wants me off the mountain and I think you know why. You said something back there about keeping Callum safe. And I think it has to do with more than just jealous male friends or a mother's fierce need to protect her child. You're hiding out from someone. Am I close?"

She looked down at her hands. "I don't know who's messing with you, Jared, honestly. And I hope they aren't doing it because of me. I'm not involved with anybody, not in that way. I don't want to be involved." Glancing back at the baby, she added, "I'm not hiding out. I'm just trying to start over."

Jared got that sinking feeling in his stomach. Because he thought he knew why she was so skittish. "This has something to do with your husband, doesn't it?"

She nodded again. "We…we weren't always a happy couple." She glanced out the window at the rolling hills and the yards abloom with all the signs of spring. Tulips and daffodils lined the sprawling yards and dotted the side of the road. "You know, we lived this beautiful facade, all flowers and light to the outside world."

"But inside?"

She wouldn't look at him. "Inside, things were very different." Finally, she cast a quick glance over toward him. "I had to get away. Too much light, too much noise. Too many memories."

Jared absorbed that bit of information, wondering just how far he should push her. "What about the azaleas?"

Her head shot up. "What about them?"

"You've received two plants now, but refuse to put them in your yard."

She nodded, then leaned her head against the window. "I thought you...I wondered if you'd left them for me."

"Me?" He shook his head. "Why would I do that?"

"I know it wasn't you," she admitted. "But I don't know who left them there. I...I don't like azaleas."

"So you're telling me somebody deliberately left you a plant you don't even like?"

"I don't know." She threw up her hands, then let them fall in her lap. "I hope it was just a thoughtful, innocent neighbor, being kind."

Jared didn't think kindness had anything to do with the happenings at *his* cabin.

Deciding since they were alone and he had a captive audience, he said, "Somebody left an azalea blossom on my table earlier today."

She went utterly still, her face turning so pale, Jared thought she was going to faint. "Alisha?"

When she looked up at him, his heart slammed to a halt. He'd never seen such dread, such fear, in a woman's eyes.

"I'm sorry," she whispered, a hand going to her mouth. "And you're right. This is obviously about me—somebody doesn't like you being nice to me—and I can't talk about it with you."

"I need answers, Alisha."

"I know you do." She turned away again, to look out the window at the hills and pastures. "But I can't give you what you want, Jared." Then she lifted her head, her eyes locking with his, her words a plea that pierced his heart. "You should go back to Atlanta and forget about me."

He sat staring at her.

Alisha could feel Jared's dark eyes on her, could see the questions there in the chocolate-colored depths. She felt torn between the need to rush into the safety of his solid arms and the need to turn and run away before he got too deeply involved in the sordid details of her life.

Jared had insisted on coming into the examining room with them, and Alisha hadn't had the strength to protest. To keep busy, she checked Callum's diaper once again while they waited for Dr. Gaddy to tell them what was wrong.

The good doctor had already questioned her home birth, warning her she should have had proper follow-up. Jared had defended her, stating that she had both a family doctor and a midwife checking on the baby daily.

Grateful for Jared's support, Alisha still felt the guilt of her decisions weighing heavily on her now. "I should have been more prepared for things like this."

"We're learning together," Jared replied, his tone warm and sure.

Alisha wasn't used to warm and sure, calm and knowing. She closed her eyes, remembering shouts of anger, words of condemnation, a demanding tone that always expected submission and guilt.

"He's a tough little fellow," Jared reminded her.

"He's still fussy," she said, watching as Callum grunted and squirmed. "What's taking that doctor so long?"

"I'm sure Callum is fine," Jared said, the rich texture of his words moving over her like a soft blanket. "Dr. Gaddy seemed to agree with Geneva. Probably an ear infection."

"But he's so little and so young."

Jared reached out a hand in the air. "I don't have children. Haven't been around many, I admit. But I do know from hearing my secretary and some of the other workers back home, ear infections are common in newborns."

"Really?"

"Really." His smile was lopsided. "Being a parent is scary, isn't it?"

She nodded, watched as little Callum's hand wrapped around her index finger. "Especially knowing I'm on my own. Thank goodness for my friends."

"You don't have any family?"

"No. My parents died five years apart when I was married. My aunt lived in the cabin, but now she's in a nursing home. She doesn't even recognize me when I get a chance to visit her, which is too rare, I'll admit." *Because I don't want to be traced back to Dover Mountain.* "She was the last of the four sisters." She shrugged. "My cousins are scattered here and there throughout the South. We're not close."

"What about your husband's family?"

She pulled away from Callum so abruptly, the baby jumped. "I'm sorry, honey." Grasping his hand again, she said, "Mommy's here."

"Alisha?"

"They don't live near here," she explained, hoping Jared would just leave it at that.

But he didn't. "Where do they live?"

Alisha swallowed, prayed. "South of Atlanta."

Jared held his hands at his knees, his eyes on Callum. "You don't have to explain any further. Whatever happened between you and your dead husband is between the two of you." Then he looked up at her, his dark eyes so open and honest, Alisha knew in that one minute she could trust him if she'd just have faith. "I have my secrets, too, you know. That's why I came back to Dover Mountain."

"Back?" The trust she'd just felt disappeared like a ray of light being shut out by a curtain. "You've been there before?"

"When I was very young. Throughout my growing-up years, I spent some time there a few summers with my grandfather Murdock. He got too sick to come back and I got too busy running my company. I haven't been here in close to twenty years. When he died two months ago, for some reason that got me to thinking about this place."

Relief washed over Alisha even while her heart went out to Jared. He couldn't know anything about her. Her mother had moved away from the mountain before Alisha was ever born. "I'm sorry to hear that about your grandfather," she said, meaning it. "I never knew my grandparents. They were long dead before I was born." Recalling Jared's words, she asked, "So you came back to the mountain? Why?"

"I have no idea," he said, getting up to pace around the tiny examining room. He studied the teddy bear designs on the red-and-yellow wallpaper before turning back to her. "His death hit me pretty hard, and then I found out a few things about myself, and my business partner. Ugly things. I just needed to find a place where the memories were good."

"Me, too," she said, her heart going out to him. "I knew I'd be safe on the mountain."

Jared leaned back against the sparkling-clean counter. "I didn't need to be safe. I made some bad decisions, and I guess I lost out on so many things. I wanted a new perspective. Some think I'm having an early mid-life crisis, but I just needed to be away, lost in my own thoughts. Or my own self-condemnation."

"Me, too," she said again, her smile bittersweet. "We seem to have a lot in common. Miss Mozelle would tell us to go ahead and throw a pity party, then get over it."

He took her completely by surprise then as he pulled her up to her feet, his eyes locking with hers. "Yes, we do have a lot in common. But you don't seem to be pitying yourself." He held his hands on her shoulders, his gaze searching her face. "That night we delivered Callum, that night made me think about all the things my grandparents tried to teach me. About Christ and the Bible. About believing. About faith."

Alisha's eyes grew moist with tears. "You came along exactly when I needed you, Jared."

"I know. And I didn't even know you needed me. Or that maybe I needed you."

Alisha didn't know how to respond, so she spoke the truth. "But God did. He knew we needed each other that night."

Jared leaned close. Alisha could smell the soft, clean scent of the evergreen soap the Wilkeses always left for guests in the cabins. She breathed in the scent, wondering so many things, wishing so many things.

"Do I scare you?" Jared asked, the question husky and soft as his breath flowed over her skin.

"Yes," she admitted. "And no."

"What does that mean?"

She looked up at him, saw the goodness in his eyes. Saw that he wanted her to tell him her secrets. "The way I feel when I'm with you—that scares me. But you've been so good to me, Jared. I don't deserve you."

"Don't say that. It's the other way around."

"Oh, no." She tried to pull away, but he held her there. "You have to be careful. You should go back to Atlanta. I'm not what you need."

"I think I can make that decision for myself."

She shook her head. "But it's not just about us. Someone is threatening you. I don't want to be responsible. I don't want something bad to happen to you because of me."

"Nothing bad is going to happen," he said, his tone sure and steady. "This is probably just a jealous man trying to stake a claim on you."

"That can't happen. I won't allow anyone to claim me. And I won't allow you to get caught in the middle of it."

"Do you have any idea who it might be?"

She thought about that. "I know Hank Burgess has tried. But I've pushed him away." She thought of Jimmy Barrett and his suggestive remarks. Even Doc Sloane, twenty years her senior, had flirted with her, when he was too drunk to remember doing it. "And Deputy Parker asked me to a church picnic when I first came here."

Jared actually chuckled. "Well, none of those men seem too inclined to become my best buddy, that's for sure. But I think I can handle their jealous rages."

Alisha shuddered. "I wouldn't be so sure."

"But I am sure. About you and me, at least. I'm sure that I won't let anyone come between us."

He leaned even closer then and Alisha knew he was going to kiss her. It had been so long since she'd been this close to a man. So long since she'd *wanted* to be close to a man. But she couldn't let it happen.

"Don't," she said, lowering her face.

Jared lifted her chin, his fingers warm against her skin. Then he bent his head and touched his mouth to hers in a kiss that felt like the flutter of a feather over her lips. "Don't be scared, Alisha. You don't ever have to be scared again."

Then he pulled her into his arms. Alisha fought the feelings rushing through her, but they were too over-whelming to control. Like a spring waterfall after a long winter freeze, all the emotions and feelings she'd held frozen to her heart melted and came pouring down on her in a whitewash of wonder. She wrapped her arms around Jared's neck and lifted her head, her eyes meeting his just before she kissed him.

Two seconds later, the door swished open and a grin-ning Dr. Gaddy entered the room. "Now that's what I like to see. One big happy family, a set of loving parents."

Alisha's flush heated her body as she pulled away from Jared. "Oh, no. Jared is not—I mean he's—"

"Don't be embarrassed," the doctor said, waving a hand in the air. "You two are obviously still in love, even with sleep deprivation and Callum's first ear infection. We'll give him some antibiotics and he'll be right as rain."

Alisha was so relieved to hear her son was all right she didn't try to explain to the doctor that Jared wasn't her husband. "Thank you," she told Dr. Gaddy as he handed her some prescriptions and some samples of children's pain reliever.

"Not a problem," the hurried doctor said, already on his way to the next little patient. "But I want to see Callum back in a week, just to be sure."

"We'll get him back," Jared said from behind Alisha, his tone cool and calm.

After the doctor left the room, Alisha whirled to Jared, and saw that in spite of his calm words, he looked as flustered as she felt. "I'm sorry," she said, waving a hand at the door. "I should have explained to Dr. Gaddy."

Jared grabbed her hand in midair. "Don't apologize, Alisha. Because I'm certainly not going to."

✤ Chapter Thirteen ✤

He refused to apologize for kissing Alisha.

So over the next week, Jared did something else entirely. He avoided her. Not that he wanted to avoid her. He wanted to see her, touch her, hold little Callum close.

But there was a hesitancy in Alisha that caused Jared to keep away. He'd seen it often enough, had felt it even when she'd responded to his kiss there in the doctor's office. And he thought he'd figured out what that meant. He was beginning to believe Alisha's husband had been abusive. That would explain her need for privacy, her need to protect her child. That would explain her hesitant, almost shy nature. It would also explain her strength.

Was Alisha rising up again, after so much suffering?

Jared had wondered all of this over the last couple of days, while he toiled beside Hank Wilkes in the spring sunshine, removing debris and straightening up the yards and woods around the rental cabins. He'd remembered that kiss over and over again as he sat in the Hilltop Diner, making small talk with Langford and Dorothy Lindsay, while cranky Dr. Sloane had sat in a booth, red-eyed and disheveled, listening and coughing over his cold coffee. Jared thought about Alisha day and night, while fishing and hiking, while eating and sleeping, and all the while, he'd kept an alert, open eye toward those in the village who didn't want him to think about Alisha.

It didn't help that she was inside the Wilkeses' trailer right now, visiting with Loretta and Geneva, letting them take turns holding and spoiling little Callum. He knew she was in there. He'd seen her and Geneva walking up the road about an hour ago, taking turns pushing the baby stroller along the rutted terrain.

So he'd suddenly decided now would be a good time to check up on David's math homework and offer some help. He'd found the boy out in the yard, working at his assignments.

"Are you woolgathering, Mr. Jared?"

Jared looked up from his spot underneath the great oak tree in the Wilkeses' yard. David Wilkes sat staring at him, his chewed-up pencil in one hand, his battered math notebook in the other.

"Woolgathering?" Jared laughed, one hand rubbing across the splintered gray wood of the old picnic table. "I guess I was. I'm sorry, David. Did you finish the problem?"

"Yep. I mean, yes, sir." David glanced over his shoulder toward one of the open windows, with an age-old aversion to having his ears boxed for lack of respect for an elder.

"Let's see how you did," Jared replied, his mind centering once again on the word problem they'd been going over. He studied David's bold scribbling, then said, "I think you got the right answer."

David shrugged. "I don't get why we have to decipher things like this. Who cares how many hours it takes for a train to get from one spot to another three different ways. When you're there, you're there, right?"

Jared chuckled again. "I can't argue with that kind of logic, but your math teacher probably would. The idea is to find the fastest way, and learn calculations and critical thinking, too, I believe. So it's important that you understand how these problems work."

David took a noisy swallow of lemonade. "I only understand why they call them *problems.*"

Jared was about to launch into the next problem when they heard a motor revving up out on the road. David dropped his pencil, his eyes going wide.

"Jimmy," he said, shaking his head. "My mama says that boy's gonna kill himself in that fast car one of these days."

Jared glanced toward the sound of the car as it rounded the winding hill on two wheels. "He does drive way too fast for these curving roads."

David jumped up, his fists clutching at his side. "And he's got my sister in there. My daddy's gonna go ballistic."

Jared echoed that statement, since he felt on the verge of going "ballistic" himself. Jimmy was being way too reckless with both his own life and that of his girlfriend and her unborn child.

They watched as Jimmy pulled the Camaro to a grinding halt, tires spewing rocks and dirt, right in front of the double-wide. Rayanne got out of the car, tears streaming down her face, then turned and shouted, "I hate you, Jimmy Barrett. I hate you and I hate this baby."

Jimmy hopped out, his unbuttoned plaid workshirt flying open to reveal his flat stomach as he ran to grab

Rayanne by the arm. "That ain't even my brat, so don't blame it on me."

Rayanne gasped and put a hand to her mouth. "How can you even say that? I haven't been with anybody else!"

"I'm not so sure about that," Jimmy said, his expression murderous, his big hand grinding a red spot into the girl's arm. "I've heard things, Rayanne."

Rayanne hiccuped a sob. "From who?"

"I ain't saying, but I'm beginning to wonder, is all."

Rayanne tried to jerk away, but Jimmy dragged her close. "If I find out——"

"That's enough," Jared said, unable to allow the man to treat a pregnant woman this way. "Let go of her, Jimmy."

Jimmy turned on Jared, dragging Rayanne even closer. "Oh, you gonna make me?"

"If I have to," Jared said, his voice perfectly calm. "You don't need to be so rough, so just let her go."

Jimmy lifted his chin in defiance, his blue eyes tinged with fire. "What's it to you, mister? Ain't none of your business."

"You're right," Jared agreed, his eyes centered on Jimmy. He caught a glimpse of a movement inside the trailer, then Loretta, Geneva and Alisha all stepped out onto the rickety side porch. "This isn't my business," Jared continued, keeping his tone even and steady, "but I won't stand here and allow you to treat Rayanne that way."

Jimmy snorted, his hand still bearing down on Rayanne's skinny arm. "I've heard things about you, Murdock. Rich city fellow. You think you can come up here, do a little sightseeing and fishing, make some new friends——" he flicked his eyes over Alisha, then back to Jared "——and suddenly, you get to boss everyone around. Well, that ain't how things work here, mister. So just back off." With that, he jerked Rayanne to his chest, his face red with anger as he glared down at her. "We'll take this discussion into the house."

He was dragging the girl toward the back of the trailer when Jared caught up with him. "Let her go, Jimmy."

"Jared?" Loretta called from the porch. "It's okay."

"No, it's not," Jared said, a hand grabbing Jimmy's broad shoulder.

Jimmy did let Rayanne go, pushing her toward the house so hard she stumbled and almost fell. He turned on Jared then, his fists in the air. "You wanna go a round, man?"

Jared could hear Rayanne's sobs, could see Alisha trying to comfort the girl, her own green eyes filled with fright and anger. Geneva stood close, her hand on her sister's back.

"Murdock, you ready for a fight?" Jimmy shouted, a teasing, daring light in his eyes.

Jared stood perfectly still, every fiber of his being alert. "Not really. You're not worth the effort. I just want you to learn to respect women. Especially a woman who is pregnant with your child."

"Not according to what I keep hearing," Jimmy said, the words a loud snarl. "But why am I explaining this to you? Tell me again?"

"Okay, I will," Jared said, his patience wearing thin. "You will respect Rayanne. You will treat her with dignity. You will not handle her in that way again."

Jimmy jumped like a scared cat toward Jared. But Jared was ready for him. Deflecting the blow with a hand in the air, he grabbed the other man's right arm and twisted it behind his back, whirling Jimmy around so that the younger man had to crash back against Jared's chest while Jared held down his free arm in front of him. Twisting the back arm, Jared said, "See how it feels?"

Jimmy grunted and tried to break free, but Jared held him in an iron grip.

Loretta came down the steps then, reaching out to Jared. "Let him go, Jared. Before Tate gets home."

Jared loosened his grip, but leaned close to whisper in Jimmy's ear. "Do you understand what I'm telling you, Jimmy?"

Jimmy snarled. "You're gonna regret this, Murdock."

"I doubt that," Jared replied as he sent Jimmy spinning away from him. "But if you ever treat Rayanne that way again, you'll regret it much, much more. Now, get in your car and leave."

Jimmy pointed a finger at Rayanne. "We ain't through talking about this, Rayanne. You hear me?"

The girl only whimpered and buried her face against Alisha's sweater.

"And you, Murdock. You'd better watch your back."

With that, Jimmy hopped into the Camaro and gave it a loud, rocketing crank before he backed up and whirled back out onto the road, the car spinning and spewing dust back into the yard.

The quiet after the roaring of the motor was eerie and still.

Jared turned to Alisha. "Is she all right?"

Alisha nodded, the disgust in her eyes coloring them a deep forest green. "She's just shaken." She looked down at Jared then, and with a sickening feeling, he realized the heat and loathing he saw in her eyes was aimed at him.

"Alisha?" he said, holding his hands out to explain.

Alisha urged Rayanne inside. "I have to check on Callum," she said over her shoulder.

"Alisha, I had to stop him," Jared called.

"I know you did," she said, her words falling on the still air. "I understand all about how men deal with these things, Jared."

Jared watched her go, wishing *he* could understand how women coped with such things. His grandparents had taught him to respect women, to be a gentleman, to use his fists only as a last resort to settle a score. And he'd tried to do just that with Jimmy.

Well, sometimes violence begot violence, didn't it?

Loretta touched him on the arm, tears in her eyes. "Thank you, Jared. Nobody's ever taken up for my daughter that way. Nobody." She let out a heavy breath. "Tate, he tries to talk to Jimmy, but the boy just snarls at him. Tate only tolerates Jimmy for Rayanne's sake." She looked out toward the road, her arms hugging her body. "Of course, Jimmy rarely acts like that when Tate's around. If her daddy had come up on that, I think he'd have killed the boy right here on the spot."

"I had to stop him," Jared said again. "Tell Alisha—"

"Alisha will be okay," Loretta replied. "Just give her some time."

"I don't want her to think—"

"She knows, she knows," Loretta said, her expression cautious but sympathetic. "Alisha knows you're a good man, Jared."

Jared watched as Loretta whirled and hurried into the house, then he sank back down on the bench by the picnic table, frustration and confusion making him feel weak now that the adrenaline rush was gone. David came to sit beside him.

"And we thought math was the problem," David said, his teenage eyes wise beyond their years.

Two days later, Jared was in the Mini-Mart, talking to Warren J. and Letty Martha, when Alisha came in. He looked up and into her eyes and saw both doubt and denial in the forest-green depths. She was still leery of him.

He'd wanted to gain her trust and instead he'd only caused her to fear him. But how else could he have stopped Jimmy?

"Hello, there, suga'," Letty Martha said, rushing to greet Alisha. "It's about time you brought that pretty young'un in to see us." She leaned down, her pink plaid silk windpants rustling as she admired Callum. "Hello, sweetheart. My, I think you've grown two inches since I saw you a couple of weeks ago."

"We needed some fresh air," Alisha said, her gaze roaming over the store. "Hello, Warren J., Jared."

She looked at Warren J., but didn't look at Jared.

"How you doing, honey?" Warren J. asked as he came to stand by his wife. "We sure do miss you around here."

"I'll be back in about a month," Alisha said, smiling. "Miss Mozelle says I'm healing up nicely. She came by to examine both of us, then pushed me out to get some exercise, so I decided I'd pick up a few things. I've got plenty of room in this big stroller y'all gave me. Callum sure loves it, too."

Jared noticed the sturdy plastic gingham covering on the elaborate stroller. "Callum has a first-class ride," he said by way of opening a conversation. "Aren't you due to take him back to see Dr. Gaddy this afternoon?"

Alisha nodded, her eyes downcast. "Geneva's going with us."

"I thought I was."

"No, that's fine. Geneva needs to pick up a few things in Dalton. She doesn't mind."

"I wanted to go with you."

Alisha looked up then, her expression full of a silent plea. "You don't need to do that, Jared."

Jared saw a speculative glance pass between Warren J. and his wife. It looked as though they both had a hand to an ear, listening. That and the fact that they were both suddenly still, indicated they wanted to hear more of this particular argument.

Jared didn't give them that satisfaction, however. "Okay, then. Let me know if you change your mind."

"I won't," Alisha replied. Then she turned to Letty Martha. "Would you like to help me gather the things on my list?"

"Of course, honey." Letty Martha rustled off in a flurry of almond-scented delight, cooing down to Callum as they moved up the front aisle of the store.

Warren J. chuckled then scratched his balding head. "That Alisha, she's sure protective of that little fellow."

"So I noticed."

"She's a sweet thing. We just love her around here."

"I've noticed that, too."

"You've been a help to her, though. That's for sure."

Jared rounded on the other man, his frustrations coloring his words. "But now I need to back off? Is that what everyone wants to tell me?"

Warren J. lifted two bushy salt-and-pepper eyebrows. "Probably," the old man admitted, his sharp eyes meeting Jared's glare head-on. "We just ain't used to someone from the city being so all-fire friendly."

"So that makes me suspect?"

"That makes you one unique fellow, I reckon," Warren J. replied. "We don't mean to be standoffish, Jared. But it's just the nature of this place. Tight-knit, closed off from the world. We don't like change. We fight it at every breath."

"I can certainly believe that," Jared said, relaxing a bit. It wasn't Warren J.'s fault that everyone here, including Alisha herself, wanted Jared gone. "And I promise, I'm not going to bother Alisha. I can clearly see that she's not interested in either my help or my friendship."

"It ain't what you think," Warren J. said, then brought a hand to his face, stretching it down his beard stubble.

"I can see that, too," Jared said on a dry note. "In fact, nothing around here seems to be what I think. Nobody wants me to interfere, I get little warnings here and there, and yet, I'm the kind of man who sees things that need to be changed and I try to change them."

Warren J. poured two cups of coffee from the industrial-size coffee machine behind the counter, then handed Jared a cup emblazoned with "Brasstown Bald" and a depiction of the famous mountain to the east. Jared took the cup of coffee, nodding his thanks.

"I hear you been talking about that old factory," Warren J. said as he stirred three spoonsful of sugar into his milk-clouded coffee. "Letty Martha says you got some right good ideas for reopening that old place."

Jared was glad to turn to a subject somebody wanted to discuss. "I did mention it," he said, recounting how he and Tate Wilkes had driven by the closed factory a couple of days ago. "In my past life, it was my job to help companies with their images, and sometimes that meant creating new business ventures to turn things around."

"You sound like a smart man," Warren J. said, tipping his coffee cup in a salute. "Wanting to reinvent this old town."

"I know business," Jared said, suddenly missing the thrill and challenge of taking a failing company and bringing it back to life. He looked around the big store. "Just think about it, Warren J. You've got handmade quilts in here, homemade jellies and breads, crafts made by the local artisans." He shrugged, one ear tuned to the laughter coming from the ladies across the way. "You're sitting on a gold mine here."

"We do sell a lot of that junk to the tourists."

"But it's not junk," Jared replied. "Junk is what you find in a flea market beside the road. You've got things here that would sell for a small fortune back in Atlanta."

"We ain't Atlanta, son," Warren J. said as he leaned over the counter. "And remember, we don't like change."

"Even the kind of change that would give people jobs and pump dollars into the community?"

Jared heard the squeak of stroller wheels and turned to find Alisha's eyes on him. "What are you talking about?" she said, her tone full of accusation and mistrust.

"Your deliverer here wants to turn Dover Mountain around," Warren J. said, grinning. "Got some high notions about opening that old carpet outlet."

Alisha's eyes went to that deep shade of green Jared was beginning to know and understand. Her mistrust cut him like a briar. "Why would you want to do that?"

"It was just an idea," Jared said. He put down his half-empty coffee cup and held out his hands, palms up. "It's what I do—what I did for fifteen years. I'm a consultant, mostly for media companies, but we had several retail clients, too. And I've seen this work. Instead of hiding your assets in a basket, you bring them out and show them off."

"By opening up the old factory?"

He didn't like the way she dared him to explain. "Yes. It would be a combination sporting goods store, rental store—you're located right by the river, but you don't offer any tube or canoe rentals around here—and a place to show off the talents of the local artists and craftsmen. Once we get going, we could bring in outside vendors, too. I've seen these type of stores in other places and they're highly successful."

"We're not like other places," Alisha retorted, her eyes shining brightly against the dark interior of the store.

Jared felt as if he were beating his head against a mountain. "I understand that only too well," he said, his anger overtaking his better judgment. "And I was only making a suggestion, based on observations, and based on the fact that half the people in this village are out of work, or have to drive many miles to make a meager salary." Tossing up his hands, he said, "But hey, if you don't want my help or my suggestions, then that's just fine, too. I only came here to get away from the city, to find some peace and quiet. But it seems as if I've found anything but. That's easy enough to remedy, though. I'll stick to the woods and the trails."

With that, he pushed past Alisha and the open-mouthed, but silent Letty Martha and headed out into the bright afternoon sunshine.

* * *

Alisha watched Jared stalking away, her heart pushing her in an uphill battle to go after him. It wasn't his fault that she needed to avoid him. It wasn't his fault that Jimmy had provoked Jared to an angry showdown. After all, Jared had protected Rayanne, had stood his ground with Jimmy Barrett when no one else in this town would. Torn between the need to explain everything to Jared and the need to keep silent and safe, Alisha let out a pent-up sigh.

"I think we made him mad," Warren J. said.

"But he does have some good ideas," Letty Martha replied, a hand on her hip. "As mayor, I'm obligated to listen to any and all suggestions."

"That's for sure," Warren J. agreed, his expression bordering on urgent as he gave Alisha an "aren't-you-going-after-him?" look.

"He's a nice man, so polite," Letty Martha said, her eyes centered on Alisha as she tried to plead Jared's case. "Such manners. You can just tell he came from good stock." She rubbed her hands down the silk of her wind pants. "Yep, yep. Sure a nice fellow. And now we've done gone and made him madder than a fox in a trap."

Alisha dropped her hands to her side. "Okay, okay. Will you watch Callum for a few minutes?"

"Be glad to."

"Well, sure."

They collided with each other in their rush to get to the baby.

Alisha didn't stop to think. Instead, she hurried up the aisle. "I won't be long. There's a bottle in the diaper bag on the back of the stroller."

"We'll be just fine," Letty Martha called out. "You don't worry about a thing."

But Alisha was worried. She was worried that she was making a big mistake. Why couldn't her heart listen to her head?

"Jared?" she called, rushing down the street toward him, her broomstick skirt flying out around her legs. "Jared, will you stop?"

He turned, a puzzled look on his face. But he stood still, waiting for her by the tiny town square. "Are you all right?" he asked as she halted a couple of feet away to catch her breath.

"I'm fine. No, I'm not fine."

Instantly, his expression changed to one of concern. "What's wrong?"

"We need to talk," she said, motioning to a wooden bench underneath an ancient oak tree.

Jared was the one being standoffish now. "Do you think that's wise?"

"I have to explain about the other day."

"You mean when I jumped on Jimmy?"

She nodded as they walked toward the bench. "Yes."

"I thought I was the one who needed to explain."

Alisha sank down on the bench, waiting for him to do the same. The wind lifted and she could smell that clean scent that seemed to cling to him. He looked good, and he smelled good. She remembered his kiss.

"Jared, what you did—"

"—was wrong," he interrupted, holding up a hand. "You don't have to tell me that."

"No, it was right," she replied, her gaze moving over the few people out on the street. "I was wrong to get so upset, but you have to understand that seeing that whole scene between Jimmy and Rayanne was very unsettling."

He looked over at her, his dark eyes glimmering with questions. "Did that happen to you? Did your husband push you around, treat you like that?"

"Yes," she said, nodding as she lowered her head. She felt the shame of it in that one admission.

"Look at me," he said, his tone gentle.

"I can't."

He lifted a finger to her chin, bringing her head around. "Yes, you can."

Alisha looked into his eyes then, afraid of what she'd see there. But there was no judgment, no condemnation. There was only an abundant understanding.

"Do you think, do you believe I'll think less of you, Alisha, because your husband abused you?"

Her heart fluttered like a crushed flower in the wind. The pain of her secrets wanted to burst forth, but she held it back. "Some do, yes."

"I'm not like that," he said, his hand moving to cup her face. "You have to know I'm not like that."

She bobbed her head, savoring the warmth of his fingers on her cheek. "I think I do know that. But, Jared, you have to understand, I've never known gentleness in a man. I've never seen tenderness in a man's eyes. I only know what I saw in that yard the other day. Anger and accusation." And violence. "That's what I know."

She watched as he swallowed, leaned close. "When I kissed you the other day, did you feel…did you understand…that a man can be tender and gentle?"

"Yes," she whispered, closing her eyes to the need coursing through her system. It wasn't just a physical longing. It was a soul-weary need to be held and nurtured, to be touched and healed. "Yes." Then she opened her eyes and looked at him. "And that's what I'm fighting against. Your tenderness, Jared. I can't allow myself to give in to that."

"Why not?"

"It's not right."

"It can be right."

"You need to go back, you need to get away."

His eyes went cold. "From what? Is someone threatening you, because of me?"

"No," she said. "But we can't be sure. I can never be sure."

Even here, in the bright sunshine, she felt as if she were being watched. And condemned all over again.

"I'm sure," he said as he pulled her close and hugged her to him. "I'm sure. And I won't let anyone come between us, Alisha."

He watched them from the woods. Watched as Alisha let that stranger hold her close. She wasn't acting the way a mother should act. She'd left her baby with those two old befuddled storekeepers. Just left what she'd called the precious little one to run after a man. Maybe her baby wasn't so precious to her, after all.

But then, that's what women did. They left. They went away.

He'd placed such high hopes in Alisha. She was beginning to disappoint him. That would never do. He'd have to do something very soon. He'd have to send out another warning to Jared Murdock. Because if *he* couldn't have Alisha, if he couldn't convince her to help him with his plan, then no one would have her. Nor her brat.

He'd see to that. One way or another.

❦ Chapter Fourteen ❦

"It's all over the mountain, Alisha."

Alisha watched as Hank Burgess stalked around the small office she used to counsel teenagers at the church. "Hank, I told you, I was there. I saw what happened. Jared did not provoke that fight with Jimmy."

Hank jammed a finger toward her. "He stuck his nose in where it ain't needed," Hank said, his eyes snapping fire. "I don't trust that man—all high and mighty and wanting to open a new factory or something. There's talk that he came up here to buy everybody out and take over. He'll ruin all of us, you just watch."

Alisha tried to stay calm. She took a long, settling breath to rid herself of the disturbing currents running up and down her spine, then looked down at her desk. She'd come to the church for a couple of hours, bringing little Callum with her, just to get out of the house. It was a lovely spring day. Or at least it had been until Hank had shown up with an armful of mail he'd taken from the mailman on his way in.

"Jared means well," she said, hoping to set the record straight. Though with Hank, that might not be possible. He was too full of hatred and a narrow-minded attitude to listen to reason. "He's heard and seen how this town is suffering and, well, he's an idea man. He didn't come here with an agenda, but he does have some valid suggestions for helping the economy around here. That's what he did back in Atlanta. He consulted companies on how to change their image and invest in the right properties."

Hank shook his battered work cap in the air. "Then he needs to go on back to Atlanta. We don't need his kind here."

"Don't we?" Alisha asked. "People need work. Letty Martha has been trying her best to turn this town around. But no one wants to do the job, and we certainly don't have the funds to invest in any new venture. No one wants to be the leader. Jared *is* a leader, and his idea about a combination sporting goods and arts and crafts store in that old factory has some merit."

"He's getting to you, ain't he?" Hank asked, his gaze slipping over her in a possessive way that left her feeling exposed. "None of us is good enough, but he is, right?"

Alisha didn't like the accusing glare in his eyes. "I don't know what you're implying. Jared has been a good friend, nothing more."

"*More* than I've ever got from you," Hank retorted, waving his grease-stained hands. "I'm just a mechanic, though. I don't drive a fancy Cadillac SUV or live in some hoity-toity blue-blooded neighborhood."

"Hank, we've been over this. I—I'm not ready for anything like that right now. I have to think about Callum."

Hank glanced down at the sleeping baby as if Callum were a bug on the rug. "Yeah, whatever. I just don't like that man. I'm warning you, Alisha, he's messing around where he ain't welcome. Somebody's gonna get him sooner or later."

It was a threat. Alisha knew that from looking into Hank's eyes. And she had to wonder if he'd had anything to do with breaking into Jared's cabin. Hank was full of such uncontrolled anger, it scared Alisha. And reminded her of Trevor. But then, Trevor's anger had been the cold, calculating kind. He hadn't lashed out in the heat of the moment. He'd planned his revenge, carefully and thoroughly. Hank was more inclined to go into a quick fit of rage and then be done with it, from everything she'd heard and seen. Which would explain the mess apparently left in Jared's cabin.

Could Hank really be that jealous of Jared?

Any anger was still dangerous, no matter what form it came in. Alisha wanted no part of it. And she certainly didn't want Jared to come to any harm because of her. She thought about questioning Hank, but decided that might just provoke him even more. Better to remain silent and watchful. She'd have to be careful.

"I have to get these letters answered, then head home," she said to Hank, hoping he'd take the hint and leave. "Callum just got over an ear infection, so I don't want to keep him out too late. But I appreciate you bringing in the mail for me."

Hank nodded. "Just wanted to say hi. Maybe when you get back on your feet, we can finally make that trip into Dalton and have a decent dinner."

"Maybe," Alisha said, a shudder of revulsion shimmying down her backbone.

She didn't want to encourage Hank. She actually felt sorry for him, but that didn't mean she wanted to be his best buddy or his number one girl. She'd tried to counsel him when she'd first started helping out at the church, but Hank had taken her kind words as flirtation. Instead of coming to church, he'd shown up unwelcome at Alisha's home on several occasions. Reverend Stripling had warned her that Hank could be violent at times. He was still very bitter about his wife running off with another man.

A man very much like Jared Murdock.

Oh, Lord, Alisha thought as she watched Hank get into his high-powered truck, *help me get through this.* She'd promised herself that if she could just get to a safe haven and have her baby, she'd walk the straight and narrow. She looked around, the sanctuary of her church giving her a sense of security.

"I came back, Lord," she said out loud. *"I came back to You."*

Alisha remembered the horrible months after Trevor had died, remembered turning away from God's open arms. She'd been scared, disillusioned, confused. She'd wandered in limbo, like a stranger lost in the wilderness.

Until she'd come back here.

She got up now to peek at her sleeping baby. His round, rosy face held perfect peace. Callum was warm, his tiny belly full. He had a good home, a mother who loved him, a town that would watch over him.

And he has a protector.

Alisha remembered Miss Mozelle's words. But could Jared be a protector for her son? Not if someone out there knew something about her, not if someone wanted to use that information to bring harm to her baby. Who could protect Alisha from her own past?

She turned away from the purple-and-green-tinged mountain vista to the east and started sorting through her mail. Most of it was newsletters and information on youth retreats and workshops for counselors. Then one package caught her attention. It was marked Alisha Emerson—Important. The heavy black writing looked as if it'd been scrawled by a child, but there was no return address.

Curious, Alisha wondered if one of the youths she associated with had sent her a gift for the baby. She tore into the gold paper envelope, then touched her hand to the papers inside, pulling them out to read them.

Her heart slammed against her ribs, coming to a halt, then picking up tempo as her pulse quickened.

Her whole body shaking, Alisha threw down the papers, her hands going to her face as she stared down at the newspaper clippings from her past. Feeling as if she might be sick, she pushed away from the desk, then quickly grabbed the offending copies and shoved them back inside the envelope. No one could see this. No one.

Her gaze hit on the piece of floral paper someone had tucked inside the envelope. The paper was embossed with azalea blossoms.

And the message written in that same scrawling handwriting was very clear.

To replace what you've lost.

This time, the messenger had added another statement underneath those haunting words.

And to replace what I've lost.

"You look lost."

Miss Mozelle slipped into the booth, sitting across from Jared with queenlike grace in her turban and colorful layered shawls and scarves. "Why do you keep staring into that coffee cup, Jared?"

Jared's smile took more effort than he was willing to give. He couldn't tell her about the subtle little messages someone continued to leave at his doorstep—the azalea blossoms, the footprints ground into the mud in the yard, or the fact that someone was still managing to get inside his cabin. Jared couldn't be sure, but he felt as if someone had been back there several times. He always left a light on when he went out at night, but for the last two nights, the light had been off when he'd returned. True, the socket was loose and the connection faulty on the lamp by the door, but then, he'd thought he'd fixed that.

"I was just thinking," he finally told Miss Mozelle.

Miss Mozelle folded her hands primly together on the table. "Too much of that and you will be in trouble."

Jared was already in trouble. Trouble that had kept him awake last night and brought him out early this morning. And it didn't just have to do with being teased and taunted by one of the overbearing locals who wanted him out of town. But he didn't feel like divulging that to this wise woman. "You headed over to church?" he asked, his gaze scanning her frilly blue and red headdress and her navy-blue jumper.

"Yes, sir, I am that," she replied, fingering the pearls that lay against one of her knotted scarves. "Why don't you come, too?"

Jared glanced around the near-empty Hilltop Diner. "I guess that's where everyone else is this morning."

She nodded, the bright red flower centered on her headdress shaking with each bob of her head. "Langford only keeps this place open on Sundays for the church crowd. We gather here before church, go hear the message, then come on back over here for a good Sunday meal."

Jared lifted his nose. "Chicken-fried steak today, according to that wonderful smell."

From the nearby counter, Dorothy let out a chuckle as she adjusted her own black straw hat. "Now, Jared, you know you already asked me what was for lunch. And what did I say?"

"Chicken-fried steak," Jared admitted, a sheepish grin cracking his face. "But it sure does smell great."

Dorothy came around the counter, pulling at her apron. "Well, come on then. We're gonna close up for a couple of hours. But we'll be back when the church bells ring at noontime."

"You do that?" Jared asked, once again struck by the simplicity of the life on this mountain. "You just shut down and then open back up after church?"

"And why wouldn't we?" Dorothy asked, her eyes wide underneath the saucy brim of her pillbox hat. "Ain't nobody gonna be around during church. Most of the sinners are still asleep and the rest of us poor souls will be in that building across the way, hoping to get a spot on that train that's coming."

"Train?" Jared looked from Dorothy to Miss Mozelle.

"The Lord's train," Miss Mozelle said, exasperation clear as she clasped her hands together on the table. "Man, when was the last time you heard a good sermon on the Word?"

Jared felt like a sitting duck, cornered and ready to be shot and defeathered for dinner. "Uh, it's been a while."

"That's too long," Miss Mozelle said, not bothering to inquire any further. "Get up and come on with us."

Jared knew when he'd been beaten. "I guess I don't have anything pressing this morning."

"The Lord is calling you, that's what you got pressing," Miss Mozelle said with the assurance of one who knew. "You gonna be blessed today, Jared Murdock. Mark my word."

Jared had a feeling she might be right. He'd been sitting here, a pressure building in his chest as he remembered his grandfather's gentle teachings and his grandmother's tender urgings. They'd both been churchgoers, but then his grandparents had been pillars of the community in every way. He didn't know how he'd ever live up to that, and he hadn't really tried. He gave money to worthy causes, minded his own business, but for the most part, he'd been drifting through life. Then his grandfather had gotten old and sick. Jared had cared for him, in spite of Meredith's pointed protests. Jared didn't regret that decision, but after Meredith had broken things off and then his grandfather had died, Jared had felt empty and bitter. And lost.

Until he'd come here and met Alisha.

Rising up out of the booth to follow the two women out the door, he asked, "Do you think...?" He hesitated, then plunged ahead. "Will Alisha be there?" he asked Miss Mozelle, hoping his tone was casual.

The look the woman gave him was anything but. "She might. But I'm thinking she'll want to keep that baby home. Just got over that ear infection. She might not want him around all the children in the nursery."

"I saw her just yesterday," Dorothy said as they strolled toward the whitewashed country church across the square. "She stopped in for a glass of water. Said she'd been clearing her desk at the church. She looked a little pale and tired, said she was okay. But her hand was trembling when she took the glass from me."

"I haven't talked to her since Friday," Jared said, concern warring with self-control as his mind raced with questions. Yesterday, he'd wanted to see her, but Tate had needed him to help out with fixing some rotten boards on one of the vacant cabin porches. That had taken most of the morning. Jared had gone by Alisha's cabin that afternoon, but she wasn't home. Geneva had greeted him, telling him Alisha had walked into town. Jared thought about chasing her down, but then thought better of it. There were too many prying eyes around the square. He didn't want people to speculate about his relationship with Alisha.

As the two women with him were obviously doing right now. Jared couldn't blame them for the sideways looks and sly glances. He'd been sitting in the diner, doing some speculating himself. Maybe sitting in church would help him decide what to do about his future.

And Alisha.

Jared heard Miss Mozelle's intake of breath, then turned to see what the woman was looking at. He followed her gaze up the street.

"He's drunk again," Miss Mozelle said, pointing a long finger. "That man is going to kill himself or somebody else one day."

Dorothy leaned her head around. "Poor fellow. He's sure a pitiful sight."

"Pitiful?" Miss Mozelle huffed another breath. "We all got hurts, baby. Dr. Sloane needs to clean up his act and get right with the Lord."

"Why doesn't he come to church?" Jared asked as he watched the doctor tottering along in a sloppy stroll.

The man's clothes were rumpled and dirty, as if he'd slept outside.

"He hates God," Dorothy explained in a low whisper as if just saying it were a sin. "He blames God for his wife's death."

Miss Mozelle stopped as they reached the church steps, her turban fighting for attention against the backdrop of pink- and salmon-colored azalea blooms on the nearby hedges. Pinning Jared with a direct look, she said, "His wife died in childbirth about twenty years ago. The wife and the baby died while he was helping in the delivery. He blames himself."

Jared couldn't help but feel sympathy for the man. "Was he drinking then?"

"Oh, no." Miss Mozelle shook her head. "He was as straitlaced and decent as they come back then. But he loved his wife with a fierceness that's hard to explain, even though he wasn't too keen on having a baby just yet. It happened during a bad storm, kinda like the one that hit the night you came. So bad that the roads were flooded and he couldn't get her down the mountain to the hospital. He tried to deliver the baby at home, but something went bad wrong. She bled to death and took that poor baby with her. They're buried right here behind the church."

"And he hasn't set foot in the church since that night, except to bury her," Dorothy added.

Jared watched as the doctor made his way up the steps of his house, still teetering like a broken ship lost in a storm. "That explains a few things." Jared wondered how a man handled that kind of pain, that kind of blame.

"He needs to turn back to the Lord," Miss Mozelle said, "but he won't. He's stubborn and full of hatred, mostly for himself. So he drinks to forget. But it's all there when he wakes up. It's still all right there."

From up in the belfry, the church bells began to ring away, while the sound of a door slamming softened to an echo out over the hills and bluffs. Dr. Sloane had entered the dark bleakness of his house, effectively shutting out the beautiful Sunday morning, and the ringing of the bells.

Alisha had heard the church bells ringing about an hour ago.

She wanted to be there, to soak up the tranquillity of God's love and protection. But she was gripped by a fear so vivid and real, that she could almost feel the evil breathing the very air she tried to breathe.

To replace what you've lost.

Those words haunted her, laughed at her, echoed around her each time she heard the wind tapping at her window, or felt a draft moving through her cabin. Someone knew about her past. Someone was trying to scare her.

Well, it was working. She was terrified. Not so much for herself as for Callum. She had to keep him away from the legacy of his father's past. Her past. She had to keep the truth about his father away from her baby.

Alisha turned from the kitchen sink to stare down at the envelope on the table. She'd sent Geneva to church, and now she had to face what was in that package. Slowly, she pulled out the clippings, her mind reliving each horrible minute of her last hours with her husband.

Closing her eyes, she could feel the snap of azalea bushes falling all around her, could hear her own screams as Trevor pushed her down into the broken branches, her skin scratching and rasping and itching as he shoved her into the thick foliage, holding her face there amid the pink and fuchsia blossoms until she couldn't breathe, couldn't call out, couldn't see the sky above her.

Alisha's azaleas had stood six feet tall, full and lush and blooming in a glorious array of bright colors. Those colors now darted through her head in a blinding profusion of fear, causing her to take in a gulp of breath as she opened her eyes and remembered she was safe now.

Or at least, so she had thought.

She had to face this. She had to deal with her past, so she could give her son a future. Whoever knew about her, whoever was doing this, wanted to scare and intimidate Alisha.

"Well, I've had enough of that," she said out into the still air. "I've had enough." With a purposeful intent, she went out onto the back porch to the spot where Geneva had placed the two potted azaleas. Grabbing first one and then the other, Alisha took the plants down to the road and placed them in the garbage can she kept there. Brushing her hands on her jeans, she stared at the plants, their wilted tips just peeking out of the partially closed lid. "I don't want any azaleas in my yard," she said, her words echoing out over the hills. "Never again."

Let them bloom all around her. Let the whole countryside be filled with them. Azalea blossoms only lasted a few short weeks. She could live with that.

She just couldn't live with having them close by.

And she wasn't going to live in fear anymore.

He watched her from his spot on the hill. Watched as she dumped his gifts right into the trash. That certainly wasn't very nice. He'd sent her the plants out of love and concern, hoping to win her over with a reminder of something she'd once loved. He'd waited until everyone was in church, just so he could come here and have some quiet time with her.

But she'd tossed his gifts away.

Well, she wouldn't toss him away. He'd go to her soon and tell her of his plans for them. He'd tell her she needed to get to her money—to keep him quiet until they could get away from Dover Mountain. Then they'd take the small fortune and go far away, just the two of them and the precious baby. And if she didn't get the money, well, then he'd have to remind her of what he knew. And what he now needed.

"To replace what I've lost," he said as he watched Alisha stomp back to the cabin, her hands wrapped against her midsection. He watched, hidden by trees and bushes, as she glanced around and looked straight up toward where he sat hunched over. He didn't dare move, but he felt sure she couldn't see him. He knew how to hide, how to stay almost invisible. He was just imagining things, probably.

She looked up, and then she quickly disappeared back into her little cabin.

She thought she was safe there.

But he knew better.

✎ *Chapter Fifteen* ✎

Jared liked Reverend Stripling. The man had a round-faced grin that gave him an air of mischief, but his sermon held a note of reverence that left no doubt he was truly a man of God. The robust reverend with the salt-and-pepper hair talked of being lost, then being found.

The sermon hit home with Jared.

As he sat in the Hilltop Diner, enjoying chicken-fried steak, mashed potatoes, fresh vegetables and sweet iced tea the color of rich caramel, Jared once again had to marvel at the people of Dover Mountain. They shared their bounty without question, without condemnation or expectations. It was a new concept to him.

In the city, people had assets. Here they had bounty. They didn't have impressive portfolios or huge companies, but they had honest feelings and a willingness to take care of each other. Those were the same values his grandparents had tried to instill in Jared. And he supposed it had worked to a certain degree. He'd always been honest in his business dealings; he'd tried to lead a good life.

But something had been missing. And losing his grandfather had brought that emptiness into a sharp focus. That and his breakup with Meredith had caused Jared to reach the end of his road.

But look where you wound up, he told himself now.

He liked the idea of putting down roots, of creating something on this mountaintop. Maybe that was why he'd been drawn back here in the first place.

"Have you given any thought to my ideas?" he asked Letty Martha, who sat across the table from him.

"You mean, about that catch-all store you want to open in the old factory?" Letty Martha asked, her blue eyes going wide as she looked at him over her bifocals. She wore a bright teal dress with a white silk flower attached to one shoulder. Her shoes were teal-and-yellow-striped. She was the picture of spring, very prim and proper. But her expression now was all business.

"The very one," Jared replied, grinning. "But I wouldn't exactly call it a catch-all. It's more of a mini mall—something for the avid sportsman and the avid woman shopper to boot."

"A man after my own heart," Letty Martha replied.

"And you think that kind of thing could fly here?" Warren J. asked before spearing a chunk of steak from his plate. He grabbed a flaky biscuit from a wicker basket in the center of the table, then dipped it into the rich brown gravy swimming around his mashed potatoes.

Wondering what the *J* in Warren J. stood for, Jared said, "I believe so. I'd have to do some research, bring in some data to back me up. The factory is in a good place, just at the bottom of the mountain and right off Interstate 75, so we wouldn't have to worry about rebuilding roads. But if we present it just right, the state would probably want to make some road improvement leading up to the village. That could be part of the package."

"I hear that," Warren J. said, hitting his hand on the blue-and-white-checkered tablecloth so hard, it caused the centerpiece, a soda bottle filled with gerbera daisies, to shake and rattle. "Been needing that for a long time now."

"I agree," Jared said. "And I can vouch for that from personal experience."

That brought a round of chuckles from everyone who'd been listening. Everyone except Hank Burgess, who sat in a corner, nursing a cup of coffee.

"You're just determined to change the face of this old mountain, ain't you, city fellow?"

Jared glanced over at Hank. The hostility on the other man's face was obvious. Hank's features had gone red and splotchy. "I'm proposing an idea," Jared replied. "It sure would bring in a lot of needed revenue."

"And bring you business, too," Warren J. offered up to Hank.

"I got all the business I can handle," Hank replied, his eyes still on Jared.

"Do you?" Dorothy Lindsay asked from her perch behind the counter. "Then why are you always saying you want off this mountain, Hank Burgess? Didn't you tell me just the other day you had big plans? Gonna move away forever, or some such nonsense."

Hank jumped up, glaring over at Dorothy. "You don't need to go repeating everything you hear."

Langford came up beside his wife, his barrel of a chest puffing out, his big round eyes centered on Hank. "You got a problem with my wife, Hank?"

Hank simmered down, but his eyes were tinged with a red ring of anger. "No, but I got a problem with outsiders coming in here, trying to tell us what we need to be doing. Can't y'all see this man is out to get something?" At the silent stares, he added, "He comes in here out of nowhere, claiming he just wants to fish and hike, but all of a sudden, he's knee-deep in our business and trying to rebuild the town. Am I the only one who finds that strange?"

"Maybe Jared is just trying to be helpful," Miss Mozelle said as she twisted in her chair to face Hank.

"And maybe I got some swampland in Florida I can sell all of y'all," Hank said as he pushed out of his chair and headed for the door. "Y'all are all crazy."

Dorothy waited until Hank had left, then said in a low voice, "Speak for yourself."

Letty Martha rolled her eyes. "That man has sure got a chip on his shoulder."

Dorothy nodded. "Yeah, and one day, I'm afraid somebody's gonna knock it right off." She gave Jared a purposeful stare.

Jared felt the same way. He'd like nothing better than to see Hank Burgess set straight. And he might just have to be the one to do it. But right now, he needed to ask a question of the collective group sitting around the diner. "Do you all believe I have an ulterior motive?"

Miss Mozelle bobbed her head, surprising everyone. "Yes, I do." She waited for a beat or two, then pinned Jared with a look that could cut granite. "I think you're trying to impress Alisha." Then she slapped her hand on the table and let out a whoop of laughter.

Jared let out a breath, embarrassment coloring his next words. "I care about Alisha, that's true. She's a good woman. But I think it will take more than opening a tourist store to impress Alisha Emerson."

"You got that right," Letty Martha interjected, grinning. Then her expression changed. "Alisha has her reasons for being cautious toward men."

Warren J. sent the now-familiar warning look toward his wife. "Let's get back to talking about this business venture."

Jared took a swig of tea, his eyes cutting to Letty Martha's blushing face. "Yes, let's get back to business. I'm not suggesting this just to impress Alisha, although that would be nice. I'd like to have her respect, and the respect of all of you. I came here..." He stopped, threw up his hands. "Actually, I don't know why I came back here. I just had good memories of being here a few times with my grandfather when I was young. I needed to cling to those memories. He just died a few months back and well..." He shrugged, a dark emotion curling inside him like water churning through a rocky riverbed.

Reverend Stripling, sitting behind Jared, touched a hand to his shoulder. "We understand, Jared. You don't have to explain your grief. You came back to this mountain because this mountain holds part of your grandfather's soul. You had good times with him here. If he loved it here, then he must have left a part of himself here. It's hard for outsiders to understand that, but that's why we stay on, fighting the good fight for the home we love. We might not have much money or material things, but just look outside. The dogwoods and azaleas are blooming, the forest is ripe with spring and those mountains out there offer us comfort and peace every day. Who wouldn't want to keep a part of that for himself?"

Jared was overwhelmed by the compassion in the room. He could only nod, blink, long for something just out of his reach. "Maybe I'm just trying to stay busy," he said at last, his voice hollow and raw. "If I pour my-self into this project, then I'll feel as if I'm still in control of my life."

Just then, the door to the diner opened and Alisha walked in, pushing little Callum in his souped-up stroller. All eyes turned to her and she stopped, taking in the people in the room. "What's going on?" she asked, her eyes going wide before they settled on Jared.

Jared saw the fear in her eyes, saw the hesitant way she stood at the door. She was still wary of him. The darkness in her green eyes reminded him of the center of a deep mountain pool, rich and never-ending, with something hidden deep down inside.

To reassure her, he said, "We were just discussing the possibility of me investing in Dover Mountain, maybe opening the old factory as a store—sportsman gear and things that women can appreciate, too."

"Oh, that," she said, clearly relieved. Pushing the stroller inside the room, she added, "That sure sounds like a big undertaking."

"It would be," Jared replied, sensing her distraction. She looked beautiful in her floral full-skirted dress and white sweater, but she also looked tired, her eyes cloudy. "I'd be willing to invest in it myself, and I have connec-tions back in Atlanta, people who are looking for just such an enterprise."

"Atlanta?" She glanced around the room, her gaze touching on Letty Martha, then Miss Mozelle. "I'm not so sure we'd want a coalition from Atlanta coming in to run our town, Jared."

Jared frowned. "But that's where the money is."

"Then keep the money there," Alisha retorted, push-ing at the auburn curls escaping around her face.

"You sound like Hank," Langford said, shaking his head. "I would have thought you'd be all for this, Alisha."

Jared didn't miss the looks that passed between Dorothy and Letty Martha. The caution was back, a silent reminder that these people had their own secrets to protect. He looked at Alisha, questions battering his mind.

Alisha's eyes stopped on Jared, but a wall of resistance covered her gaze. He wished he could read that dark resistance. "I'm all for progress," she said, "but I don't want a lot of outsiders taking over. I came back here because I like my privacy."

Miss Mozelle seemed to take that as her cue. Getting up, she hurried to smile down at Callum. "How's his ear, honey?"

"He's well," Alisha replied, her eyes still on Jared. "I just needed to get out and get some air. I bundled him up, but it's rather warm out today."

Jared watched her. She was fidgety and nervous. She kept glancing around, as if expecting someone to come inside the diner. She adjusted the cover on Callum's stroller twice. Something was wrong. Alisha was usually so calm. Except when—

He got up to move toward her. "Want me to hold him?" He pointed down at the baby.

"No, let's just let him sleep."

Jared started to speak, but Dorothy interrupted him. "Want some steak and peach cobbler, Alisha?"

"That would be nice," Alisha said as she sank down on a chair. She was clearly tired, her freckled porcelain skin pale.

Jared shot a look at Miss Mozelle. Okay, she looked worried, too. "What's wrong?" he asked Alisha in a hushed tone.

"Nothing."

She refused to look at him.

"You've had another scare, haven't you?"

"What's he mean, a scare?" Miss Mozelle asked, her dark eyes beaming in on Jared.

"Nothing," Alisha said under her breath, her gaze beseeching Jared to let the matter drop.

Miss Mozelle picked up on her concern, but respected Alisha's need for discretion. She turned back to the group and started talking about the weather. "So nice out there today. Dorothy, want to take a walk with me before I go home to get my Sunday afternoon nap?"

Dorothy flicked her gaze toward Alisha. "Yep, that sounds like a good way to burn off that peach cobbler. You don't mind, do you, Langford?"

Her husband chuckled, the sound rumbling like a train up his broad chest. "Not one bit. I'll get the boys to help me finish up the lunch dishes." He nodded toward where three busboys sat finishing their own noontime meal.

One of the boys, tall and lanky, jumped up to protest. "Coach, you said we might shoot some hoops today."

Jared looked toward Langford, but the boy was talking to Dorothy. "Who's the coach?" he asked, curious.

The boy pointed to Dorothy Lindsay. "She is. And she's tough, too."

Dorothy grinned, then gave the youth a gentle shove. "Get this place cleaned up and we'll see about basketball later." Then she shrugged. "I help out at the high school, part-time."

Langford laughed, then nodded toward Jared. "Things ain't never as they seem around here."

Jared shook his head. "This place is just full of surprises." Then he looked back at Alisha. "But I'm learning to go with the flow."

Langford patted Jared on the back. "That's the best way to accept the world." He hurried the boys about their business. "Y'all get things in shape, and I'll get a plate for Alisha."

After that, the crowd began dispersing, each helping out Langford by clearing away their own tables. Jared helped, too, his eyes on Alisha as she sat staring at the plate of food Langford had put in front of her. She wasn't eating. Just staring. She held one hand on the stroller, as if afraid to let go, unconsciously pushing it back and forth in a pattern that resembled pacing.

After everyone but the hustling busboys, a waitress and Langford had left the diner, Jared sat down beside Alisha. "Have you ordered phone service yet?"

She nodded. "Yes. They're coming tomorrow."

"Good." He waited, hoping she'd open up to him. She didn't.

"Alisha, I can't help you if you won't talk to me."

She looked at him then, the expression in her eyes bordering between despair and resolve. "You can't help me, Jared. This is something I have to fight on my own."

"Why? Why can't I help?"

"I don't want to get you involved in my problems."

"But if someone is threatening you—"

"I won't be intimidated by threats, not ever again."

"Okay, now you're scaring me. I don't like the tone of your voice."

Her smile was small, just a twist of her lips. "Do I sound resigned? Frustrated? Determined?"

"Yes. But that can be dangerous. You can't get reckless with whoever is doing this."

"I won't be reckless."

The fire in her eyes scared Jared more than seeing fear there. "You can't fight this kind of thing on your own, you know."

She sent him a look full of sorrow. "You're wrong there. I've been fighting this kind of thing all my life. Or at least since I got married ten years ago."

He leaned close, his eyes holding hers. "Tell me about your marriage."

She shook her head, toyed with a carrot stuck on her fork. "There's not much to tell. I really don't want to talk about it."

Frustration colored Jared's words. "Why is it that everyone here seems to distrust me so much?"

"We don't distrust you," she replied, her head down. "We just like to keep our personal business close."

"But somebody knows something about you," he reminded her. "Why don't you go to the sheriff, at least?"

"And tell him what? That someone brought me two azalea plants? That the person harassing you might really be after me?"

"That might work, for starters."

"I don't trust law enforcement."

Jared heard more in that one statement than he'd ever heard in her words before. "Was your husband a police officer?"

Again, she shook her head. "He was a businessman. But he knew people in high places."

"But he's dead now."

She finally looked up and into his eyes. Jared would never forget the raw honesty of that gaze. "Yes, he's dead. But his parents aren't." Then she whispered, "And they don't know where I am."

Before he could delve into that statement and all it implied, the door to the restaurant burst open, bringing in Miss Mozelle and Dorothy. And Rayanne.

The girl's nose was bleeding.

"Langford, get me some ice, quick," Dorothy called out, her arm around Rayanne's sagging body.

With Jared's help, Miss Mozelle managed to get the sobbing girl to a booth. "There, there, honey. Sit here. We'll get you home in a bit."

"What happened?" Alisha asked, running over to sit next to Rayanne.

The girl fell into Alisha's arms. "Jimmy," she managed to hiccup. "He...he got so mad at me."

Jared got up, a dark rage coursing through his system. "Jimmy did this to you?"

Rayanne nodded, then grabbed Jared's arm. "It's my fault. I made him mad."

Jared saw a flash of fire in Alisha's eyes before they became distant and vacant. "That's what they want us to believe," she whispered to Rayanne. "It's always our fault."

Jared felt so sick, bile rose up in his throat. "Where is Jimmy now?" he said, his voice clear in spite of his shaking hands. He didn't condone violence, but someone needed to stop Jimmy Barrett from beating up women.

"He left," Rayanne said. "Put me out and just took off."

"We saw it," Miss Mozelle said, her own usually steady voice shaking. "We were walking around the square, toward that wooded park down the mountain, when we heard him a-roaring up the road. Then we watched as he yanked open her door and told her to get out of the car. She wouldn't, so he hit her square in the face, then shoved her. Poor little thing almost fell down the hill." She placed a hand on Rayanne's shoulder. "I hollered at him, then he threatened *me*." She pounded her chest with one finger. "Just let him do that again— he'll regret that, I'm telling you."

Jared imagined Jimmy *would* regret that, from the look in Miss Mozelle's eyes. But he also saw the caution and worry in Alisha's green eyes. And remembered how upset she'd been with him the last time Jimmy got violent and Jared had tried to confront him.

"Are you hurting anywhere else?" Alisha asked Rayanne, her gaze flying to Miss Mozelle. "Is the baby okay?"

Rayanne bobbed her head. "I'm just scared and my nose hurts. I think the baby's fine. I caught myself before I fell."

"We brought her straight here," Dorothy said, wiping the blood from Rayanne's face with a clean towel. "Miss Mozelle checked her over when it first happened. I think the baby's all right, but if she stays with that idiot, that could change."

"Yes, it could," Alisha said, her arms still around the girl, her expression grim. "Do you want to go home, to your mama?"

Rayanne nodded. "But I'm afraid Daddy will go after Jimmy."

Langford stepped forward then. "I'd be glad to do that for your daddy, baby."

Jared could see the pulse throbbing in the big man's jaw. He felt the same. "We can go and find Jimmy, haul him back here. We can press charges."

"No," Rayanne said with a wail. "That would just make him even madder at me."

Jared couldn't grasp that logic. "The man hit you, Rayanne. He needs to be held accountable."

"I shouldn't have made him so mad," the girl said, gulping back yet another round of tears. "I just wanted him to go to church with me this morning. Just hoped he'd maybe change his mind about me and this baby." She burst into tears again, leaning into Alisha. "I guess he ain't gonna ever marry me."

Miss Mozelle let out a grunt. "I'd rather see you single than married to that monster, baby."

"I'm so ashamed," Rayanne said, sniffing back tears. "I'm so ashamed. I never wanted to get pregnant."

Alisha pulled the girl close. "We're here to help you, Rayanne. The reality is that you *are* pregnant, but we can't blame this child for the mistakes Jimmy has made. This is a human life, an innocent little baby. We have to protect you and your child. And we can't do that if you continue to let Jimmy abuse you."

Jared stared down at the scene, wondering why Alisha couldn't take her own advice. She'd obviously relived her own nightmare, sitting there trying to comfort Rayanne. Had she once been the same, wanting to take the blame for a man hitting her? Wanting to piece things back together instead of getting away from the shame and abuse?

Maybe that was why she couldn't trust him now. Maybe she'd been hurt so badly, both physically and mentally, that she'd never be able to trust another man again. He stood there, his heart breaking for both Alisha and Rayanne. He'd never felt so helpless.

Alisha looked up at him, that cold determination sealed in her green eyes. There was also something else there. He saw grief and pain etched in her expression.

He saw a resolve that made him want to hold her close and protect her. She looked from him to her sleeping child, tears misting her eyes as she rocked Rayanne back and forth in her arms.

Jared thought back over the little bits of information Alisha had given him about her marriage. Then it occurred to him: Alisha had never said exactly how her husband had died.

❧ Chapter Sixteen ❧

"Do you want me to stay a while longer?"

Jared looked over at Alisha, half expecting her to ask him to leave. After taking Rayanne to Miss Mozelle's house so the girl could get cleaned up and get some rest underneath Miss Mozelle's watchful eye, Jared had walked Alisha and Callum back to Alisha's cabin. Geneva was having Sunday dinner with her family in the Wilkeses' trailer, so they were alone.

They'd all decided Rayanne would be safe with the midwife for a while. They'd call her parents to tell them she wanted to visit with Miss Mozelle and get some advice about being a parent. The Wilkeses hadn't questioned this, since this was the way of the mountain. It was expected that Miss Mozelle would play a big part in the delivery and care of Rayanne's baby. But Rayanne had insisted no one tell her parents about what had happened. She was afraid her father would go after Jimmy.

Jared wanted to do the same, but knew that wasn't the answer. He prayed he'd find the answer soon.

"You don't have to do that," Alisha replied to Jared's question. "I'll be fine."

"You don't look fine," Jared said, determined to get to the bottom of what was bothering her. Seeing Rayanne hurt had only added to Alisha's frantic demeanor. She was obviously fighting for control, but Jared could see the anxiety in her eyes, in her gestures. "And I'm not leaving until we talk about it."

"Let's go sit on the porch," Alisha said, turning to grab the baby monitor to take it with them. "Do you want some tea or lemonade?"

"No, nothing for me," Jared said as he followed her out onto the long, planked porch. He pulled one of the rockers up close to the porch railing; really, he moved the chair just so he could be closer to Alisha. "Are you all right?"

"I'm okay," she said, shifting the matching rocker so she could see him better. "I just wish…I wish a lot of things."

Jared nodded. He wished she would talk to him. "We have to get Rayanne away from Jimmy, don't we?"

"Not we, Jared," Alisha replied. "You need to stay out of this."

"And let you fight it alone, the way you seem to want to handle everything? The way you're handling this person who's harassing you? I don't think so."

Alisha watched him for a moment, her expression changing from apprehensive to aggravated in the afternoon sunlight. "What are you doing here?" she asked, her anger as clear as the sky west of the mountains across from them.

"What do you mean?"

"I mean, what's in this for you? Why can't you just stick to the woods and fish and hike, like you said you were going to do?"

"I've done that, and I've helped Tate out some, and I'm helping David with his math. I've tried to stay busy and out of people's business," Jared said, refusing to be defensive about caring. "But you can't expect me to see an injustice and not try to fix it. It's not in my nature to ignore this. That man is dangerous—he could have seriously hurt Rayanne and the baby." He got up to stomp to the porch railing. "I just don't understand why someone doesn't do something about it."

He heard the anger draining out of Alisha in a long sigh. "We've all tried. I've talked to Rayanne. I've talked to her parents. And I've tried to talk to Jimmy. He's had a bad upbringing, and I'm pretty sure he's just following the same pattern his own father has set."

Jared whirled around to stare down at her. "So that gives him a good excuse to abuse his pregnant girlfriend?"

"No, it's not an excuse. It's a reaction." She stopped, stared out over the woods. "I'll try to reason with him again, for Rayanne's sake."

Jared didn't like the thought of Alisha being anywhere near Jimmy Barrett. "Be careful with him."

"You don't have to tell me that," she said, the steady rocking of her chair the only sign that she was still shaken. "I'm very aware of what kind of man Jimmy Barrett is."

"Because he reminds you of your husband?"

Her head shot up then. "Jimmy is nothing like Trevor."

"Trevor?" Jared wrapped his arms across his chest. "Do you know that's the first time you've said his name to me?"

She stopped rocking, her sudden stillness an indication that she didn't want to take this topic any further. "I didn't think you needed to know the specifics."

Jared threw his hands up in the air, then dropped on one knee in front of her. Placing a hand on each arm of her chair, he held her captive as he looked into her eyes. "You've got to see how I feel. You have to know that I'm attracted to you. That makes me want to know the *specifics*."

She turned her head away. "You just feel an obligation—"

Jared reached up to force her head around, his thumb gentle on her chin. "This is not an obligation, Alisha. I helped you bring Callum into this world. Don't you see, until that night, I had given up hope."

She looked into his eyes then, and Jared could clearly see that she had feelings for him, too. But he also saw the resistance she pushed toward those feelings. It reminded him of some of the rock faces he'd climbed over the past few weeks—etched in granite and just as unrelenting. "Don't pin your hopes on me," she said, the words washed with a whisper of regret and longing. "We can't do this. You'll be leaving in another week, right?"

He hadn't thought that far ahead. "Yes, I suppose so. But I know the way back."

"You don't need to come back here. I'll be going back to work soon and my life will settle down to a nice, normal routine."

"Not with someone threatening you."

"I'm hoping that will stop when—"

"When I leave?" That notion floored him. "So you *do* think whoever is doing this, is doing it because I've shown an interest in you?"

"It started when you showed up here," she said, the honesty of her words sounding in an echo out over the woods. "No one has ever bothered me before."

Jared let go of her, then rocked back on his knees. "You don't think I—"

"I know it's not you," she said, shaking her head, alarm brightening her eyes. "I actually thought that it might be you at first, but now I know better. But you've triggered something in someone. I don't know what's going on, but I do know that I'm not going to cower or hide anymore."

"And what about Callum?"

"I will protect my baby."

The steely quality of that statement jarred Jared to his bones. "How? You need better security around here, a cell phone maybe."

"I'm getting a phone tomorrow."

"That's good for starters. And do you have a gun?"

She pushed him away, then shot out of her chair, her steps causing floor boards to creak and moan. "No. I don't want a gun."

"You could protect yourself. I could show you how to fire it properly."

"I know how to fire a gun," she said, her words rushing out in a breath of air over her shoulder.

Jared didn't understand how to get through to her. "So what are you going to do? Just wait for this person to make his next move?"

She was silent for a long minute, then she said, "He already has. He sent me something. Something from my past."

Jared spun her around, his hands on her arms. "What?"

Alisha looked up at him, her eyes guarded and full of pain. "Don't make me tell you. I won't tell you."

Jared pulled her close, hugging her to him, his need to protect her so strong, he seriously thought about packing her and Callum up and taking them off this mountain. "Please let me help you."

Alisha relaxed against him, her tense body going slack as she leaned into his arms. "I don't want you to get hurt. You shouldn't have to deal with this."

"But I'm a part of it now, you said so yourself. If this person is jealous of me, he might try to get even by hurting you or Callum."

"Just give me some time," she said into his shirt. "Just let me think how I can figure this out."

"You don't need to put yourself in danger," he reminded her. "I'll stay here, and we'll find a way to end this." Touching a hand to her hair, he added, "Or I'll go, if it will make all of this go away."

Alisha lifted her head then, her eyes full of honesty. "I do feel safe with you here."

"Then I'll stay as long as you need me."

Jared stared down at her, the need inside him blossoming like a bud opening for the first time. Then he leaned down and kissed her, the touch of his lips on hers making him long to be here always to protect her. Alisha responded to his kiss with a tenderness that bordered on tentative, as if she wasn't sure how to kiss him back, how to respond to his need. Jared showed her how he felt by deepening the kiss, by pulling her into his arms to hold her tight. He tried to make his touch tender and reassuring, even though inside he wanted more, much more. He was rewarded when she lifted her hands up to run them through his hair.

Then she stood back, her hands coming to his face. "You are a good man, Jared."

"I want to be a better man," he admitted. "For you."

Tears misted in her eyes. "No one's ever said that to me. No one's ever wanted to be better, just for me."

"Well, I do. I do, for you and for Callum."

"Maybe you are my protector."

"I intend to be," he said. "I'm spending the night on your couch."

He didn't spend the night on the couch.

Alisha had convinced Jared to go back to his own cabin, but only after she'd promised to leave a light on.

He could see that light through the trees now, at midnight, from his vantage point on the front porch of his cabin. He couldn't sleep and the night was sweet with a fresh spring air that carried the sound of chirping crickets and hungry frogs. The woods seemed to be alive with the coming of spring, the rustling of leaves lifting in the night breeze, the snap of a twig causing some furry creature to scurry away. In the bright moonlight, he could make out the stark-white blossoms of a dogwood tree buried deep beneath the tall pines and old oaks of the mountain. Jared wondered what else—who else— was out there in those moonlit woods and hills.

He looked back at the soft glow of the yellow light coming from Alisha's cabin and remembered their earlier conversation.

"My grandmother kept a lamp on at night," he explained. "She said it was so I could always find my way home again."

"So if I leave a light on—"

"I'll know you're safe."

"Geneva will be here."

"I still want to know you're safe."

In the end, Alisha had agreed, more for her own security then to appease Jared. She intended to leave a light on, she promised him. She intended to keep alert and watchful, because she had a feeling, just as Jared did, that her tormentor was going to get even bolder. What did this person want? To expose her, to humiliate her, now that she'd been home for a while and safe?

Jared just wished she'd clue him in on the why of this situation. But he also knew he had to tread lightly. Alisha was learning to trust him, day by day. And as the days passed, he felt less inclined to rush back to the city. He intended to stay here until he found out who was harassing her. And until he sorted through this maze of new feelings twisting through his mind.

She knew she was no longer safe here. But Callum was too young for her to leave right now. And some of the villagers knew her situation, she'd explained to him. Maybe if she alerted them—but then, it could very well be one of them.

Jared remembered going over a list with her.

"Who knows about you?" he'd asked.

Alisha hadn't wanted to tell him, but then, she had to turn to someone. Jared was relieved that she at least trusted him enough to divulge this information.

"Miss Mozelle knows almost everything. I had to tell her, so she'd understand my concern for the baby. Dr. Sloane knows I was abused. He and Miss Mozelle nursed me back to health and probably saved me from having a miscarriage—and during that time, I told them most of it. Then the Wilkeses—they know the basics. And Letty Martha and Warren J., they only know that I don't want my in-laws to find me. Langford and Dorothy know that, too. So they're all very careful about what they say around strangers."

That explained why they'd all been so tight-lipped around Jared. And why some of them had questioned his intentions regarding starting a new business here. A new venture would bring in a lot of outsiders, and possibly expose Alisha to even more danger.

Jared thought back over this as he leaned a hip against the porch railing, his eyes and ears alert to all the shadows and sounds of the mountain. He thought about taking a flashlight and hiking around the perimeter of the woods, but then, he might scare Alisha and Geneva if they happened to be up with the baby.

He'd just wait and watch for now.

And wonder what else Alisha was hiding.

He was hiding up on the ledge behind Alisha's cabin. He could just see the faint light from a single lamp in her little den. She must be up feeding the baby right now.

If he inched a little closer…

But no, he'd better just stay up here. He'd seen the stranger with her again today. Jared Murdock, always lurking around her. Didn't give any other man much of a chance to get near Alisha. But he knew she must have received his little package. To remind her that she couldn't hide here forever. He hoped it had frightened her into believing she needed to leave the mountain.

With him.

He'd give her a few more days. He'd watch and wait and make sure that Murdock fellow didn't pester her too much.

Because if *he* couldn't have Alisha, no man would. That's just the way it had to be. It all made sense to him now. They'd take Alisha's money and leave this mountain. He'd help her raise little Callum.

Jared Murdock had to stop interfering.

He'd see to that.

Maybe it was time to give Murdock another warning.

"I'm warning you, I won't take no for an answer."

Jared stood staring at Alisha, a stubborn expression etched on his handsome face.

Hoping to convince him differently, Alisha said, "I told you, Geneva can take us into Dalton for Callum's checkup."

They'd been arguing for a good five minutes, while Geneva hovered in the kitchen with a knowing smile on her face. Wisely, her friend had decided to stay quiet and let Alisha do the talking. Or rather the persuading.

But the look in Jared's dark eyes told Alisha that he couldn't be persuaded. "Look," he said, his hands on his hips, "I let Geneva drive you last time. Today it's my turn. I told you I was going to stick around, and I mean it."

Alisha pushed a hand through her loose hair. "I have a phone now, Jared. That makes me feel more secure. And Geneva and I were going to look at used cars in Dalton today."

"Oh, so that's why you don't want me tagging along." He glanced at Geneva, then back to Alisha. "Geneva, what do you know about cars?"

Geneva giggled and started talking. "My daddy has worked part-time for Hank Burgess most of my life, Jared. And my husband—that man knows his car parts. I've picked up a few tips here and there."

Alisha grinned, feeling triumphant. "We aren't helpless, you know."

Jared nodded, subdued but not beaten. "I can tell that you are both strong, capable women. But—"

"Don't say because you're a man, you know more," Alisha replied, winking at Geneva. "I'd have to throw a wet dish towel at you if you do."

"Okay, then, I won't say that," Jared retorted. "But I can help you find a good deal. And you need a car that will survive these brutal mountain roads. What can it hurt if I offer my advice?"

Geneva shrugged, turned back to washing dishes.

No help there, Alisha realized. And Jared did have a point. What could it hurt? She enjoyed his company, it was another beautiful day, and Callum was growing and thriving.

But what if someone saw them together?

Jared's sharp expression mirrored her thoughts. "If we stick together I'll know you're safe."

Alisha considered that for a moment. He did make her feel safe. Too safe. And yet, she wanted to spend some time with him. Maybe getting away from this place would help calm her frazzled nerves.

"We can't take too long," she said by way of giving in. "I don't want to keep the baby out."

"If we find something, we'll go back tomorrow for a second look," Jared said. "Maybe Geneva would be willing to watch Callum then."

"I sure would," Geneva said, whirling so fast she sent soapsuds flying out in an arch over her head. "Don't mind one bit. I'll get Mama to come and sit with us, just so you won't fret any, Alisha."

"Gee, thanks," Alisha replied, thinking there was a feminine conspiracy traveling around this mountain, intent on getting Jared and her together. If only she could relax and enjoy it. That made her think of the ever-present fear of being stalked. She glanced at Jared and said in a low voice, "What if—"

"If he's out there, he'll know you're with me," Jared replied. "He wouldn't dare confront both of us."

"But what if he retaliates by doing something to you?"

"I'm more concerned about you," Jared told her.

Geneva turned to stare at them. "What are y'all whispering about?"

"She doesn't know?" Jared asked.

"I didn't want to worry her," Alisha responded, feeling as if she'd done something wrong. "This is my problem."

"What?" Geneva walked over to them, her gaze questioning.

"Someone's been harassing Alisha," Jared said, his expression brooking no argument this time. "You should be aware, so you don't open the door to anyone suspicious."

"Anyone, period," Alisha said, angry that Jared had blurted this out to her friend. But then, Geneva did need to know, for her own safety.

"What's been going on?" Geneva asked, alarm clear in her blue eyes.

"Just some gifts and some unwelcome mail," Alisha replied. "That's why I got the phone. And that's why I'm going to buy a car." Then she touched Geneva's arm. "If you're afraid to stay here—"

"I won't leave you by yourself," the girl responded. "Besides, Ryan taught me some self-defense techniques just before he left. I feel more secure, knowing what to do in that kind of situation."

Jared nodded. "That's good, but sometimes things don't work the way we want them to. Both of you need to be very careful."

"That's why it would be smart if you have someone here with you when I'm not here," Alisha said. "Or you and the baby could go to your mother's to stay, if and when I do have to process buying a car—you know that kind of thing can take a few hours. I'd be worried sick if I thought you and Callum were here alone." She looked at Jared. "Maybe I should just take the baby with me anyway."

"We'll take care of him," Geneva said, her smile reassuring. "Daddy's off tomorrow anyway. He'll be in and out most of the day. Should I tell him?"

"Not a bad idea," Jared said, nodding. "Tate could watch out, too, around the cabins."

"Okay," Alisha said, the feeling of being able to share her burdens as foreign to her as having Jared take over some of the responsibilities in her life. "But no one else needs to know. We don't know who this is. It could be someone real close, just waiting for a chance."

"I won't tell anyone but Mama and Daddy," Geneva said.

Then she looked at Jared. "And I promise, I won't ever leave Alisha and the baby alone."

"Good," Jared said.

Alisha pushed away the shard of resentment at his masterful handling of her problems. The man truly was a godsend. Why couldn't she relax and accept that?

She wondered that all over again a few minutes later, as they headed down the mountain toward Dalton. Glancing over at Jared, she said, "You know how to maneuver people, don't you?"

He watched the curving road, then lifted a brow. "What do you mean?"

"You told Geneva about my problem. I would have rather done that myself. And you managed somehow to talk me into letting you take us to Dalton."

His expression turned impassive then. "Well, excuse me for caring about you."

"Do you—care about me?"

"Can't you see that?"

Alisha stared at the ridges and hills, the sun-dappled mountainside changing and dipping in a dizzying array of green trees and gray rocks. "I'm not used to being cared for, I guess."

"Didn't your husband show you any kindness?"

"At times," she replied, her memories as vivid as the mountain ridges, and just as puzzling. "That's why I stayed so long, I think. At other times—"

Jared reached across the seat. "Don't talk about it. It will only make me angry."

She could see the pulse throbbing in his jaw. "I thought you wanted to know everything."

"I do, but this—I can't condone this, Alisha. I can't condone what Jimmy is doing to Rayanne, and I certainly can't understand why you stayed with your husband for ten years."

"Then I won't try to explain it," she replied. "At times, I don't understand it myself." She shrugged, glanced back at Callum. "But I'm free now, free and clear." Then she thought about the clippings she'd received. "Or at least I thought I was."

She heard the frustration in Jared's sigh. "You could be, if you'd only let me in. If you'd tell me what you're trying to hide. I've got a pretty clear picture of what your husband must have put you through, but I don't have a clue as to what really happened."

Alisha's heart was beating to a tempo that rivaled the soft rhythm of the tires hitting against the rocky, rutted road. She was alone with Jared, with no distractions, with no well-meaning friends around. Maybe she could tell him everything, at last, and maybe that would be a good way to gauge his true feelings for her. If Jared could handle the truth, then maybe she could too.

She turned to him, her pulse quickening with fear and dread, but also with a sweet relief. "Jared?"

He looked over at her, hope in his dark eyes. "What?"

"I—"

Jared's expression changed from one of hope to one of shock and alarm. He gripped the steering wheel, his eyes centered on the road.

"What's wrong?" Alisha asked, watching as his gaze darted to the steering panel.

Then she knew with a sickening feeling what was wrong. She heard his foot frantically pumping even as she felt the vehicle accelerate in speed. "Jared?"

"Hold on," he said, his face grim as he held to the steering wheel and tried to control the careening vehicle as it sped down the mountain road. "Alisha, hold on. The brakes are gone."

❧ Chapter Seventeen ❧

"Jared?"

Alisha screamed as the vehicle gained speed around a sharp curve.

Jared had both hands on the wheel, his whole body alert as he held the SUV on two wheels and managed to keep it on the narrow road. Alisha didn't dare look out the passenger side. She knew what was down there. The trees and rocks and deeply dropping ravines whizzed by in a blinding speed that was only increased by the fear pounding in her heart.

"Callum," she said, unfastening her seat belt to haul herself over the seat and into the back, her head hitting the ceiling as she struggled to stay on her feet.

Jared didn't even try to stop her. Instead, he barked orders. "Fasten your belt, and make sure Callum is secure," he said, screaming the words at her. "Just hold on. Hold on."

That last was said in a plea. Alisha knew the situation. There was no hope. No hope. How could Jared control the big vehicle on this twisting, treacherous road? Especially now, when they'd reached a sharp drop-off midway down the mountain, which only increased their speed.

"What about the emergency brakes?" she shouted, hoping to find a way to stop the vehicle.

"Too risky," Jared said over his shoulder, his eyes still on the road. "We'd jackknife and pitch forward."

And over the edge, Alisha thought.

Fear for her sleeping baby coursing through her like a great river, Alisha closed her eyes to the nausea moving inside her stomach and began to pray. *Dear Lord, help us. Help us. Don't let my baby die this way.*

She said the prayer in silence, because the words were stuck in her throat. With each jerk of the SUV, she prayed hard, focusing on her son's sweet face, her mind reliving everything she'd been through just to have him. *Don't let it end this way. Lord, I know I've sinned. I know I will carry the burden of that sin to my grave. But don't let my innocent baby suffer because of me. Spare him, Lord. Spare him.*

That became her mantra as she braced and bumped and held her breath with each twisting, winding curve. Her body was jolted back and forth so much, the seat belt began cutting into her shoulder, but Alisha ignored the pain to concentrate on her son.

Jared sat up in his seat now, his hands gripping the steering wheel as he turned it and straightened it, then turned it again. They were rounding a sharp S-curve, causing the vehicle to swerve dangerously close to a straight drop into the canyons below. Alisha felt the wheels careening on rock, felt the jolt of the skidding tires as Jared quickly jerked the SUV back to the center of the road.

"Alisha," he called over his shoulder, his eyes holding to the road. "Alisha, we're coming to that bad spot. You know, the overlook of the river on the right and that narrow field of wildflowers just past the cliff on the left?"

"Yes," she said, the one word coming through a shaking voice. "Yes, Jared."

"Listen to me," he called. "I'm going to try and send the SUV to the left, past the rocks and over into the wildflower field."

"O-okay." Alisha pictured the spot in her mind. The jutting cliff hung out over the road on a curve, obstructing the view of the field beyond. Jared would have to guess at when to take the SUV off the road. If he missed, they'd either wind up hitting solid rock or go careening off into open space…and down, down, down.

"Spare him," she heard herself whispering, her mind back on Callum. Her whole body was shaking now, but she gripped Callum's padded car seat with all her might, ready to throw her body over him when the impact came.

Jared's loud shouts brought her back to reality. "I want you to hold on, do you hear me?"

"Yes."

Sensing her obvious shock, Jared repeated the words. "Alisha, I need you to hold on. Hold on to Callum's seat, and don't let go. Just hold on."

"I will. I promise."

Tears were coursing down Alisha's face as she watched the road and then her baby. She wanted to remember his face. She wanted to remember spring and Jared's kiss and all the good things she'd found on the mountain. She wanted—

Jared's voice stopped her memories. "Now, Alisha. Hold on."

She felt the car lurch sharply to the right and as her body shifted from the force, her eyes caught a glimpse of what lay beneath them on that side. Jagged, glimmering rocks and sharp-limbed trees fell off straight into the shallow river and rock bed below. It all became a blur that merged with Alisha's screams as Jared quickly jerked the wheel back to the left and straightened the SUV.

"Here we go," he shouted in a rush of breath.

Alisha looked up at the jutting rock approaching them on the left. What was beyond that rock? Death or salvation? Another car coming around the curve, to crash right into them when they veered? Then she looked to the right and saw the azure of the spring sky, saw the puffy clouds of a perfect day, saw the trees brimming with new buds. She imagined herself falling, falling into that vast sky. Falling into nothingness.

Her prayers became silent screams then, as she turned to focus on her baby. Then she felt the SUV propelling forward and for a moment, it felt as if she were as light as air. Alisha laid her upper body across her baby, her eyes on his beautiful, angelic face. In that one split second, Callum opened his eyes and seemed to smile up at his mother.

Everything became a blur after that. Alisha felt the impact as the SUV hit something solid, heard the crash of tires to dirt, felt her body shifting and bumping against Callum's seat. Her head came up to hit the top of the SUV, then her whole body slammed down again. Alisha knew she was crying, knew she was going to die. But she landed back across her baby, the smell of baby powder merging with the smell of dust and rubber and gasoline as the vehicle rushed forward and down. It seemed to go on forever, this feeling of being on a fast-moving roller coaster.

In the next instant, she heard the whine and click of the emergency brake, and felt the screech of tires as the vehicle protested and plowed into the earth. Then everything stopped.

For a moment, Alisha thought she had died. The silence screamed brilliantly white inside her mind. She didn't even realize she had her eyes tightly shut until she heard Jared's voice from far, far away.

And then, the door was flung open and he was beside her, his arms reaching for her, his body warming her.

"Alisha, let go, honey. You can let go now."

"No!" She wailed the one word through a sob of fear and gratitude. She didn't want to leave her baby, even for heaven's welcoming call.

"It's all right," Jared said, his voice soothing and close, his breath warm on her shivering skin. "It's all right. We made it." She felt the pull of his hands on her arms and realized she was holding to Callum's car seat with a death grip. "You can let go now, Alisha."

It was the gentleness that brought her back to reality. Jared had such gentle hands. She'd never known that kind of touch from a man's hands.

And it was the gentleness that caused her to turn quickly and fall into Jared's arms, her sobs echoing out over the still countryside in a keening purge of horror and fear, relief and redemption.

Jared didn't ask her to stop crying. He just held her there in his own tight, tender way, and let her sob. Then finally, when the last of her sobs had turned into hiccups of exhaustion, Jared held a hand to her chin and said, "Look at your baby."

She glanced down at her son, a new fear coursing through her, followed by a quick, fierce relief as she touched a hand to her son's face. He was awake and wide-eyed, his little blue booties kicking in the air. Callum was safe.

"He's fine," Jared assured her. Then he tugged at her shoulder. "Now, look outside."

She finally tore her gaze from her baby, then looked up and out the door of the still vehicle.

Wildflowers, tiny dancers in the soft afternoon wind, swirled out before them in a summer symphony. In a field of deep yellows, hot pinks, and pure stark whites, buttercups and lily of the valley mixed with black-eyed Susans, bachelor's buttons and Queen Anne's lace, shimmering as they lifted their faces to the sun.

It was as if God had thrown out a colorful quilt for them. Alisha had never seen such a beautiful sight.

"Tate will be here with the tow truck in about an hour," Jared told Alisha a few minutes later.

She nodded as she leaned back against the SUV, which was once again stuck—this time in dirt and flower blossoms. She'd just fed and changed Callum in the privacy of the big truck, while Jared had tried calling Tate on his cell phone. Luckily, they were far enough down the mountain to reach a signal. He'd managed to get through to the Tate home.

"Callum's asleep," she said, her voice still raw and raspy, her body still shaking with little aftershocks. If she closed her eyes— No, she wouldn't do that. Not yet. Instead she looked at Jared, saw the grim cast of his tight jaw, saw the dark worry in his eyes. "Thank you."

Jared lifted a brow. "I think I'm going to trade this vehicle in. It's bad luck."

"No, it's not. Not entirely. It brought you to me. And now you've rescued me twice. I owe you so much."

He shook his head. "But if I'd let you come with Geneva instead—"

Alisha placed her hand to his face. "Hush."

She looked into Jared's eyes and accepted that she needed him. Why had it taken a near-death experience to make her see things so clearly? But that need was overshadowed by the solid fear moving like a shadow behind her feelings. "I'm sorry, Jared."

"For what?" he asked, moving closer to her, his dark eyes touching her everywhere.

Alisha looked at his broad shoulders, then back up at his face. He still looked pale and shaken, in spite of his deep suntan. Suddenly, the need to protect not only her son but this man raged through Alisha. "For almost getting you killed."

"What are you saying?" Jared asked, a hand on each of her shoulders.

"I'm saying I don't think this was an accident."

Jared nodded, glanced off into the field. "That thought did cross my mind, but you're certainly not to blame if that's true."

"Yes, I am," she said. "If someone did this, then that's a clear message that you're in danger. You could have been killed because of me."

"Me?" He punched at his chest with a finger. "Me? What about you and Callum?" The rage darkened his eyes to an ominous black. "If I find out—*when* I find *who* did this, I promise—"

Alisha held a finger to his lips. "Don't, don't say it. I've had enough of violence and retaliation. Do you hear me? I need for you to be safe."

"I'll be fine," Jared assured her, his eyes sweeping her face with a clear longing. "But I will not leave you and Callum alone until we find out who is doing this."

"So you agree this was deliberate?"

Jared nodded. "I checked the engine and the brakes while you were feeding Callum. The brake line seems intact, so that means someone either drained some brake fluid or put air or water into the system—enough to cause the brakes to go out."

Alisha closed her eyes, reliving the moments before the crash. "I feel sick," she said, dizziness overcoming her as she leaned into the truck. "Just the thought—"

Jared held her steady. "We're okay. We're safe. Tate is on his way, and I won't trust anyone else to examine this vehicle. Especially not Hank Burgess."

Alisha lifted her head. "Do you think Hank would do this?"

"He's a mechanic. He certainly has the ability to empty the brake fluid."

She nodded, feeling sick all over again. "That makes sense, but I can't believe Hank would deliberately try to kill us. Not if he's interested in me. That *doesn't* make sense."

Jared's expression turned merciless and dark. "Maybe he was going after only *me*."

That brought a new realization pouring through Alisha's mind. "Oh, Jared. No. No. If you'd been alone, you might have crashed into a ravine and we would never have known."

"Exactly. That would certainly clear the way for your stalker."

Alisha pushed past Jared to walk out into the field, hoping to find a cool spot of wind to clear her mind. "My baby almost died today. You almost died today." She couldn't get past that.

Jared pulled her around. "Yes, we *all* came close to being killed, but Alisha, we survived. We survived. Don't you think it's time you let me in on all the things you're fighting so hard to hide? It's the only way I can help you. You have to see that now."

Alisha nodded, reached up to touch his arm. "You helped bring Callum into the world, and today you saved my life and my baby. I owe you the truth, at least, for that."

Jared leaned in to check on Callum. "He's still sleeping. Let's sit down by the door and talk while we wait for Tate."

Alisha nodded, then glanced around to Callum. He was such a good baby. He would never know the fears that had coursed through her soul just a short while ago. She thought back, remembering how he'd opened his little eyes and looked up at her, so trusting, so innocent, but in that brief moment, so reassuring, too. Maybe God was sending her a message, after all.

She watched as Jared opened the back hatch of the SUV and tugged out an old blanket. "I brought this in case I decided to sleep out underneath the stars," he explained, a sheepish grin on his handsome face. "My grandfather used to let me do that when we came to Dover Mountain."

Alisha was comforted by that image. "You must have loved him a lot."

"I did," Jared replied, a dark swirl of regret coloring his eyes as he offered her a hand and pulled her down onto the blanket. "His death was hard on me."

"I can imagine. You lost your parents when you were so young. Then your grandmother. He was the last one you could turn to."

"Yes." He picked at a lush yellow jonquil, broke it and handed it to her. "I was engaged to a woman named Meredith. We'd been together a while, and finally, I decided I wanted to marry her. But when my grandfather had a stroke and required constant care, she balked."

Alisha's heart went out to Jared. Here was the darkness she'd sensed in him, the secret he kept inside himself. He'd been hurt, by death, by love. "She didn't want to marry you then?"

"She wanted to marry me," Jared said, his smile twisted. "She just didn't want to put off the wedding while I nursed my grandfather back to health."

"That's sad."

"It was sad. I hired nurses to sit with him, of course. And therapists, too. But I wanted to be there, to give him a sense of hope, you know? To show him that I still loved him and respected him."

Alisha nodded, wondering when this had become Jared's time to share, instead of hers, but grateful for the reprieve. She felt as if she needed to hear this, to understand him. "Of course, you wanted to help him. Family members are important after a stroke, after any such illness."

"I tried to explain that to Meredith, but she insisted I was being silly and overprotective. She said he had professional people to help him. Then she rather crudely pointed out the obvious—that he might not ever recover anyway, so I needed to let go."

"Oh, goodness," Alisha said, her tone sarcastic. "She sounds like a really understanding person."

"I thought she was, until she said that. We had words, and I broke off the engagement. I couldn't abandon the man who'd raised me and cared for me, even to get married. It just wasn't right."

"And then he died, and you came here to recover."

"Not exactly. My grandfather died a few months after Meredith and I had that fight, but surprisingly, we did try to patch things up. But I didn't feel the same. Next thing I knew, Meredith was engaged to my partner. I found out she'd been growing closer to Mack the whole time we were engaged. And Mack was more than willing to give her his undivided attention, while I worked and went to visit my grandfather each day. She seemed to take pleasure in pointing out to me that while I was sitting with my grandfather and trying to teach him how to speak again, she was out having fun with my best friend. I got so frustrated, I sold out my half of the business to him and that's when I wound up here. I just needed to get away from everything, but unfortunately, my grief and bitterness chased me up this mountain."

He shifted on the blanket, his muscular arms folded on his bent knees. "Then I met you and Callum. So many good, caring people, too. I found hope again." His eyes turned a misty deep brown. "I'm willing to fight for that hope."

Alisha watched his face, saw the changes and shifts in his expression. He went from blank and uncaring to sharp-edged and resentful. He moved from grief to relief and back again. But he had been honest with her.

"I guess now it's my turn, huh?" she said, almost glad that this moment had finally come. Jared would understand. Jared wouldn't judge her. She had to believe that.

"I think so," Jared agreed, his eyes now a warm, liquid brown. "I need to know, Alisha. Not only to help you, but to understand you. I need to know for myself, too."

"Okay." She took a deep breath.

And that's when they heard an engine roaring across the field toward them.

Tate had arrived with the tow truck.

Jared shook his head. "Perfect timing."

Alisha wished they could sit here a while longer. She grabbed at Jared's arm. "Tonight," she said as he helped her up. "Come to see me later. I'll tell you the whole story then, I promise."

Jared's dark eyes searched her face, a hidden regret deep in their depths. "I'm going to hold you to that promise."

Alisha prayed that once he knew the truth, he'd still keep his promises, too.

∝ Chapter Eighteen ∝

The night was full of noise.

The wind whipped through the trees, startling the leaves and tossing redbud and wisteria blossoms all around him. He thought he heard thunder off in the distance. He stood on the worn spot above Alisha's cabin, watching.

He hadn't meant for her to be in the Escalade.

Neither her nor the baby.

With a shaking, jerking hand, he pushed at his pounding head. This was bad. Very bad. When he thought about how close he'd come to messing things up, he shuddered and cursed underneath his breath. He felt so sick, he had to bend down to control the bile rising in his throat.

It should have been Murdock. *Just* Murdock. That man should have been long gone, but Jared Murdock refused to take the hint. What to do now?

He paced and watched, his breath fanning out into the cool spring air. Should he go down there and confront Alisha now? No, better to wait and think things through. This plan had seemed so simple. So very simple. It had been brewing in his mind since he'd first met Alisha Emerson. And then the storm had come. The Easter storm. That had been a sure sign that he was doing the right thing, the only thing he could do.

But that same storm had brought Jared Murdock.

The protector, that old biddy Mozelle had called him.

Everyone liked the man, even if they didn't quite trust him. Well, almost everyone.

He'd just have to come up with something else to get Jared Murdock out of the way. A diversion of some sort.

He thought about that for a while, then, tired and confused, he sank down on a rock and held his head in his hands. He'd almost killed Alisha today.

But he didn't blame himself. He blamed Jared Murdock. If Murdock hadn't been butting in where he wasn't wanted, this wouldn't have happened. Alisha wouldn't have been with him.

That man had to leave this mountain. Dead or alive.

"Yep. Gotta have brake fluid to make brakes work."

Deputy Sheriff Dwight Parker stood staring at Jared's truck as if it were a dead body, his ruddy face scrunched up in what might have passed for concern. "But I'm not ready to call in the CID boys just yet."

Tate glanced over at Jared. Jared could see even in the waning light that Tate didn't have very much faith in the deputy's abilities. "Uh, Dwight, we've already established the brakes were tampered with," Tate pointed out. "I examined them myself. Somebody punctured the brake line, which caused fluid to leak out. It was a slow leak, but the mountain road took its toll, too. I'm surprised they weren't all killed."

The deputy took his time before replying, his eyes downcast as he carved a rut in the gravel with one booted foot. "These old roads are hard on a vehicle, even a fancy one like this. Maybe you should have checked your brakes before you came here." Then he looked over at Jared, his gaze lazy and shuttered. "Or maybe somebody did mess with your vehicle. After all these coincidences, you might want to consider cutting your stay short, Mr. Murdock."

"This isn't just coincidence, and I'm not leaving until I know Alisha is safe."

"Maybe she will be, if you go."

Jared glared at the man, his patience snapping. "If you'd do your job instead of asking me to leave, we might get to the bottom of this. I don't suppose you've received that fingerprint report back from the state crime lab, either."

"Seems to have gotten lost in the backlog," the deputy said, a grin splitting his face. He shrugged. "I reckon you'll expect us to go over this vehicle with a fine-toothed comb, too?"

"Oh, you think?" Jared asked, wishing he could just punch the chunky deputy and be done with it. Knowing that wouldn't solve anything, he braced a hand on the SUV, his eyes on the deputy. "I trust Tate. I'll let him give it another thorough inspection in the morning, but you should make a report on what we find, at least. And I'd appreciate it if your criminal investigations division started taking this seriously, too." He lifted his head toward Tate. "Does Hank know you towed us up the mountain?"

"He's away on business," Tate replied. "Been gone a couple of days." His expression indicated he didn't intend to tell Hank what was going on.

"Good. Let's keep this between us for now," Jared said, the dare in his eyes causing Deputy Parker to smirk.

"You don't think Hank—"

"I think someone is either trying to scare me to death or kill me outright," Jared replied. "And since I can't depend on the local law enforcement to find out what's going on, I will just have to do it myself."

The deputy chewed his gum, his jaws smacking. "Hank Burgess is a friend of mine. He's a hothead, but he'd know better than to do something like this."

"He knows all about brakes," Jared reminded the deputy. "And I intend to ask him if he knows about this."

"Don't go taking the law into your own hands," Deputy Parker said, his chest puffing out in indignation. "That could really get you in hot water."

"Barreling down a mountain at breakneck speed kind of makes my blood boil," Jared said. "I'd say that puts me in hot water already."

The deputy hitched his tan pants and lifted his head, like a turtle coming out of its shell. "I reckon I can check around, ask a few questions. And I'll call the boys on up here."

"That would be mighty nice," Tate said, shaking his head. "Honestly, Dwight, I know we don't have much crime here, so you're not used to actually investigating stuff, but could you be a little more serious about this? Jared has had break-ins and now Alisha is being threatened. And today…well, I think this is pretty obvious."

"I am serious," the deputy replied. Then he shrugged. "You know how it is, Tate. I cover a broad area, and we don't have the manpower or the money to do fancy CSI work around here. We have to go on hunches and whatever information we can glean out of witnesses and citizens. And in both the break-in here and now this, I don't have any witnesses, any proof. And Alisha hasn't filed a complaint. I just got *his* word." He squinted at Jared.

Tate's face turned as red as the redbud blossoms in the woods. "I saw the damage done to the cabin, Dwight. And I checked these brakes. Whoever did this knew what he was doing. This SUV is practically new and in mint condition. Think about it. Why would Jared bring it up here if he didn't think it would run? This had to be deliberate."

"Yeah, or he bought a lemon and didn't know it."

"I had the Escalade thoroughly checked before I ever left Atlanta," Jared told him, throwing up his hands. "Look, thanks for stopping by, Deputy. I'll take it from here."

Deputy Parker adjusted his hat. "Well, don't be stupid, now, Murdock. I said I'd check around."

"Fair enough," Jared replied, not believing it for a minute. "And I said I'm going to find out who's doing this and put an end to it, before someone does get killed."

A few minutes later, Jared waved goodbye to Tate and the deputy, then turned to go inside his cabin. He wanted to call Alisha. Tate had dropped her and the baby at her cabin, then brought the Escalade here to Jared's cabin. Jared hadn't wanted to leave Alisha, but Tate had already called ahead and had Geneva and Loretta waiting for her. She'd be safe with them until Jared could get back to her.

"I don't know what's going to happen next," Loretta said as she stared out into the night.

Alisha was rocking Callum and Geneva was baking oatmeal cookies. Geneva put down her spatula and came over to where Alisha sat. "Do you want another cup of tea?"

"I'm fine," Alisha said, her eyes on her son. She couldn't seem to stop looking at him. "When I think—"

Loretta joined them, sinking down on the sofa. "Don't think about it, honey. You're safe now."

"But I'm not safe," Alisha replied, a sick dread coursing through her system. "I had grown complacent, you know, living here. I forgot to be careful. And somebody out there knows something about me. I just keep waiting for the next thing to happen." She rocked back and forth, the creaking of the old oak rocker matching tempo with the ticking of the cuckoo clock on the mantel. "I had decided I'd face this, that I wouldn't run this time, but after today, I keep expecting the very worst...but that can't happen. Trevor is dead. He's dead."

"Oh, honey. You know it's not him," Loretta said, patting Alisha's hand with hers, concern etched on her face. "You're just frightened and shook up. This is somebody's idea of a sick joke. Jared and Tate will get to the bottom of this."

Geneva nodded. "My daddy will watch out for us. And Jared, well, that man is so head over heels—"

Alisha stopped rocking. "What do you mean?"

Loretta chuckled. "He's in love with you, sugar."

Alisha shook her head, then started frantically rocking again. "He can't be. He can't."

"And why not?" Loretta asked, her eyes wide.

"I'm no good for Jared. He deserves better. And besides, I can't ever tell him the truth. I thought I could. I thought I needed to, but he'll just turn away."

Loretta gave Geneva a worried look. Alisha could tell the two women were baffled. "Honey, you're not making any sense," Loretta said. "Why don't you let me put Callum in his crib and you go lay down and get some rest?"

"I can't sleep," Alisha said. "I have to figure out what to do."

"Just rest," Loretta repeated. "We'll both stay here tonight. Do you want me to call Miss Mozelle or Dr. Sloane?"

"No," Alisha said. "No, I'm okay. I'm just still in shock. Still wondering who would do something like this. I won't allow some misguided idiot to harm my baby, I can tell you that."

The phone rang then, causing all three women to jump.

"Want me to get it?" Geneva asked.

"No, it might be Jared," Alisha said, handing the baby to Loretta so she could grab the cordless phone from the table next to her chair. "Hello?" she said, needing to hear Jared's voice.

The voice wasn't Jared's. "You threw away my gift."

Alisha gasped, her gaze flying to her two friends. "Who is this?"

"You'll know soon enough."

She thought she recognized the voice, but it sounded distorted and distant and breathless. It was definitely a man. "What do you want from me?"

"You'll understand everything very soon."

There was a click, then the dial tone pierced the line with a resounding intensity that shot fear and anger through Alisha's insides.

"Was that him?" Loretta asked, still holding Callum.

Alisha nodded. "He's getting bolder. He said I'd understand everything soon. How did he even get my number?"

"Did it sound like anyone we might know?" Geneva

asked, her eyes wide, her brow furrowed as she glanced over at her mother.

Alisha saw a look pass between Loretta and her daughter. "What is it?" she asked. "Do you know something? Tell me."

Loretta tugged at the tie on her blouse. "It's just that Jimmy has been bragging to Rayanne...about things."

"What things?"

Geneva crossed her legs, one foot swinging. "Oh, that he'll be leaving Dover Mountain soon. That he's got something going on the side, a way to make big money—or as he put it, a way to get some money out of someone."

Loretta fidgeted with straightening things, her hands moving over the table to pick up books. "And, well, Rayanne says he's always asking about you. She thinks he has a crush on you. That kinda hurts her, even though she doesn't blame you."

"Did it sound like him?" Geneva asked.

Alisha shook her head, trying to absorb this new information. "It's hard to say." She reached up for Callum and took him back into her arms, holding him tight as she remembered how Jimmy had appeared in her backyard that day. Could he have left the azaleas or sent the clippings? He was a big flirt, but this? "You don't think Jimmy is the one threatening me, do you?"

"We just don't know," Loretta said, twisting her hands. "We hope it ain't him, but you know how he can be."

"And he's always online searching for games and information," Geneva pointed out. "He told Rayanne he knows how to hack into files and get all sorts of information, too. If he dug deep enough—"

"He could find out anything about me he wanted," Alisha replied. "All about my past."

Loretta nodded. "Honey, we don't know the particulars, and we don't need to know. But we know enough from what little you've told us. If anybody could find something to hold over you, though, it'd be Jimmy Barrett. That boy is no good, no good at all."

"I wish Rayanne had never hooked up with him," Geneva said.

"Too late to cry over spilled milk," Loretta told her. "We've got to take care of Rayanne and that baby."

Alisha nodded. "Yes. Do that. Don't force her to marry Jimmy Barrett. Just let him go on and leave. That would be the best thing for Rayanne for now." The graphic memories of her own forced marriage seared through her soul, and Alisha suddenly realized why she was so afraid to let go and turn to Jared. She would never be forced again. And neither should Rayanne. "She's better off without him. Especially if he's trying to scare me with these nasty tricks."

"Try telling her that," Geneva said. "She's still holding out hope that he'll change."

"He's not going to change," Alisha replied. "Trevor never did."

Loretta leaned forward, her hands clasped. "What happened to you, Alisha? Tell me, so I can warn my daughter."

Alisha looked up at her friend, saw the apprehension in Loretta's eyes. Loretta was a good woman, a hard-working woman who tried to do the best for her family. Alisha had to tell someone, and Loretta could be trusted. Besides, if Jimmy Barrett was the one harassing her, things could get dangerous, very dangerous, for all of them. She didn't want to live through that again, and she wouldn't put her friends at risk.

Taking a breath and saying a silent prayer that she was doing the right thing, Alisha said, "I killed my husband."

"Oh, my." Loretta's hand flew to her chest. "Oh, my goodness."

Alisha lowered her eyes, ashamed of the disgust and dread she saw in Loretta's eyes.

But Loretta didn't let her end it there. "You must have had a very good reason, sugar."

The compassion in those words caused Alisha to break through her pain. "It was an accident," she said on a low whisper, her gaze moving from Loretta to Geneva. "We were in the backyard. He chased me around the house, and he kept shouting that he was going to kill me. He had a gun, and he kept coming for me. I tried to get away, but he whirled me around—and then, somehow I grabbed for the gun and it went off and then he just crumpled to the ground." She swallowed the bile in her throat, her heart beating in a rapid cadence. "Several neighbors watched the whole thing. Someone called the police—the neighbors testified that it was self-defense. There was a hearing, but they let me go."

She didn't, couldn't tell them the rest. About the azaleas, about having to protect her unborn child. She couldn't tell them the very worst, the horrible things that had happened shortly after the marriage, the things she'd been talked into forgiving, over and over again. But she could see it in her mind. "It was an accident," she repeated. "But his parents still blame me. They don't know where I am. And they didn't know I was pregnant when I left."

Geneva gasped. "So if Jimmy knows that—"

"He can tell them everything," Alisha said. "He can tell them that they have a grandson, and I might lose

Callum." She touched a kiss to Callum's head. "What if Jimmy plans to blackmail me or something like that?"

"We need to call Jared and Tate," Loretta said. "This is much worse than we imagined."

Alisha nodded, numb now, her fear gone, her resolve slipping. She was tired, so tired. And she'd fought against this all on her own for too long now. She had to trust her friends and she had to trust Jared.

Her protector.

But mostly, Alisha had to trust God.

It was all about to happen now. He'd found a way to take care of things. This would actually work much better for him. It would all be tied up in a tidy bundle, and then he could convince Alisha to leave Dover Mountain with him.

She wouldn't have a choice. She'd have to come with him now. Then it would all be over, and he'd have her and the baby and that trust fund she was hiding, at last.

At last.

"The phone's not working," Geneva said, panic in her words as she pushed at buttons, then put the cordless back on its receiver. Picking it back up, she tried again. "It's dead."

"What do you mean?" Alisha rushed to her side, staring at the phone, her numbness kicking in. "I just had it installed. It worked fine yesterday. And we just got a call—"

"The line is dead," Geneva said, her eyes going wide.

"Maybe I should just run over to Jared's cabin," Loretta suggested, already heading for the front door.

"No." Alisha grabbed at her arm. "He...somebody might be out there."

Loretta stopped, wrapping her arms together. "I don't like this."

"Jared was coming by to check on me," Alisha said, the numbness clearing and blessedly rational thoughts taking its place. "He promised." She stopped, looked outside. "And Jared always keeps his promises."

Jared had just gotten out of the shower and tossed on his clothes and shoes when he heard a knock at the door. Thinking Tate had forgotten something, he opened it with smile.

Which quickly died on his lips.

Hank Burgess stood at his door with a gun pointed right at Jared's forehead.

"Hank?" Jared asked, alert to the other man's agitated state. Hank's face was flushed, and his breath smelled of whiskey.

"Shut up," Hank said, pushing his way into the door, the big revolver gleaming as he waved his free hand in the air. "I just need to tie you up for a little while."

Jared backed up, a deadly calm taking over his shock. "So you can go and harass Alisha?"

"What are you talking about?" Hank said, his eyes darting here and there, his breath huffing in nervous excitement. "I'm just doing a favor for a friend of mine. Didn't mind helping out one bit, either, let me tell you."

"What friend?" Jared asked, still standing, his whole body filling with a heavy dread.

"Just sit down in that chair and shut up," Hank said. He fished an old roll of duct tape out of his jacket pocket.

Jared sat down, his every fiber screaming that Alisha was in trouble. "Look, Hank, I don't know who talked you into doing this, but Alisha could be in real danger. We need to go and check on her."

"We?" Hank scoffed. "Nice try, city fellow. All you need to do is stay out of the way. Once you get the message and leave here, Alisha and I can pick back up where we started. My friend is going to help me see to that."

"Where is your friend now?" Jared asked, all sorts of dark images moving through his mind. "Maybe we can talk to this friend together."

Hank wasn't listening. "Pull off some of that tape," he ordered as he tossed it to Jared. "Now put that around your ankles, real tight. And don't try anything. I know how to use this thirty-eight. Got it straight out of my collection just for you."

"Thoughtful of you," Jared said, trying to sound reasonable and friendly in spite of the rage and panic churning inside his system. He had to keep his head so he could get to Alisha. After ripping the stubborn tape with fingers and teeth, he carefully placed the tape around his ankles, making it look as if he'd tightened it. "That's a Colt right? Vintage, too, from the looks of it."

"Pull off some more tape," Hank said, watching and holding the gun dangerously close while Jared did his bidding. "Now hand me the piece of tape and put your hands behind you, over the chair back." Hank took the piece of torn tape Jared offered up him, the gun jerking in his right hand. "Vintage, I reckon so. And I got plenty more where this one came from. What do you know about guns? You with your money and houses."

"What do you know about my money and my houses?" Jared said, tossing the question back.

"I know a lot about a lot of things," Hank replied, his feverish actions making him sweat in spite of the cool night. "I know my wife left here with a man like you. He had money and looks and he just took her away. He took everything from me."

"So you're getting even through me?"

"I'm getting what should have been mine. I want Alisha. I can make her a good life."

"What if Alisha doesn't want you?"

"She will, once you're gone. My friend promised me that. Said he'd help me."

"You really need to tell me more about this friend," Jared said as Hank came toward him with the tape.

"Shut up." Hank was behind him now. "Don't move. I got to do this. Don't make me have to reach for this gun."

Jared cut a glance at the table where Hank had put the gun. He'd have to take a chance on getting shot by going for the gun before Hank could get the tape around him.

Because there was no way he was going to let Hank Burgess tie him up. No way.

"We can't just sit here," Geneva whispered, her face pinched with fear. "I could sneak out the back way, head up the footpath behind the cabin. I can be at our place in fifteen minutes."

"That might be a good idea," Loretta said, glancing at Alisha. "Tate thinks we're settled in for the night. Him and the boys don't have a clue that we might be in any danger."

Alisha glanced out the window between the drawn curtains. The night had grown so still, as if the whole mountain was waiting for something to happen. Not a rustle, not even a snapping of a twig. Off toward the west, lightning flared just once, but then even it was gone. Alisha counted, waiting for the thunder to follow.

Was someone really out there? She knew it. Alisha could feel him watching her, waiting for the right time to attack. She didn't plan on going down without a fight. She'd had to fight once before and through that tragic, horrific day, she'd saved her unborn baby. She aimed to save him tonight, too, one way or another.

She could just make out the light from Jared's cabin. And she had her light on for him. "Jared said he'd be here. We have to stay calm and wait on him." Then she got an idea. "Geneva, turn off the lamp."

Loretta shot her a panicked look. "We can't sit here in the dark."

"Yes, we can," Alisha replied. "If Jared sees the light's not on, he'll know we're in trouble."

"But what if whoever's out there thinks we've gone to bed and tries to get inside?"

"We'll be waiting," Alisha said, a new determination filling her with courage.

Geneva turned off the lamp, then in the moonlight, touched a hand to Alisha's arm. "I'm sure Jared will be here, but let me go just in case. I'll be careful. I know this mountain like the back of my hand. And remember, I won first place in the hundred-yard dash my senior year in high school. I might be older, but I can still run."

Alisha turned from the window, apprehension making her skin crawl and her nerves twinge into awareness. "I don't want anything to happen to you."

"It won't," Geneva said. "I can do this, Alisha."

Finally, Alisha nodded. "Are you sure you remember those self-defense techniques Ryan taught you?"

"Every one of them," Geneva replied. "We practiced a lot...in between other things." Her grin belied the tension in the room.

"You be very careful, honey," her mother warned. "Look all around before you even step off the porch." Then she reached for a paring knife from the counter. "Take this for good measure."

Geneva took the knife, then slipped out the back door. Just as the front door burst open.

❧ Chapter Nineteen ❧

Jared rushed down the footpath, his breath leaving his body with a searing burn as he hurried toward Alisha's cabin.

Her dark cabin.

He'd knocked Hank over the head and tied the man up. Hank really was all bluster and no bite. Before Hank got the tape around Jared's hands, Jared took his loosely tied feet and slammed them against the table, causing his chair to fall back against Hank's chubby midsection. The unexpected action caused Hank to lose his grip on the tape, and caused the tape to stick to Hank's arm and shirt. That gave Jared enough time to twist around, grab the gun and hit Hank over the head. Once Hank was out cold, Jared shoved the tape off his feet and took care of the unconscious man.

Jared tied Hank up and then debated whether to call Deputy Parker to come and get him. But when Jared hurried to the porch and glanced toward Alisha's cabin, he decided there was no time to call the authorities. The lamp wasn't on at Alisha's cabin.

A sure sign of trouble.

Now Jared was running for that dark cabin.

If she was in there with Geneva and Loretta, the three women wouldn't be sitting in the dark. And it was way too early for all of them to go to bed. Jared knew instinctively that something was terribly wrong. And Hank had a "friend" helping him. Was that friend after Alisha right now?

All of this raced through Jared's mind as he sprinted down the mountain, his heavy hiking boots hitting against jagged rocks and twisted centuries-old root systems. He rushed so fast, he almost stumbled. But he regained control and stopped at the base of Alisha's property to take in much-needed air, Hank's pearl-handled revolver still in one hand.

That's when he heard the crash of the front door slamming open and saw a shadowy figure through the muted moonlight.

And that's when he heard the screams of the women inside.

Clinging to the loaded gun, Jared ran to the front yard of the cabin, then stopped to regain his breath. He kept to the shadows, careful not to make too much noise. He didn't want whoever this was to overreact and hurt someone.

"What do you want from me?" Jared heard Alisha asking, her voice sounding firm and strong, and way too determined.

"Jimmy, why are you doing this?"

That was Loretta. Jimmy? Jimmy Barrett was the friend Hank had bragged about? This was going from bad to worse, Jared decided. Both of those men had had it in for him since he'd shown up on this mountain. But why were they tormenting Alisha? Because of jealousy? They sure were going to extremes to make their point. But Jared intended to put them both to a stop. Tonight.

While Jared listened, hoping to find the right time to make his move, Jimmy answered Loretta's question. "Why do you think? I need money to get off this stupid, backward mountain," he said through a hiss of breath. "And I ain't taking anyone with me. Not even Rayanne."

"You're threatening me for money?" Alisha asked, her voice rising out onto the night as Jared moved silently closer. "Sorry to disappoint you, Jimmy, but I'm fresh out of money."

Jared crept up onto the porch, careful to avoid the squeaking second step up onto the old planked floor. He clung to the porch railing and slipped to the side of the open door, his eyes adjusting to the gray-washed interior of the cabin. Two women were sitting down near the fireplace. He could make out Alisha's long thick hair and Loretta's short bob.

And Jimmy stood in the center of the room, holding a gun toward them.

Two women. Somebody was missing, Jared realized. Had Geneva gone for help? Or was she hiding in another part of the cabin?

"I know some things," Jimmy said. "I know some things and so do a few other people. You're a rich woman, Alisha. Why do you want to live like a hillbilly in this old place, when you could have a dream house anywhere in the world?"

There was a moment of silence while Jared stared through the window, needing to hear the answer to that question himself.

"I had a dream house once," Alisha replied, her voice calm and still. "It turned out to be a prison."

Jimmy's snarl of laughter sounded skeptical. "Oh, is that why you shot your husband and then came to this mountain to hide out?"

Jared heard Alisha's sharp gasp of breath, and suddenly, standing there in the darkness, he knew what she'd been trying to hide, what she'd wanted to tell him.

"It was an accident," Loretta said.

Jared took in that bit of information, and believed it. Alisha wouldn't deliberately kill another human being. But she might shoot someone in self-defense. And she might still feel guilty over having done it. Guilty enough to hide out on a mountain, with people around her to protect her and her baby.

"I did some digging," Jimmy said. "For a friend. He paid me a tidy sum to dig up everything I could about you, Alisha. You—so high and mighty, always preaching to the young people around here—telling Rayanne what's good for her—getting your pretty nose into *my* business—and all along, you're the worst hypocrite on this mountain. You murdered your own husband, then left with his fortune. Man, that's cold, real cold. I don't think I want you around Rayanne anymore."

"How much do you want?" Alisha said, her tone sounding numb and defeated.

"That's more like it," Jimmy replied. "My partner and me, we gotta split it, you understand. But he sent me to collect. I'd say out of a cool quarter of a million, you could spare around a hundred thousand, don't you think?"

"Are you crazy?" Loretta asked in a high-pitched voice.

"No, I'm smart," Jimmy answered. "I know a good thing when I see it. Alisha will pay, because she wants to keep her past quiet. And then I can leave this place knowing she'll never come after me."

"You won't get away with this," Loretta said. "We'll go to the authorities."

"No, you will *not* do that."

Jared watched, ready to spring, as Jimmy pressed the glinting gun close to Loretta's head, causing Alisha to lurch forward. Jimmy grabbed Alisha and shoved her back in her seat, but Jared didn't dare move. It was hard to see with the clouds drifting over the moon, blocking out what little light there was. If he spooked Jimmy, the man could very well shoot Alisha. Jimmy had the gun aimed in her face now.

"Neither of you will breathe a word of this, if you know what's good for that whining, conniving Ray-anne." Then he inched toward the wicker crib nestled by Alisha's chair. "Alisha won't talk. She wants to keep this kid safe, right, Alisha?"

"You're right about that," Alisha said, her voice still calm. Deadly calm, to Jared's mind. "I protected this baby when I was carrying him, and I aim to keep protecting him. If that means I have to give his savings account over to you, well, then I guess that's what I'll have to do."

"Oh, I get it," Jimmy said, shuffling his feet. "The money is for the baby, right? Yeah, tell that to somebody who believes it. You killed Trevor Emerson and then you got your hands on the family stash. That's the way I see it, and I'm sure that's the way Trevor's grieving parents see it, too. I have their phone number. Want to call 'em up and ask 'em?"

"We should leave them out of this," Alisha said. "I inherited the money, according to Trevor's will. He set it up as a trust fund for our baby. It'll be hard to get to the money—I just want you to know that."

Jimmy leaned close to her again. Jared could see his shadow hulking over Alisha. It made Jared's blood run cold, but he didn't want to provoke the idiot just yet, so he tried to stay calm and think about how to get inside and stop this. And he prayed.

"I know you'll find a way, though, won't you?" Jimmy said to Alisha. "Do the Emersons even know they have a grandson?"

She leaned away, one hand on Callum's crib.

Jared didn't have to see her face to know the answer to that question. Alisha had been secretive because of the baby. She was trying to protect her son.

And now this lowlife was trying to blackmail her. Jared's anger was so strong, he was sure Jimmy could hear his heart racing with rage.

"And what about your mysterious partner?" Alisha asked, her words low and monotone. "Will he leave me alone, too, if I pay this money?"

Jimmy laughed again. "Don't know about that. He kinda digs you, if you get my drift. He talks about all the things you and him can do together. Once he takes you away from here. I forgot to mention that's part of the deal, didn't I?" He laughed again, and Jared could see him waving the gun in the air. "He only wants you and the baby. And part of the cash—but just to start a new life with y'all."

Jared wished now he'd called the deputy. But apparently, Jimmy was expecting someone else to show up.

"He oughta be here any minute. Once we finish our financial exchange, he's going to take you away. Far away."

Jared wasn't surprised. Obviously, Jimmy and Hank were in on this together, so Hank probably thought if he couldn't win Alisha over by conventional means, he'd kidnap her. But since Hank was trussed up like a Thanksgiving turkey back at Jared's cabin, Jimmy was the one in for a surprise. Make that two. Jared was about to give him the surprise of his life.

Jared waited two beats, then decided he couldn't depend on Deputy Dwight. He had to get in there and get Jimmy away from the women and little Callum.

After all, he had a gun, too.

Alisha stared up at the silvery steel of the gun Jimmy flashed in the moonlight, her heart ripping as she thought of the day her husband had died. She could remember *that* gun, *that* day, with such a vivid clarity, that she seriously thought it was about to happen all over again. It happened in her head each day of her life. And each night. The nightmares never went away.

Could her guilt, her shame, ever go away?

Lord, will I ever get through this? Will it ever truly be over? What can I do to make it up to You? What can I do to put it out of my mind? How can I let this go?

She looked up at Jimmy. His face, full of shadows laced with a sinister grin, looked evil in the gray-washed light of the moon. If she gave him the money, she'd have nothing, nothing to offer her son. That was Callum's money, his legacy from his shrewd father's business dealings. Alisha didn't care about the money. That's why she'd hidden it away, safe in a bank in Chattanooga, so it could grow into a small fortune until Callum was ready to use it. That trust fund was the one gracious act of a father who would never know his son, of a husband who had never overcome his controlling, abusive ways.

But if it meant her child's life over the money, there would be no question as to what she had to do. "I can't get the money right away," she told Jimmy, all the while hoping Geneva had gone to get Jared and Tate. Jimmy didn't need to know that it was an open trust fund, to be used whenever Alisha felt the need. But she'd refused to touch it. And she refused to hand it over to Jimmy without a fight.

"Yes, you can, sugar," he said, leaning low again, his beer breath pouring over her. "That's what we have the Internet for—you know, online banking and all of that."

"What do you mean?" Loretta asked, her voice shaking.

"I mean, you can do all sorts of transactions over the Net, if you have the right codes and passwords. And I'm here for the passwords."

"I won't give them to you," Alisha said, stalling for time. "Not until I talk with this partner you keep mentioning. I want to see who I'm up against."

"He should be here soon," Jimmy said, the nervous quiver in his tone telling Alisha the boy was losing confidence.

If she could just keep Jimmy talking, keep him bragging, maybe Geneva would bring help. Maybe Jared would find her. "How'd you hook up with this partner?" she asked, needing to know, but also needing to buy some time.

Jimmy's smirk looked ghoulish in the ashen light. "He came to me, actually. Needed help doing research."

"You hacked into somebody's computer, didn't you?" Loretta asked.

"I just played around some. He wanted to know all sorts of things about Alisha. Didn't take long to dig up the whole story. But there's one piece missing—the money. Where to find the money?" He laughed, waved the gun. "We were working on how to get that when that Murdock man showed up and put a kink in everything."

Loretta shook her head. "Jimmy, think about what you're doing. You're wasting so much potential—"

"Shut up," Jimmy shouted. "Don't tell me about potential. I don't see a whole lot of that on this piece of rock. He offered me a lot of money and promised me more, once we found out how much Alisha had." He leaned close again, his eyes glimmering like two blue-tipped coals of fire. "He really, really digs you, Alisha."

Alisha shivered at that implication. A madman was on his way here to kidnap her, and she didn't even want to think about what he might do to her and her child. "Can't you tell me about him, Jimmy?" she asked. "So I can be more informed and prepared."

"I told you," Jimmy said, his words hitting like pellets in the air, "he's coming here to get us. Then we're going to find a computer and get into that bank account."

"And after that?"

"After that, I'll get my cut and be on my way."

"And what about me and my baby?"

"What about you?" Jimmy said on a snarl. "He said he'd take good care of y'all. That ain't my concern."

"It should be," Loretta said, her eyes wide with fear. "Jimmy, he might hurt them."

"He won't," Jimmy said, shaking his head. "The man's obsessed with her and the baby. He plans to take good care of them." He glanced around, shouted, "If he ever gets here, that is."

Alisha could tell Jimmy was getting more nervous and jittery as the minutes ticked away. And so was she. She wasn't leaving here with a maniac. She cut her eyes to the door. She thought she saw a shadow there. Was it Jared or her tormentor?

Alisha wanted to find out, one way or another. "I think he is here, Jimmy. I think someone's on the porch."

Jared took that as his cue. He knocked loudly on the wall then shouted in a gruff voice, "Hey, it's me."

"About time," Jimmy said, cursing under his breath, his eyes on the women, his gun aimed at Alisha. "Where have you been, man? I'm ready to get this over with."

"I've been right here, listening to your interesting conversation."

He turned to face the shimmer of Jared's gun.

"Yes, it is about time," Jared continued before Jimmy could speak, contempt and disgust causing his pulse to burn through his veins. "It's about time I finish your business here, once and for all."

Alisha breathed a sigh of relief, followed by a gasp of fear. Jimmy and Jared were now squared off in a showdown, gun to gun, and she was reliving her worst nightmare all over again, the shadows of the night leaping and laughing at her each time the wind moved through the trees.

"Jimmy?" she said, the name a plea. "Jimmy, please stop this now. Just stop and leave. We won't tell anyone."

"I can't leave," Jimmy said, the angry words hissing out of his mouth. "I'm in too deep. He'll hunt me down and do me in."

"He, who?" Jared asked, his gun aimed at Jimmy's glistening blond head. "Just tell me who set this up and I'll take it from there. Was it Hank?"

"Hank?" Jimmy laughed. "Yeah, right, Hank."

Alisha looked up at Jared, her worry and concern settling like a jagged rock against her stomach. Jared had heard everything, every terrible thing she'd tried so hard to hide. And yet, he was here. Her protector. "Jared, I—"

"No need to explain," Jared said, his words soothing. "I think I understand a lot of things now. And I want Jimmy to fill me in on the rest."

Jimmy let out a sharp breath. "Man, you are *not* supposed to be here. He said you'd be out of the way."

"I realized that when Hank tried to tie me up."

"Hank? Hank ain't got a thing to do with this."

"Don't lie to me," Jared said, advancing a step, his gun steady while Jimmy's hand begin to shake. "I left Hank in my cabin, unconscious and tied with the duct tape he tried to use on me. So you might as well give up while you can."

Jimmy muttered an oath, pushed one hand down his sweat-covered face. "I don't know why Hank did that, man. Hank ain't in on this, I'm telling you."

"I don't believe you," Jared said. "How much?"

"How much what?"

"How much do you want? How much money?"

Jimmy shifted, groaned. "I want what I was promised."

"By Hank?"

Jimmy shook his head. "If you give me the money, I'll be outta here."

"How can I take your word on that?" Jared asked, and Alisha saw the deadly cold in his dark eyes. They now held the same flash of fire she'd seen the first time he'd confronted Jimmy.

Jimmy stuttered. "Man, I just...I just want to get away from this place. He promised me—"

"He isn't coming to help you," Jared said, advancing inch by inch into the room. "You're on your own here, Jimmy. And you won't be able to hide. Not from him, and certainly not from me."

Loretta was crying. Alisha heard the other woman's soft sobs as Loretta pleaded with Jimmy. "Jimmy, please don't do this. You're going to be a daddy, soon. What about Rayanne and the baby?"

"I don't care about them," Jimmy said, the words rising out on the night air. "I don't care, do you hear me?"

Alisha saw tears moving down his face now. "I think you do care," she said. "I think you're just afraid to grow up and accept responsibility. Because you never had it taught to you. But now, you're in a mess of trouble. Let us help you, Jimmy."

Jimmy pivoted then, the gun back at her head as he grabbed her and pulled her in front of him. "Drop the gun, Murdock." When Jared hesitated, Jimmy crushed his hand against Alisha's windpipe. "I'll hurt her."

Alisha's breath was cut off as she stared at Jared and saw the dread in his eyes. Jared dropped the gun.

Jimmy pushed Alisha toward the crib. "Get the baby."

"No," Alisha said, digging in her heels. "I'll go with you, but I won't let you take my baby."

"Get the kid," Jimmy retorted, the gun moving over the crib. "Just do it, Alisha. Plans have changed. I have to take you to him." Then he let out a stuttering sigh. "I'm sorry."

Alisha reached down, her hands shaking as she lifted her son out of the warm crib. Callum shifted in his sleep, his soft sigh echoing through the still room. Alisha held her baby close, fear for his life clouding out everything else. "Don't hurt him, Jimmy, please."

"Jimmy, let them go," Jared said, his hands out, palms up. "Don't do this."

"I don't have a choice," Jimmy said, his voice quivering as he yanked Alisha back in front of him. "He *will* kill me if I screw this up."

"I'll kill you if you don't let her go," Jared said.

Alisha shivered, felt the nightmares closing in on her. She remembered being held like this before, being choked and suffocated, being trapped, unable to breathe. She remembered her face being buried against the soft, sweet touch of azalea blossoms, her skin being ripped and torn by broken stalks as she was pushed over and over again into the chopped, crushed bushes. She'd survived that, for her child. She couldn't let Jimmy hurt him now.

"Can't...." she tried to say. "Can't...breathe."

Jimmy started toward the back of the cabin, his arm around Alisha as she held tightly to Callum. "I have to take her. I have to. He—he'll want them."

"Hank is not coming," Jared said, his eyes on Jimmy and then Alisha. She saw the plea there in the dark depths, saw the message—*Hang on, don't give up.* If she focused on Jared, she might make it out of this alive. If she focused and prayed, the way she had the night Jared had come to her and helped her deliver Callum, maybe she could breathe again.

Callum. She gulped back a sob, repeating herself as she swallowed in air. "Jimmy, don't hurt my baby, please?" Her chest tightened, constricted by fear and memories. "Please, Jimmy."

"I don't want the kid," Jimmy said, pushing, pushing her toward the back door. "But *he* does. He does."

"Who?" Alisha asked, anger replacing the sick dread in her stomach. "Who would want to harm a little baby? "Hank? My in-laws? Did they hire you and Hank?"

"They don't even know where you are," Jimmy said into her ear. "But they will, if you don't cooperate."

"Just take *me* then," Alisha said, her gaze flying from Jared's face to her sleeping child as she fought against the dizziness and darkness. "Just take me and let my baby stay safe." Then she looked back at Jared, tried to lift Callum toward him. "Will you take care of Callum for me?"

Jared didn't answer at first. Then when he did, his voice was raw with...hope, fear, reassurance? She thought she heard all three. "We will take care of Callum together, I promise."

Jimmy jerked and skidded toward the door. "Got to get her to him. Something's wrong. He shoulda been here by now."

Jared advanced, his hands still out away from his body. "He's not coming, Jimmy."

Loretta sobbed quietly in her chair, her prayers lifting out into the night. *"Father, help us. Don't let him do this."*

"I'll give you fifty thousand dollars," Jared said, his voice a calm buffer against Alisha's erratic heartbeats.

Jimmy stopped just at the back door, forcing Alisha's body back against his. "Yeah, right. I guess you carry that kind of cash around in your pocket."

"I can write a check," Jared said, holding up one hand. "Or better yet, I can give you a charge card. You can leave right now, with the card and my blessings. It has a large line of credit for both charges and cash advances."

Jimmy shook his head. "You'd trace me."

"No, I wouldn't," Jared said. "I'll make you a deal. You take the card, use it to get the cash advance, then we'll call it even. I'll approve the transaction, pay it off and then we're done. If you try to use it again after that, I *will* come after you."

Jimmy still held Alisha, but thankfully, she felt him slacken his grip. She tried to keep her eyes on Jared, tried to stay ahead of the tight darkness cutting off her breath, her arms wrapped around her baby.

"How can I trust you?" Jimmy asked, glancing around, then back to Jared.

Jared shrugged. "It's your only option. The card and the money will get you far enough away, that Hank can't find you. You can't ever come back here, though. And this is a onetime offer, with a onetime cash advance. You can trust me on that, but only that. I'll give you a PIN number, then after you've gotten away with the money, I'll cancel the card and we'll call it even."

Jimmy stood there, his harsh breathing permeating the room with a sense of fear and indecision. Finally, he held out one hand. "Hand over the card and number, and I'll be out of here."

Jared reached into the back pocket of his jeans. "I've got it right here." He found the card and held it in the air. Alisha saw the flash of silver and blue, glistening like diamonds in the bright moonlight. "The number is—my mother's birthday—2-3-44."

"2-3-44. Got it," Jimmy said, waving the gun again. "Give me the card."

"First, drop the gun and let Alisha and the baby go."

"I'm keeping the gun," Jimmy said as he pushed Alisha forward. Jared caught her to him, pulling her out of the nightmare and into the shelter of his warm, welcoming embrace, his free hand wrapped against her waist.

"Loretta, would you take Callum?" Jared asked, his voice quiet, his eyes still on Jimmy.

Loretta sniffed, got up, and reached for the baby. Alisha hesitated, but she was shaking so badly, it probably was a good idea for Loretta to relieve her. She kissed Callum's soft head, then handed him over to Loretta. His little body stretched, then he settled back into a peaceful sleep. Loretta sank down in the rocking chair, her tears filled with joy now as she whispered thanks to God.

Jimmy held out his hand. "I need to go."

Jared walked over to him. "Use it wisely."

"You'll probably call it in as stolen the minute I leave," Jimmy said, his voice still raspy with nerves.

"I could," Jared replied, his hands on his hips. "But I'll consider it money well spent if you never come back here. We'll take care of Rayanne and your baby, don't worry. You just stay away from Dover Mountain."

Jimmy's eyes held a flash of regret. "Not a problem," he said, already moving toward the front door. "But y'all still have a problem. He won't give up, you know. He's crazy."

"Hank won't be bothering Alisha again," Jared said.

Jimmy turned at the open front door. "I told you, Hank didn't have anything to do with this." Then he rushed out into the night without a backward glance.

❧ Chapter Twenty ❧

"I'm telling you, he's gone."

Deputy Parker glared at Jared, his stance unyielding, his expression condemning.

"I had his hands and feet taped," Jared said, lifting his hands out then dropping them at his side. "Between that and the headache I gave him when I hit him, I don't see how the man could have gotten away."

The deputy chewed a wad of gum, blew a bubble, then gave Jared the suspicious eye again. "Hank Burgess was not waiting for me in your cabin, Mr. Murdock. But I did find the tape and some signs of a struggle. Want to fill me in on what's really going on here?"

They were in Alisha's cabin. Jared had managed to get just enough signal on his cell phone to call the deputy. In a static-filled message, he'd told Parker to get here quick.

Tate Wilkes came rushing through the door, his eyes wide with worry. "Are y'all all right? I went by Jared's cabin and then I saw the deputy's car here."

Loretta looked from the deputy to her husband. "Did you see Geneva? She went for help about an hour ago."

Tate shook his head. "Geneva? I thought she was here with y'all."

Jared glanced at his watch, amazed that so little time had passed. It had seemed as though they had tried to reason with Jimmy for an eternity. He quickly filled Tate in on what had happened. "Geneva managed to get away for help just as Jimmy came in."

Tate shook his head, anxiety in his eyes. "Why'd you let her do a crazy thing like that?"

"She insisted she'd be okay," Loretta said, her voice beginning to quiver. "Now I'm so worried. What if Hank—"

"I...we weren't thinking straight," Alisha said. "It's been a long night." She looked at Jared and he could see the remorse and fear in her eyes. "We got rid of Jimmy, but we need to find Hank. He might come back here for me. And now, I'm wondering if Geneva ran into him somewhere." She sank down on a chair, her head in her hands. "It's never going to end."

Jared sat down beside her and took one of her hands. "We'll find Hank and we'll find Geneva, too."

Loretta's gasp filled the tense air in the tiny cabin. "What if he's got her?"

"Honey, she's smart," Tate said. "I bet she's hiding out somewhere, or she's gone into the village for help."

The deputy put his chubby hand on his hips, his eyes back on Jared. "I told you not to take the law into your own hands. Now I got two people missing, and one on the lam."

"Just let Jimmy go," Alisha said. "He won't be back."

They heard a commotion outside, then a scream.

"That's Geneva," Loretta said, jumping up to run out the door before Tate could stop her.

Jared took in the grim sight. Jimmy lay curled upon the ground. "You were right, Alisha. He didn't get very far." Everyone followed him out into the dark front yard.

Geneva was standing over Jimmy. "He had a gun. He came around the corner and he scared me. I stabbed him."

"Oh, honey," Loretta said, grabbing her daughter in a tight hug. "Are you okay?"

Geneva bobbed her head, sobs racking her body. "He was trying to tell me something and then he just slumped over. What if I killed him?"

The deputy bent down to check Jimmy's pulse. "He ain't dead yet. Look's like you just nicked him on the shoulder." He stood with a grunt, then stalked to his car. "I'll radio for an ambulance and some backup to find Hank. Don't anybody leave here. You've all got some explaining to do."

Jared bent down over Jimmy. The boy's breathing was shallow and he looked sickly pale in the moonlight. A bright spot of blood was oozing from his left shoulder. "Jimmy?" Jared said into his ear. "Can you hear me?"

Jimmy moaned, "Make sure Rayanne is okay. I do love her, you know," then drifted back into unconsciousness.

Jared stood, sympathy for Geneva making him wish he had listened to the deputy's warnings. "I think he'll be okay, Geneva," he said. "Maybe we should call Dr. Sloane. He'd probably get here before the ambulance from Dalton."

"He's not home," Geneva replied, wiping a hand across her tears. "I tried calling him when I got to Mama and Daddy's place." She crossed her arms. "When I didn't find anybody there, I panicked. I tried calling everyone I knew."

Tate put a hand on her arm. "I'm sorry, honey. We must have just missed each other." Then he looked at his wife. "I got worried when I couldn't get anyone to answer the phone here. I sent the boys to Miss Mozelle's so Rayanne could watch out for them, then I came here right away."

"They cut the phone line," Alisha said, a wry expression on her face. "So much for getting a phone for protection and help."

Jared could see the weariness shrouding her. "Sit down," he ordered as he guided her to the porch steps. Then he turned to Geneva. "How did you meet up with Jimmy?"

"I hid outside on the back porch when he came in the front door. When I realized who it was and that he had a gun, I ran as fast as I could to your place. But it was dark there and nobody answered, so I went to get Daddy."

Tate shook his head. "I should have dealt with that boy a long time ago."

"We thought he was gone for good," Loretta said. Jared didn't miss the secretive glance she cast toward Alisha. It wouldn't do to tell the deputy that Jared had paid Jimmy off, just to get rid of him.

"After I couldn't find any help, I ran all the way back here and right smack into Jimmy," Geneva explained. "He had the gun—I had the knife—I didn't mean to stab him. And I don't think he intended to shoot me."

"But why was he coming back here?" Alisha wondered out loud. "Maybe he found Hank and helped him escape. Or maybe he was trying to warn us."

Jared wished this would all make sense. Maybe Jimmy had decided he wanted more money, or maybe he'd decided to finish them all off before he left for good. "We'll have to ask him when he's better," he said.

"He tried to tell me something," Geneva said again. "He seemed to really want to say something, but then—" She burst into tears again. "I can't believe Jimmy and Hank would try to do something like this."

"It's all right, honey," Tate said. "It's all gonna be fine. We'll get Hank and put an end to this mess."

The deputy came back then. "Okay, folks, ambulance is on its way, and so are the investigators who've been working this case already. And after all of this, I imagine the sheriff will be here soon, too." He put a booted foot on the porch step and leaned forward, his beady eyes on Alisha. "Now, I want to hear the whole story, from start to finish. Who wants to go first?"

Alisha woke with a start, her eyes adjusting to the pinkish-blue hues of the dawn outside her bedroom window. At first, fear clawed at her body, making her shiver in the cool morning air. She remembered the rain coming in the middle of the night, a soft gentle rain that had washed the mountains and trees in a shimmering, crying shower. Then she remembered Jared was here. She was safe. Glancing around, she sat up to find Callum sleeping in his little crib next to her bed. He'd had his 4:00 a.m. feeding, so he'd sleep for another hour at least.

Alisha also knew that Jared was keeping watch in the other room, just as he'd done the first night he'd come here. He'd told her he wouldn't leave her.

Alisha felt tears springing to her eyes. He knew everything now, and he was still here.

But she needed to tell it to him again. He hadn't heard it from her, and she hated that he'd had to overhear the worst details of her past from Jimmy Barrett.

"Jared?" she called, her voice raspy and raw from fear and crying.

He jumped straight up, his body going on full alert. "What?"

"I'm fine," Alisha said as she grabbed her robe and tied it over her nightgown. "But we need to talk. I'm going to make coffee."

She went into the kitchen, comforted by the pad of his bare feet against the old plank floor of the cabin. Remembering the horrible details of the past night, she focused on making the coffee while she waited for the sun to crest over the hills behind her house.

"It's a beautiful morning," Jared said from behind her.

"Yes."

The sun lifted through the trees, its bright light flowing out in golden-yellow rays, making everything seem fresh and green and misty with hope.

"You'd never know that last night these woods were full of fugitives," she said. "Including me."

She turned and Jared pulled her into his arms. "It's over now," he told her, kissing her hair.

"But Hank's still out there."

"The sheriff is in on the hunt now," Jared reminded her. "He's put a whole team on this. Finally."

"After I finally told Dwight the truth."

He lifted her face with a finger. "They'll find Hank. Then it will be over for good."

Alisha pulled away to pour their coffee. "But I need you to understand, Jared."

He nodded, silent and alert, his eyes a soft, rich brown. "Tell me."

Alisha sank down in her chair, staring into her coffee. "I fell in love with Trevor right out of high school. We'd both planned on going to college. I wanted to be a social worker and he was going to follow in his father's footsteps."

Jared nodded, took a sip of his coffee. "What did his father do?"

"He was a minister."

Jared put his cup down. "Your husband was a minister and he abused you?"

"Trevor never made it through seminary. He had a few discipline problems, which his father managed to smooth over, but basically, he wasn't cut out to be a minister. So he got a job with a big company in downtown Atlanta while I went to school nearby. He worked in finance. But he didn't want me to go back to school after the baby."

Jared's head came up. "The baby? Alisha—"

"We had to get married. I got pregnant my freshman year of college." She lowered her head, the shame heating her face. "His parents insisted. And my parents kind of went along with it, because they didn't know, they didn't know that Trevor was a control freak with a bad temper and a drinking problem. Neither did I until it was too late."

Jared's face went still in the light of the morning sun. Still and questioning. "And the baby?"

"I lost the baby." She looked down at her hands. "Trevor resented having to marry me. And he took it out on me." She looked up at him again. "I lost the baby."

"Because of the abuse?"

She nodded, the sick feeling of terror and disgust making the coffee turn sour on her stomach. "It was just too much, too much. His parents, they tried everything to keep it quiet. They sent him through counseling, begged me to stay with him. You see, the church is huge. His parents are very well-off and very well connected. They didn't want the scandal—"

Jared shot up then, his own rage coloring his eyes to a dark burning brown. "The scandal? You're telling me a man of God forced you to suffer through his son's abuse just to avoid scandal?"

Alisha's heart beat like a battered bird against her chest. "They convinced me he would change. And I was so afraid, so in awe of them, I believed he could change."

"So you stayed with this man for ten years?"

She nodded. "I'm not proud of it, Jared, and I don't know if I can explain it. But when you're in an abusive situation, you can justify a lot of things. I prayed, I hoped, I tried to be a good wife. I gave up my dreams of a career and stayed home, by the phone, always within reach, thinking he'd stay calm and rational if I was the perfect wife."

"And just what does being a perfect wife require?"

"I had to give up my books," she said, waving a hand around at the many books scattered here and there in the cabin. "And my music—he didn't like my gospel music or my mountain music. Trevor liked hard rock, in spite of his father's disapproval. He'd play it really loud...whenever he—" She stopped, wringing her hands in her lap.

"Whenever he beat you," Jared said, leaning down to stare at her. "Alisha, why did you stay?"

"I told you, I rationalized it in my mind. At first, I was afraid to leave him. He always said he'd come after me. He resented marrying me, but he didn't want to let me go. It was a matter of pride for him. And then, his parents would come into the picture—trying to change him, trying to pray him well. Our prayers didn't work. We tried, but it just wouldn't work. He'd get better and for a while, things would be pretty good. And then I'd slip up—"

Jared slammed his fist down on the table, causing her to rise up out of her chair and move away. "I'm sorry," he said, pulling her back. "I just can't listen to this. I can't think of you with this man."

Alisha pushed Jared's hand away. "Well, I *was* with him. I had all sorts of excuses. All sorts of reasons for trying to make my marriage work. Things did get better, though, for a while. We bought a new house in a nice neighborhood. I planted azaleas and decorated the house—always with Trevor's approval. He seemed pleased with that. His career was taking off and he wanted a pretty yard and house to show off to his business associates. Then I started volunteering at the YWCA, helping unwed teenagers and other abused women. I knew what they were going through and I thought we were over that.

"My azaleas—" she stopped, a shuddering breath moving down her body "—my azaleas had just finished blooming all over the yard—six feet tall and so lush, so beautiful, but they were beginning to die back. Trevor didn't like the dead heads, so he kept fussing at me to get out there and get rid of the spent blossoms. I wanted to work in my garden, but I hadn't been feeling well. I had just been to the doctor the week before and found out I was pregnant again. I was so happy, and Trevor seemed pleased. He made all these elaborate plans for the baby. That's when I first learned about the trust fund. That day, I went by the Y and worked awhile, then stopped by the grocery store. I wanted to make a special dinner."

She looked out the back window, her gaze taking in the dogwoods and redbud trees, the daffodils and tulips. But no azaleas. "When I got home, Trevor was waiting. He was so angry because I was late. So angry. He'd had a bad day at work and he'd been drinking." She hitched a breath, crossed her arms against her chest. "We had a terrible fight, and then he went out into the garden and started chopping down my azalea bushes. He just kept on chopping, then he got the riding lawn mower and mowed down what he hadn't chopped."

Jared was beside her, a hand on her arm. "You don't have to tell me this."

She nodded, wiping at a lone tear. "Yes, I do. I do. I tried to stop him, tried to talk to him about the baby, but he was in a black rage. He'd held it in so long, you see. He'd tried to change, but something snapped. I begged him to listen to me, and he got so mad, he grabbed me and pushed me down into the azaleas, pushed my face into the dead, wilted flower blossoms and the bushes." She stopped, putting her face in her hands as tears rushed down her face. "I couldn't breathe. I couldn't breathe."

Jared urged her around and held her, not tightly, but softly, gently, against his chest. "It's all right. It's all right."

"He finally let me go, then he left. He was gone a couple of hours. I went inside and sat in the dark, but I knew then that I had to leave. I was packing when he came back."

Jared's grip on her arms tightened. "He didn't like that, did he?"

Alisha lifted her head. "No, he didn't like me trying to leave. But I told him it was over, that I had to protect *this* baby." She paused, swallowed. "I told him I wouldn't allow him to *kill* this baby. That made him even more angry. He took me outside and pulled me through the yard, sometimes by my hair, other times by my neck. The neighbors were home now and watching, telling him to stop. Someone called 911. I could hear them talking into the phone.

"Trevor went to his car and got a potted plant out, then tossed it on the porch. He kept telling me I didn't appreciate him, that he'd gone and bought me a new azalea bush to replace the ones I'd lost. Then he went back to the car and got a gun, so none of the neighbors would dare approach us. He was just so mad...so mad. I tried to run, tried to get away. He caught up to me, told me he'd kill me before he let me go, and I turned and grabbed at the gun. I was shouting at him, telling him not to hurt me because of the—"

"—the baby," Jared finished for her.

Alisha sank down against his body, her sobs coming in great gulps as she struggled for air. "The gun went off and he slumped to the ground. I held him there, begging him not to die. He tried to tell me he was sorry. He kept telling me that he'd replace the azaleas. That he'd replace what I had lost. I saw one tear falling down his face, then he just...went to sleep. I fainted. When I woke up, the police were there. And his parents. I had killed my husband."

Jared guided her over to the sofa. "Loretta was right, Alisha. It was an accident. It was self-defense."

Alisha bobbed her head. "That's what the judge decided. After the hearing, I was free to go, so I did. I never mentioned the baby, never. I turned my back on everything and everybody, even God. My parents had died in those ten years and all I had left was this cabin that had been passed down through my family. This cabin, Jared.

"But before I left Riverdale, I got a call from a bank where we'd never done business. That's when I found out about the secret bank account. Trevor's father had set it up for the first baby, and Trevor had taken it over after he started making money. But he'd moved it to a different bank. He'd made regular deposits and hidden it from me, but when he found out about the second baby, he'd decided that money would be for the baby. When I came here, I had it transferred and set up as an open trust fund, just in case the baby needed something early on. Then I hid away here, sick and broken. Dr. Sloane and Miss Mozelle and Reverend Stripling and Loretta and Tate, the Langfords, they fixed me. They made me see that God would forgive me, made me see that I still needed God. And they guarded my secret—my baby."

She looked up at him, hoping he'd understand. "But no one knew about the bank account. Not even Trevor's parents. They just assumed Trevor had spent the little bit of money they'd given him all those years ago. I signed all the assets over to them, except that one account. That was my insurance policy for Callum."

Jared nodded. "It's obvious you never used any of that money, Alisha. And I don't blame you for wanting something for your child."

"But do you blame me for the rest? For killing my husband, for staying with him for so long?"

Jared tugged her back into his arms. "I can't blame you for anything. I would have probably killed him with my bare hands." Then he rocked her against him. "But that's not the answer is it? That's why you got so upset with me the time I strong-armed Jimmy."

She nodded. "I was afraid. Afraid you'd be just like Trevor." Then she looked up at him, her smile beaming through her tears. "But I can see you aren't that kind of man."

"No, I'm not," Jared said. "I'm not."

Then he leaned down and kissed her, the touch of his lips to hers as soft and gentle and warm as the coming day. And just as full of bright promise.

The sun hung over the sky to the west, just tipping the mountains. He had to finish this off by himself. He couldn't depend on anyone else. He looked down at the body in the ravine, disgusted and sickened by what he had already done and what he was going to have to do. But he didn't have a choice. They had all betrayed him.

"Sorry, Hank," he said as he remembered pushing at the heavy man's flesh, remembered the sickening thud of bones hitting rock. "Sorry." He glanced around, sure that no one had seen him, then he took one last look down at the spot where, late last night, Hank Burgess had landed amid the rocks and shrubs of the creek bed.

Now all he had to do was find Jimmy Barrett and take care of him, too.

Then he'd be free to go to Alisha and take her away from here. She'd go. She'd go, whether he had the money or not. She'd go, because he'd make her see reason. She'd understand and she'd be glad to go with him.

He'd make sure of that.

Late that afternoon, the deputy was back at Alisha's cabin.

"Well, folks, I've got good news and I've got bad news," Dwight Parker said, scrunching one booted foot in the dirt at his feet as he looked up onto the porch at Jared and Alisha.

Jared held his breath. "What did you find, Deputy?"

"We found Hank Burgess," the deputy said, his eyes narrowing as he glared up at Jared. "That's the good news."

"And the bad?" Alisha asked, her hand on Jared's arm.

The deputy took off his Stetson, shook it against his khaki pants. "We found him dead, at the bottom of a ravine just beyond Mr. Murdock's cabin."

Alisha gasped, grabbed the porch railing. "Jimmy? Is that why Jimmy came back here? Did he kill Hank?"

The deputy shook his head. "I talked to Jimmy down at the hospital in Dalton, 'bout an hour ago. He said he didn't kill Hank Burgess. Said he was coming back here to warn y'all. But, since then, Jimmy has decided not to talk."

"Then who did kill Hank?" Jared asked, his mind whirling with possibilities, none of them making sense.

The deputy put his hat back on his head and nodded up at Jared. "Well now, it looks like you did, Murdock. You're our number one suspect. That's why I'm here to take you in."

❧ *Chapter Twenty-One* ❧

Alisha rushed down the steps. "You can't possibly believe Jared had anything to do with this."

"I can, and I do," the deputy said, already turning Jared around toward the squad car. "I'm just taking the man into the sub-station for questioning, Alisha. I need some answers."

Jared didn't resist, but he turned when the deputy was through. "And meanwhile, there is a killer out there. He could come back for Alisha, too."

"We'll put a deputy on her," Parker replied. "Right now, the sheriff wants a word with you."

"I won't leave her," Jared said, backing away from the deputy. "Her phone line hasn't been repaired yet. She'll be all alone here."

"Leave your cell phone with her," the deputy suggested with a blank face.

"Oh, come on," Jared said, shaking his head. "You know it barely works in these mountains."

"Yeah, lucky you got through to me last night."

Jared crossed his arms. "I won't leave until I know she's safe."

Deputy Parker took out his gun. "Murdock, don't make me have to use this."

Alisha hurled herself in front of Jared. "Dwight, put that gun away. Jared didn't do this. Think about it. There's no way he could have done this. He was trying to get here to help me."

"He had time before leaving his cabin last night. He thought Hank was trying to kidnap you, and he knew something was up. It would have been easy for him to throw Hank over that bluff, just to get away from the man."

"But why would I have called you, if I'd just killed Hank?" Jared said, anger coloring his face.

"That's part of what we'd like to know. You made it look like Hank had escaped. Maybe hoped we'd think he accidentally fell off the side of the mountain trying to get away. But you had Hank's gun. Mighty interesting, don't you think?"

"I gave you the gun," Jared replied, rolling his eyes. "Why would I do that if I'd used it to kill him?"

"Was Hank shot?" Alisha asked, her eyes flying to Jared's face.

"We're waiting for the autopsy report on that," the deputy replied. "But, no, we didn't see signs of a gunshot. He could have been pushed, or fallen, I reckon."

"Well, maybe he did fall," Alisha said. "Or maybe Jimmy *did* kill him."

"Or maybe Murdock was so angry and afraid for you, that he just lost control. Maybe Jimmy's covering for Murdock, seeing as how we found Murdock's charge card on Jimmy."

"I gave him the card. I'll admit that," Jared said. "He was trying to blackmail Alisha."

"So *you* paid him off, so to speak?"

Jared nodded. "I just wanted him away from Alisha, for good."

"And maybe you just wanted Hank gone for good, too. Only, maybe Hank wouldn't settle for being paid off."

"That's crazy," Jared said. "If I had killed Hank, I wouldn't have called for help at all. Someone's guilty, but it isn't me."

"But you'd want to establish that you left him in your cabin, supposedly. Make it look like somebody else did the deed. You left all the evidence right there, too."

"Which shows I didn't hurt Hank," Jared replied, his dark eyes flashing at the deputy. "Somebody helped him escape and whoever that somebody was must have pushed Hank over the edge and into that ravine. Don't you see that?"

Deputy Parker scrunched his brow. "I see that you've had trouble with both Jimmy Barrett and Hank Burgess since you came to Dover Mountain. I see that Jimmy is hiding something. He ain't talking, except to swear that he didn't kill Hank. And I see that you threatened both these men, in front of witnesses."

Alisha grabbed at the deputy's arm. "Dwight, be reasonable. Both Jared and Loretta saw Jimmy threatening me. And several witnesses heard Jimmy and Hank arguing with Jared. Most of those witnesses could testify for Jared. He had right on his side each time he was confronted by Jimmy and Hank."

"Well, right or not, I still need to take him to the sheriff," Dwight said, shaking his head. "I'm just doing my job, folks."

"Well, you're doing it wrong," Alisha replied, her eyes holding Jared's. "I know Jared didn't do this."

"But somebody did," Jared said, his expression grim. "Look, Parker, you can't leave Alisha here by herself. Let me stay until the other deputy arrives. Or have the sheriff come here to question me."

"Nope. Can't do that," Parker said, shoving Jared toward the patrol car. "Sheriff wants to see you right now, and he wants me to bring you to him."

Jared gave Alisha a look full of resolve, then handed her his cell phone. "Alisha, take this and go to the Wilkeses' place. Stay there until I can get back here."

Alisha nodded. "Do I need to call a lawyer for you?"

"I don't need a lawyer," Jared said, his eyes cutting to the deputy. "I didn't do this. Try to get someone to talk to Jimmy. He's probably afraid he's next."

Alisha nodded, watching as Parker put Jared into the back of the squad car. She could see the uneasiness in Jared's eyes. That same feeling shrouded her in a paralyzing fear. But she couldn't let that fear take over. "I'll be okay. I'll hurry to Tate's before it gets dark, I promise."

Parker looked at her over the car's top. "I'll radio for another deputy right away, Alisha. But I think you're safe with Jimmy in the hospital and Hank dead." Then he lowered his head toward Jared. "Maybe this is the one you should be worried about."

Half an hour later, Alisha had Callum bundled into his stroller and was heading out the door to walk to the Wilkeses' place when Miss Mozelle showed up on her porch.

"Where you off to, child?"

Alisha didn't want to alarm her friend, but she had to tell her the truth. And she needed to be away from here before darkness fell. "I'm going to stay with the

Wilkeses. They found Hank Burgess dead a little while ago, and Jimmy's in the hospital and—"

Miss Mozelle held up a withered hand. "Slow down. What on earth is going on?"

Alisha quickly filled her friend in about the night's events. "So Jared sent Geneva and Loretta home to get some rest, and he was here with me all day, but then Dwight came and took him away. I have to get away from this cabin. Whoever this is—he's still out there. It wasn't just Jimmy and Hank. I don't know who it is."

Miss Mozelle sucked in a breath. "Mercy, so much going on. I came to visit the baby, and to see if you'd heard from Doc Sloane. He hasn't answered the door or the phone in two days, but Letty Martha said she thought she saw him walking down this way earlier this afternoon. I thought maybe he'd come to pay you a visit."

Alisha shook her head as she hurried to lock up the cabin. "No, I haven't seen him since last week when he came by to look in on Callum." Then she stopped, staring over at Miss Mozelle. "Do you think he's drunk himself into a stupor again, and he's just not answering the door?"

"Thought that might be it," Miss Mozelle said, bending to baby-talk to Callum. The baby kicked his feet and gurgled his delight. "Or worse," the midwife said, her words low and full of concern. "He's missed several appointments at the clinic, too. I'm really worried."

Alisha wanted to reassure her friend, but right now, she was more concerned about her son's safety. "He's done this before, right?"

Miss Mozelle nodded. "Yep. Disappears for days on end, then shows back up, sober and ready to take on the world."

"Maybe he went on a trip."

"The doc never leaves this mountain, you know that."

Alisha had to agree there. Dr. Sloane kept to himself and rarely traveled. Then her heart hit against her ribs in a rapid-fire pace. "I hope this killer hasn't hurt him, too. I mean, Dr. Sloane knows things about me, things I could only tell my doctor. But if someone wanted information.... Maybe we should check his house, see if something's wrong."

Miss Mozelle brought a hand to her face as they headed out of the yard, her dark eyes squinting toward the approaching sunset. "I'm so used to his black moods, I hadn't even thought about that. I just figured he didn't want to be found, but now with all this going on, you might be right. He could be hurt or in trouble."

They were out on the road when they heard a rustling in the blackberry bushes across from Alisha's cabin. Already nervous, Alisha whirled around to find Dr. Sloane standing there. He looked disheveled and disoriented, as if he'd slept in his lightweight suit.

Alisha motioned to Miss Mozelle. "Look."

Miss Mozelle turned around in the road. "Well, there you are, old man. I was worried sick about you. You can't go missing appointments. And I need you to check on Rayanne. I think that girl's about ready to have that baby."

"Shut up," Dr. Sloane said, waving a hand at Miss Mozelle.

Alisha looked at the doctor, saw the fevered cast in his blue eyes. "Are you all right, Dr. Sloane?"

"I will be," the doctor said as he approached them at a slow gait. "I will be now, my dear."

Then he collapsed on the road.

"We need to get him back inside," Miss Mozelle said as she rushed forward to touch the doctor's forehead. "He's burning up."

Torn between the need to get Callum to safety and the need to help her friends, Alisha could only nod. She'd be okay here for a while with the doctor and Miss Mozelle. "Okay," she said, turning Callum's stroller around. "Can you get him up?"

Miss Mozelle nodded, already bending to help the doctor. "Doc?" she called down to him. "Dr. Sloane, can you walk?"

The doctor opened his eyes and looked around, confusion apparent in his expression. "Water," he said in a weak voice. "Just need some water."

"C'mon," Miss Mozelle said, struggling to help him up. She was a strong woman, so, with little effort, she managed to half drag, half walk the gaunt doctor to the porch. "Sit here while I go get you a glass."

Alisha lifted the stroller back up the steps and placed it by the door. "I'll wet a cloth," she said as she hurried to unlock the door, then followed Miss Mozelle inside the cabin.

They both came back, Alisha carrying the cloth and Miss Mozelle steps ahead of her, carrying a glass of cool water.

Alisha stopped when she heard the glass crash against the porch steps. Then she looked down and saw that her baby was gone from the stroller.

"What—" She looked to the steps and saw that Dr. Sloane was standing in the middle of the yard. He had Callum in his arms, cooing to him. The expression on the doctor's face brought a silent scream to Alisha's throat. He had a look that dared her to come any closer, a look of pure malice.

"You threw away the azalea bushes," Dr. Sloane said, a reprimand in his eyes. "You threw away my gift."

"Oh, no," Alisha said, her heart stopping as her blood ran cold and her knees went numb.

Dr. Sloane glared up at Alisha and Miss Mozelle, his eyes lighting with a mixture of madness and hopefulness. "It was the only way, Alisha. I lost my family. You lost your husband. You've suffered, and so have I. Don't you see? If you and Callum come with me, I'll have everything I've lost. And with your money, I can start a new practice. We can replace everything we've both lost and start a new life together. It's the only way. I hope you can see that. I hope you won't make trouble. I don't want any more trouble."

As he said this, he held Callum tighter against his chest, one dirty hand rubbing the baby's head. "I don't want any more trouble," he repeated, the look in his eyes full of warning. "I just needed Murdock out of the way. I didn't mean to hurt you or Callum."

Alisha swallowed her fear, all sorts of horrible thoughts rushing into her head as she realized this man had tampered with Jared's car. "I told you about what happened the day Trevor died, about what he said to me."

The doctor nodded. "He tried to tell you he was sorry. He wanted to replace your azaleas. I remembered all of it, my dear. And I had Jimmy find out the rest. You were hiding a lot of secrets. But I don't want any more trouble," he repeated as he rocked back on his heels, slowly swinging Callum in his arms.

"And did you have Jimmy cut the brakes on Jared's truck?"

The doctor shook his head, his whole body seeming to shiver and jerk, his grip on Callum tightening. "Oh, no. I paid Hank to do that. He'd do anything if it meant he'd get a chance with you. Only, he won't get another chance."

"You killed him," Alisha said, her stomach churning, her mind racing, her eyes on her baby.

Dr. Sloane let out a shuddering sigh. "He became belligerent. He didn't want to cooperate." He held Callum close, smiling down at the baby. "I didn't want to kill him, but he was getting in the way of my plans. He didn't understand what I wanted."

"What *do* you want?" Miss Mozelle asked, her voice calm, her head high, even as the lightweight floral scarves tied over and around her throat and dress shook with her quickening pulse.

"I want a wife and a baby," the doctor said. "I want my wife and my baby back." Then he kissed Callum's head, his lips wet, his eyes red-rimmed and rounded. "I've waited so long for the perfect wife, the perfect son. I know Alisha will go with me. She doesn't want any trouble either. She doesn't want the Emersons to find Callum—the grandson they didn't even know about. They might try to take your baby away, right, Alisha?" Then he nodded toward Alisha. "Get some things together. We have to leave right now."

Jared sat in the hot, musky sub-station, which was just a trailer backed up to a parking lot at the bottom of the mountain. A trailer with a tiny holding cell and two battered desks, a few rusty file cabinets and an ancient rotary phone. A trailer that he had to get out of.

He'd told the sheriff everything. Then he'd used his one phone call to try to get through to somebody back on the mountain, to send help to Alisha. No one answered at the Wilkeses' place, and he didn't know the number for the Curtises' store. He'd asked a deputy to bring him a phone book, but so far that wasn't happening. They couldn't hold him. He knew it and they knew it. And in the meantime, they were just stalling. While Alisha could be in danger.

They'd left him sitting here at this desk, while they whispered and conferred in a tiny lounge in the back, Deputy Parker cutting his eyes back to Jared every now and then.

They'd left him unsupervised, and with the keys to Deputy Parker's patrol car lying where he'd tossed them, within easy reach.

Jared didn't hesitate. He got up, grabbed the keys and rushed out the rickety front door. He was peeling rubber before Deputy Parker even made it down the broken concrete steps, his gun aimed for Jared's head.

Jared heard the ping of bullets hitting the back of the car as he gunned the gas pedal and headed up the winding mountain road. Back to Alisha.

"I won't let you do this," Miss Mozelle said. She inched down the porch to face Dr. Sloane, her hands wringing the long, braided fabric belt tied around her waist. "Think about what you're doing here, man. You can't take Alisha and this baby."

"I can and I will," Dr. Sloane said, his grip on Callum causing Alisha's whole body to turn to jelly. "And you'd better stay out of my way. You and your prayers and herbs. You don't need to get involved in this."

Miss Mozelle lifted her face to the sky. *"Help him, Lord. Help this poor, pathetic man see that this is wrong."*

"Do not speak to the Lord about me," Dr. Sloane said, his eyes flaming with a mad rage. "God took my family. Took the woman I loved and my baby girl. I will not let you ask God for any favor on my account."

Miss Mozelle glanced at Alisha. Alisha didn't dare move for fear that the doctor would hurt her son. She tried to speak. "Dr. Sloane, why don't we go inside and talk about this? I'll make you some coffee and feed you."

"No," the doctor said, stepping back, Callum tight against his dirty suit jacket. "I said to come with me, Alisha. And I mean it. I'll just have to take Callum without you, if you don't."

Alisha nodded, her hands out, a shiver of sickening apprehension moving up her spine like a crawling spider. "I'll go with you. I'll go. Just please don't hurt Callum."

"I'm not going to hurt the boy," the doctor said, his tone moving from defiant to petulant. "I want to raise him. I want us to live somewhere far away from this mountain. I can't stay here. I can't stand having to see that cemetery every day. I have to leave them...I have to leave them there and start a new life. With you and Callum."

Miss Mozelle shook her head, then looked toward the heavens. "This is wrong."

"No," Alisha replied, calmness taking over her through the echo of her silent prayers. "No, Miss Mozelle. This is exactly right," she said as she grabbed the diaper bag from the stroller and moved down the steps. "I'll go with Dr. Sloane. We'll be fine, just fine. You should go on back to your house." She stressed this last, hoping Miss Mozelle would get help as soon as she was away from them. And in the meantime, she'd try to hit the 911 button on Jared's cell phone.

"She ain't going anywhere," the doctor said. "Except down the mountain with Hank."

Alisha gasped as Miss Mozelle lifted her head high, her whole countenance defiant.

"You can't hurt Miss Mozelle," Alisha said, getting between the doctor and the midwife. "She's your friend. She's stood by you when others turned away."

"Yeah, stood and harped at me, worried me sick, tried to take over my clinic—"

"I was just trying to help you," Miss Mozelle said, her eyes widening. "I'm trying to help you now."

"Well, I don't need your help," the doctor said. "You got to come with us. Just till we get to that bluff across the way."

"You aim to throw me over the mountain?" Miss Mozelle asked, still calm, still standing tall.

"Yes, I do." Dr. Sloane came forward then. "Both of you will do whatever I say, or I'll have to toss Callum right over the mountain with you."

"Please, you said you wouldn't hurt Callum, remember?" Alisha looked at her friend. "Miss Mozelle, come with us. I need you." She gave Miss Mozelle a look that was both a plea and a warning.

"Yes, I reckon you do at that," Miss Mozelle said. "Okay, then. I'll walk a ways with y'all. But, he ain't gonna throw nobody off this mountain."

"Let's go," Dr. Sloane said. Then he stopped, as if listening. "But let's go around back. We'll take that trail that winds around the village."

Alisha knew what that meant. The trail was long and treacherous, and rarely used by anyone. Only someone who knew the mountain well could find it.

Jared wouldn't know where she was.

No one would know where they'd gone.

Her only chance was to distract the doctor enough, to calm and reassure him enough, that he'd give her baby back to her. And then she'd have to find a way to run, run away into the night.

But first, she had to get Miss Mozelle and Callum away from Dr. Sloane.

Jared hit the brakes on the squad car, rocks and grass spewing up as he fishtailed into Alisha's driveway. He left the door open, then rushed onto the porch and through the unlocked door of the cabin.

The silent, dark cabin.

"Alisha?"

He went into the bedroom, noticing the diaper bag and stroller were gone. Maybe she'd made it to Tate's.

Jared looked around the den, saw that everything was in order. Then he went back out to the porch. That's when he saw the stroller sitting there, empty. No baby and no diaper bag.

Alisha wouldn't have left without the stroller. It wouldn't make sense that she'd carry the baby and a diaper bag up the mountain road. This didn't feel right. Jared was heading back to the car when his foot brushed against something on the steps. He leaned down and touched the object.

One of Miss Mozelle's colorful scarves lay like a fallen butterfly, crushed and crumpled, at his feet.

Did she accidentally drop it?

No, Miss Mozelle never did anything by accident. Her scarves were always tied precisely either at her neck or around her head.

She'd left this as a sign. As a signal.

It was dark now, so Jared hurried to the squad car and opened the trunk, hoping he'd find a flashlight there. When he did, he grabbed it and turned it on. He could hear sirens coming up the mountain road, so he rushed to shut the car door then ran toward the woods at the back of the property. He'd have to hide out there and work his way toward the Wilkes house. Maybe he was overreacting and Alisha was safe there already.

But in his gut, Jared knew that she wasn't safe.

"Where are you taking us?" Alisha asked Dr. Sloane a little while later. They'd been walking since dark, steadily working their way up the slender, threading trail. The sounds of the coming night lifted in echoes all around them. Crickets chirped and mosquitoes buzzed. The bushes rustled with the scurrying of nocturnal animals. And the wind carried the scent of honeysuckle and wild orchids. She thought she smelled the hint of rain coming again.

"I have to get you away," Dr. Sloane said, repeating himself. "I have to think."

"You been thinking way too much, if you ask me," Miss Mozelle said in a winded breath.

"I didn't ask you," the doctor replied, his arm on the older woman as he pushed at her. "I told you to stay quiet."

He'd made them walk ahead of him, while he carried Callum. Alisha had tried every tactic to make him give her son, but the doctor wouldn't let go of Callum.

"Can we rest for a minute?" Alisha asked. "It's almost time for Callum's seven o'clock feeding." She could get to the cell phone if he'd let them stop.

"We'll feed him when he frets," Dr. Sloane said, the words coming out in a grunt as he lifted up onto a rocky step. "He's such a good boy. So sweet. I've watched him sleep so many times, you know."

A shiver of fear and revulsion slid like cold water over Alisha's body. "You mean, when you came by to visit?"

She heard his grunt. "No, my dear, I mean when I watched from the woods. And sometimes, through the windows. I had to keep watch. I had to make sure you were all right."

Alisha cut her eyes to Miss Mozelle. Even in the moonlight, she could see the look of disbelief on her friend's face. "I appreciate that, Dr. Sloane," Alisha said, her prayers and hopes centered on keeping Miss Mozelle and her baby alive. "I need someone to help me out. I need someone strong and sure."

"Not that Murdock fellow," the doctor replied, clearly assuming he would be the one to take care of Alisha.

"No, no. He was just being nice. He's just someone who helped me deliver Callum. He's leaving next week."

"We don't need to discuss him," Dr. Sloane said, his words dismissing the subject. "He's been taken away. They say he murdered Hank."

"But he didn't," Miss Mozelle said, looking over her shoulder. "You did that. You killed poor Hank Burgess. It ain't right—"

Alisha felt the swish of air as the doctor advanced and grabbed Miss Mozelle's arm. "I told you to stay quiet. Next time you speak, you will go off the side of this mountain."

Alisha watched in horror as her son was jerked and shifted, held tentatively in one arm by the doctor, against the backdrop of dark woods and jutting bluffs all around them. Callum didn't like being jostled and cried out in protest. "Let me hold him," Alisha said, her nerves twisted like tree vines, her mind reeling with shock and anger. "I'll go wherever you want, if you'll just let me carry my baby."

"No," Dr. Sloane said, releasing Miss Mozelle to get a better grip on Callum. "He's fine. Just fine. We're almost there. You can feed him soon."

Alisha didn't argue. She had to stay calm, had to find a way to get her baby out of this sick man's arms.

As they climbed higher, out of the corner of her eye, Alisha saw a soft flutter of fabric. Miss Mozelle dropped a small handkerchief scarf onto an outstretched cropping of bramble. She did it with the ease and grace of a ballerina moving through a dance. In the moonlight, Alisha saw that her friend was missing her colorful cloth belt and two of her neck scarves.

Miss Mozelle was leaving a trail.

And Alisha was praying that someone would find that trail.

∾ *Chapter Twenty-Two* ∾

Jared found the second scarf at about the same time he heard Deputy Parker calling his name below. He also heard rumbles of thunder off in the distance. Another storm was brewing, just what they needed.

He wasn't about to stop now. Picking up the bright-orange-and-aqua calico material that he had caught in the beam of the powerful flashlight, he breathed in the scent of Miss Mozelle's special goat's-milk lotion—a soft vanilla scent. It brought him a measure of comfort as he worked his way up the rocky incline behind Alisha's house. Jared hoped he was following the right trail. He prayed this truly was Miss Mozelle's way of guiding him, rather than the killer's sick way of throwing him off the path.

Hearing footfalls and voices down below, Jared glanced around and down. He could see uniformed officers circling Alisha's cabin. Then he heard the back door slam.

"Nobody in there," a deputy said, his own flashlight beaming through the trees.

"Spread out," came the command. "Let's comb the yard and woods. Then we'll work our way up the footpaths."

"This could take all night."

"Well, we've got to find Murdock. I didn't trust that man from the minute I met him." That would be Deputy Parker, dependable soul that he was.

"And the Emerson woman."

"What if he took her hostage?"

"Then we'll bring him in," Parker barked back to the underling who'd had the guts to suggest the worst.

Jared had to prove them wrong. He had to help them bring the real killer to justice.

Before that killer did something to Alisha and her baby.

"We have to break into the general store," Dr. Sloane said, his voice calm, his eyes burning like candle flames in the moonlight. "We'll need provisions."

"Provisions? How far are you planning on taking us?" Miss Mozelle asked, her mouth flying open.

"I have to get us off this mountain," the doctor explained. They were resting under the umbrella of an old mushroom-shaped oak. While Alisha fed Callum, she listened to the steady drip, drip of a gentle rain falling off the tree leaves.

Alisha only half listened to Dr. Sloane's ranting. They were close to the village now and she had her son back in her arms. She wasn't going to give him back to the doctor without a fight. And she had managed to dial the bright red nine on Jared's cell phone. She thought she'd heard a voice at the other end, but she didn't dare take the phone out of the diaper bag. Instead, she tried to engage the doctor in a loud conversation.

"Dr. Sloane, would you explain to me again why you've kidnapped Miss Mozelle and my son and me? And why are you taking us the back way up the mountain to the village?"

Dr. Sloane gave her a look of utter impatience. "I'm not going to explain anything again, Alisha. I've given you reason enough to trust me. I'm going to take care of you and Callum."

"To replace what we've both lost?" she asked, her back to the doctor for modesty's sake, her voice high-pitched and clear in spite of her shaking limbs. She clung to Callum with both arms, rocking him against her as he greedily finished his evening meal. She'd managed to get his diaper changed, and as much as she hated to leave trash on the mountainside, she'd gently placed the soiled diaper next to the rock where she sat, hoping someone would spot it.

When Dr. Sloane didn't answer, she chanced another glance at him. "You want to take us away from here, because of the memories? We both have bad memories."

"Yes," the doctor said, rising up to pace back and forth, averting his eyes from her as he pushed a hand through his thick gray-tinged hair. "Would you please hurry before this drizzle turns into another storm. I'm so very tired of storms."

Alisha nodded, then quickly put her clothes back together while she held Callum on her knees. "So we're headed to the general store—I mean the Mini-Mart? That is the only store in *Dover Mountain*."

Dr. Sloane started to speak, then abruptly stopped pacing, his keen eyes centering on Alisha as he stepped toward her. Her heart went still, her pulse beating rapidly. What if he'd figured it out? What if he found the cell phone?

"No, I think we'll just go into the diner instead. We'll get Langford and Dorothy to make us up some sandwiches. A break-in will be messy and could bring attention to us. We'll just pretend we ran into each other and that we're having a late meal at my place."

Miss Mozelle huffed a breath. "Oh, so we're going to go in and order takeout with a smile on our faces? You know something? You are completely off your rocker."

He grabbed for her, holding a wad of one of her scarves in his hands. "That's exactly what we're going to do, old woman. Or somebody will pay later. Probably you, since you're getting on my very last nerve."

He let her go, then reached for the silver flask in his jacket pocket. He'd started drinking about halfway up the mountain, and now he was reeling drunk. No way was Alisha going to hand her baby back over to this lunatic.

No way.

Jared found the third scarf nestled like a sleeping white bird on some brambles near an overlook. He grabbed at it, taking it into his hands as he shone his flashlight beam up the winding path. They were steadily traveling up the backside of the mountain. He didn't know this path, but he was going to have to get to know it.

He thought he'd heard voices up this way earlier.

And he knew there were voices beneath him. He had to find Alisha before the sheriff's department found him.

Whoever had Alisha and Miss Mozelle was probably trying to get back to the village to get a car. If he didn't find them soon, the chances of rescuing them would drop significantly. So would their chances of surviving.

She was going to survive this.

Alisha decided that when Dr. Sloane tried to take Callum back. "No," she said, her protective instincts kicking into overdrive as she held her baby close. As if sensing something was wrong, Callum made a grimace and let out a wail. "I told you, I'll go wherever you want, do whatever you need me to do, but I'm not letting you near my baby again."

"Give him to me," the doctor said, teetering on his dirty loafers.

"You're drunk," Miss Mozelle said, coming to stand by Alisha. "I'll fight you myself if you come near this child."

Dr. Sloane made a swing at them, but it ended up just being a weak jab in the air. "We can stay here all night, then. Let the bugs bite us all, let the heavens soak us. See if I care. I'll just take him when you both fall asleep."

"Hmph." Miss Mozelle advanced a step. "You'll be out cold before either of us blinks an eye."

That made him stop and think. Alisha watched as the doctor slowly realized that by handing over Callum to her, he had lost any leverage here. The only thing he could do would be to push one or all of them off the side of the steep path. Which he just might decide to do.

"We can all walk to the *Hilltop Diner*," she said in a calm, loud voice, praying the 911 operator had heard their location. "We'll get you some coffee and something to eat. We won't make trouble, *Dr. Sloane*. No one will have to know anything is wrong. We can let Miss Mozelle go, then you and I and Callum can leave from there together."

"Sounds like a sane plan to me," Miss Mozelle said, giving the man a look of disdain that dared him to do anything foolish. "And to ensure Alisha's safety, I won't tell a soul what you've told me. You know, about Hank and all that other."

"Okay," Dr. Sloane said on a rush of breath, the word shaky and unsure. "But we're walking it together, me in the middle with an arm on each of you. I'll push the first one who makes a move. And if one of you runs off, I'll just have to be that much meaner to the other one, you understand?"

They both nodded, giving each other reassuring looks. Then Miss Mozelle leaned close to Alisha. "I'm 'bout outta scarves, baby."

Alisha glanced up to find only one fringed floral scarf draped across Miss Mozelle's neck, and a gingham handkerchief still on her head. "Save it for an emergency," she whispered. "Because I doubt he's going to let any of us stay behind."

"Stop talking and let's get going," the doctor said, his words slurred and broken. "I want to be on the road before dawn."

Alisha shuddered to think of going down the mountain in a car with this drunkard. She wouldn't do it. She wouldn't subject herself or her baby to that kind of reckless disregard.

She glanced into the diaper bag and saw that the cell phone was still on. And active. Up this high, they were getting a weak but steady signal. She only hoped that someone was monitoring their conversation on the other end of the line.

Someone was.

Jared hid in a cluster of thick blue spruce trees just off the path, where he could clearly hear the sheriff and his men talking around a curve a few feet below. In spite of the clouds drifting in and out, he could just make out the silhouettes of the men. But that meant he had to stay in the shadows.

"The 911 operator says she's getting an open cell phone conversation—static—coming in and out, but it looks like we have something. A hostage situation on or near Dover Mountain. If it's Jared Murdock's phone, the woman talking could be Alisha Emerson!"

The excitement in the junior deputy's voice didn't match the wrath in Deputy Dwight Parker's angry reply. "Murdock!" he shouted, the one name echoing eerily over Jared's head. "Murdock's the only one around here with a fancy cell phone."

"No," the other man said. "Something about a doctor. She's smart. She's been feeding details, and she called him by name—Dr. Sloane. Something about the Hilltop Diner."

Jared stumbled. His sudden move caused a few loose pebbles to slip down on the path, which in turn caused Deputy Parker to glance up. "Let's go."

The deputy barked orders, telling the men to spread out. "We need to get back into town by way of the road, too," Jared heard the man shouting. "I'll radio the sheriff to give him an update. We need to seal off the road out of here."

Jared had to make a run for it. Dr. Sloane must be the person holding Alisha. And that would mean Dr. Sloane, quiet, disturbed, alcoholic Dr. Sloane, was the man who'd been stalking Alisha. And the man who'd threatened Jimmy and murdered Hank Burgess.

But why, Jared wondered as he pushed up the narrow path toward the village, snatching at low-hanging limbs and pushing through thorny blackberry bushes as he dodged rocks and crannies. Why?

To replace what you've lost.

Those words seemed to materialize from somewhere inside Jared's screaming brain. Could it be that the good doctor was trying not only to replace what Alisha had lost, but also what he had lost?

His wife and baby.

Maybe Jared could head them off at the diner, *if* that was where they were headed.

Jared kept running, running through bramble and branches, crashing against thick honeysuckle vines and heavy thickets of spruce trees and tall pines, his clothes damp with rain and perspiration. He could hear the lawmen gaining on him, shouting into the night as they pushed toward their quarry. Lightning hissed and danced across the sky, highlighting the growing tension on the mountain.

He had to find Alisha and the baby before the doctor took Alisha away from this mountain for good.

In the end, they all converged as one.

Dr. Sloane wobbled on the last few yards of the path, then slowly guided Alisha and Miss Mozelle down the steep embankment toward the back of the diner. Jared saw them from a spot on a bluff, then hurried off the path, through the covers of trees and rocks, down and around, to the front to try and warn Langford and Dorothy.

Making sure he wasn't being followed, he rushed through the front doors, saw Warren J. and Letty Martha sitting there with tense looks on their drawn faces, saw Langford's warning look, saw Dorothy's questioning eyes. Saw Reverend Stripling's salt-and-pepper head bent in prayer.

And felt the barrel of a gun aimed at the back of his head.

"Mr. Murdock, you left without saying goodbye."

Jared took in a long breath, his gaze moving over the people he'd come to love and respect, as the determined deputy stepped out from behind a wall partition with his gun centered on Jared.

"I didn't kill Hank," Jared told Deputy Parker, tossing him a look over his shoulder. "And I didn't kidnap Alisha and Miss Mozelle, but I think you already know that." He found some sense of relief as one by one, the people in the diner looked up at him with sincere belief in their eyes.

"That remains to be seen," Parker replied as he shoved Jared into a nearby chair. "Where's Alisha Emerson?"

Jared tried to stand, but the deputy pushed him back down. "You know where she is!" Jared shouted, frustration rattling through his system like a rock slide. "She's on her way here with Dr. Sloane. He's the one—he's taken them hostage and he wants to take Alisha off this mountain. I've been tracking them, and look—" he held up the scarves he'd collected "—Miss Mozelle left these on the path, so we'd find them." When the deputy looked skeptical, he added, "I even saw a disposable diaper up there. Alisha left that, I'm sure."

"She wouldn't leave litter without a very good reason, that's for sure." Letty Martha got up, her orange-and-turquoise nylon windsuit crinkling, her tennis shoes squeaking as she glared up at the deputy. "Deputy Parker, can't you see you have the wrong man? Jared is obviously trying to help Alisha. And we all know Dr. Sloane lost his marbles the night his wife died. No wonder Jimmy is cowering in that hospital in Dalton, afraid to speak out. Listen to us, please, and let Jared go, so we can save Alisha."

Jared saw a sliver of doubt pass through the deputy's eyes. "It's true," he said, determined to get back out to Alisha. "I heard one of your men telling you that Alisha has a cell phone, that she's giving out information so you can find them. You've got to do something."

"The sheriff has men up on the trail and surrounding this building."

"Well, good for the sheriff," Jared said, amazed at this man's stupidity. "But they have to be careful. Dr. Sloane, he's not stable. He might hurt the baby." Jared stood up and advanced toward the deputy in spite of the loaded gun. "You need to get out of the doorway. If he sees you he'll run with them and then things could get even worse."

"He's right," Langford said. "Parker, get in back. We have to all act natural, so we don't spook the doctor."

After what seemed a lifetime, Deputy Parker finally put his gun away and stalked to the kitchen, mumbling into his radio as he went. But he whirled at the swinging doors. "There's still the matter of you stealing my squad car, Murdock."

"I left it in Alisha's yard," Jared said, his patience as crusty as Dorothy's pie. "Can we talk about that later, please?"

"We sure will." He held up a finger. "Let us handle this. My men know what to do. They're out there watching and waiting to move in. And I'll be watching you."

Langford snorted then pushed the deputy into the kitchen. "That man is so full of ego—he wants to be the next sheriff of this county, only he couldn't see the truth if it pinched him on the nose."

"He just wants to blame Jared, 'cause Jared's an outsider," Warren J. said with a sniff.

"Jared is not an outsider anymore," Letty Martha replied, daring anyone to question her.

No one did.

Jared slumped into a chair by the door. "I can't stand this. I can't stand this waiting. I just saw them on the ridge. They should be here by now." He got up, paced around, then looked outside. He could hear the wind whining and the rain hitting against the roof. "I'm going out there to find Alisha."

He was out the door before anyone could stop him.

"Why are we stopping?" Alisha asked the doctor, her voice carrying out over the roar of approaching rain.

They'd made it down the path and were now out of sight at the base of a sloping foothill just behind the tiny diner. The village was eerily quiet, as if the whole mountain was holding its breath. The parking lot of the diner looked deserted and desolate. The other buildings were dark and drawn into themselves like giant hulking shadows. Every now and then, a great gust of wind and water assaulted Alisha, causing her to hold Callum close in his blankets.

"I...I need to think," Dr. Sloane said, his hands on his knees as he leaned over. "Don't either of you try anything."

"You ain't one bit steady," Miss Mozelle said. "We could both run right now."

"You can't run. Your arthritis would do you in. And besides, if I can't stop you, I can still take this baby."

The words sent a chill of warning scraping down Alisha's spine. He *would* take them. Dr. Sloane was demented, sick, drunk with grief and pain. She'd been that way herself when she'd turned to this man and Miss Mozelle for help. And she'd been too wrapped up in her own grief and pain to see that Dr. Sloane was mentally unstable.

"We don't have to do this," she said to Dr. Sloane, her arms around her baby as she stared over at the man. "We can end this right now." Louder, for the benefit of the 911 operator, she added, "We're *right here* at the diner. We'll get you some help. You need help."

The doctor straightened, then grabbed her so quickly she let out a scream, the diaper bag falling off her shoulder and to the ground, while she held to Callum. "I'm tired of playing games. You and I are leaving this mountain tonight. I've waited for this too long to end it now."

"And you got too many people involved," Miss Mozelle said. Alisha watched as her friend fiddled with the one scarf left around her shoulders. "You done killed for this, and 'bout scared poor Jimmy Barrett to death with your threats. We can help you, but you in a whole heap of trouble, friend. You gonna go to jail for that murder."

Dr. Sloane's ruddy face was wet, his hair plastered to his skin. "Not if they don't find me."

Alisha heard the desolation in his voice. "Why did you kill Hank?"

"I had to. He was making noise. I had to. I thought they'd blame Murdock."

"They did," Alisha replied. "You had to get everyone out of the way, one way or another."

"Yes." He bobbed his head. "And now, I've succeeded. We're leaving together, at last. We'll drive to Chattanooga in the morning to get your money."

"It's Callum's money," Alisha reminded him, watching as Miss Mozelle continued to untie her shawl. "I have to save it for him."

"I'll take care of you," the doctor said, his eyes on Alisha and the baby. "I'll cherish both of you."

At just about the time Miss Mozelle threw her scarf over Dr. Sloane's head, Alisha heard a grunt and looked up to see Jared crashing through the brush on the foothill. She screamed and backed away, watching as the floral cotton scarf fluttered over Dr. Sloane like a shroud, temporarily leaving him disoriented and confused. While Dr. Sloane struggled with the scarf, Jared tackled the man to the ground, then sat on top of him, holding the scarf tightly so he could lift the doctor's head off the ground.

"You didn't get rid of me," Jared said into his ear, yanking on the scarf, twisting the doctor's neck. "And you are not ever going to bother Alisha again."

Dr. Sloane groaned and struggled, then slumped his head back to the earth, his sobs echoing out over the rain. "I'm sorry, Alisha. I'm so sorry. I only wanted—" he stopped, dropped his head down "—I only wanted a family."

Alisha couldn't speak, couldn't look at him. And right now, she couldn't give him the compassion he needed.

Jared waited, taking long breaths, then released the pressure he had on the material. "Miss Mozelle, there are deputies all around this place. Could you let them know we have Dr. Sloane?"

Miss Mozelle bobbed her head. "I heard that." She waved her hands in the air. "Hey, anybody out there. Hey, we're back here, behind the diner. Don't shoot. We're okay. We're okay now."

In seconds, the place was swarming with uniformed men and concerned citizens. The angry sheriff and a sheepish Deputy Parker took a disoriented, ranting Dr. Sloane away while Letty Martha and Dorothy comforted Miss Mozelle and Alisha. Jared stood watching, waiting for Alisha. She was a few feet away, her body rocking, swinging softly from side to side as she tried to comfort her crying baby.

Miss Mozelle motioned to Letty Martha and Dorothy and the three women moved aside, giving Jared a clear path to the woman he loved.

"Alisha," Jared called, his voice raspy with emotion. "Alisha."

Alisha looked up, her tears shimmering in the bright glare from the security light on the side of the building. She didn't say anything at first, just stood there, rocking and staring at Jared. Finally, she said, "You promised me you'd be back. You promised, and here you are. Sorry I've been so much trouble."

Jared rushed to her, careful not to crush her into his arms. He stood a foot away, his hands on her arms, staring down at the sight that had caused him to fall in love with her.

Mother and child.

"I'm here, and I'm not leaving you, ever again," he said. "No matter the trouble."

Her laughter was tinged with tears. "Another promise?"

"No, a lifetime commitment." Then he looked down at Callum. "May I?" Alisha didn't hesitate. She offered her son to Jared. He gently lifted Callum out of her arms, then kissed the baby's downy head. "A commitment to both of you."

* * *

"Is it really over?" Alisha asked a couple of hours later as they all sat around the diner. Langford had made coffee for everyone and Dorothy had issued free pie to anyone who had an appetite. They'd all gone over their statements with the sheriff. And Deputy Parker had grudgingly apologized to Jared.

Now the diner was closed, except for the crowd of regulars. Dorothy had made Callum a soft bed, complete with clean dish towels, in a huge, scoured dish tub they'd found in the kitchen. Everyone just sat, staring in the muted light, the night's events too fresh and raw for words.

Jared took Alisha's hand in his. "It's over. Dr. Sloane is locked up now. You're safe."

"But Hank's dead."

Her words were full of doubt and despair. Jared wanted to lift that burden away from her. "It's not your fault. Dr. Sloane is a very sick man."

"He played all of us," Langford said, shaking his head. "Had Jimmy doing his dirty work, and apparently, hired Hank to do what Jimmy couldn't do—"

"Put a hole in my brake line," Jared finished, his eyes still on Alisha. "He had each of them thinking they'd get a cut of the money. And he had Hank believing he'd get you."

"Without letting the other one know—they had no idea about each other being involved," Letty Martha said. "You just never know about people."

"I knew," Miss Mozelle said. "Or I should have known. I was there the night Dr. Sloane's wife and baby died. I'll never forget that man's grief. He didn't want that baby at first, you see. So that made it even worse when the child didn't make it. I should have seen this coming from the first time I found him passed out drunk in his clinic."

Alisha reached for her friend's hand. "No one could have predicted this, Miss Mozelle. He had it all planned out and he might have succeeded if—"

"If Jared hadn't come along," Dorothy said, her eyes wide with wonder.

"The protector," Miss Mozelle added, nodding toward Jared. "I shudder to think if that man had delivered Callum that night. Alisha might not be sitting here right now. I don't believe in chance. I believe God sent you to us for a reason."

Jared shook his head. "But I was the catalyst for all of this. If I'd stayed away—"

"I might be dead right now," Alisha said to him, her eyes wide and a pure forest green. "Think about it, Jared. A storm, no way of getting to Dr. Sloane. He might have taken us that night if things hadn't happened the way they did. He was already scheming even then. He just had to rush things because of your interference."

Langford let out a chuckle. "No, because of your *persistence*. You don't mess with a man in love."

Everyone looked at Jared, their faces expectant. "I am in love," he said, smiling over at Alisha. He saw that love returned in her eyes. "The lightning didn't just strike the power lines that night. It struck me, too. It just took me a while to see that."

"Don't you mean—to make Alisha see that?" Miss Mozelle asked.

Alisha smiled. "Okay, all right. I was afraid. You all know what I've been through."

Reverend Stripling spoke up. "As Jared said, it's over now. God has given both of you a second chance."

"Amen to that," came the chorus.

Jared saw a dark emotion pass over Alisha's face. "That is, if Alisha wants me."

"I do," she said, lowering her head. "But there's something I have to take care of before I can put my life back in order. I have to take Callum to see his grandparents." At the gasps around the room, she held up her hand. "No, it was wrong of me to try and keep him from them. They're good people, honestly. They wanted to help me, they wanted to help Trevor. But he was beyond their help. I can't punish them for that. And I owe it to Callum to let him get to know his grandparents."

"What if they try to take him?" Dorothy asked.

"They won't," Jared said before Alisha could speak. "I have some very powerful lawyers back in Atlanta."

Miss Mozelle clapped her hands. "The protector is here to stay."

"They won't," Alisha said, a hand in the air, "because I'm trusting God to show me the way, the right way, to handle this."

"Amen again," Letty Martha said, then she turned to Jared. "But keep those lawyers handy, just in case."

They all started moving to leave, ready to call it a night. Langford went to the door to unlock it. "Hey, there's Tate Wilkes."

He opened the door to let Tate inside. "Tate, you okay?"

Tate's face was flushed, his words breathless. He nervously waved his hands. "It's Rayanne. She's going into labor. I need Miss Mozelle. And where's Dr. Sloane?"

Langford glanced around the room, then back to Tate. "The doc, he's been taken away. He's real sick."

"We'll explain it all later," Miss Mozelle said, springing into action. "Get me to your house, man."

Alisha looked at Jared. "I need to go, too."

"Okay." He picked up the tub with little Callum. "Guess we've got another baby to deliver."

Tate grinned, then went straight-faced again. "She's asking for Alisha and...she wants Jimmy."

"Hmph," Miss Mozelle said, her hands on her hips.

Alisha touched Jared on the arm. "Do you think Jimmy can change?"

Jared shrugged. "I certainly hope so. He did say he loves her."

Reverend Stripling came to stand beside them. "I'll go to Dalton and talk to Jimmy, make him see the error of his ways. Tell Rayanne I'll try to get the sheriff to bring him to her."

"Okay, thanks," Alisha said.

Jared guided her out of the diner, then turned. "I don't have a car."

Langford threw him the keys to his late-model Chevy. "Take mine. It has a car seat—for our grandchildren."

Jared thanked Langford, then helped Alisha secure Callum in the infant seat. Soon they were on their way to the Wilkeses' house.

Alisha glanced at the digital clock on the dash. "It's after midnight." Then she gasped, a hand flying to her mouth. "Oh, oh, Jared, I just realized something."

"What?" he asked, his body going on full alert again.

"It's Mother's Day," she said, her smile cresting like a coming dawn. "And the storm has passed."

"So it has," Jared replied. "Happy Mother's Day, Alisha."

She smiled again, nestled close to him. "Thank you."

Jared took her hand in his as he held the steering

wheel with the other one. "You know, the gardens back at my grandparents' estate have lots and lots of azaleas."

Alisha closed her eyes. "Really?"

"I can have them removed. Or I can sell the estate. I was thinking of a place a little more remote."

"You were?"

"Yes. I was thinking we could add on to the cabin, make it a little roomier. We could make it a home."

"We could," she said, her hand squeezing his. "Will you give me some time to get used to the idea?"

"Okay. I can be patient. I've got lots of ideas, both for us and this mountain."

"Okay then," Alisha said as he pulled the car up the drive toward the Wilkeses' trailer. "But right now, we have to help deliver another baby."

Jared laughed, his whole being humming with a new awakening, a new awareness, and a new faith. "I think I'll sit this one out, if you don't mind."

"Just so you're there when I'm done," Alisha replied, her hand still in his.

"I'll be there," he promised.

Jared got out and glanced up at the moon and the stars shimmering over the rim of the distant mountains. The night was cool and clear again, the wind refreshing and pure. The woods were filled with the scents of earth and night and water. They had been nurtured and protected by the hand of God, through sun and storms, through rain and wind, and heat and cold.

Jared felt the solid strength of the mountain rising up to touch him, to hold him, to protect him.

"No more doubts," he whispered to God. *"I'm in Your hands from now on. And I will do my best to be a worthy servant. I promise."*

Then he took Callum from Alisha, and together
they walked inside to help Rayanne bring a new life
into the world.

* * * * *

SDH535MM

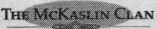

THE McKASLIN CLAN

SERIES CONTINUES WITH...

SWEET BLESSINGS

BY

JILLIAN HART

Single mom Amy McKaslin welcomed newcomer
Heath Murdock into her family diner after he'd
shielded her from harm. And as the bighearted
McKaslin clan and the close-knit Christian community
rallied around him, the grief-ravaged drifter felt an
awakening in his soul. Could the sweetest blessing
of all be standing right before him?

The McKaslin Clan: Ensconced in a quaint mountain town
overlooking the vast Montana plains, the McKaslins rejoice
in the powerful bonds of faith, family...and forever love.

Don't miss SWEET BLESSINGS
On sale April 2005

Available at your favorite retail outlet.

www.SteepleHill.com

LISBJH

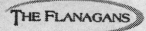

Love Inspired®

THE FLANAGANS

SERIES CONTINUES WITH...

HERO DAD

BY

MARTA PERRY

Firefighter and single dad Seth Flanagan was looking
for a mother for his son. Then he met photojournalist
Julie Alexander. The introverted beauty made him
wonder if God was giving him a second chance. As he
watched his toddler son break through the barriers
around Julie's guarded heart, Seth realized he was ready
to love again. But would their budding relationship
be destroyed when he learned her real identity?

**The Flanagans: This fire-fighting family
must learn to stop fighting love.**

Don't miss HERO DAD
On sale April 2005

Available at your favorite retail outlet.

Love Inspired

PAY ANOTHER VISIT TO SWEETWATER WITH...

LIGHT IN THE STORM

BY

MARGARET DALEY

After raising her three siblings, teacher Beth Coleman was finally free to see the world. She planned to do mission work in South America...until a troubled teen walked into her classroom. Beth's caring nature wouldn't let her say no to the girl or her handsome father, Samuel Morgan. Soon her heart was in danger to Samuel and his ready-made family....

The Ladies of Sweetwater Lake: Like a wedding ring, this circle of friends is never-ending.

Don't miss LIGHT IN THE STORM
On sale April 2005

Available at your favorite retail outlet.